PARACHUTES

PARACHUTES

a novel by

MARIANNE
MIDDELVEEN

CORMORANT
BOOKS

The publisher wishes to acknowledge the generous financial
assistance of the Canada Council, the Ontario Arts Council, the
Government of Ontario through the Ministry of Culture and
Communications, and the Department of Canadian Heritage.

Very special thanks to Chris Scott for reviewing the manuscript,
and for his critique and suggestions, his limitless encouragement,
and his belief that *Parachutes* would fly.

Many thanks to Rob Allan and to my family for their support.

Cover photograph © Robert Barclay Allan.
Author photograph © Robert Barclay Allan.
Cover design is by Artcetera Graphics in Dunvegan, Ontario.
Edited by Gena K. Gorrell.

Published by Cormorant Books Inc.,
RR 1, Dunvegan, Ontario, Canada, K0C 1J0

Printed and bound in Canada.

CANADIAN CATALOGUING IN PUBLICATION DATA
    Middelveen, Marianne, 1960-
      Parachutes : a novel
    ISBN 0-920953-83-2
      I. Title.
    PS8576.I44P37 1995   C813'.54   C95-900291-X
    PR9199.3.M43P37 1995

To my panas in Venezuela

Prologue

All the ends of the earth
will remember and turn to the Lord,
and all the families of all the nations
will bow down before him,
for dominion belongs to the Lord
and he rules over the nations.
Psalms 22: 27-28.

Ronald Elliot could scarcely understand the yells of Captain Zambrano above the racket of the outboard motor, "It's here, I think." There was a break in the thickets overhanging the water, a black forbidding hole. Beyond, the forest was dark, impregnable. Zambrano, a bulky military man in camouflage, cut the engine and Ronald Elliot heard the roar of howler monkeys. God gave man dominion. He willed that this green fortress be subdued to the progress of civilization.

Ronald took off his glasses and massaged the bridge of his nose. His glasses fitted too tightly, pinching his nose and behind his ears, and sometimes they gave him a headache—one of the many things to attend to on his next leave to Caracas. Perspiration glazed his fingers and mingled with the smeared remains of a mosquito. Despite his total fatigue, he felt happy. Doctors Baumstark and Marshall were both out of the country, out of the way, so to speak. All obstacles were gone. Soon, at this site, another remote outpost for the teaching of the Gospel would be built—a testimonial to God.

As they glided to shore, Ronald saw a silty beach in the shadows of the thickets. The captain rose unsteadily to his feet and the small aluminum boat tilted precariously from side to side. He grabbed a liana, pulled the boat closer to shore and stepped out. Ronald waited as Captain Zambrano secured the boat, then followed.

They sloshed for fifteen minutes along a muddy overgrown path, the mud as thick and sticky as an oatmeal gruel. Just when Ronald thought they had disembarked at the wrong spot, the trail opened to a clearing. Few traces of the previous inhabitants remained: a circle of charred posts on the perimeter, a couple of half-burnt Yanomami baskets, a few metal cans and charred flashlight batteries. The site was near perfect, a little far from the river perhaps, but few trees, if any, would need to be cleared for housing. A large area must be felled for the airstrip, of course, but the natives, who did not understand money, would be paid a token sum to do most of the labour.

Ronald noticed a square patch in the ochre dirt that must have once been the foundation for a small hut. Part of a mud wall remained standing, and some blackened papers stuck out between partially burned support poles. He picked up some sheets. "Cranial capacity estimated to the nearest cubic centimetre", "grams of animal protein consumed daily". So that was what the demonic doctor had been up to. He put down the notes and poked through the scorched mess with a stick. A booklet surfaced, the proceedings of an international meeting. The edges of the paper were charred, the print still quite legible:

Ethnocide in the Orinoco-Ventuari Region
J. Marshall Ph.D.
Instituto Central para Investigaciones Antropológicas
Apartado 134, Caracas Venezuela

Abstract

The diverse ethnic groups in the Orinoco-Ventuari region are in danger of being integrated into national life, thereby opening up the Amazonian rainforest for resource extraction. Integration consists mainly of religious conversion, colonization and cultural change.

Missionaries are allowed free access to even the most remote areas and catalyse integration, affecting the economic base, social life, family structure, environment, nutrition and health of entire communities. The survival of indigenous people is seriously threatened by resource utilization, agricultural development, tourism and introduced diseases. Prompt action is needed if their extinction is to be avoided.

"What have you there, Ronaldo?" Zambrano's bulk loomed over him.

"Propaganda, Communist ramblings written by our American anthropologist friend. It's as well we're rid of him, and that whore who helped him." Ronald tucked the booklet into his knapsack. "This location is perfect, Máximo. With your help we can at last bring God's salvation to these unfortunates who have lived in ignorance and darkness for so long."

"Ronaldo, I don't give a damn about the Indians. Let them rot. That's not why I agreed to help you, and you'd better not forget it."

1

Debra Baumstark didn't need her Spanish-English pocket dictionary to decipher an account of five "carbonized" bodies recovered from the burnt-out hull of a car. Her imagination continued past the vivid description and the smudgy photograph displaying five dark blobs—charred skulls, eyeless sockets, flesh consumed by flames, clumps of charcoal-like residue, the once white teeth sooty grey, exposed rib cages, ashes blowing in the wind of passing cars. Even less of her and her fellow passengers would be left for identification if this old commercial jet didn't make it off the runway. No matter how much she travelled, she could never calm her thoughts during takeoffs and landings.

She was glad to be leaving Caracas. The small, dirty fingerprints on the newspaper in her lap remained from the boy who had sold it to her, one of a multitude of scruffy waifs, tattered clothing, hair covered in an earthy crust pulled into filthy spikes, who wandered the streets of Caracas. They stood at intersections inhaling exhaust fumes, roasting under the blazing sun, peddling candy and stolen hubcaps. Or they begged.

When Debra had first arrived, she had been puzzled by the sound of children's voices — "*Muuunndddooooo, Muuuuunnndddooooo*"—the cries tapering into echoes between the modern office buildings. They were just selling the newspaper *El Mundo* for a few coins. Many were missing arms or legs, or were in some other way physically disfigured. She remembered reading that beggars (was it in Brazil?) would intentionally maim their children to make them pathetic enough to elicit sympathy. Did they do the same thing here, or were the injuries the consequence of living in intersections?

El Mundo, like most of the local papers, filled its pages with typical city life: graphic accounts of stabbings, shootings, stranglings—mostly domestic disputes—and brutal vehicle accidents. She had thought Miami, her home for most of her adult life, noisy, violent and dangerous. Her three months in Caracas almost made her miss the tranquillity of home. But now she was headed to a less refined area of the country, a rough frontier, she'd been told. It was too late to have reservations now that she sat on board the Aeropostal DC-10 which in less than two hours would deposit her in Puerto Pedriscal. Would she be able to last a year in Amazonas, in isolation, her umbilical cord to civilization severed?

Had she made the correct decision when she accepted the position at the new medical research station? At the time she had thought of the glamour of working in tropical rainforest, the giant rivers, anacondas and stone-age native cultures that she knew only from coffee-table books and television. The excitement now retreated behind a mounting panic.

The plane, against all expectations, made it safely into the air. She put the gory headlines of *El Mundo* out of sight in her carry-on bag and pulled out the more comforting *Daily Journal*, the English-language newspaper.

True to its American heritage, *The Journal* gave the sorry state of Venezuela's economy second place to President Reagan's colon. The International Monetary Fund was imposing strict economic controls and the local currency had in recent months been devalued from four to forty bolivares to the dollar. Reports of financial scams involving preferential exchange rates incriminated unnamed government officials.

Debra lifted her eyes from the paper and looked out the window. The forested coastal hills that cradled Caracas had given way to a flat, dry landscape speckled by scrubby brown miniature trees. Nothing green and friendly as far as the horizon, no lakes, no rivers, no hills, no people. She was adventurous, ready to handle a challenge. After all, she had survived a gruelling residency. She would look back when she was settled in a successful suburban practice and be glad that she'd had this experience, that she had really lived life when others merely existed. She looked down and tried to read, but her mind wouldn't co-operate.

ॐ

It was her father's doing. Debra was thirty years old and had been settling into a supporting role in her father's lucrative Miami clinic, pursuing an interest she had found in dermatology. One day they discussed the dramatic increase in unusual and often puzzling lesions in travellers returning from the tropics. He thought it would be beneficial for the practice if she were to get first-hand experience with some exotic diseases, and suggested Venezuela; he had some friends at an institute of tropical medicine in Caracas who would be glad to show her around.

She had spent a month in the Hospital Universitario in dermatology, another month at the Instituto de Medicina Tropical in parasitology, and was in the middle of a final month at the instituto in medical mycology, where daily work with the most grotesque corruptions of human flesh sparked the enthusiasm of the doctors in the department. In Miami, athlete's foot, jock itch and candidiasis were about the limit of Debra's experience with fungal infections. Here, they could cause gruesome disfiguration and even death.

Under the microscope the organisms that caused such suffering were fairy gardens of spirals; clusters on the tips of delicate branches; ornate pods; chains; plumes. The tissue sections from grotesque lesions were processed in a burst of royal blue and fuchsia. Ghostly yeast cells and mycelium peeked out among host cells. One species, growing in pus, was converted to exquisite asteroid bodies, little stars, from crystalline immune deposits.

The peace and fascination discovered in the laboratory were

12

interrupted a few hours daily by practical classes for medical students that Debra observed. The atmosphere was much more relaxed than in the regimented classes she had endured at the University of Miami, and she realized one morning that she had probably dropped her professional air too much when a pimply student attracted her attention by calling her "mi amor". She decided it was time for a break to reconsider her approach, and she slipped out to the cafeteria.

A brick lattice-work, open to a gentle breeze, enclosed the cafeteria. Lush tropical plants, dark green as ripe avocados, filtered the dappled light from the lattice. White figures sat around white tables, sipping coffee and speaking softly. An unwritten code of conduct required doctors to wear lab coats at all times, even in the cafeteria. The coats, like stethoscopes, distinguished physicians from other staff. She meandered among the tables wondering what virulent tropical microbes adhered to the coats around her.

She ordered a tea from the swarthy waiter behind the counter. He wore a white tee-shirt topped by an apron stained indelibly with deep-frying residues, and a pack of cigarettes pocketed in a fold of his sleeve. His eyes took in her breasts beneath the white coat, then he glared and abruptly shoved the order across the counter. A plastic thimble, the type used for espresso coffee, was stuffed with a teabag and filled to the brim with hot water.

"Por favor, I need a bigger cup. There is no room for liquid in here," Debra explained.

"Then you should have ordered a long tea, doctora," he answered. "That is a short tea! The long tea is a bolívar fifty. The short tea is one bolívar. You owe me fifty céntimos." He leaned heavily on his hands and stretched his beefy face towards her.

She handed him the difference and he pushed a larger plastic cup full of hot water across the counter. "Gra-ci-as," she said, enunciating each syllable distinctly and flashing him a smile she hoped looked sarcastic. She transferred the teabag

13

to the tall cup and scanned the room for an empty table. A customer sitting alone at the table beside her smiled.

"Venezolanos do not often take tea," he said in clearly pronounced Spanish, "and it is particularly difficult to order a hot tea with milk." He stirred his cafecito with a red and white plastic straw. "Would you care to join me?"

She sat down opposite him. He was a distinguished-looking man, his composure elegant. He was definitely her idea of handsome: mid-forties, black hair silvered just enough at the temples, a warm smile revealing flawless, glinting teeth.

"Visiting English scientists often order tea with milk. They are surprised when they receive a teabag served in a glass of scalding whole milk instead of hot water. I am Doctor Diego Velázquez." He offered a hand, a very well manicured hand; the cuticles had been pushed back and the fingernails spotlessly cleaned, evenly filed and brushed discreetly with clear polish.

Fingernail polish didn't strike Debra as being very manly and, having noticed the impeccably groomed hand, she wiped the sweat off her palm on her lab coat before she took his. "Doctor Debra Baumstark, Debra."

"Debra. Do you work here?"

"I'm visiting from Florida, to learn about tropical dermatology. I have just two more weeks in medical mycology, then I'll be heading back home. I haven't seen you around the institute before. Do you work here too?" No white lab coat, she noted. He wore an open-necked short-sleeved shirt.

"I am on salary as a professor here at the institute, but I also direct a new research centre in the Amazon Territory. The university provides an office for me here if I give an occasional lecture. International communication is difficult from the Amazon frontier so, out of necessity, I work most of the time in Caracas, writing grant proposals and setting up collaborative research with institutes abroad." Velázquez had only one visible flaw, a tiny lump on the sclera of one eye.

"What type of research does your centre do?" Debra asked. She sat up attentively.

"At this stage we are looking mostly at the epidemiology of diseases in native Amazonian populations—malaria, tuberculosis and such. The communities are so isolated from normal medical help that I hope to find new ways to control the diseases," he said. Debra chewed her plastic straw while she listened to his meticulous pronunciation. "It is most curious you should mention mycology," he continued. "I have been looking for someone with clinical expertise in precisely that area and I have not found anyone suitable. Qualified doctors will not leave the cities. I employ some young and enthusiastic biology graduates, but they need insight and direction from someone with advanced medical knowledge and I am not available enough to guide them." He looked straight at Debra and smiled warmly. "Would you be interested?"

"You said you worked with native groups. Does that include the Yanomami? I learned a little about them from television documentaries, and they've interested me ever since." She bent the straw around her finger.

"Yes, they are the most exotic group we work with. However, most people are not aware that there are actually sixteen distinct ethnic groups in the Amazon Territory. We work with only a few of them at the moment." He watched her, waited for a response and took a sip of his cafecito.

"It sounds intriguing." She shifted her eyes around the room, at professionals engaged in quiet intelligent conversations, then down at the badly mangled straw in her hand. She couldn't imagine her father's reaction if she were to phone him saying she was off to work in the Amazon.

"It really is interesting work," he prompted. "Difficult and uncomfortable at times, yes, but never boring." He folded his napkin neatly and waited.

She just couldn't believe what was happening. "Let me get this straight. Are you offering me a position?"

"Would such a position be of interest to you?"

"It's certainly tempting."

"Naturally, I would have to formally interview you and

review your qualifications. And I'm afraid you could not officially practise medicine except in the most isolated areas, at least not without ratifying your medical degree. You would be a medical adviser of sorts, and you could get involved with our original research. Shall we schedule an interview?"

"Oh," she inhaled deeply, "all right. This is just too good an opportunity to miss. And I wouldn't have to make up my mind until after the interview, would I?"

"Most certainly not," he said. "But I should warn you that there are two things you must consider. First, you may have to apply for Venezuelan citizenship. We draw salaries from the Ministry of Health and it prefers to employ foreigners who at least look as though they want to become nationals. Having said that, you would not actually have to become a citizen. The application process takes at least two years, and you would probably be moving on before then, I expect."

"Sounds reasonable. And the other?"

"The Amazon Territory is isolated. My staff get very lonely. Some of our people have even broken apart emotionally. People behave, sometimes, in ways they ordinarily would not."

He became serious when he said this, yet here she was, already isolated from family and friends in the U.S. How much more isolated could she get? And what a tremendous opportunity, a chance to do original medical research while she had fun, and to get some of those publications so important to a future career away from her father's clinic. She decided to do precisely as she pleased for once in her life, not what her father had ordained.

The interview had been a formality and now, three weeks later, the events she recalled did not quite seem real as she sat on the plane taking her south to the jungle. She folded the *Daily Journal*, leaving it in her lap. She swallowed her panic and tried to regain the excitement that had brought her this far.

❦

Jeff Marshall sat in the aisle seat. He wore dirty, bleached blue jeans and a University of Michigan tee-shirt. He wasn't bad-looking, in a rugged kind of a way, stocky but athletic. Reddish-brown hair, freckles beneath a deep tan. Pale crow's feet and blue-grey eyes contrasted with his tan. He inspected the blonde beside him—suspiciously gringa, early thirties, he guessed, and nice long legs, though perhaps a little thin in the calves. After his years living with brown people she was a bit pale for his taste, but she did look damned attractive after the months he had spent in celibacy. He wanted to strike up a conversation with her. Hell, it was difficult. He wasn't used to social niceties and small talk any more. She did seem to be aware of him, though. He swirled the little square cubes around his plastic glass of Coke, glanced around the aisle and then took another look at her knees. She caught him looking and Jeff turned his eyes away. She twirled a strand of her shoulder-length hair around her finger and scanned the limitless grasslands beyond the scratched window, trying to look casual. He was sure she was just trying to pretend she hadn't noticed him.

Probably a tourist, he thought, yet there seemed more to her than that. She had an air of independence, of self-confidence, that attracted him. She definitely wasn't a missionary, not wearing a skirt like that, and not with makeup. Thankfully, there was no trace of Christian modesty in those blatantly revealed legs.

A group of Venezuelans a few rows up had begun to sing cheerful folk-songs accompanied by a four-stringed instrument called a cuatro. The musicians provided a festive atmosphere that relaxed him, very different from the old American utilitarian approach to air travel, and he decided to make a move. "'Scuse me." He tapped her arm. "I noticed you reading the DJ." He glanced down at her lap. "You an American?"

She turned away from the window and smiled. "Yes, I am. Is it that obvious?" Just the reaction he'd hoped for.

"Yeah. DJ or not, I'd take you for an American. Could I see it, the DJ, that is, after you've finished? It's been a long time

17

since I've had news from the U.S. of A."

"Sure, I can't concentrate on it anyway. Why have you been out of touch for so long, if you don't mind my asking?" She handed over the newspaper.

"I'm an anthropologist. I've been in Amazonas for the past five years. The name's Jeff Marshall." He placed the paper under his table on his lap and extended his freckled brown arm.

She accepted his hand and looked directly at him. "I'm Debra Baumstark. I've been in Venezuela for just a few months."

"Are you joining a tour around Puerto Pedriscal?" he asked. A pocket of turbulence sloshed his Coke and he drew his hand back to stabilize it.

"No." She smiled slightly. "I'm a physician. I'm going to Puerto Pedriscal as a medical adviser."

He grinned at her. "What do you know, you're a quack. I'm a Ph.D—a real doctor. You must be working for that new tropical disease institute in Puerto Pedriscal."

"Yes, INSA. Are you familiar with it?" The plane heaved and the musicians filled the cabin with a chorus of squeals.

"Yeah, I know it well. INSA has expeditions to the Yanomami territory where I work, and they've paid me to help them sometimes as an interpreter."

"Oh, you're working with the Yanomami," she said excitedly. "I've been fascinated with them ever since I read about their ritual violence. Is it true that they shave a patch of hair off the back of their heads so that they can show off battle scars? It must be so interesting."

"Yeah, it has its moments, but it's not all fun. I lived with them a year before I knew enough language to ask them the simplest questions. And then I couldn't understand their answers. It's as well there was always plenty of activity to watch or I would have gone loco. You know they never sleep? I lie in my hammock among them and they talk all night long. I used to wonder what the hell they could find so interesting that they could talk about it so much." Jeff felt breathless. It had been so long since he'd spoken to anyone freely in English.

18

"So what do they talk about?"

"Everything. It turns out that their nights are like a community parliament, when everybody's together and gets to have his say about how things are running. It's also when the headmen, the elders, organize the next day's activities. It's all very casual—no orders're given out, just suggestions like 'I think it would be a good idea if a couple of the guys around here went hunting tomorrow,' and sure enough, some hunters will disappear at dawn."

"I don't know if I'd have the courage to live with them like that, but I want to at least see them. How did you end up down there?"

"Just luck, I guess, if you can call it that. When I taught in Michigan I married a foreign grad student—mine, unfortunately. I had tenure, but talk about unlawful carnal knowledge. That's what the department called it, anyway. Just couldn't stand the chitchat, so I got residence here through my wife and headed south. The Yanomami live about as far away from Michigan as I could get."

Debra straightened her mouth and looked at him from the corners of her eyes. "And does your *wife* work with the Yanomami, too?"

"You gotta be kidding! She wouldn't live in Venezuela, let alone in a hammock in the jungle. She says she can't stand to live in an underdeveloped country any more. Last I heard of her, she was off screwing a shrink in San Diego. I'll get round to divorcing her one day."

"I'm sorry to hear that," Debra said.

He shrugged it off. "No big deal. It's better for both of us this way." He was thinking of himself and Debra, not himself and his wife.

"I know INSA also works with some of the other tribes around Puerto Pedriscal," she said, "and I'll probably be working mostly with them. Do you have any experience with them?"

"Not really. By the way, it's not considered politically correct to call them tribes any more. Ethnic group sounds a little more polite. There are a lot of different groups in the Territory, each with its own unique language and culture. Well, they used to have, but most of them have been around criollos, whites and missionaries so long that they now don't know where they belong—'acculturated' and 'assimilated' we call it in sociological jargon, just polite words for alcoholic, disease-ridden misfits. 'Decultured' would be a better term."

"Surely it can't be as bad as that."

"You bet your sweet little ass it is. You don't know how frustrating it is to be studying cultures that have survived unchanged for twenty thousand years or more and probably won't last another twenty."

"Then why do you work there, if you think it's a lost cause?"

"Shit, I've wondered about that myself. The Yanomami live in an area so remote that they're only now having significant contact. They're a big group, maybe twenty thousand between Venezuela and Brazil. There're even some communities around the border, that we've spotted from the air, that no one has yet found a way to get to. There's still a slim chance for them."

"But I thought the Yanomami were protected. I was told you have to get special permits to study them, even for medical studies."

"That policy was made during the rich old petroleum days, when they could afford restrictions. Now their oil's worth fuck all. But in Amazonas there're plenty of rich mineral deposits, hardwood trees and other stuff. Politicians now see it as a vast untouched resource just waiting to be exploited. The Yanomami don't fit into the pretty development picture. The government wants to get them out of the way, so to speak. Missionaries, especially the New World Mission, are a cheap way to do it. Missionaries never have trouble getting permits." He picked up his Coke and crunched an ice cube. He needed to cool off. He'd been called into the U.S. embassy during his stay in the capital and the ambassador had told him to lay off harassment of the New World missionaries. He knew he'd get himself into deep shit if he didn't learn how to back down. He didn't need another fucking lecture from Mr. Mighty-Ass Ambassador on how to behave like a gentleman while visiting a foreign nation.

Jeff leaned in front of Debra, his head very close to hers, and pointed out the window at an expanse of water below. "We're close to Puerto Pedriscal now. That's the Orinoco River. You see all those large black boulders, and the beaches? We're just getting into rainy season. Once the rains get going full blast the boulders will be gone, completely inundated under fifty feet of water."

Her eyes followed his finger. The river was impressive even at this elevation, so wide it took up the entire window. The sky and brilliant sun reflected from the water's surface, the colours of a blue and gold macaw. Gigantic, charcoal-coloured granite boulders were scattered across the landscape—the river-bed, its banks and beyond—their size revealed by dwarfed buildings among them. In places, the boulders perched on smooth black domes protruding from beige silt. The scale of the boulders was revealed in the distance, where more bare black domes, like massive boils, erupted out of a smooth carpet of thick forest. Far beyond, near the horizon, the muted outlines of vertical-walled, flat-topped tepuis thrust above the forest. The plane swept through a big arc, changing the view to the other side of the river. An abrupt strip of dark green vegetation hugged the river's edge and separated it from a sea of green-gold savannah, the flatness broken only by the perfect counterpoint of an isolated mountain in the distance. The DC-10 dipped slowly and Jeff's ears popped.

"It's breathtaking," Debra whispered.

"No shit!" Jeff answered. "It's the power of the river that amazes me. It drains this whole territory, yet here, over a thousand miles from the ocean, it's only a hundred feet above sea-level. There's almost no gradient at all in its entire length. Have you heard of the Casiquiare channel?" She nodded vaguely. "Well," he continued, "it's a few hundred miles upstream from here. It connects the Orinoco to the Río Negro, one of the main tributaries of the Amazon River in Brazil. In the dry season, the Río Negro runs through the Casiquiare into the Orinoco. In the rainy season, the Orinoco rises and backs up so much that the flow in the Casiquiare reverses and about one-fifth of the Orinoco's water runs into the Río Negro. In the height of rainy season the Casiquiare becomes a vast, shallow lake covering maybe twenty percent of the land mass between the Orinoco and the Amazon. Fuckin' blows you away, doesn't it?"

"Yes, put like that it does," she answered. She pressed her forehead against the window. "Is that Puerto Pedriscal?" She pointed across the river to a ramshackle riverside development enveloped by greenery.

"No, that's El Pichirre. Sort of a sister community over the border. It exists for the sole purpose of selling cheap clothing to people from Puerto Pedriscal. And we think Venezuela's economy is bad. That," he pointed to the near side of the river, "is Puerto Pedriscal, where pretty well everything, except for the daily newspaper which is underneath us now, is brought upriver at highly inflated prices."

She had to strain to see it, as it lay almost directly underneath them. A scar of exposed red earth lay amid the greenery, all trace of vegetation scraped away. Houses and small buildings became distinguishable, topping the scar in a linear, well-organized pattern.

They hit the ground with a thump, wheels screeched and the plane gave a final rush of speed before it rolled in front of a small terminal. A rustic hangar with a corrugated metal roof stood to one side. The musicians applauded enthusiastically and charged to the exit before the plane had come to a complete stop.

2

A sponge of tropical air enveloped the passengers as they staggered down the steps to the tarred runway. Under the glaring sun, the airport boiled with human activity, small brown people desperately pushing and straining to recognize family and friends. The daily arrival of the DC-10 was an important event, and every disembarking passenger had a welcoming congregation of twenty. Debra and Jeff shoved their way through a wall of people to a spot on the rubbery asphalt where handlers dumped luggage and boxes off the plane.

A group of North Americans, conspicuous by their hyaline white skin, kept to one side of the mêlée. They were New World missionaries, men dressed in plaid shirts and full-length pants and a few women dressed to conceal rather than to flatter, most of them shiningly blond. They moved around with a sense of urgency, grabbed boxes from the asphalt and loaded them into jeeps, all the while giving curt orders to submissive brown men. A tangible wall of isolation surrounded them.

"Ronaldo, la caja está por aquí," a short-sleeved brown man called. A stocky man spun round in recognition. His eyes, small even after magnification through thick glass lenses, glinted as he looked towards the unloaded luggage. The arms of his black-rimmed glasses fitted too snugly and pressed into his head, indenting the padded flesh at his temples. His long-sleeved brown and black plaid shirt and long brown pants looked freshly laundered but entirely wrong for the stifling heat, and his forehead shone with sweat. His chunky build and big barrel chest made his legs look undersized, and he looked massively strong.

Almost four years ago Ronald Elliot had learned about the Yanomami people from his brother Luke. Luke had returned to Oklahoma each year scarcely able to contain his excitement as he recounted his jungle adventures as a missionary bush pilot. Ronald and his other brother Stanley had listened in fascination. One time Luke's plane had stalled in the middle of hostile territory. The plane had glided so close to the treetops before he could restart the engine that he could see the whites of the Indians' eyes as they shot arrows at him. Another time he had whacked his way through an overgrown jungle trail and a deadly bushmaster snake slithered out of the bushes in front of him, only inches from his feet. It was killed by an Indian guide as it struck out at Luke. Then while Luke and the other missionaries were out leaving gifts in the jungle for the Indians a jaguar had visited their camp to hide a dead wild pig in Luke's sleeping bag. Dinner was delicious, and the jaguar provided a bonus of its beautiful skin when it came back looking for its meal that night.

Luke described the Yanomami in lifelike detail—their pagan superstitions, their hunger for salvation and the joy they felt once they heard His word. Ronald had fretted when Luke explained that there were still so many unfortunates who had not yet heard the Gospel. He had sold his profitable vending machine business and enrolled at Briarcliff Bible Institute to become a missionary. There he had met and married Esther, the institute's librarian. Ronald's business skills and Esther's expertise in Indian linguistics made them ideal candidates for running the Ventuari mission headquarters. The Lord had willed Ronald to make good Christian homes in the middle of this jungle tangle; to establish a place of devoted Christian worship. Immediately after their wedding, he and Esther had found themselves on their way to Puerto Pedriscal. Yes, it had been about two years ago that they had arrived at this same airport.

Ronald and Jorge, a Guahibo convert, separated the supplies for the mission headquarters from the supplies that Luke would be flying on the mission Cessna out to Kovӓta-teri and Porohóa. Esther's tall, thin frame cast an elongated shadow alongside the jeep as she and the other mission wives watched the men work.

"Ronald, you have Jorge load that box carefully, on the top, please. It has breakables in it," Esther reminded him curtly.

Ronald picked up the box and personally loaded it in a safe place. His life would be a misery if any of Esther's mom's milk-glass broke. He looked up through sweat-splotched lenses and saw Jeff Marshall standing with an indecent woman who sinfully displayed sexuality. The woman smiled at him. Ronald did not return the smile. He couldn't prevent these fellow Americans from making contact with the Indians. He could only try to teach the Indians that foreigners who didn't know God were evil, and pray that they would understand. Satan did his bidding through those like Jeff, disguising their malevolent deeds in the name of science. Jeff Marshall had spoken publicly a month ago against the Lord's work, and a destructive article, full of scientistic lies, had been published in a militant Indian publication. Ronald had had no choice but to speak to the American ambassador in Caracas, a good Christian man, about Jeff's interference, and the ambassador had assured Ronald that he would take care of the matter personally. Still, Ronald felt his old fears resurface with Satan's power represented so close at hand.

Ronald prayed that the Indians might learn and understand the word of Christ, and that they might find salvation and good living rather than feral brutality in an unavailing wilderness. He concentrated on the words of His saving knowledge, and the power of God's love again ran through his body. Only prayer could move the arm of God against those who courted sin. Greater be He who lives within the faithful than Satan's agents, cowardly disguised as scientists.

God answered Ronald's prayers. "My son Jesus Christ was

murdered, yet He forgave His enemies and showered them with love. Have trust in Me to deal with My enemies. Ronald, rejoice not when thy enemy crumbles. Retribution is Mine and I repay My enemies in full. Replace your hatred with My love and forgiveness." God said that he must love and forgive his enemies, but God did not command that he go out of his way to be friendly to them.

"Ronald!" Esther said, in a voice that ruptured the surroundings like a razor blade to a balloon. "It is very impolite to stare."

Ronald turned away only to see another who had fallen into the dark service of Satan, a brown-skinned, sooty-haired man in a red shirt who handed out pamphlets—the Communist. He smiled deceptively at everyone and everyone smiled in return. Everyone in town knew this man, not surprising in such a small place, but not only did people know him, they liked him. Men slapped him on the back affectionately, joked and laughed. Women smiled at him politely. Never had the prospects of bringing salvation to this God-forsaken region been so bleak; the promise of deliverance faded. Tonight, he would lead the others in prayer.

Debra saw a man who commanded her attention. He was tall for a Latin American, with a lean, sinewy build. His posture was remarkable, so straight he might have been held up by a pole through his spine. He wore a red shirt and handed out some sort of papers.

She turned away from him and looked for her ride. Velázquez had assured her he would be in Puerto Pedriscal this week and, yes, the second of May would be ideal for her to come, and if he couldn't meet her personally he would send someone down from INSA. The crowd thinned and she suspected she'd been forgotten. Jeff had located the last of his belongings, and dragged himself up to her, overloaded with boxes, no suitcases. Cardboard boxes tied with rope served as luggage here.

"They didn't come for you? You know, you'll never be able to get up to INSA in a taxi," he said. "It's on top of a steep hill accessed by a dirt road. The drivers won't go up there."

"Wonderful! Then what am I supposed to do?" She squinted at the road from the airport to see if someone had arrived late.

"You could try the telephone but they're usually impossible here. The one up at INSA regularly gets struck by lightning. Or you could spend the night in the Hotel Las Palmas and look around town for someone you know."

"This is not the sort of welcome I envisioned."

"This is Puerto Pedriscal, hon. It's a small town. Don't worry, the news of a tall blonde gringa doctor will travel fast. Wanna share a taxi?"

Maybe he was right. She had met some of the staff at her interview and perhaps she would recognize one of them. She didn't know what else she could do. The thought of spending the night in town made her feel better, less overwhelmed. Debra felt comfortable and safe with Jeff, someone from her own country who knew how to survive here. She could be introduced to her new job and place of residence more gradually. "Sure, why not," she answered.

Jeff whistled for a taxi by expertly sticking two fingers in his mouth and blowing sharply. Politely waiting for service in this country, as Debra did, often meant being ignored. A red fringe above the windshield and a clutter of religious icons—a serene Virgin Mary, a crucifix, Christ dripping bright red paint, and some local saint with a halo around his bowler hat and a moustache similar to the driver's—decorated the taxi's interior. This shrine protected driver and passengers from the perils of the journey.

Puerto Pedriscal was very much a frontier town. The taxi bounced down the uneven road churning up clouds of terracotta dust. Jeeps and trucks far outnumbered the old clunker cars. The traffic was incredibly chaotic for a town of just ten thousand residents, the majority of whom could probably not afford to own a vehicle. The backs of Debra's thighs stuck to the vinyl upholstery with a gritty paste of sweat and red dust.

The driver hung his cigarette out the window and tapped off the ashes to the *tin, tin, tin* of the cowbell punctuating the salsa rhythm that blasted from the radio. The ashes flew back into Debra's face, and she sputtered and closed her window. A cloud of dust blew in from Jeff's window. "Jeff, would you mind closing your window? There's a lot of dust."

Jeff raised his eyebrows as if she'd taken leave of her senses. "You crazy? It's too hot. You'll never adapt if you don't get used to a little dust, hon, because there aren't many paved roads around here."

Desiccated grasses and trees were dulled with dust. Debra's eyes couldn't focus well while they vibrated over pebbles and depressions. "It doesn't look as if there are any."

"There are a few in town, and there's one paved stretch of highway. You see, Puerto Pedriscal was founded as a base camp for construction crews when the Puerto Pedriscal/Puerto Olvidado highway was built; it bypasses the Gran Raudales rapids." He had relaxed completely even as they lurched and swerved around the bigger pot-holes. He slouched, and rested his bacon-brown arms on his lap. "If it makes you feel any better, the rainy season's just started. Then the dust will settle and this place will be swamped in mud. Take your pick."

"Isn't there a paved road to Caracas? It looks like it on the map. Or is the only way in and out of here by that plane?" Debra felt dew on her upper lip. What if something happened, a revolution or a coup, and there was no airline service and she was stranded?

Jeff nodded his head to the cowbell like a pecking rooster. "Sorta! The plane is the only easy way out of here. There're boats. Supplies are brought as far as Puerto Pedriscal that way, but it would take days to get to Ciudad Bolívar. Then there're the roads. The ones leading out of the Territory are all dirt roads. Most're pocketed by holes so large they call them 'come carros', you know, car eaters, and sometimes they're passable only in the dry season."

"Really?" she asked, dazed. She rolled her window down a crack.

"Yeah. Last time I left Amazonas, I hitched a ride in Velázquez's Toyota Land Cruiser. You know Velázquez, I suppose?"

"Yes, of course. He's the director."

"Anyway, it took us two full days to reach the border of Bolívar state. We had to cross a few rivers, none with bridges. Some of the larger ones have float ferries, chalanas. We tried one river without a chalana and waited the entire day for a truck to come pull us out of the river, and another day for the engine to dry out. Velázquez was pissed about his upholstery. He was lucky it was just his upholstery. A friend of mine lost his Volkswagen Beetle in the same place. It just floated downstream and sank in a hole."

"Wonderful!"

"That's called Tarzan's house, a local landmark." Jeff pointed out his window. Debra ducked down and glanced up at an enormous forty-five-foot black boulder scoured by chalky white horizontal water-marks. A metal staircase balanced precariously up the height of the rock led to a small house perched on the boulder's summit. The rock towered above the trees, with no shade.

"Who would want to live up there? It must broil."

"An architect who moved here thought it would be a way to get above the bugs," he explained. "No one lives in it now. Gets struck by lightning all the time so it's not really inhabitable."

Most of the houses were uniformly assembled from concrete breeze-blocks, metal beams and corrugated metal roofs. The town was prettier towards the centre, where many houses were painted white and blue and the road became paved. The only outstanding beauty to be found within town boundaries was the giant mango trees with their large, glossy green leaves, umbelliferous deep-shade refuges from the bleaching sun.

A busy intersection, centred by an anachronistic bronze sculpture of an Indian adorned with feather diadem and loincloth, seemed to be the town's hub. The taxi swung around the Indian, his eyes fixed somewhere far beyond the gasoline station and derelict Don Juan movie theatre, down a narrow pot-holed sidestreet and through wrought-iron gates into the Gran Hotel Las Palmas.

Although not quite Debra's idea of grand, the Gran Hotel Las Palmas had a surprisingly pleasant ambience, with polished black-and-white tile floors, and high arched ceilings supported by Spanish pillars, all open coolly to the outside. They checked into separate rooms, clean, functional and sparsely furnished with no adornment on the white walls. Debra quickly found out that the blank white walls facilitated mosquito hunting. She smacked a fat one full of someone else's blood and left a ragged sanguine splotch on the wall. She took a quick shower, all she could stand because the water, controlled by a single faucet, was frigidly cold. She wondered where such cold water could come from in such a blistering environment. She collapsed naked on the bed and let a gentle buffeting from the ceiling fan dry her body. Her skin tightened deliciously with goosebumps and her nipples hardened.

The semi-aroused state stayed with Debra as she dressed and made her way to the pool to meet Jeff. The anxieties that had plagued her had evaporated and left her excited; apprehension was transformed into anticipation, and she regained her old confidence with the glow remaining from the shower.

The swimming pool, inviting from a distance, lost its appeal up close. Stagnant green water—its only recent patrons the green frogs, mosquito larvae and microscopic beings that enjoyed it with obvious relish. The frogs mated enthusiastically, the males gulping air, then releasing it with a croak in hopeful sexual display; the females responded to the ample choice with placid contemplation. Mosquito larvae squiggled up and down, zigzagging between Lilliputian strings of algal slime.

Jeff felt cool and refreshed as he sat by the pool with an iced bottle of Polar in hand. The ubiquitous beer with its trademark dignified polar bear sitting on an iceberg was a national institution. No one asked for just a beer; the choice was a Polarcito, a small one, or a Polar grande, the pint version, and it was invariably served ice-cold in the bottle. It was unthinkable to ruin the Polar ceremony by decanting it into a glass, no matter how well chilled the glass might be. A considerable mystique surrounded the temperature of a good Polar. The bottle had to be frosted with ice and the beer as close as possible to freezing. The slightest trace of ice in the beer itself was an abomination and the bottle would be returned with disgust to the bartender. Debra came from the general direction of the bar with a Polarcito in hand and sat down facing the pool beside Jeff, semi-reclined in his chair, strumming his fingers on his Polar bottle to the tintinnabulation of merengue. He spread his legs, one foot resting upon his knee, and held onto his beer loosely. Music, the croak of frogs and the electric hum of cicadas vibrated the air.

"You look great, hon. You must've been ready for that beer," he said.

"Thanks. The beer is good, and now that I've finally made it to Amazonas I feel suddenly quite calm. I think meeting someone as well adapted as you has helped me get things into perspective. I've decided to relax and enjoy the experience."

"Congratulations!" He extended his bottle. They clinked brown glass together. "You've just taken the first step to survival down here. Don't take anything too seriously. Take my word, you're going to face a lot of frustrations, and the more you let them get to you the more miserable you'll become. Shit, I've been here over five years and almost every day I could have found a reason to pack it all in and go back to the States. Not many outsiders stick it out for long, and that includes Venezuelans who come from up north. Who knows, maybe tomorrow's trip will be my last."

"Tomorrow?" she asked. Jeff thought he detected a trace of disappointment.

"Yeah. I've got to get back upriver. I've been away too long and I might not be welcome back there. I'll be hitching a ride on a Ministry of Health Cessna to Topochal first thing in the morning. That's where I left my boat. Two days from there I'll be back in my little hut—that's if the Yanomami haven't destroyed it."

"I'm sorry you have to go so soon. I was hoping we could spend some time together and you could introduce me to Puerto Pedriscal. Can you give me any quick tips?"

"You'll want to meet the governor. He's the one person you want to know and get along with in the Territory. It's a political appointment from Caracas, but while he's in power he can do pretty well anything he likes. If you want some rules bent or something done fast, he can do it. You should get along well with him. He's an MD turned politician so of course he's a bit dumb"—he grinned—"but that makes him easier to handle. INSA is his big showpiece right now. He thinks the whole lot of you have the sun shining out your asses. And he likes pretty asses, one big advantage you have that I don't. In fact, most people in power around here are men, so don't be afraid to flirt a little. It can help lubricate things, if you know what I mean," he explained with a leer. "You're on the frontier here so there's a large army and naval presence. You'll definitely run into Capitán Máximo Zambrano, who heads the División de la Selva. In fact, you may have to go through him if you want permission to go upriver. I've heard local gossip that he runs some shady private business operations, some even claim he's on the CIA payroll. I kinda doubt it, but it doesn't hurt to play it safe, to keep a safe distance anyway." Jeff polished off his beer. "Another?"

"Yes, please. I don't normally drink much beer, but it really is refreshing." Debra took a big gulp. "I guess it's hard for anyone to keep secrets in a town this size."

Jeff motioned the waiter to bring another round. "Ain't that the truth. Well, mostly the truth, 'cause you don't get to know everyone's business in town. For the most part the wealthy who invest in Puerto Pedriscal live outside the Territory, so forget trying to get to know them."

"Hmmmm," she said. She burped quietly. "Excuse me. I noticed in the newspaper yesterday that the Judicial Police are investigating some rich family from the capital who own a hacienda down here."

"Yeah, there's a big stink going on. The allegation is that native people had squatters' right on the bigwig's hacienda. They were forced off by some hired cowhands, the women raped and the men beaten. There's a rumour that stolen military guns were used in the assault. People here say the federal investigation is biased because the investigators stayed at the hacienda and they were wined and dined at the bigwig's personal expense. The investigators' report declared the cowhands to be innocent. 'Course nobody around here believes that's true."

3

The first time Debra woke up, Jeff had thrown a hairy arm across her breasts and a big hairy leg over her pelvic bones. They prickled and she had developed intolerable itches that she couldn't reach. She tried to move, but he had her pinned and he tightened his grasp like a boa constrictor. His leg and arm were very heavy. After her escape attempt Jeff snuggled his face deeply into her hair, his mouth against her ear. First she heard a rhythmic *pphhuuu, pphhhuu,* which gradually increased to a raucous snore. It was hot. The room had an air-conditioner but Jeff hadn't allowed her to turn it on (not used to that shit any more, hon) and she felt dirty and sticky. The copulating frogs outside made a din that flooded the gaps between snores and she felt a dull ache start about one inch behind both eyes. If that wasn't enough, people walked up and down the corridors all night long, slamming doors behind them. If Debra could so clearly hear noises in the hallway, then she had probably been quite audible to anyone passing by. The air-conditioner would have masked the sound. Damn him!

A brief interlude of restless sleep was rudely interrupted by someone bouncing on the bed. "What the . . . ," Debra asked groggily, levering herself up on her elbows. Jeff crawled on all fours, naked, rear end thrust towards her, penis and testicles dangling in front of her nose as he rummaged through the sheets.

He turned and stunned her with a light beam coming from the middle of his forehead. The head-lamp made him look like a lunatic gynaecologist, and instinctively Debra's legs snapped shut. "Ants, hon. There's fucking hundreds of them crawling all over the bed. They woke me up when they started biting." She leapt out of bed with a cry and switched on the main light. Sure enough, ants scurried everywhere, no doubt snacking on secretions. Debra helped brush them off the bed and Jeff wound Scotch tape around the bed's legs, sticky side out.

"Take that stupid light off your head before we get back into bed," she said. "On second thought, Mr. Gynaecologist, leave it on for a while."

❦

In the morning, Debra danced around in her own shower trying to avoid the frigid water while trying to wash thoroughly. She cursed her stupidity and the damned alcohol. She had totally lost her inhibitions, and although it had been a lot of fun she was worried now. Jeff hadn't used a condom and she wasn't on the pill. She had thought there would be no need for contraception in the middle of the jungle. And now, she thought with regret, Jeff would probably spread it around town that he had screwed the gringa quack.

As she mentally calculated the date of her last period (just a few days and she'd be able to relax again), she set off to town to look around and try to locate a familiar face from INSA. She strolled down Avenida Río Negro, a pitted lane leading to the main plaza. The two-storied white buildings surrounding Plaza Bolívar were blinding in the morning sun. This was the administrative centre of Puerto Pedriscal: the municipal council, the Ministry of Justice, the Judicial Police station, the Ministry of Indian Affairs and the Salesian Church and Mission House. White walls contrasted dramatically with the plaza's deep shade, where mature mango trees encircled the omnipresent effigy of Simón Bolívar. Every town in the country had its Plaza Bolívar in homage to the Great Liberator of the Americas, and one had to be very careful about appropriate comportment in the plaza. In Caracas, a policeman had once made Debra detour around the entire perimeter of the plaza rather than cross directly through it because she carried a paper bag containing acetaminophen that she had bought at a pharmacy. The policeman informed her firmly that to carry a paper bag while inside the plaza's boundaries constituted a "lack of respect for the Liberator". Likewise, Jeff had mentioned that he had once been reprimanded for holding hands with his wife while admiring a magnificent bronze statue of Bolívar on horseback.

Debra took another sidestreet to Avenida 23 de Enero, the town's commercial street. January 23, her guidebook said, was an important public holiday commemorating the overthrow in 1958 of the country's last dictator, Pérez Jiménez. During his dictatorship, Pérez Jiménez, who loathed loud noises, had outlawed the use of car horns in downtown Caracas and had renamed El Centro to El Silencio. During her stay in Caracas, Debra noticed that some drivers still thumped the roofs of their cars rather than use the horn. Pérez Jiménez would have hated Avenida 23 de Enero. The avenue bustled with jeeps, trucks and people, mostly men. They stopped and stared openly as Debra passed. A hissing sound could be heard above the growl of engines. A few women hurried by, looked straight ahead and ignored any hisses that came their way. A wave of hissing followed Debra. Someone in a dark doorway hissed, *"Pssst, psssst,* catira." She had been called that before—blonde, light-coloured, offspring of mulatto and white, said her dictionary. Here it didn't sound too complimentary. Suddenly, a friendly male Spanish voice spoke behind her.

"I should have known that only a catira could provoke such a commotion."

Debra turned. "Fermin," she said. "I'm so happy to see you. I thought I'd never find someone from INSA." Debra had met him at her interview in Caracas. He worked in parasitology, mostly picking apart human faeces. He carried a fanny-pack— in his case a pene-pack, for he wore it in front like a sporran, quite low under a thickening waist. Debra wondered if he was trying to conceal or accentuate what lay beneath.

36

Fermin's head reached only to Debra's shoulders. His curly black hair had receded although he was still in his early twenties, and round wire-rimmed glasses circled his eyes. He blinked several times, squeezing his lids tightly together, a nervous twitch. "Debra, what are you doing here in Puerto Pedriscal?" he asked. "No one was expecting you so soon."

"So soon? Doctor Velázquez told me to come. He said I would be met at the airport."

"I think he forgot. He mentioned it to nobody, and as usual there is trouble up at the centre. The ministry objected about your being a foreigner and Doctor Velázquez has been meeting all week with local health officials on your behalf. We thought you wouldn't be coming until he had straightened things out."

"What? You mean I may not be able to work?" Had she come all this way, gone to so much trouble, even so far as applying to change her nationality, for nothing? By this time, the sun baked the streets from directly above. Debra drooped and shifted her weight from one sore foot to the other. Her high heels had become uncomfortable. Her feet had swollen and sweated, conditions ripe for blisters, and she realized much of her Miami fashion was useless in this environment.

"Why don't you come with us to INSA. Osvaldo, our driver, is here with the transport jeep. Don't worry about the small problem. I have no doubt the doctor will resolve everything. He is very skilled at political relations and we at INSA are accustomed to dealing with many a crisis." Fermin smiled and guided Debra around a corner to a dusty mustard jeep with the centre's logo painted on its side, an *Anopheles* mosquito with "Instituto Nacional de Salud Amazónica" printed in a circle around it.

A man stood leaning against the jeep. "Debra," said Fermin, "this is Osvaldo. Osvaldo, this is Debra, the doctora gringa I told you about."

Osvaldo beamed welcome. His brown eyes scintillated with enthusiasm, framed by lightly etched laugh lines when he smiled. His brown skin was stretched taut over unpadded cheekbones. "Doctora, I am pleased to have you join us," he said. His smile was infectious.

The jeep could seat around ten passengers. By now Debra's armpits were ringed with sweat and her hair clung to the sides of her face. Fermin and Osvaldo also sweated, but not as badly.

"You are now a mosquito doctor. Local people see the institute's logo on the jeep," Osvaldo said. He inserted the key and the engine coughed to life. "They don't know exactly what it means, but because we have a mosquito on the jeep they assume we operate a hospital to cure infirm mosquitoes. They ask me, 'Why do you heal mosquitoes when there are so many, and they bite and cause us pain and malaria?'"

"They know little of the scientists who work high above them on top of the hill," Fermin added.

"Time is bringing change," Osvaldo continued. "Some now come up for medical help, those who are desperate enough and don't trust the hospital."

"Yes, but the misperception continues," Fermin said. "Last week Tour Amazonica brought up a tourist group to see the mosquito hospital."

The jeep strained up the arduous hill to INSA. Puerto Pedriscal was spread below, barren earth and granite capped by cloned houses surrounded by fecund greens, opulent golds, and vivific water—a harsh and vibrant scenery. The roadside had eroded in deep rust fissures running down to the hill's base, emphasizing the fragility of the lush vegetation.

The road levelled out towards the hilltop and became a channel through thick forest. Two dead trees jutted above the foliage at the tunnel's end. A white paste plastered the naked upper branches and the source occupied the topmost branches—black, hunched silhouettes of vultures that guarded the entrance to INSA. The jeep approached an open gate in a tall chain-link fence and a larger silhouette loomed out of the shadows, also on guard. Closer, the features were discernible: a swarthy, pock-marked policeman, holding a machine-gun at the ready as he watched the jeep pass. He gave no sign of recognition or response to Osvaldo's wave. How had tourists slipped by him to see the mosquito hospital?

Beyond the fence all forest stopped abruptly. Any vegetation that had ever covered the plateau had been scraped off. In its place were expanses of bare red earth surrounding a small complex of low modern buildings, with lots of glass and white walls punctuated by red doors and yellow doors. The largest blank wall facing the entrance gate had a stylized depiction of the centre's acronym entangled in an abstract web of circles and lines, horrible sixties art in orange, blue, yellow and red.

The buildings were arranged in a square facing a small central yard, a small Plaza Bolívar, in fact. An honoured centrepiece, the Liberator's head on a pedestal, emerged from the weeds. Roofs extended to form a covered pathway around the plaza. Debra stared at strange heavy chains hanging from roof to ground every few yards. Might they be supports for climbing plants that had never been planted?

"It rains bullets here, Debra," Osvaldo said, as if she'd asked the question. "If not for the chains, the rains would chew up the ground and spit it into a million pieces."

"They direct the water flow from the roof during storms," Fermin clarified further. He ran his hand down a length of chain and set it swinging slowly. "The doctor's office is this one." Fermin said "the doctor" with a peculiar reverence. He knocked on the door and, hearing a response from within, slipped inside.

If not for his fingernails and aloof formality, Debra would have found Velázquez to be tantalizing. He had told her in Caracas that he had come originally from Buenos Aires. He had received his Doctor of Medicine from an Argentine university and later obtained his Ph.D from the Heidelberg Institute of Hygiene.

The centre was a remarkable accomplishment in an area as isolated as Puerto Pedriscal. Jeff had told her that its existence was due solely to years of determination and political dealings by Velázquez. He wheedled money successfully from both national and international sources, demonstrating his talent for getting exactly what he wanted. Velázquez possessed a charismatic quality in addition to his extreme good looks. He intimidated people while he smiled graciously, leaving his opponents with the impression that he was infallible. Every word he uttered had been selected, carefully scrutinized, before being spoken. He habitually told women who might be politically useful that he was single, when in fact he lived with a common-law wife.

Fermin re-emerged. "You may enter now," he said.

Doctor Velázquez's office was dark in comparison to the bright light outside. The windows had been covered with aluminum foil, keeping the sunlight and heat out. A wall-mounted air-conditioner filled the room with noise and gave it a synthetic chill.

❦

The doctor had meticulously orchestrated a play for Debra to step into. In this way he could command any verbal intercourse from the onset. He sat at a desk with his hands folded together on top, every scrap of paper stacked in perfect alignment. He wore a waist-length, short-sleeved white lab coat, pressed perfectly, instead of a shirt. Such coats were fashionable among lab techs and doctors in Venezuela, and were perfect for the Puerto Pedriscal heat. He allowed his curly black chest hair to creep up above the top button. He had been friendly during her recruitment for his centre. Now it was time to change his demeanour, to emphasize his authority.

"Doctora Baumstark, welcome. Please seat yourself," he said. He swept his hand to indicate a chair.

"Thank you," she replied, and sat opposite the expanse of his desk.

He suddenly dropped his warm smile. "I sincerely express my apologies for not having personally met you at the airport."

He spoke slowly and clearly in his impeccable Spanish. "The situation at INSA is a little tense politically at the moment." He explained that he had been occupied with political turmoil involving the centre. Political relations in the Territory required skill, finesse and his undivided attention. He shifted his weight in the chair and once again poised himself. "The seriousness of our current political situation demands that I inform you of a few things. First, INSA has many enemies. To work here you must constantly guard against people from outside our centre. They are jealous of my success and will stop at nothing to handicap me. The latest disruptive effort comes from an official in the Ministry of Health, whom I will for the moment leave unnamed. He has officially objected to my hiring you despite the fact that we have searched five years to assign the position. Fortunately, the territorial governor has been sympathetic to my needs." What he didn't add was the fact that an American medical doctor was ideal for his needs. An American doctor looked good when it came to acquiring international funding, and an American, not understanding the institutional politics here, wouldn't get involved in them and become overly ambitious. Velázquez could effortlessly keep such a person in line.

"I am very sorry to have caused you any problems," said Debra. She sat stiffly, feet pressed together in parallel.

He smiled a fraction of a second. "I assure you there is nothing for you to be concerned about. I am disposing of the difficulties personally. I merely want you to be aware of the situation so that you will monitor your behaviour accordingly. These are difficult times. You must always be vigilant, and until the situation has been defused I think it would be wise if you were to keep your presence here in the Territory quiet. Don't draw attention to yourself."

"There is no need for you to worry," Debra said.

"Good." Velázquez smiled with deliberation.

"But why did you not let me know that there were problems before I flew down here?" Debra asked.

41

He spread his hands apologetically but his poise didn't waver. "There are so many problems with telephone communication that I can't contact people from here when I would like to. That's why I must spend most of my time in the capital. It is the only way to keep informed of the actual situation."

"You could have at least sent someone to meet me at the airport," she protested.

"We have just one vehicle available for errands," he explained calmly, "and I needed Osvaldo for urgent work yesterday." He paused. His supreme control of the meeting had left her with nothing more to say. "You have been assigned a consulting suite beside the laboratories. Are you acquainted with the staff yet?"

"No, today I have met only Osvaldo, and in Caracas I met yourself, Fermin and a few others."

"Then you should feel at liberty to spend the afternoon meeting people. There is a chain of command here which is necessary for maintaining the smooth operation of the centre. Your official title is Co-ordinator of Medical Services. I have biologists who co-ordinate various research areas, and technicians beneath them who perform routine laboratory tasks. In addition to doing research I have created a diagnostic facility. This not only provides a much-needed service to the community, but provides us with clinical materials that we use for experimentation. Your first duties will be to visit patients at the local hospital and to identify those afflicted by the diseases in our research areas. You must accompany all research expeditions and you'll be expected to take blood and biopsies. In remote areas without medical services, there is no problem with ratification of your credentials, and you will provide limited medical aid. You should work closely with the other co-ordinators whenever clinical research is conducted. The majority of cases you see in Puerto Pedriscal will most probably be of tuberculosis. Reina is our Co-ordinator of Microbiology and she must be informed of any cases you encounter. Additionally, she and the other co-ordinators can arrange diagnostic tests if you deem them necessary for the procurement of a definitive diagnosis. You will act as an intermediary between my centre and the local hospital. A general practitioner, Doctor Amador Pantaleon, will be your contact there. I plan to have you concentrate on routine clinical work initially, but later I expect you to participate in research and publication. I think I need not stress the importance of timely publication to a research institute."

"That sounds very reasonable, Doctor Velázquez," Debra said.

"Lastly, I made arrangements for you to stay at a house leased by the centre. At the moment two of my researchers live there—an immunologist, Wilfred, who is conducting research in the area of immunoparasitology, and a medical entomologist, Yadira, who studies anopheline mosquitoes. Unfortunately, you will not be able to meet Yadira today as she is in Caracas, but Wilfred is here and will answer any questions you may have concerning accommodations. Originally I leased the facility to house visiting scientists, but most have shown a preference for the Gran Hotel Las Palmas and I have decided not to renew the lease. It's imperative that you, Wilfred and Yadira promptly find your own accommodations in town."

"Thank you, Doctor Velázquez," Debra said. Her voice sounded weak. "I appreciate the arrangements you made for me."

The pervading hum of air-conditioning didn't hide the silence as Velázquez planned his next words. "The problem with the ministry has, for the most part, been resolved, but I want to remind you again that you must maintain a modest profile."

"Of course," she replied. "Is there anything else you wanted to discuss with me?"

In her crude Spanish she had addressed him as "tu", the informal pronoun, rather than "usted", the respectful term. A vein on Velázquez's forehead throbbed. He recovered instantly, forcing his lips back into a tight smile, and nodded graciously. "Yes, there is. I will need protocols outlining the methodology you will use to fulfil your job description on my desk by tomorrow morning. Make a list of all supplies you intend to use and have it ready for Luz María, our administrator, by the beginning of next week. I need you to become a fully functional staff member as soon as possible. That should put the ministry's complaints to rest." It was an unreasonable request, one he knew she could not possibly meet in such a short time. It would, however, keep her out of sight and out of trouble for a while.

"I will do my best," she assured him.

"In that case, I am most pleased to welcome you to my institute. I expect your appointment to be of mutual benefit to us both. Do not disappoint me and do not forget the protocols."

"Thank you, Doctor Velázquez," Debra said, easing herself from her seat. One final formal smile and he gently encouraged her, his hand on her back, out of his office. The air-conditioning chilled her damp back. Velázquez wiped his hand on his short white coat.

A restful quiet settled on Debra. The facility was spotless, modern and well equipped, and her consulting suite could have been transplanted from any clinic in the U.S., although the location made it seem almost surreal. She was used to windowless rooms where the only decorations were yellowed posters displaying cross-sectional noses, eyes peeled away in layers like fruits and colourful drug-company calendars. Here, one entire wall of louvred glass gave a stunning panorama from the vast flaxen Colombian savannahs to the distant jungle-smothered tepuis she had seen from the plane. The Orinoco River braided through the centre of the landscape in ribbons gilded by the late-afternoon sun.

Both her office and an adjacent private examination room

were decorated with intimate black-and-white photos of Yanomami: a family in hammocks around a fire; an old lady with sagging stomach and flaps for breasts, laden with a staggering load of plantains; young girls with flower pompoms in their pierced ears and thin sticks through pierced noses and lower lips, smiling unselfconsciously at the camera; stern, muscled warriors painted in exquisite patterns, dressed only in tight bands below the knees and around the upper arms and strings around their waists holding penises erect by a knot around the foreskin.

"Hola! Velázquez told me to go with Osvaldo to take you to your house," Fermin said as he stuck his head through the door. "The doctor will take you to dinner tonight. He said to expect him at your house at seven."

Osvaldo drove her to a residential area of nearly identical concrete-block houses with tin roofs, close to the base of the INSA hill.

"Not very inspiring architecture," Debra said.

"They are all Department of Malariología houses built by the Ministry of Health as part of an effort to eradicate malaria," Fermin said. "The concrete can be dusted easily with DDT. Female *Anopheles* mosquitoes always rest soon after a blood meal and should be killed by the DDT. The concrete blocks also have fewer entrance points for mosquitoes than thatch and mud construction does."

"My God, they didn't dust the house I'll be staying in, did they? Please tell me they're not still using that stuff," Debra said. "DDT was banned in the U.S. years ago."

Osvaldo chuckled. "In the countryside DDT is used by the bucketful. Even the children grab it with bare hands and have snowball fights."

"Fortunately," Fermin interjected, "in town there are very few cases of malaria so they don't use it here any more. But they do spray a diesel-oil mist to kill the larvae. The fogger comes to this area every Tuesday night. As far as I know, the mist is not too harmful to people."

Osvaldo slowed the jeep and pulled up in front of the last cement-block house on the street. "Here it is, tu casita."

They stepped through a small front yard of cracked dirt and limp weeds, up concrete stairs to the unpainted breeze-blocks of the house. A neat, modest church stood on a rise next door, its presence silent, watchful.

"That's the Evangelist church," explained Fermin, as if he thought Debra would be comforted by the strong American presence. "And think of the keychain as a welcoming gift," he said, smiled, and held out a key with a clear plastic case dangling from it. The case enclosed a rolled-up condom and written on it was "Para Emergencia—Prevenir Es Proteger".

"What are you trying to insinuate?" Debra asked, fixing him with a cold stare.

His glasses lay across his nose, a little askew. He quickly squeezed his eyes shut and reopened them. "Actually, I received it at a community development seminar in Caracas. They were passed out as souvenirs and, speaking as one single person to another, it pays to be prepared in Amazonas. Sexually transmitted disease is epidemic here."

"What makes you think I need to be protected?"

He inserted the key into the lock. "I went to the airport to pick up a shipment and found Doctor Marshall there, his vuelo delayed on account of the weather. He complimented me on Velázquez's choice of médicos and gave me a look, the kind that one man gives to another to show him exactly what he means."

"I think you've said enough," Debra said.

He smiled. "Debra, this is a very small town and discretion is advised. I too have found myself the victim of gossip, and Doctor Velázquez will display your head on a stake for all the town to see if you become the object of local talk."

Fermin opened the door and Debra's anger died in the bleak room in front of her: a bare, battleship-grey concrete floor, a single grimy window barred heavily with black wrought iron, green iron beams supporting the corrugated metal roof, cobwebs. A bare lightbulb hung from exposed wires. The grey sitting room had been adorned with cracked, brown vinyl chairs that spewed foam at the corners.

She walked slowly around. The sitting room opened into a kitchenette with a tiny two-burner propane gas stove, a peeling mother-of-pearl formica table and four chairs. Past the kitchenette lay a long, narrow room with large hooks sunk into the walls at intervals. A hammock hung, strung between two of the hooks. Three small rooms lay off the hammock room, each with a cot-like single bed. Two contained personal belongings; the smallest did not.

Her stomach lay heavily on her intestines. If Fermin knew about Jeff, how many others did? The whole town, probably. If Debra had managed to get pregnant, she wouldn't have to offer many explanations. And at least nothing from now on could possibly be more embarrassing.

Velázquez picked up Debra in his gleaming black Toyota Land Cruiser, a custom vehicle befitting the distinguished director of a research centre in Amazonas. Osvaldo had washed and polished it that afternoon. He had managed to rub out most of the watermarks on the upholstery, and only traces and a faint smell of mildew remained.

Velázquez took her to the Salón Rojo, which he assured her was the best eating establishment in town. It lived up to its name with red brocade walls, red upholstery and red plastic tablecloths. The menu had even been translated into English for the convenience of English-speaking patrons:

Ración de jamón Serrano—Mountaineer haw ration
Bistec muchacho a la plancha—Slab of boy to the metal plate
Yuca frita—Yucca in the oil

At the bottom of the page was "please, but left behind a 10% gratuity would be thanked much for, when you leave".

"Debra, would you care for a drink to celebrate the beginning of a productive professional relationship?" Velázquez asked, noticing her smiles as she read the menu.

Debra looked at the red brocade walls. "I feel I'm incubating *in utero*. A Bloody Mary would be appropriate," she answered.

He didn't laugh with her. He had thought his intimidating tactics during their earlier meeting more successful. This girl would obviously need a different approach from his other staff. A waiter in a burgundy jacket and a black bow tie laid a dish of butter and a basket on the table. "Un Chivas Regal con hielo, por favor, y un jugo de tomate con vodka para la señorita," Velázquez said. He took an arepa from the basket, delicately broke off a piece and dabbed it with butter. "Do you like arepas?" he asked.

She picked one up and broke a piece off. "It's a bit heavy. Corn, is it?"

Velázquez nodded. "How did you get on with the staff?" he asked.

"It was difficult to meet so many new people all at once. Most of them were very friendly. That is, except for the three women co-ordinators. They seemed a bit reserved."

"It is a difficult social situation here. Puerto Pedriscal is a small town. There are few you will have anything in common with. The laboratory staff, particularly the researchers, will be your social life, and because they spend so much of their time together, there can be a great deal of friction."

The waiter came and quietly placed their drinks on the table. "A few of the staff have been reluctant to accept your appointment," Velázquez admitted. "They may be xenophobic at first. They think foreigners lack the ability to adapt to the heat and isolation. Handle the social situation prudently. Relationships can become caustic, and everyone has had difficulties with another staff member at some time.

"As a foreigner, the onus is on you to make a favourable

impression. Learn from Wilfred's example. I had high expectations for him. He's German, from the Heidelberg Institute, with the utmost in professional qualifications for one so young. However, the cultural change and isolation have been too much for him, and his research ambitions are far too sophisticated for the kind of things we can currently accomplish at my centre. He has not adapted well."

Throughout the meal, Debra sipped at her drink nervously and picked at her food. The fact that she drank more than she ate did not escape Velázquez's notice.

"Excuse me, Doctor Velázquez," she said as a waiter cleared the table. "I need to visit the rest room."

They had sat at a table close to the entrance, so Debra had to walk to the rear of the restaurant to the ladies' room. The restaurant had filled up while they talked.

As she wove back through the tables towards him, Velázquez saw people stare at her, some with their mouths gaping. He tried to motion to her but she just looked puzzled, completely unaware of her predicament. She took her seat.

"Debra . . . my signals . . . all the people staring," he said. He could barely speak, and swallowed his outrage the way he would a rancid prune. This was not his idea of a low profile.

"I must seem pretty unusual to them," she answered.

"You would find yourself to be far less conspicuous if you were to untuck your skirt from your underwear, Doctora Baumstark."

4

"I hate it here," Wilfred said. Sunday night, and he sat at the pearly formica table with Debra. It was the first opportunity he had had to speak with her in confidence since she had moved in from the Hotel Las Palmas. The blond fuzz of his moustache barely accentuated his thin lips, and his fine, limp hair drooped across one eye in the day's accumulated heat radiating from the ceiling. "It is impossible to work here. All the fancy equipment and none of it works. It's so backward. I have wasted a year of my life, pouring with diarrhoea, living in this hell. Finally, I tell someone." He stressed the point with a thump of his clenched fist on the tabletop.

He had tried to do an enzyme-linked immunosorbent assay just last week. He had tried to detect *Leishmania* antigen in patients' sera but the electric current had kept shutting off and he couldn't even calibrate the ELISA machine, a sophisticated French apparatus that was useless here. Debra smiled back sympathetically. He knew she would understand. Only a fellow foreigner could relate to the frustration of trying to do real science in such primitive conditions. An American, used to efficiency, would quickly become as disgusted as he.

The musky onion smell of body odour mixed with clouds of cigarette smoke masked the aroma of roasted coffee beans steaming from the mugs in front of them. He had never had this problem with body odour in Germany. Never had he been able to adapt to the infernal heat here. The smell had once been so severe that the técnicos refused to ride the transport jeep with him. Osvaldo had had to make two separate trips to take the staff home. Osvaldo told him to wash daily with a laundry soap, Las Llaves. "Like this, Wilfred, under the arms,"

Osvaldo said as he grabbed an imaginary bar of soap and rubbed vigorously up and down his armpits. "Remember, Wilfred, JABON LAS LLA-VES." Las Llaves was guaranteed lethal to microbes; it could also digest fabric. The experience was utterly humiliating to Wilfred. He quickly bought a motorcycle so that he no longer had to take abuse from Osvaldo and the técnicos.

He sat hunched over his coffee, a cigarette dangling from his lips. Too bad Debra hadn't come to work here a year ago, when he had been desperate for non-Latin company. Now he had almost finished his contract and he could soon go home to Germany. He would be there before Christmas, and he was counting the days. In a little over four months he'd be home for good, home where his lovely fiancée waited patiently.

Debra nervously picked at a fraying piece of plywood on the table's edge, as if she had picked up his mood. A moth fluttered around the bare lightbulb that hung above them, casting giant shadows around the dismal room.

"Perhaps you could work on a simpler project, something easier technically," she said.

Suddenly, the front door burst open. A stocky, dark-haired girl barged into the room and looked in horror at the cosy kitchen-table scene.

"Wilfred, I caught you. Huevón!" she screamed. She flew out the door as quickly as she had come in.

"*Verflucht!*" He had forgotten to tell Inés not to come, that he had a new roommate. He tried to keep his relationship with Inés a secret. There was now no telling what she would do. Probably not let him sleep with her for a week or, worse yet, tell her husband about the affair. "Inés, it's not what you think! Come back," he called out to her as he leapt from his chair. "Pardon me," he said to Debra, who hadn't moved throughout the outburst.

Inés roared her bomber car to life and it backfired as it screeched around the corner. Wilfred's motorcycle ripped the air, seconds behind her.

Reina arrived at the house in the exaggerated silence left by Wilfred's exit. She co-ordinated the microbiology lab, which worked almost exclusively with tuberculosis. She was a pretty girl in an insipid way. She had regular features and a trim figure. Her Madrid genetic heritage provided her light colouring, which was enough to attract the attention of most local men. She permed and cropped her hair in a cap of curls, a functional approach to managing fine hair in the tropics, although her bangs still separated into strings revealing her too-round, shiny forehead.

She was apprehensive about having another foreigner on staff. Not that she was xenophobic, as Velázquez had accused, but working with Wilfred had been next to impossible. God forbid that the centre should be burdened with another person like him. He complained continuously and he always considered himself so superior to those around him. And he smelled. Reina knew her country had problems, but she didn't like a smelly foreigner, a misiú, coming here and saying so. Her country needed to find its own answers to its problems. What could the misiús, ignorant about Latin America, hope to contribute?

Still, if she and the other researchers had helped Wilfred more in the beginning, he might have adapted better. Reina felt she should make an attempt to be friendly to this new doctor, who at least seemed to be interested in the centre's research. She stopped at the house just in time to see Wilfred's motorcycle tear around the corner. She tapped on the door.

"Buenas noches, Doctora Baumstark. I am Reina. We were introduced at the centre."

"Reina. Doctor Velázquez told me we would be working closely together. Come in. And please drop the doctora title and call me Debra. I was about to make myself some dinner. Would you care to join me? I think there's just enough in the refrigerator to make us an omelette." Reina followed Debra to the small kitchen area and looked in disgust at the dirty sink, the crumbs being carried off by a procession of ants, and the overflowing ashtray.

"I see Wilfred is as tidy here as he is in the laboratory," Reina said. "Yadira will be angry with him when she returns from the capital. She is very exigent. I too lived here for a short time when I first came to work for the centre, then I was lucky to find a small place just outside of town. It has an iron roof so it's hot during the day, but it's fresh in the evenings, and I have privacy when my husband comes to visit."

The only food Debra had in the house was eggs, bread, overripe tomatoes and Cheez Whiz (Chee Wee, Reina called it). Reina cracked the eggs one at a time into a cup, sniffing each one before sliding it into a bowl. She was an expert on local eggs. She cultured her tuberculosis bacilli in a medium prepared with fresh hens' eggs. Fresh eggs were difficult to find, and she regularly scoured the surrounding ranchitos to buy them for her Lowenstein-Jensen medium; the fastidious bacilli refused to grow if the eggs were more than a couple of days old. That was how research had to be conducted here, with perseverance. Why, she could remember the days when the centre didn't even have distilled water. The scientific advances the centre had managed to achieve in only a short time were remarkable.

"Where was Wilfred going in such a hurry?" Reina asked.

"A girl came bursting in, screamed and ran out. It was most peculiar," Debra replied.

"Inés," Reina said with a smile. "Wilfred's girlfriend. She thinks, for some reason I can't understand, that all women chase Wilfred. She's a simple girl. Perhaps she thought you were a German girlfriend who had arrived to take him away."

"But I only just met him."

"She's married and Wilfred thinks he has kept their affair a secret. He made a mistake befriending the pharmacist. That man is a big gossip, and horrible, completamente putañero, I think. People here call him Huevo de Pava—Turkey Egg, you say in English."

"I don't understand."

"He has red hair, very unusual here, and his freckles make his face look like a big turkey egg."

"Does the word 'huevón' have anything to do with 'huevo'?" Debra asked, diligently cutting black spots from tomatoes.

Why did misiús always pick up swearwords before they could even speak the language correctly? "Huevones are large eggs, but the word is used in reference to testicles. It should never be used in polite company. Who has been teaching you such groserías?" Reina asked.

"Wilfred's girlfriend called him that tonight," explained Debra, looking quite amused.

The eggs steamed, ready to be eaten, but before a fork could be lifted a frantic pounding and screaming sounded from the front door—"*They killed Wilfred, they killed Wilfred!*"

A fuzzy dark form showed through the frosted glass window. Reina's fork clattered across the floor as she rushed to the door.

"Inmaculada," Reina cried, "what happened?"

Inmaculada stood panting, her eyes opened so wide that the whites haloed her dark brown irises. She was a very dark girl, a chocolate brown with darker knees and elbows. Her lips—normally purplish, almost black—were now bloodlessly pale. Inmaculada had given birth not long ago, and dark patches on her orange tee-shirt showed where milk had seeped through her bra.

"Who killed Wilfred?" prompted Reina. "Tell me. Calm down."

"They killed him!" Inmaculada wailed. "He's at the hospital. Come quickly. Osvaldo is waiting to take us. Doctor Pantaleon needs Doctora Debra to help him."

❧

Dead? Debra strove to understand Inmaculada's hysterical ramblings in the back of the transport jeep. How could Wilfred be dead so soon after running out of the house? If he had been taken to the hospital, and where Doctor Pantaleon, already on the scene, was asking for her help, he must surely be alive. But why was her help needed at all? She wasn't licensed to practise medicine in Venezuela, and everyone knew it.

The jeep skidded to a stop behind the ambulance in front of the emergency entrance. The ambulance, a white jeep embossed with a red cross barely visible through a layer of dust, looked as if it hadn't been used in a decade.

A small crowd had gathered at the entrance. Debra recognized most of them as staff of INSA. Out of the babble that greeted her, she understood that Wilfred, following Inés on his motorcycle, had been struck head on by the drunk driver of a pickup truck. From the animated gestures, it was clear that Wilfred had sustained head injuries.

"Reina, don't you want to say goodbye to Wilfred?" choked a pear-shaped girl, her eyes puffy and red from crying.

"No, Blancanieves. I prefer to remember him the way he was," Reina replied.

"It may be your last chance," Blancanieves sniffed. She put her chubby arm around Reina and urged her towards the door. Reina resisted and frowned as if repulsed.

A thin, nervous voice spoke rapidly. "She doesn't have to go if she doesn't want to, Blancanieves, but I think Doctora Baumstark should go in now to help." Debra looked at the small, bird-like head tilted to one side. Marisol, the blackfly expert. Marisol stared at her intensely through dry eyes, wide and strangely dark.

Debra glanced around the faces watching her and then down at her wristwatch. "You know, I really don't think I should interfere. There's nothing I can do medically. I don't think anyone else should go in there either. Have they started operating?" she asked.

"Operating?" Blancanieves blinked incredulously between

sniffles.

"Blancanieves!" Fermin said sharply. He nudged her none too gently with his elbow. "She doesn't yet know!"

Blancanieves burst into tears again, chin quivering. Fermin unzipped his fanny-pack, took out a handkerchief and handed it to her.

"You're right, Fermin. I'm sure she doesn't," said Osvaldo, and put his arm around Debra protectively. His eyes shone, reservoirs of saline solution. "Debra, Wilfred se desapareció."

"He disappeared?" Debra asked, totally confused. "You said before he was in the hospital with Doctor Pantaleon."

Fermin spoke with exaggerated patience. "Debra, Osvaldo is tactfully informing you that Wilfred is dead. Actually, he died the instant the truck hit him. You should go inside now, because the doctor is waiting for you." He shook his head. "Gringos estúpidos!"

"Dead? Then why is the doctor asking for my help?" Debra challenged, her arms folded across her chest. What the hell was going on with these people?

In the background, INSA staff members stood at the emergency entrance, sobbing and embracing. Others went back and forth through the emergency door.

"Look, Debra, you're a médico. Start acting like one," said Reina, who at this point still maintained better emotional control than anyone else. "You have seen a cadaver before. Now go help preserve the body or it can't be flown to Germany. Decomposition occurs rapidly in the tropics. Osvaldo already brought the phenol and formalin down from the lab but Doctor Pantaleon says he doesn't want to perform the procedure alone." She pressed her lips together authoritatively.

"What?" gasped Debra. "You're not serious. I'm a doctor, not a. . . ." She didn't know the word in Spanish for a "mortician". She felt sick. Wilfred had died and these crazy people expected her to embalm him!

"You are familiar with anatomy, with blood vessels," Fermin said. "There are also contusions to be cleaned up. There's no one else. Velázquez left for Caracas on this morning's flight, so you are the only physician at INSA right now."

"Is there no one who could assist instead? What about the doctors at the hospital? I've never done anything like that before." There was no immediate answer. She heard only crickets chirping from the darkness.

"Lamentablemente, the hospital's surgeon and coroner, Doctor Aguirre," explained Reina patiently, as if enunciating for a child, "is on vacation. The other doctors have all gone home for the night. Anyway, they are newly graduated pasantes on rural service and they have little in the way of practical experience. You have been a practising physician for several years. Bodies rot quickly here and cadavers are usually buried immediately, so no one in Puerto Pedriscal has had experience of embalming. There is no one else."

Fermin patted Debra's shoulder softly. "It's more difficult for Doctor Pantaleon. He knew Wilfred longer than you did. You know, if you are going to work with us at INSA, you must learn how to manage a crisis," he said.

The mysterious biochemical sparks that had maintained Wilfred's life were extinguished. Debra tried to think of it scientifically, all the biochemical reactions, the electric impulses that made a body come to life. But the complexities of thought and emotion made a mockery of her detailed knowledge of physiology and anatomy.

Of course, death didn't happen all at once. Even when death came "instantly", it was incremental. Molecular reactions slowed at different rates, controlled by hundreds, thousands, of independent variables. A brain deprived of oxygen had only minutes until it exhausted itself irreversibly; kidneys, tough and durable, lasted for hours. At that moment, some of Wilfred's organs and tissues were still alive and, if antigenically compatible, could have been successfully grafted to last another lifetime.

Whatever it was that had made Wilfred a unique personality had died. Eventually all of the cellular functions, in each and every compartmentalized cell, would cease, microorganisms would convert Wilfred's tissue to more microorganisms and decomposition would proceed rapidly. Even so freshly dead, some decomposition had started, another kind of life already feeding on Wilfred's corpse.

He had been generally unpopular and Debra, herself, had known him for only a few hours. Yet his death had prompted an outburst of grief from those around him. Did his death reinforce personal fears of transience? She shuddered at the thought of a time when her body, too, would decompose, and her thoughts cease to exist. What a comfort it must be to truly believe in God, in eternal life, but somehow she couldn't do it—couldn't believe in an immaterial existence with no scientific proof, no physical reality, which, above all, required blind faith.

❦

Amador Pantaleon had cloaked himself in a green surgical gown. There was no need for a mask; infecting the patient was not an issue here, and covering up was to keep himself clean, not the patient. He was beginning to wonder what was keeping the gringa doctor when she finally walked in. She looked unstable on her long legs. He could see that her already pale face was further drained of colour.

A bright spotlight dramatized the corpse sprawled on the steel operating table. Blood had clotted in maroon splotches on the light cotton shirt. The head was mangled, the blond hair matted with clotted blood, the skull crushed concave on top, the face swollen so that it was not easily recognizable. That at least made the task less personal.

"Chama, catch!" Amador said as he threw Debra a gown. He thought maybe he should try to lighten the situation. He hoped she wasn't going to faint. "Gloves are in the box there. Let's finish this business quickly. It is unpleasant for both of us." She was clearly squeamish, had no kidneys. He wondered how she had made it through medical school.

"I've never done this before," she said, sliding on the greens. Latex closed tightly on her wrists with a snap.

Latex gloves, they reminded Amador of condoms, the same rubbery smell that clung long after they had been removed. "I haven't either." Out of morbid curiosity he had watched an embalming once at the university anatomy department. "But I think we can make it work. If you expose the femoral artery and vein for me, and catheterize the artery, running the tubing into that drain in the middle of the floor, then I'll do the rest." He pointed to the drain with a bloody finger. "I'll prepare the solution—formalin, a little phenol, some glycerine to keep the tissue soft, and water to dilute. Chama, go and start on the German." His nostrils burned and he choked on acrid fumes as he poured formalin from a brown bottle into a heavy-duty cleaning bucket.

Debra unzipped Wilfred's pants and tugged half-heartedly. Nothing budged. "I need help. His legs are very heavy."

Amador left the bucket and they heaved off the soiled pants together. Debra sliced open the blue-tinged skin at the inner side of the thigh with a sharp scalpel, exposing the artery and vein. The cadavers used in anatomy classes had already been fixed; the tissue was less fleshy, more rubbery. They were always old when they died, their insides layered with greasy fat that had to be scraped off. Students could divorce themselves emotionally from what they were doing. This cadaver was young and still smelled of his last cigarette. Debra catheterized the artery and ran the tubing to the drain.

Amador stood on a chair beside a supply cabinet and Debra handed him the cleaning bucket. He placed it on top of the cabinet and inserted an end of catheter tubing into the embalming fluid. He sucked the tubing to get a siphon started, which he knew was a stupid thing to do with embalming solution, but there were no pumps available here. He attached a wide-gauge needle to the end of the tubing and inserted it into the vein. Hydraulic pressure pushed the solution into the body, and Wilfred's blood flowed very slowly down the drain. "I don't know what to do about his face, chama. It will be hard to make him pretty once the tissue is fixed."

When the last of the fluid had drained into the body they wrapped Wilfred's body in black plastic garbage bags. There was no telling how effective the embalming would be. They could only hope the bags would contain some of the smell and the fluids draining from the body.

❦

Rain poured down from the heavens in sheets, ruthlessly pounding the sun-baked earth into rivulets of mud. It crashed upon the corrugated metal roof, the noise reverberating through the house like a funerary drum dance. Reina had left the clothing on Wilfred's bed when she took Debra home. The pants Wilfred had died in were not only bloodstained; Amador had spilled embalming fluid on them and the blood was now fixed permanently to the cloth. Acrid formaldehyde fumes from Wilfred's pants and Debra's clothes diffused throughout the house. His unmade bed waited for him and Inés to slip between the sheets. Instead his body lay in a corner of the hospital surgery, wrapped in garbage bags, his circulatory system full of embalming fluid. Never again would he complain about the centre's inefficiency.

Debra shivered, alone in the empty house. The pounding rain deafened her and the smell of formaldehyde choked her. She was afraid to turn off the lights in the house, afraid to sleep. A bolt of lightning killed the lights. She felt her way around the dark kitchenette, frantically searching for a flashlight or a candle, but found none. She sat alone at the formica table in darkness, except for the stark blue-white illumination of intermittent lightning flashes that exposed two

60

congealed omelettes. She picked splinters off the exposed plywood where the formica had chipped. What was she doing here, in this strange, hostile place so far from home?

Doctor Velázquez managed to telephone Wilfred's parents in Berlin, and told them to expect the body in a few days. But there was much to do, an entire week's work, before the body could be sent to Germany. The various government bureaucracies required a mountain of paperwork, and since no one had ever tried before to ship a body overseas from Puerto Pedriscal, no one was certain how to do it. Every official had a different opinion and the experts, it seemed, all lived in the capital. Luz María, INSA's administrator, and Rosalia and Milagros, the secretaries, worked nonstop on written documents and eventually, with the governor's assistance, completed them to the satisfaction of all the bureaucrats. Velázquez stayed in the capital, where he could solicit funds from the German embassy for the shipment.

Reina helped pack Wilfred's personal effects. She even folded and packed the bloody clothing. Debra said it should be discarded, but in Reina's opinion the parents should be given all their son's belongings. She neatly folded his other clothing into cardboard boxes and a trunk she found in his room. He had collected some native artifacts: woven baskets, pottery, arrows and an ocelot's skin strung on a wooden frame. She packed everything he owned, even packs of cigarettes, matches, a toothbrush, his hairbrush matted with fine blond hair, a half-finished box of condoms, pots, pans—absolutely anything at all that she identified as his. "This was his favourite frying pan," she said as she held up a cast-iron pan, wrapped it in newspaper and gently placed it in a box. She carefully erased every trace of his existence from the house. Except for his books. Velázquez had telephoned earlier from the capital and forbidden any books to be shipped, in case they contained information belonging to the centre.

The técnicos and Horacio, the maintenance man, constructed a shipping crate. A body couldn't travel by air in an undisguised coffin because the sight of it could frighten passengers. But Reina had been told the body could be shipped inside a crate without a coffin if it was well wrapped in plastic. She thought this news would please Velázquez, when he discovered that he didn't have to buy a coffin. The money could be more usefully spent on scientific research.

❦

On shipping day the mosquito-sided INSA flatbed truck served adequately as a hearse. Wilfred's few friends and the entire INSA staff followed in a procession of assorted jeeps and trucks with headlights on. At the airport gates the sobbing started all over again when Soledad and Inmaculada laid flowers on the crate.

Behind a chain-link fence, men in khaki coveralls fork-lifted a pallet with the crate, flowers and all, into the DC-10.

The pharmacist, Huevo de Pava, slid into an available viewing spot not far from Reina and Debra. The red hair didn't look quite right on a Latin. Genetically he had been programmed to have olive skin, but somewhere the coding had gone wrong and he had ended up as a bleached-out phenotype spattered with melanic blotches. He had a fiendish-looking grin, gaps between his teeth, dark eyes and reddish-blond lashes.

"Debra, that's Huevo de Pava," Reina whispered. "You can see how lecherous he is, look."

"I don't think he's lecherous, Reina," said Debra. "He simply has a hyperactive thyroid gland that makes his eyes protrude a bit, and he can't very well help that. He displays other symptoms of thyroid hyperactivity too—thinness, nervousness."

"Buenos días, señoritas," said Huevo de Pava, addressing

Debra and Reina. "Un día muy triste. I told him from the beginning that a married girl would amount to nothing but trouble. Although she killed him, that woman didn't even have the decency to aid him at the scene of the accident. She just ran home to her husband as if nothing had happened. And smart as you please, she knew better than to show her face at the hospital, where people would talk. I really did try to warn him. I truly did. Just look where he is now." Huevo de Pava pointed his spotty upper lip at the forklift. "And where is she today? Perhaps she lacks the strength of character to bid him a final farewell."

"Sinvergüencería! It's not nice to talk about people that way," Reina said. She pressed her forehead against the chain link and watched the plane taxi on the runway. Her curls obscured most of her face, except the tip of her nose.

"I know he made love to her because he bought his paracaídas at my pharmacy," he said. He jutted out his speckled chin.

Debra nudged Reina. "What are paracaídas?"

Reina lifted her head. "Debra, a paracaídas is a device made out of silk to slow your fall if you jump from an aeroplane, but in slang it refers to condones, profilácticas, preservativos, cubiertos de látex para un hombre para prevenir la concepción y la transmisión de enfermedades sexuales."

Reina knew from previous experience that it was better to explain these things quickly and bluntly to Debra, who was otherwise likely to use the words inappropriately. One really did have to be very careful using the Spanish language. A perfectly innocent word in one country could have sexual connotations in another. She recalled the grocery shopping trip she had made with Debra the weekend after Wilfred died. Debra had asked if there were any papayas for sale. Reina had pinched her arm hard—"Be quiet. That means female genitalia. The correct word for the fruit in this country is 'lechosa'." Later, she told Debra not to be too embarrassed, just to be more careful. She told her about the time that she had gone to Puerto

Rico for a tuberculosis conference and had seen some fruit she knew as mamones. Reina had announced in an enthusiastic voice to the entire store, "I really love mamones," which in Puerto Rico meant that she very much enjoyed oral sex.

"Transactions in a pharmacy are supposed to be confidential," said Reina, loudly enough for Huevo de Pava to hear.

Huevo de Pava shrugged. "He's dead now. He'll never know."

The DC-10 shrank until it faded in the distance to the north. Wilfred would arrive in the capital in the afternoon. His connecting Lufthansa flight to Germany left the next morning, a long time without refrigeration.

Reina started to leave. The Communist, in his red shirt, caught her eyes as he handed out propaganda. He was standing beside Debra, smiling muy simpáticamente, and he asked her, "I suppose you would like one too?"

"No thank you," Debra answered too quickly.

Reina didn't know the Communist very well, although he was a prominent figure in town. He was the head and only member of the Communist Party in the Territory. He was tolerated by the government and military, but anyone else showing interest in joining the party soon found himself escorted to the airport by the National Guard. The authorities maintained tight control of leftist influence to inhibit the spread of Communist and terrorist activities from neighbouring countries. Such groups were known to be active in drug smuggling through the Territory, and their proclivity for blowing up oil pipelines and storage tanks was not wanted here.

The fear of spreading Communism probably explained the tacit official support of the American missionaries in the Territory. Reina watched Ronald Elliot talking to one of the mission pilots, a clean-cut all-American boy, beside their immaculate Cessna— "Wings of God" was written on the side. She had heard that they weren't really missionaries at all, but agents of the CIA. How else could they be so efficient, not to mention so rich? As if they would choose to live for years in such remote isolation in the jungle just to bring Yanomami people the Bible. She knew the CIA worried about the spread of Communism through Latin America. It made sense to her that the CIA wanted a strong American defence on the frontier. There were also many rich mineral deposits, minerals that the Americans would surely like to get their hands on.

5

One Sunday, a month after Wilfred's death, Velázquez gave Osvaldo the use of the transport jeep on condition that he take the new American doctor away from Puerto Pedriscal for the day. Velázquez claimed that she had been shocked by Wilfred's death so soon after her arrival, and that her "crisis de nervios" was not being helped by constant exposure to the noisy and incessant grieving.

Osvaldo was a survivor. He knew it was important to his future with the centre to be available whenever the doctor required him, even on Sundays. He was also not averse to having a good time, especially if it was subsidized, so if he had to take the doctora out it might as well be for something he and his panas would enjoy too—a fishing trip. Of course, his wife and four young children would have to be left alone at home again, but they were used to it by now.

He left home at first light and gathered up Salvador, Cheo and the doctora from different corners of the town. She asked him to pause at an abasto, where she bought a case of Polarcitos to contribute to the trip, and she loaded them into one of the deluxe coolers the científicos normally used to transport blood and tissue samples back from field expeditions.

Osvaldo drove up Avenida Orinoco, past the port where a crane unloaded another week's supply of Polar from a barge, and turned down a sandy track to a mud and thatch hut perched on the edge of the Orinoco. Osvaldo left Salvador and Cheo to barter with a man for a dugout canoe and outboard motor while he and the doctora watched chickens scratch for food. A scrawny cock strode from hen to hen, interrupting their search with overt sexual advances. He displayed, spreading his iridescent wings, arching his ruffled neck, then tried to mount. The hens squawked and sprinted away, until he finally ran one down and pecked at her until she gave in. A few seconds later he strutted off contentedly and started scratching for scraps to replace his spent energy.

Osvaldo grinned at the doctora. "Un gallo bien macho, no? See how a little persistence can wear a woman down."

Hints of blue peeked out tentatively from behind a cloud-littered sky. The river here was a mile wide and the colour of light coffee. Salvador steered the dugout into the current. Osvaldo had known him ever since Salvador had come to work as a técnico in the mosquito lab. He looked Asian, but Osvaldo recognized the thick, straight hair, broad face and almond-shaped eyes of Piaroa blood. Salvador was very reserved and kept to himself at INSA. It had taken Osvaldo a year to gain his trust. Not that he was unfriendly, for he smiled easily; but he was wary of those from outside the Territory.

Cheo, Osvaldo's closest pana at INSA, was at the other extreme, an extrovert, black with a woolly afro and a mocking smile. He often complained to Osvaldo about his technical work in the blackfly lab, claiming his co-ordinator was a slave-driver. Everyone at INSA knew that Cheo was partially responsible for his boss's dissatisfaction. It was common knowledge that he overindulged in alcohol and women. He dragged a leg shrivelled by childhood polio, but it didn't deter him from successfully pursuing the opposite sex. He was rarely inclined to work enthusiastically the day after a night of bonche. Official reprimands, "memoranda", had been issued to him on two occasions. Once, his co-ordinator caught him in her lab mixing up cocktails for a party he was giving—citric acid, glucose and absolute ethanol. Cheo told Osvaldo the only alcohol you could drink at the centre was "absoluto", the stuff in refrigerated glass bottles. The others, he said, contained poison. Osvaldo would never forget the hangover from after one of Cheo's bonches. The doctor himself issued Cheo's other memorandum, the time he caught Cheo kissing Rosalia in a supply closet.

The river had swollen, impregnated by the rains. Silty currents undercut the banks and rough thickets sagged towards the flow. Salvador cut the engine suddenly and the deceleration slid them forward in their seats. Something surfaced in front of the canoe with a *whhooooosshh!* like pressurized steam bursting from a pipe.

"What was that?" Debra asked, grabbing Cheo's arm. Cheo and Osvaldo smiled and Osvaldo held a finger to his lips. Salvador pointed ahead. A shallow dorsal fin cut through the surface without a ripple. A blow hole opened with another *whhooooshhh!* and the dusky form slid back into the water, leaving small swirls that disappeared into the current. Cheo rubbed the crescent-shaped fingernail depressions on his arm.

"A river dolphin," Osvaldo said quietly as it surfaced again beside the dugout. The mammal had the same intelligent eyes as its salt-water relative, but sad, with no happy grin from its long snout.

"My people are direct ancestors of the tapir, and close relatives of the river dolphin," said Salvador. "We are related to all large mammals and also to the balentón catfish, which grows up to six metres long. For us to kill any large mammal or balentones is taboo. We hunt only small mammals."

Cheo paddled the dugout into the calm of a tributary where a granite slab tilted gently into the river. The canoe tipped precariously as the three disembarked.

The doctora stripped off her shirt and shorts and lay on the water-smoothed granite in her bikini. Osvaldo brought her a Polarcito and he, Cheo and Salvador sneaked looks at her exposed white skin and the fine line of fair hair running from her navel down her belly. He had never before had a chance to examine a gringa so closely. She would look pretty good once she was bronceada, although it would take a lot of sun to bronze skin pale as peeled yucca, and there wasn't much sun that day. It was cool for Amazonas. The rains had brought milder temperatures and a heaviness to the air. Mosquitoes and blackflies now flourished. The doctora soon squirmed and slapped her skin, already erupting in raised white welts and blood blisters left behind by satiated blackflies.

"Doctora," Osvaldo said, with a smile, "the native people believe that the irritation is helped if you pinch the bite and suck the poison out. Would you like me to try the remedy on you?"

She grinned back at him and quickly pulled on her shorts and shirt. "Let's see if you can catch any fish."

A baited hook and line wrapped around an index finger did the job. The slightest nibble could be felt by the naked finger, and a quick yank would hook the fish before it stole the bait.

"Chévere, Salvador! A caribe," Cheo said.

"Doctora," Osvaldo called. She had told him to call her Debra but he found it uncomfortable. "Come and see the caribe Salvador caught." Salvador rapped the fish sharply on the head and removed the hook. The fish had pointy little teeth, and was flat and roundish, greenish-grey, lightly blushed with orange.

"Pana, you will be simplemente encarpado tonight," said Osvaldo to Salvador, who smiled shyly and turned a rosy brown.

"Encarpado?" Debra asked.

Cheo said nothing, but grinned and lifted his pants at the groin into a little tent. "Chamo, I envy you! You will have hard huevones tonight," he teased Salvador. "Dancing on three legs all night long."

Debra stooped closer to better see the fish endowed with such potent powers. Its unblinking eye couldn't help but stare. She touched a fingernail tentatively to the teeth.

"Doctora, be careful!" Salvador grabbed her by the waist and pulled her away from the fish.

"Are you worried that I'll get the erection meant for you? I think it's highly unlikely, Salvador." She laughed.

"No, doctora," Osvaldo said. "But you must never touch the teeth of a caribe."

"Why not? Does the fish cause pregnancy in women?"

"A caribe can snap the fingers right off you," Cheo said.

"With those little teeth? You must be joking." She laughed.

"You gringos call these fish 'piranhas'," Cheo continued. "I once saw an American film at the Don Juan before it shut down. We all laughed at it. It was a very stupid film. They showed piranhas with wings flying in the air and ripping out people's throats. Simplemente ignorante."

"Epa, pana!" Osvaldo interjected. "I saw that movie too. Qué broma! They showed the fish sawing off people's faces. They looked nothing like caribe, either, more like big grey moths with dogs' teeth, and they flew fast, like mata caballo wasps." He turned to Debra. "We swim in the Orinoco with them and they don't bother us. They attack only in small tributaries in the dry season, when they're trapped in pools without food, and only when they smell blood. You have nothing to fear swimming, but you must never stick your fingers into the jaws. The fish was stunned but it could still have bitten your finger off."

While Salvador concentrated on catching enough for lunch, the others collected firewood and set a large cast-aluminum pan to heat. By the time the oil was hot, a half-dozen fish were cleaned and ready for the pan. Most were caribes; however, Salvador had caught a large rayado, a spotted and striped catfish famous for the quality of its meat, and that was reserved for the doctora. Osvaldo remembered a time when rayado and other prized fish had been more plentiful. Salvador was lucky to have caught this one.

They ate the crisp fish simply, with just a little salt and freshly squeezed lime juice. Washed down with cold Polar, it was delicious, almost orgasmic, thought Osvaldo, watching the doctora consume slice after slice of rayado. She tried a piece of caribe and pronounced it good. She said nothing about the rayado, just kept eating and eating. She looked thin and delicate, yet she matched the guys bite for bite and beer for beer. She must have downed a kilo of fish when she stopped suddenly and groaned. They strung a chinchorro between two trees and helped her climb into it.

"Forget any ideas about using those erections when I'm helpless like this," she slurred, and then fell asleep, swaying gently in the shade.

❦

When Debra awoke she didn't move from the chinchorro. She felt completely relaxed. A breeze rustled the leaves above her and kept the insects at bay, and the lapping of the river blended with the deep murmur of male voices. She could see the men down at the shore, gutting fish and stacking them in the cooler. The pile of empty bottles beside it suggested that there was now plenty of room in it. Something had changed inside her. The guilt she had felt after Wilfred's death, that she might have contributed to it, aggravated by the endless mourning of the female staff, had receded into a less prominent part of her consciousness. She had enjoyed the company of her new male friends much more than she did the company of the fussy women at the centre. The beauty of the Amazonas was seeping into her, becoming part of her being.

6

Evading the thought of death for very long in Puerto Pedriscal was difficult. Its faint odour clung to lab coats and hung in the air of the local hospital. The mortality rate for hospitalizados in this small town was high, Amador thought, especially among the native populations, although not surprising when those suspicious and superstitious people always waited until their diseases were untreatable before they sought medical help. Still, he remembered the days when it had been much worse, during the rat infestation, when being confined to a bed was no different from being nailed inside a coffin. Improved standards of cleanliness and disinfection had helped enormously, while not totally abolishing the smell.

What Amador lacked in bedside manner, he made up for with large, sensuous, come-to-bed eyes. His skin was dark, rich brown, and his face soft. Even at the age of thirty-six, he rarely had to shave. He preferred to leave the dark downy hairs growing on his chin. Amador enjoyed mornings, fresh out of bed, the last erotic dream a fading, agreeable memory, a time for reflection after busy evenings. The gringa doctor dispelled his lingering morning thoughts and they dissipated like the current from the air-conditioner.

"Hola, Amador! What do you have for me today?" Debra remained in the doorway, indicating that she was ready to go.

"Chama," he said, "did you get some sun on the weekend? You are getting a little colour." Amador expertly conserved energy, but seeing that Debra was not about to sit and chat, he pulled himself up from his chair slowly. "I have a case in the communal room that should interest you."

The patient lay comatose, eyelids puffed shut and eyelashes

buried in a swollen face. The nose had partially decayed and blackened. A serous exudate discharged from the black smudge in the middle of the face and ran in rivulets down the cheeks. He was young, twenty years old, and apart from his head he looked in good physical condition.

"Qué opinas?" asked Amador. "This desgraciado came in last week—general malaise, frequent urination, thirst and a bit tired. We diagnosed diabetes mellitus and treated him. His health improved steadily and we were about to release him when headaches started and his nose ran. Just grippe, I thought, but while I was off this weekend, he lapsed into a coma and his nose began to decay. It all happened very suddenly."

Debra focused on the black hole for a moment before answering. "I saw this once before, at Medicina Tropical in Caracas. The patient died. Rhinocerebral zygomycosis."

"Yes, just a common bread mould but, as you know, in a diabetic it can very quickly go up the sinuses and invade the brain," confirmed Amador.

"I can take a biopsy to our lab for culture and do direct microscopic examination. You may want to start him right away on amphotericin B."

"Chama"—Amador shook his head solemnly—"let him go peacefully. He is already in the vulture's beak. There is little cerebral function: pupils no longer dilate, no reflexes." Amador pressed on the supraorbital fossa. "See, no response to pain. We have no life support here and he will quickly die." His face slackened. Years of watching people die, and often being at a loss to prevent it, had taken an emotional toll. He had learned to hide his compassion behind a barrage of blunt, crude slang. With a scalpel, Debra debrided black tissue from the hole and put it into a vial with sterile saline that would prevent it from drying until she got it to the lab.

Most of the body still lived despite the lack of brain function, though only as an empty container. An inhaled zygomycete spore had germinated, growing quickly just as it would on a piece of bread, creeping into the sinuses and then the brain. Then the mould secreted enzymes to digest the tissues for conversion to fungal filaments. If they had recognized the disease earlier, it might have responded favourably to antimycotics.

Amador took Debra's silence to be disapproval of his apparent callousness. He often found it difficult to know what went on inside her head. She had not yet fully grasped the language, and she was sometimes not a very communicative person. "Diabetes mellitus is epidemic here, chama." He maintained professional composure, his eyes disconsolate, his expression contrasting with his soft face. "There is much in the way of malnutrition. How can we hope to cure people if the causes are out of our reach? Medicine here is like treating malignancy with a Band-Aid. I grab at what I can, even if it's not the lot."

In the communal room, almost every patient was hooked up to a saline drip. Saline rehydrated spent tissues, and with the limited medical supplies available little else could be done for many cases. Patients on IV saline at least thought they were receiving treatment, and Amador was convinced that sometimes it even made them feel better—the placebo effect.

Amador recognized the skinny body of Pedro Aguirre bent over a bed halfway down the room. "Have you met Doctor Aguirre yet, chama? Come, let me introduce you." He led Debra through the parallel rows of closely spaced beds.

"Pedro, welcome back. We have a new colleague that I'm sure you will be delighted to know." Aguirre unfolded himself from the rib cage on the bed and unhooked his stethoscope from his ears. His eyes immediately passed over Amador to fix on Debra with a glint that Amador knew well. "Doctora Debra Baumstark from Miami, this is Doctor Pedro Aguirre, our surgeon and coroner—the only man in the hospital who can kill a patient and certify the death as accidental. A most useful man for a doctor in Puerto Pedriscal to know."

"Encantado, doctora," said Pedro with a slow smile, and he walked around the foot of the bed to face Debra. "Your name is Baumstark? Surely I know your father. Did he visit Caracas at any time?"

"Yes he did. It's through his friends in the Institute of Tropical Medicine that I'm here in Venezuela. I don't think he mentioned your name before I left Miami."

"That is not surprising. We didn't have the opportunity to become close friends," Pedro explained. "Perhaps I can compensate for that loss through a friendship with his daughter. We must have lunch together very soon."

Watching Aguirre in action, Amador could understand Pedro's renowned record with women. His reputation as a mujeriego was unsurpassed in Puerto Pedriscal. It would be enjoyable to see how Debra, a more sophisticated proposition than Pedro's usual conquests, responded to the inevitable campaign.

Debra and Amador passed a patient on the way out who was a jaundiced mustard colour, with an abdomen distended by ascites fluid and an enlarged liver and spleen. His eyes sank into a cadaverous face showing details of the underlying skull. There was nothing Amador could do for this man; death was imminent. Interesting, Amador thought, how one patient could have a dead brain and a healthy body, and another could have a dying body and an active brain. This man should have died long ago, yet his will to live had commanded his body to function for a few extra days.

❦

As Debra drove back to the centre with Osvaldo, the vial of tissue in her hand, her withdrawn mood stayed with her. Amador's casual acceptance of the fate awaiting the boy bothered her, although she knew it was a necessary self-defence on his part. She knew she should eventually adopt this approach if she was to maintain her sanity.

In the laboratory Reina's técnico, Soledad, cultured some of the nose tissue on Sabouraud's dextrose agar. Debra smeared some on a slide and mixed it with a weak potassium hydroxide clarifying solution, and added lactophenol cotton blue to stain mycelium. Remarkably, under the microscope there was more fungus than human tissue, and a myriad of follicle mites. The microscopic arthropods, inhabitants of eyelash, eyebrow and nose hair follicles, scuttled around like miniature cockroaches, gobbling up flakes of skin and sebum. The fungus had liberated so many nutrients that the follicle mites had proliferated out of normal proportions.

After one day's incubation at 25° Celsius, Soledad found a fluff of grey mycelium growing from a spot of nose tissue, incredibly fulminant growth. Amador sent word that the patient had died.

❦

After six weeks at the centre, Debra was increasingly disturbed by the clinical picture of the region that had begun to emerge: tuberculosis, meningitis, sexually transmitted diseases and killer flus. Almost everybody had some sort of mycosis. Malaria, both *falciparum* and *vivax*, were common, and other parasitic infections too numerous to contemplate. One man she examined had nine different species of worm living in his intestines. Weekly, she visited an out-patient STD clinic, its waiting room always overflowing, mainly with native prostitutes. Drug-resistant gonorrhoea was a big problem. Some of these women had three or four children, and they looked old and worn out; the case notes revealed many to be in their teens and twenties. Diagnosis of diseases could be difficult. The hospital's laboratory facilities were almost non-existent. INSA provided some routine lab tests but they were nowhere near adequate for the community's needs. Many with health problems, especially those in outlying communities, would sooner trust their own curanderos than the hospital where so many friends and family had disappeared. And Debra knew from conversations with the doctors that the majority of the cases went undiscovered and untreated.

Amid this misery, she wondered where the rich rituals, painted torsos and feathery headdresses of the proud Amazonian people she had seen captured in coffee-table books had gone. She had read anthropological accounts about these cultures, vividly bringing to life people so well adapted to the tropical rainforest that they lived harmoniously, in perfect balance with their surroundings. In Debra's mind, native culture had been torn away, disease and penury annihilating the traditional way of life, leaving an aftermath of spiritual and physical destruction. She was emotionally unprepared for the devastation she saw, and the apparent complacency of the Ministry of Health, the Ministry of Indian Affairs and the various religious bodies.

The evangelized Guahibos exemplified the marginal slum communities that surrounded Puerto Pedriscal. They made pottery, not for their own use but to sell to tourists or middlemen who sold it in Caracas. Reina wanted to buy some pottery for her new house and took Debra with her. The community lay about twenty minutes outside Puerto Pedriscal.

Shacks were slapped together out of assorted materials: old tires, cardboard boxes, the odd brick or stone, scraps of corrugated metal and mud. A thin (apart from a belly heavily laden with pregnancy), shabbily dressed woman made the pottery. She looked wrinkled and old but new-found experience taught Debra that she probably was in her thirties. She carried a sleeping baby on her hip, and another child, about three years old, crawled with the chickens on the dirt floor. The crawler hacked thickly and violently as she played. The potter pointed to clay plates stacked on a wobbly table. "Diez bolivares, cada uno." She coughed up a loose gob of sputum that had been rattling inside her chest, spat it out on the dirt floor. A hen raced to the gob and ate it before it could be stolen. Reina unhurriedly picked out the best six, paid the woman and thanked her. To Debra the woman's eyes looked empty and expressionless, eyes without hope.

"They all have tuberculosis," said Reina, as she drove back down the Puerto Pedriscal–Olvidado highway towards Puerto Pedriscal.

"I can believe they've all been exposed," Debra said, "especially living in such conditions, but isn't it unusual for such young children to manifest clinical disease?"

"Lamentablemente, that is not the situation here. Genetically there is little immunity, and malnutrition aggravates the weak immune response."

"Why do they not get treatment?" Debra stuck her head part-way out the window. The jeep's interior was as hot as an oven set on broil.

"The people are very poor, drugs are expensive and the duration of treatment long. Few who start the treatment complete the necessary course, which means we may be helping drug resistance to develop. They are also terrified of the hospital, and it's a great effort to get them there."

"Don't the missionaries help them?"

"They certainly have the money to do so—their own fleets of aeroplanes, networks of ham radios, nice solid houses right out in the middle of the forest, miles away from civilization. But the dollars don't seem to translate into material benefit for their charges."

"I was told in Caracas that they provide health care. Perhaps the extent of the problem is just too great."

"People here say that they're really spies working for the CIA." Reina paused to shift down a gear as she turned into town. She pushed her sunglasses higher up the ridge of her nose. They immediately slid back down on a film of sweat. Her tank top didn't cover the bra straps across shoulders reddened by the late afternoon sun slanting through the window.

"Spies, the CIA, that's ridiculous," Debra said. She shifted her weight to loosen the grip of vinyl from her thighs.

"I believe it's true. They even get fresh apples and Coca-Cola shipped to them at their stations in the middle of the rainforest. You wouldn't believe the money they have. They live the way they do in the United States. They have refrigerators and stoves run by gasoline-powered generators. They have carpeting, sofas, toilets. All of it has to be flown by small aircraft to dirt landing strips in the middle of nowhere. Have you any idea what all that costs? If they aren't CIA, how do they get all that money? Explain that one to me."

The bronze Indian in the main intersection still fixed his stare between the Don Juan and the gas station, through the narrow sidestreet, but Debra thought he was surely looking far beyond the wrought-iron gates of the Hotel Las Palmas, far beyond the town. He looked longingly to the wild, forest-coated tepuis, thinking of a time before his conception, when the very land he stood on was still unscathed by ruthless intruders.

Reina had obviously never heard about televangelism, thought Debra.

7

Late the next afternoon, Marisol stood expectantly in Debra's office. "Do you want to come look at a house?" she asked, tilting her head to one side. Her blue jeans were tight and a low-cut blouse showed cleavage. She had a sexy look that would have better suited a flamenco dress. Her appearance was grossly misleading: Marisol was far more comfortable with the company of her blackflies than she was with the company of men.

"I'm sorry, Marisol," Debra said. "I've been prodding at swollen spleens and livers, taking biopsies and drawing blood all day. I'd like very much just to relax for a while before tonight's meeting with Velázquez."

Blancanieves waited patiently beside Marisol, her pear-shaped body planted sturdily on chunky thighs and chunky legs. She looked placid, with bovine eyes. She seldom expressed her own opinion, always nodded safely in agreement with whatever seemed to be the consensus. She was very insecure but a stubborn streak would surface once she'd reached an intolerable limit of agreeability. She had taken over Wilfred's research and now co-ordinated an important area of INSA's research; the human immune response to malaria, leishmaniasis and onchocerciasis. Blancanieves wasn't even a research scientist. She had trained as a laboratory technician, which could not prepare her for so much responsibility. Fortunately, most of INSA's research in this area was accomplished through international collaboration, and her main duty would be to keep the lab organized and prepared for visiting scientists. That much she might manage.

"You and Yadira must start looking for another place,"

Marisol continued with a toss of her head. "I don't believe Doctor Velázquez will renew the lease, especially since Wilfred's gone. Blancanieves and I aren't pleased with our house, and if we rented a place I know of together we'd save money." Her words ran rapidly together with no pause.

"Yes, a house is hard to find, and we must go to see it today," Blancanieves added. "There's a long list of people waiting for Malariología houses. There're still two hours until the meeting." Her inflection rose at the end of each phrase, perpetually asking questions, seeking approval even in statements.

"What about Yadira?" Debra asked. "I haven't even met her yet."

"She could live with us too," Marisol said. "The owner has made an addition to the house and there are four bedrooms. It's owned by the Communist Party leader, imagine. Of all possible people." There was something about her so very much like a bird—rapid fluttery movements of her hands, and her tilting head.

"A Communist? A Communist owns a house in town?" Debra asked, whisking a strand of hair out of her eyes.

"Yes, the Communist Party leader has a house in town," Blancanieves said.

"Where did you expect him to live? In a commando hideout in the jungle?" Marisol twittered. "He also owns an abasto that serves as the party headquarters. He sells things such as casabe bread and cigarettes to raise funds. You must have seen it before, the ranchito converted into a little shop up on the hill beside Avenida 23 de Enero, the one with the red flag. Debra, you're living back in the McCarthy era. Realmente, I'm told he's a very nice man." Blancanieves nodded in agreement.

꽃

Marisol brought her jeep to a stop in front of a Malariología house by running into the curb with such force that Debra's head whiplashed forward.

"Perdoname," she said. "Someday I'll get used to the width of this thing." She had driven spasmodically, lurching, braking, grinding the gears and often confusing the brake with the accelerator. Unruffled by her own driving, she inspected herself in the rearview mirror. She swiped her fingertip across the tip of her tongue and used it to clean an errant smudge of mascara on her lower eyelid. Debra and Blancanieves stepped out of the jeep on shaky legs.

Buttery allamanda flowers, bracts of scarlet heliconias like lobster claws, cool lavender flowers dripping from jacarandas, paddle-leafed plantain trees and spiky pineapple plants camouflaged the front of the house. A man posed at the entrance way, propped against the wall with his arms folded. Lean bronze biceps curved below his sleeves. Immediately, he was recognizable as the straight-backed man from the airport. With his red short-sleeved shirt and beret he looked to Debra like a commando in an Italian flick. He said nothing as they approached, just followed them with his eyes. The beret's insignia, El Gallo Rojo, was a red rooster circled by the words "Partido Comunista de Venezuela".

"Es muy guapo," Marisol whispered.

"Yes, if you like a testosterone overdose," Debra whispered back. They walked up the pathway leading to his house.

"Buenas tardes, señoritas. You have come to enquire about the house?" he asked pleasantly.

"Yes. I am Marisol and these are my friends, Blancanieves and Debra."

"Encantado. I am Segundo. You are científicos employed at INSA, no?"

"You are second to what?" Debra asked. She could not keep her eyes from the Communist.

He laughed. "My *name* is Segundo. I was the second-born in my family so my father named me Segundo. My older brother—his name was not Primero—died, so I am not the second in the family any more."

"Yes, we are from INSA," Marisol said, and then fired off in a breath, "I do research on blackflies, the vectors of river blindness, a terrible disease, you know, but very interesting work. Blancanieves works on the immunology of various diseases and Debra is a doctora of the skin." Marisol's head tilted repeatedly, always to the left. The birdlike mannerism looked flirtatious but Debra knew it was just a nervous twitch.

"Valuable work. We need more people dedicated to fighting disease here in Amazonas."

"You have a beautiful garden." Blancanieves said, her cow eyes ranging over the flowers hungrily. She plucked a lavender bell from the jacaranda bush. The Communist scrutinized Debra, returning her stare. She felt herself turn warm and looked instead towards Blancanieves and the jacaranda bush. Blancanieves held the petals to her nose and sniffed.

"The native people call it guarupa," Segundo said. "The leaves and bark are used to cure infirmities of the skin and it has many other medicinal properties. La doctora of the skin should find the plant to be of considerable interest, no?" Debra glanced back at him briefly. He supported his back against the rough grey wall, watching her every move.

"Do you know much about traditional medicine?" she enquired.

He winked at her. "Please, doctoras, come in and allow me to show you my house." He leisurely pried himself from the wall.

"Why are you leaving the house?" Marisol asked.

"I need the money."

Inside, the grey floors and concrete walls of a Malariología house seemed especially drab after the blaze of colour outside. Furniture was sparse: an unfinished wooden table darkened by use, a hammock in one of the bedrooms, a few wooden chairs. The Communist posters plastering the walls provided the only character: defiant workers, fields of crops, collective labour with writing in reds and blacks, blocks of simple and bold colours. An extra room, constructed off the back of the house with walls of bamboo-like poles strung together by fibrous reeds and topped by thatch, looked very much like a secret arms depot in a war movie.

"It's a bit expensive for us," Marisol told him diplomatically. "We can't possibly afford that much, but it's a nice house and we do like the garden."

"Yes, but it has possibilities and perhaps the price could be negotiated," Blancanieves said.

Marisol shot a freezing glance at Blancanieves that effectively conveyed "shut up, you idiot". The Gallo gave Marisol a sedating smile. "I'm sorry," he said. "The price cannot be negotiated. Please advise me if you change your minds."

"It was a pleasure to meet you at last," Marisol twittered. "I have seen you so many times at the airport and we've never been introduced."

"The pleasure is all mine. At your service, doctoras."

"I like your hat," Debra said impulsively.

Marisol turned and glared at her, as if waiting for her to blurt out something even more outrageous.

Segundo took off his beret and laid it upon Debra's head, adjusting it until it had just the right amount of slant.

"Sexy, no? And it looks so much better on my camarada than it does on me." He took a step back and admired his work.

Marisol snickered. "It seems that the party has doubled in size. El Gallo Rojo now has himself a gallina."

❦

During the day a typed notice calling for a meeting of the Technical Commission had been hand-delivered to each co-ordinator by Rosalia. The notices were stamped officially with the mosquito logo and signed by Doctor Velázquez to prove authenticity, and all recipients had to initial a form to confirm their attendance. The ceremony was ridiculous in so small an institute, but Velázquez wouldn't have it any other way. He wanted drama and impact.

Velázquez always scheduled meetings after work, before the researchers could leave for dinner, and they invariably lasted hours. Everyone, he knew, hated the meetings, apart from Marisol, who enjoyed the opportunity to voice her research concerns to everyone.

Velázquez invariably made his grand entrance shortly after everyone else. He entered the room the way a priest walks to the altar to give mass. He never said hello, not even a nod. The co-ordinators gave him polite smiles and nods as he took his chair at the space left vacant at the table head. Debra sat beside him. He knew that Fermin, Reina and Blancanieves liked to arrive early so that they didn't have to sit too close to him. Debra didn't know any better. He opened a manila folder and engrossed himself in reading for a few minutes, ignoring the fact that everyone was waiting in silence for him to start the meeting. No one even whispered in his presence. He finally drew himself upright, smiled meaningfully and wove his elegant fingers together. He looked down his nose at his loyal subjects, who watched him expectantly.

"As you may know," he began in his metered and meticulous voice, "Professor David Shuttleworth, from England, will be arriving in Puerto Pedriscal to further our ongoing collaborative research. This will involve an expedition to Yanomami territory for the collection of *Onchocerca* and *Plasmodium* specimens."

"Has he confirmed his arrival?" Marisol asked, looking up at Velázquez intently.

"Yes, Marisol, he has confirmed. You will be going on the expedition to do more experimental infections. Cheo will assist."

"What kind of experimental infection? Not people?" Debra interrupted, suddenly alert.

Velázquez turned his head deliberately towards her. "No, certainly not, I assure you, Debra. We infect only simuliids with *Onchocerca volvulus.*"

"Doesn't a blackfly have to first bite an infected person in order to become infected itself?"

"Yes, you are correct. We allow blackflies to bite an infected person and then we trap them as they finish the bloodmeal."

"Doesn't all that biting harm the patient?"

"It's perfectly harmless. You might try to recall the fact that the patients already have the disease," Velázquez answered, slightly less evenly. His nostrils flared and the cleft in his chin deepened. Debra was turning out to be more bothersome than he had anticipated. Not political trouble, as a Venezuelan doctor would surely have been, but a nuisance none the less.

"But couldn't it increase the parasite load or cause hypersensitivities?"

"Debra, your line of questioning does not merit an answer. You will personally assist Professor Shuttleworth when he arrives. Your English, as well as your medical expertise, will be essential for the success of this expedition. You will take skin biopsies, remove nodules and take blood samples. It will mean temporarily discontinuing clinical duties both here and at the hospital." He saw Debra start to say something, but when he looked at her she closed her mouth and looked down at the table. Her public submission reassured him that he still maintained his authority. He turned towards Fermin. "Fermin, you will be staying here. I want you and Blancanieves ready to process blood samples as soon as they arrive off the plane."

Fermin had drifted into a daydream but he jumped to attention at the sound of his name. "Sí, sí, doctor, claro!" he sputtered. He squeezed his eyelids a few times, took off his wire-rimmed glasses and rubbed his eyes. Velázquez pierced him with a glare and his temple pulsed, just as it did whenever Debra referred to him as "tu".

Reina sat attentively and took ample notes, a model staff member. Blancanieves stared at Velázquez with loyal admiration. Some people never caused him problems.

Velázquez then allowed Marisol to dominate the meeting.

She attacked her research problems with the conviction of a military general discussing tactical manoeuvres. The head tilt became predatory like a hawk's. Unfortunately, not all the staff took research so seriously.

"I must do something about the losses before we go to Topochal," Marisol explained to the others, with double lines of worry and concentration between her eyes. "To identify the blackfly species transmitting onchocerciasis in the region I need a lot of infected blackflies, so I have to recruit as many infected volunteers as possible. But what is the use if so many of my flies die? Half of my last collection died. I keep them in vials with a strip of filter paper to stand on but they sometimes prefer to defecate on the glass vial rather than on the paper, and their wings adhere to the glass. They can't free themselves and they die. I don't understand. I have religiously followed the protocol."

"Marisol, why not just cut the filter paper bigger and roll it into a tube so that it covers the entire glass surface?" Debra asked.

"Yes, Marisol, why not indeed?" Blancanieves asked, looking nervously at Marisol.

"Because I always follow a protocol precisely," Marisol replied.

꿩

Osvaldo had taken the técnicos back to town before the meeting, and Marisol and Blancanieves offered to take Debra home. She had to endure a few minutes more, as the jeep bounced down the INSA hill, of boring Marisol in full flow about her research problems. Her blackflies spread onchocerciasis, the disease Debra knew as the river blindness of the Nile Valley from textbook photos of small boys leading chains of blind adults.

"First I want to specifically identify all the vectors," Marisol said. "Next I want to find out if the parasites themselves differ physiologically according to their geographic area of isolation, but the problem is, I am going to need a lot of infected flies, and for that I will need heavily infected patients, and there are so few patients willing to volunteer for my studies—for one thing, it takes many years for adult worms to mature in the human host, and the Yanomami, they tend to die fairly young, and even when I do manage to find a few older people with nodules, they don't always agree to participate. Fortunately for me, once I find a good candidate I can be sure my flies ingest microfilariae, because each female worm in a nodule produces millions of microfilariae and she can do so for ten years or more. Just wait till you cut open your first, Debra, you won't believe how long they get—half a metre in length."

"Marisol, you'd be disappointed if a cure was ever found. You seem to want people to suffer just so you can conduct your research."

"That's really unfair of you, Debra. Of course I care about the patients, and my work may one day contribute to disease control. It's not a native disease, you know; it's thought to have come here, along with malaria, in African slaves and it really is an interesting disease. Complicated life cycle, the parasite has, you know. You have no idea how difficult it is to get successful experimental infections, and I can only hope my flies ingest microfilariae, and then I have to wait several weeks, first for the microfilariae to go to the flies' stomach walls, then to the flight muscles—that's where they mature— then they migrate to the proboscises. That's when I kill the flies and isolate the parasite."

"It's good for people to take an interest in their work, but you, Marisol, are crazy, absolutely obsessed."

"Debra, my work can be frustrating. I spend hours collecting blackflies, cleaning their vials and feeding them sugar solution, only to find them pinned by their wings to their own excrement, their little legs waving helplessly at me. It almost breaks my heart to see them like that, after I've put in so much effort. I know all the species so well that I can tell them apart by sight. They are individuals to me."

At ten p.m. Debra arrived at her weedy yard, reeling from Marisol's verbal diarrhoea. An entire branch of bananas and some mangoes lay at her doorstep. Fresh fruits and vegetables were always in short supply in Puerto Pedriscal and, hungry as she was, she wondered who had brought her the good fortune. She caught sight of a note stuck between two bananas.

Amorcita,
Mi camarada, I am the earth, seduced by you the moon. So distant are you that I measure time by the journey of your luminescence. If you will meet me, the lonely darkness of my night will be bathed by your reflected light, and soothed. In my opinion your pale glow outshines all other brilliance in the universe. Come, lap at my shores with your cool light.
    Camarada, I await you at the kiosk down the street.
Tuyito, solito,
Segundito [*a drawing of a red rooster*].

It had to be a joke, and in exceedingly poor taste. Marisol and Blancanieves, no doubt. There was no other logical explanation. A grown man couldn't possibly write anything so infantile. Marisol had probably parked the jeep around the corner after dropping her off, and she and Blancanieves were howling with laughter, waiting to see if she would be foolish enough to go. Debra couldn't believe that they would think that she, an educated person, would fall for something so preposterous. True, he wasn't bad-looking, but so macho, and had she met him back home in Miami she wouldn't have looked twice. Still, the fruit was welcome.

8

Through the frosted window, Yadira saw a tall blonde figure lingering at the door. It had to be the American doctor who now replaced Wilfred as her flatmate. She had noticed some mess around the house when she returned from Caracas, too much for her satisfaction, but mercifully she hadn't smelled smoke. Yadira suffered from multiple allergies that Wilfred's chain-smoking had not helped. She pulled open the door. "Don't just stand there, come in," she said in English, with a mixed Venezuelan and English accent developed during a post-graduate education in Great Britain. Yadira was a sensible, mature woman. "I'm Yadira, your flatmate."

Debra had been fumbling with her key in the lock when the door burst open. Yadira saw the startled face, level with her own, break into a smile. "I didn't expect anyone here," Debra said. "In fact, I wondered if Yadira really existed. You must be fitted with dentures by now. I'm pleased to meet you at last."

"Do come in," Yadira said as she stepped aside to allow Debra to pass. She smoothed her already straight, functional blue-jean skirt. "My delay was caused by the incompetence of a cagada of a dentist here. I should have gone to Caracas in the first place, but I was in a critical part of my research. My tooth was painful and I found help where I could. I'm sure the chap who did my tooth in was no more than a first-semester student. He told me he'd done a root canal but instead he left a bloody needle inside my tooth, then sealed it up with amalgam. It became horribly infected and I didn't dare come back here until the infection had been cured for good. Care to join me for a rum and Coke?"

"Could I ever use one. I had one hell of a day."

Yadira poured soothing golden fluid over ice cubes, added Coke and freshly squeezed lime juice. They both took a long slow swallow. In the brief silence a cricket chirped repeatedly. Yadira remembered reading in an entomology journal that the frequency of the call was directly proportional to the level of humidity in the air.

"We can watch TV in my room."

"I didn't know there was a TV here."

"It was hidden in my closet so Wilfred wouldn't touch it while I was gone. We get one channel from Caracas, the educational one, and a local channel run by Catholic priests. Every night I watch a Brazilian soap opera on the Caracas channel. Don't look at me like that. I know what you are thinking, a soap opera, rubbish. But Wilfred and I never got along so hot. His bloody cigarette smoke gave me asthma and I spent evenings shut up in my bedroom. Finally I got hooked. The brasileñas are actually pretty damn good. By the way, you don't smoke, do you?"

She had made an effort to make her room comfortable, as if she really intended to settle in Puerto Pedriscal permanently. She had the largest of the three bedrooms in the house and she'd fixed it up like a sitting room, with photographs, Guahibo pottery and some white wicker furniture. Debra's room was the size of a closet, her bed was unmade and the walls were bare. Yadira sat down on her bed.

"It's funny, I never liked him when he was here but now that he's gone I almost miss him. Almost. Poor chap," Yadira said.

Debra sat in a white wicker chair and put her rum and Coke on a side table. "It must have been a terrible shock," she said thoughtfully.

Yadira switched on the TV set. It lit up with a Belmont cigarette commercial, a beach, machos throwing tanga-clad girls into the waves, lots of jiggling buttocks and rippling abdominals. "Have you seen my skillet? A thin, black wrought-iron one? It was hanging in the kitchen."

"Above the sink?"

"Yes!"

"Sorry, Reina packed it up with his personal effects. She said it was his favourite."

"That's bloody awful. It was mine. It was seasoned and it didn't stick. Have you any idea how hard it is to buy good pots and pans here?" The soap opera title came up on the screen with catchy Brazilian music. There was a knock at the door. "Bloody hell, if it isn't someone at the front door," Yadira said, getting up. "Tell me what happens."

Yadira had never met her but when she opened the door she immediately suspected who the girl was. She knew the story of Wilfred's affair and his purchase of condoms at the pharmacy. She examined the girl carefully, taking in and analysing her every feature with scientific concentration—chunky, with badly crooked teeth, one upper canine discoloured grey; she had made an effort to fix herself up, accentuated her eyes (actually quite pretty) with mascara and painted her lips. Her yellow short-sleeved blouse clung to melon-sized breasts and contrasted with her coffee skin. She was far from beautiful (neither had Wilfred been handsome) but, having had a good look at her, Yadira could understand why Wilfred had been attracted—fertile sexuality, a juicy ripe mango.

"I am Inés, Wilfred's girlfriend. May I come in?"

"What is it you want?"

"I want to feel close to him, to sit in his room. That's all."

Yadira smiled in a condescending way. "I'm sorry, but his belongings, except for a few books, were all sent to Germany."

"I have nothing left to remind me of him. Could I see the books? Maybe he left something in one of them for me."

"Very well."

Inés cried when she saw the room: the bed stripped down to the striped mattress, blotched with tea-coloured stains, and the bare concrete walls.

"If I close my eyes I can still picture him. He was not like men here. He was sensitive." She picked up a notebook, pressed it tightly against her chest so her breasts bulged out from either side and stared at the bed.

"I'll be in the room next door." Yadira shut the door behind her. She sank back onto her bed. The ice cubes were getting small and had diluted the rum.

"Who was that at the door?" asked Debra.

There was no time to answer. Inés screamed from behind the thin wall. "If that huevón were not dead, I would kill him myself, cut his liver out with my fingernails." Yadira and Debra could hear Inés crashing against the hallway as she ran, viciously cursing Wilfred. The bellow of a muffler and screeching wheels punctuated her departure.

Yadira and Debra went through to Wilfred's room and found the notebook on the stained bed, opened at a short poem in simple Spanish dedicated to Doctor Velázquez's secretary, Rosalia.

"Who needs to watch a soap when you live in Puerto Pedriscal?" Yadira said.

❦

Debra looked down at the notebook. Was attraction to the opposite sex voluntary or involuntary, she asked herself. How much did human thought and reasoning influence the selection process? Were people at the mercy of a biological jumble of sexual signals that resulted in a hormone cascade, working sometimes contrarily to their best interests?

Isolation had impaired Wilfred's judgement and loneliness had driven him into his fatal relationship. Loneliness and isolation aside, the Amazonian heat seemed to provoke sexual desire, and her own healthy sexual appetite had gone unfulfilled for many weeks now.

Maybe, she reflected, it was the survival instinct, the drive of the human species to outlast times of difficulty. Where

93

morbidity and mortality are commonplace, reproductive urges can be stimulated. Or maybe, so far away from the reality of the rest of the world, a different morality and distinct norms of behaviour presided.

❦

"Another bloody interruption!" Yadira slammed down her drink and stormed out of the room to the front door.

She quickly returned. "It's the red rooster chap who delivers propaganda at the airport, and he's asking for the doctora americana."

"Marisol, Blancanieves and I looked into renting his house," Debra explained. "He must want to know if we're still interested."

"At this hour?" Yadira growled.

Debra opened the door slightly. She saw the red-clad shoulders, enveloped by a shroud of hungry female mosquitoes. "I don't think we'll be able to rent your house," she said.

"No." He moved over and leaned his arm against the wall so he could see around the door she hid behind. "You are a médico, no?"

Debra suddenly grew suspicious. Getting ill is a sure way to get a doctor's attention. Perhaps last week's stupid note and bananas hadn't been a joke after all. "Yes, I am, but you don't look very sick to me. Whatever it is, I'm sure it can wait for the clinic tomorrow morning."

"I promise you, doctora, it's not for me. I'm here concerning a friend who is extremely ill." He did at least appear to be genuinely worried.

"You should take him to the hospital."

"I cannot take him there. The hospital is a place to die. You are a médico. Isn't it your job to tend the sick, or do you tend only those who can buy a full piñata?"

"I haven't ratified my degree and I'm not permitted to practise medicine in Venezuela."

"Could you at least look?"

"If your friend truly is ill, then he will have to go to the hospital for treatment anyway." Debra slipped on her sandals. "Yadira, I'll be back soon." She stepped out and joined him inside the haze of mosquitoes.

Segundo drove a large, new blue jeep parked under the streetlight. It must have cost him a fortune in Puerto Pedriscal. "That's a very nice jeep," Debra said suspiciously.

"I take tourists around the area so I have to own a good jeep. I do have to work for a living," he answered as he opened the passenger's door for her.

He drove past the Evangelist church, past the kiosk surrounded by men clenching Polars in their fists. "I waited for you until half past nine," he said, glancing back towards the kiosk.

"Thank you for the fruit."

"It was my pleasure." He took his eyes away from the road to look at her.

She looked away, out the window. "Why did you think I would come to meet you at that place, with all those drunks?"

They didn't speak as they passed through the town. They crested a rise on a dirt road at the outskirts. A tangle of illegally tapped electrical wires culminated in the scattered twinkling lights of ranchitos.

"My friend is a Guahibo, a curandero. He speaks no Spanish so I'll translate for you. I hadn't seen him for a long time until I found him tonight, weak, in pain and coughing. I am sure he is dying."

"It's probably tuberculosis. It's very common here," Debra said. The jeep rolled up a giant slab of granite. They stopped in front of a series of small shacks, walls of dried cracked mud loosely held upright by flimsy poles. Moonlight illuminated the walls and cast the cracks in shadow, like veins and arteries pulsing with blood, nourishing the huts.

Segundo entered one and Debra followed. Their eyes strained and their pupils widened adjusting to the darkness. A chinchorro hung from the two main structural poles of the room, a bundle enclosed in its folds—hanging heavily like a sack of plantains, coughing and muttering incoherently.

Segundo stooped over the chinchorro and spoke in a language Debra didn't recognize. He removed a hand and sheltered it within his own. He returned it to the folds of the chinchorro gently. He stood upright and turned towards Debra. "Please, could you examine him?" he asked. The dank walls seemed to swallow the sound of his voice.

She approached the chinchorro. The patient was a relic of a man with a deeply wrinkled face. Debra felt shallow, short breaths on the back of her hand and touched his hot cheek with her fingers. She reached down alongside his neck. Her fingers rolled over a firm lump of cervical node and distended veins beneath a sheath of skin, thin tissue paper. She undid the buttons of his shirt and continued down the bony torso, feeling protruding sternum and ribs. There was enlargement of the liver. She percussed his chest, an impaired thud for a response. Tuberculosis had once been called consumption. This man was all but consumed.

"Did he cough sputum or blood?"

"A green mucus with streaks of blood."

"Pain?"

"Yes, here." Segundo indicated his sternum.

"I am almost sure it's tuberculosis. Some other diseases have similar symptomatology and tests must be conducted for a definitive diagnosis. He must be admitted to the hospital for those, of course—X-rays, skin tests, cultures and possibly biopsies."

"If he were to go, what would be his chances?"

"There are excellent drugs available to treat tuberculosis, but the course of treatment is long, expensive, and the patient must take the drugs faithfully. I can't tell you how serious his condition is after such a brief examination but, in all honesty, he doesn't look good. Tuberculosis tends to settle in tissue where the partial pressure of oxygen is high, such as the lungs, but it can settle in any major organ. His liver and lymph nodes are enlarged. His neck veins are distended, which could mean involvement of cardiac tissue. The pain he feels could be explained by involvement of the bones. One thing I am certain of, if your friend doesn't receive medical attention he will die."

"I will not force him to go if he's going to die there anyway. My friend would not want to spend the last days of his life locked up in that morgue."

"Treatment is usually very effective. If you wish, I will return with you in the morning. We can take him to the hospital and I'll speak with Doctor Pantaleon. He knows the routine at the hospital and can better explain the situation to you. Who knows, maybe there's some type of financial aid available that I'm unaware of."

Outside the hut Debra could breathe again. The dust had settled, the air was clearer in the moisture-laden night. Illuminated only by moonlight, the Communist's red shirt looked blood-coloured, and Debra wondered if he had several identical red shirts or if he wore the same one day after day.

The American skin doctor said the treatment was expensive. The curandero had no money and had never had use for it. All he wanted for survival came from trade for his services. Now the healer needed to be healed—by modern medicine—and his skills could not buy that. Although the hospital was "free", patients had to provide their own sheets, drugs and even syringes and hypodermic needles. "I will accept financial responsibility for my friend," Segundo said. "But it is unjust that in any civilized nation health care should be a luxury for the rich. Such is the system in your country, Ooosah, and so we have it here. Our puppet government, as always, must emulate yours." Finding the old curandero dying had drained him. They walked slowly to the jeep. The silhouette of a large mango tree loomed out of the darkness beside them.

"In the United States we have a program, Medicaid, for the poor," Debra said. She stood almost level with him.

"Why is it then that Ooosah has one of the highest infant mortality rates among developed nations? Why do white people live longer than blacks and why do your poor people have so much more disease than the rich? I have no doubt that the finest care exists for the rich in your country, but I do not believe you about this Medicaid."

"Our medical system isn't perfect, but the poor are treated and we have some of the finest medical care available in the world. Some of those statistics are related to other sociological factors, such as violence or poor education. In any population, there are many independent variables that influence health."

Segundo opened the passenger door for her. The day she had said she liked his beret, he had thought she was a sympathizer. She was clearly not. She was an imperialista, a capitalista, una miembra de la clase burguésa. She was here to pursue her own interests, as so many others had before her: the Rockefellers, the Duponts, the Morgans, the Reynolds—the owners of his country's resources—all exploiting, economically deforming, and both commercially and politically oppressing his beloved country. He knew the type.

Moonbeams bathed the earth and created an eerie landscape in grey and black. The dirt road was transformed into a ribbon of platinum and the granite slabs were plated silver.

"When I sent the invitation, I thought you were my camarada," he said.

She turned her face to the shadowy thickets outside. "We don't have very much in common," she replied. "Where I come from, we believe in freedom, and we value this principal right above all others."

On the other hand, he told himself, she was living in a Malariología house as he was, was she not, and not in a Miami mansion. How could she not be an imperialista when she knew only the viewpoint of gringo propaganda? Was it not his duty to educate her? He might never affect her ideology, yet he found himself strangely stimulated by her, and he might enjoy trying to reach her mind and if not her mind then perhaps her body. The capitalista was particularly patuleca and he had a fondness for long legs. "Amorcita, you imply that I do not believe in such ideals? Do you not think that there are areas where our beliefs overlap, and where we can gain an understanding of one another?"

"Like the understanding we gained with Cuba during the missile crisis? Your Cuban camaradas nearly provoked a nuclear war that could have ended the world, had Kennedy not acted so intelligently." She looked at him defiantly.

He liked a challenge. The Venezuelan Communist Party ran schools where not only Marxist–Leninist philosophy was taught but also historical materialism, political economics, the history of the labour movement and scientific socialism. He felt prepared for any political debate. "First, our party broke its affiliation with Castro's revolutionary left many years ago, and secondly, that is not exactly how I remember the missile incident."

"Our satellites detected Soviet nuclear weapons in Cuba, pointing at our shores."

"Were there not American nuclear weapons planted all over Western Europe, targeting the Soviet Union? As I recall, it was Kennedy who first suggested military action in the event the missiles were not dismantled. The Soviet Union did not threaten to attack Ooosah when the missiles were first installed in Europe. Amorcita, you see it depends on what side you view it from. Personally, I do not wish for nuclear weapons anywhere."

"Yes, it's so easy for you to support the Communist Party while you live in a safe democracy like Venezuela. You don't live oppressed, lining up half the day for a loaf of bread. You have freedom here. You shouldn't be so eager to complain."

"And you, amorcita mía, are not a Latin American oppressed by disease, hunger, exploitation and lack of opportunities. I am free, yes, free to watch my friends in Amazonas eradicated, the political pawns of Ooosah and its puppet Venezuelan government. It's easy for you to support American-style democracy when you are from an elite. Democracy Latin American–style does not treat people as equals. Health and education are supposedly free here but still the poor are excluded. People must buy drugs to be cured and people must buy books and shoes to be educated. Tell me, how does a man buy drugs, books and shoes if he can't buy food for his children?"

"I'm proud to be an American."

"Every abasto promotes its own cheese as the best. Communism is a fairer system for the poor and oppressed of this country. You are an innocent, not to be blamed for your benightedness. You have never suffered, never had to do without essentials. You have the luxury to be idealistic about American democracy, but we do not live in an ideal world. The Communist Party here struggles to form a national, patriotic, popular and democratic system, where we can learn to solve our own problems by ourselves."

"People all over the world are trying to immigrate to the United States."

"True, but in the land of the blind, the one-eyed man is king." Segundo smiled at her.

"Is your whole philosophy summed up in catchy phrases and slogans? Don't you have an original thought?" Debra challenged him. "People should be free to make their own decisions, go where they want."

At the kiosk, a spotlight illuminated a Coca-Cola sign, a half-full bottle dotted with condensation and rust spots. Salsa music dinged from a radio on the countertop. A few men still drank beer but most had gone somewhere to sleep off their alcoholic tanganazos. Segundo parked in front of the kiosk. He and Debra stood at the counter and drank Polars while they argued and debated.

It was three in the morning before Debra's eyelids became

almost too heavy to lift. Segundo walked her to her doorstep. "I have a jeep and I can take you to see people who need a médico. I know you have not ratified your degree, but you can see them the way you saw my friend. They will not get medical attention otherwise." She blinked in reply, with bloodshot eyes.

"We have ideological differences," he continued, "but beneath we are both human. We have more in common—love, hate, joy, fear—than we have differences. Between us we can reach either conflict or understanding, and the only way we can reach understanding is to try to communicate with one another."

"Maybe I'll go see sick people with you, that's all. Forget any stupid romantic ideas."

"All night long you have been preaching freedom and individuality, and yet all you norteamericanos are like bleating goats. You are afraid not to conform. You stay safe within self-imposed confines. Inside your pasture there is overgrazing. If you allow, I will cut the barbed wire so that you can eat taller grasses."

She turned the key in the deadbolt. "If you can persuade the curandero to have treatment, drive up to INSA tomorrow. I'll accompany you to the hospital."

"Hasta mañana, corazoncita."

Debra woke the next morning tired and with a slight headache. She was never at her best before she had some coffee in her system. She had woken up at four in the morning in a hot sweat. She had resorted to a cold shower, one tentative toe, then the other, and with all her courage a final plunge into the frigid water, which she now knew came from the depths of the Neblina River. She had finished off with a dab of hundred-percent Deet behind each ear. It never totally stopped the mosquitoes from biting but at least it kept them from buzzing around her head. She fretted about the curandero. Segundo was obviously very attached to him, and he could be too far gone for medical help.

Osvaldo came for her before she had a chance to grab coffee. She decided to filch a cup from Reina's lab, but before she tasted it the Communist arrived at INSA. He had not wasted any time in coming to look for her.

ॐ

Pinpoints of sunlight crept through cracks in the mud walls. The curandero, spotted with light, looked even more consumed than he had the previous night. He strained to become upright when he coughed. He was too weak and he fell back into the chinchorro's sheltering folds.

Debra took her stethoscope and squatted on the dirt floor, her knees pointing up, her rear end brushing the dirt, balanced on the soles of her feet. The sound coming from the patient's chest wasn't good. She shook her head slightly and stood up.

"The savannah and the forest are his church, his home and his hospital," said Segundo. "Disease is the result of una mabita, a bad hex, the result of brujería by someone who blows harm his way. He believes that if a cure does indeed exist, then it will be found within spirituality and within forest and savannah, but he also believes the invader's brujería is stronger than is his ability to reverse la mabita. To his people the practice of brujería is a crime considered equal to murder. You realize he has agreed to go to the hospital only to placate me."

Debra helped Segundo pull the unresisting body out of the chinchorro. The woven moriche fibres moved with their heaves. The curandero muttered as his body tipped away from the security of the chinchorro. His feet dragged to the jeep, leaving a double trail scratched in the dirt.

He mumbled and coughed all the way to the hospital, with Debra beside him in the back seat. His eyes once opened wide and he grasped at her hand with his bony claws, searching for safety where there was none to be found. Debra knew that she had been thoroughly dosed with *Mycobacterium tuberculosis* by the time they reached the hospital.

Segundo made the bed for him with sheets he had brought. The old man looked pitiful in the hospital bed.

Amador joined them at the bedside, looking as he did all mornings, as if he had just emerged from a wet dream.

Segundo crinkled his nose at an unpleasant smell: the noisome hospital odour or the smell of secondary infection clinging to Amador's lab coat?

"Chama." Amador turned to Debra. "I will make sure good care is given to the viejo. I'll send sputum to INSA for culture and keep you abreast of all developments."

As they walked down the cheerless hospital corridor out into the sun, Debra felt the Communist's silence strange after his prolonged speeches in the earlier hours of the morning.

The silence continued as Segundo drove away from the hospital and turned onto Avenida Orinoco towards the great INSA hill. "I think your friend will respond well to treatment," she tried to reassure him.

"He looked stricken to me. Acceptance of modern medicine is sacrilege to him. He knows that tuberculosis and so many other diseases came to his people only after they had contact with the outside. He believes outsiders use brujería against his people in order to wipe them out and gain control of the land."

"I have confidence that Amador will be able to help him."

"I hope so, for it is I who am responsible for his admission. Should he die in hospital, I alone will carry the burden of responsibility."

"You have done the best possible thing for him." Since he had dropped all the Bolshevism she felt more sympathetic towards him. It had proved impossible to argue effectively with someone so entrenched in ideology. His logic was flawed, but he was better versed in Communist propaganda than was she in counter-propaganda, and he had it memorized, ready to spit out by rote. His firm grasp of egalitarian jargon was used as if he really knew what he was talking about, tactically obfuscating the debate.

"This weekend I could show you around, maybe take you to a Guahibo community."

Debra hadn't seen many native communities. Most of the Guahibo and Piaroa she saw were nameless, faceless, sickly representatives at the hospital. She didn't know their languages, couldn't talk to them and remembered little about them besides their clinical manifestations and the characteristics of their lesions. She didn't know them at all as real people with individual lives outside the hospital walls, but she wanted to.

She hesitated. "I would like very much to go." She half regretted her answer. She wasn't convinced she wanted to be alone with Segundo.

"How about Sunday?"

9

Debra had to complete as much clinical work as she could before the expedition. The INSA lab provided Amador with definitive diagnoses, and the steady stream of patients he sent up to INSA provided fresh clinical isolates for INSA's research. Out-patient work was more pleasant than work at the hospital—none of these patients was dying and there were usually no seriously disfiguring illnesses.

The incidence of candidiasis and other opportunistic infections was high. In the early morning, she swabbed at meaty tongues caked with solitary or confluent white plaques of *Candida albicans*. Particularly thick patches of plaque cracked liked clay, exposing inflamed tongues underneath. Predisposing factors such as a compromised immune system, nutritional deficiency or prolonged antibiotic therapy could lead to mycosis, particularly candidiasis. She knew her patients were often malnourished, and that contributed to immuno-suppression. They were also exposed to a lot of parasites, fungi and viruses. One patient had warts covering both hands, dermatophytosis all over his body, and chromoblastomycosis, a disfiguring granulomatous fungal disease that erupts like cauliflower. Any one of these conditions could happen in a healthy individual, but all three at once pointed towards immunosuppression.

Velázquez wanted to know what species of fungi causing dermatophytosis (jock itch, ringworm, tinea) could be isolated in Amazonas. He thought maybe he could get a publication out of it if the dermatophyte species isolated here were different from those isolated in Caracas. Amador's stream of out-patients provided a deluge of dermatophytosis.

To accomplish Velázquez's research goal, Debra examined wide brown feet, crotches and armpits (anywhere moist). She wedged feet firmly in her lap and snapped off chunks of dirty toenails. Infected toenails became thick and tough and were not easily snipped off so she had to use bone-cutting shears. She scraped skin from feet and groins with a flame-sterilized scalpel. Some scrapings she gave to Soledad for culture, some she examined directly under the microscope. She completed examinations by eleven-thirty and wrote up a list of positives for Amador. She arrived at the hospital just before lunch.

ॐ

Doctor Pedro Jorge Alfonso Aguirre had just returned, invigorated, from a trip to Caracas. He had supposedly been there to visit his ex-wife and children but he had enjoyed seeing his mistress too. His good mood had elevated further when the American doctor, Debra, agreed to lunch with him. An opportunity for the pleasant company of an educated woman was rare for a man of his superior standing stranded in Puerto Pedriscal. He had come here about a year ago to escape the aftermath of a malpractice suit in Caracas concerning the death of a baby and its mother during a very difficult delivery; some inconclusive porquerías of evidence from nurses suggested his negligence. His family owned a large hacienda in Amazonas, and had good connections with both the federal government in Caracas and the armed forces in Puerto Pedriscal. The town had desperately needed a surgeon, and as long as he continued to work here in that capacity, his lawyer could stall the malpractice investigation. Within a year or two his family's contacts in the Ministry of Justice would be able to quash the charges entirely. He had just to relax here until everything settled down in Caracas.

He had discovered only upon his arrival that his job description required him to double as coroner, a task he had come to very much enjoy. The outward manifestations of disease did not begin to represent the plethora of diseased tissue inside.

He walked Debra towards the centre of town. Diffuse grey clouds dulled the sky. It was hot and humid but not unbearable. Pedro predicted that it would rain today. He had acclimatized long ago and on a day like this his tall, thin body didn't sweat. He knew all the tricks for staying cool, such as wearing pastels that reflected sunlight. Today he wore a shirt with narrow blue and white stripes, a white collar and freshly starched ironed creases down the sleeves. Starching stiffened the fabric so that it didn't lie directly on the skin and trap hot body vapours. He doused himself with plenty of cologne; if by some unforeseen circumstance he did sweat, the cologne would mask the odour. Pedro stood well over six feet tall and Debra fitted in beside him nicely. He appreciated her blonde hair, a status symbol in Caracas. He chose the air-conditioned Río Negro restaurant for her benefit, as his practised eye noticed that she had begun to wilt.

"So tell me, how are you adapting to our humble town?" Pedro asked.

"To be honest, I find it can be very frustrating but I do love Amazonas. The landscape is so beautiful, and I'm intrigued by the diversity of cultures and their diseases." As she elaborated enthusiastically on the infections that filled her days, Pedro stroked his line of moustache thoughtfully, a moustache so carefully groomed it could have been drawn with a felt-tipped marker. He savoured her features, her lips and even white teeth, as he would an imported whisky.

She distractedly brushed a pale blonde strand of hair from her blue eyes, so different from the dark eyes he was used to, while she talked. The waiter waited politely, pen poised above his notepad. Pedro briefly interrupted her flow to order.

It had been so long since he had had such enjoyable female company. His wife had left him shortly after their arrival in Amazonas. He had frequented the "other" hotel in town (where one went to be discreet) with señoritas de la noche—putting on the horns, he called it, symbolized by a clenched fist with the thumb and little finger raised like a bull's head and horns. One night a "señorita" slipped something in his Chivas that knocked him out cold. He woke up alone in his hotel room, coño, with his pantalón gone. The hotel couldn't provide replacement pants for a man his height at short notice and he was forced to call his wife. She was angry, naturalmente, and she went back to her mother in Caracas in protest. She would have finally tolerated the incident, as she had done before, if she hadn't become infested with crab-lice. He smiled faintly as he imagined her face when she went to the Caracas médico thinking that she had a fungus; she had failed to believe the diagnosis and the médico had let her look down the microscope at the brown clawed bodies grasping tightly to her own pubic hair.

". . . but it's all the little things that I find so annoying," Debra said, lifting her hair up off her neck. The air-conditioning blew at the pale skin and she let her hair fall again.

"What is it you have difficulty with? Perhaps I can be of service."

"Oh, for example, last week I tried to get a driver's licence. It was suggested to me that a moderate tip, in American dollars, no less, would speed up the process. I refused to pay, naturally. I didn't get a licence."

"Debra, it's like this catarra sauce." Pedro picked a bottle up off the table and sloshed some on his rice. Debra leaned forward and peered at the tiny legs and antennae poking from between the grains of rice. "It's made from crushed ants, and cyanide juice left over from the preparation of casabe bread, from poison manioc. Rather than throw the juice away, the natives detoxify it and flavour it with formic acid from the ants. In a harsh environment people utilize whatever they can, throw no opportunity away, and use resources with creativity. I suggest you try to do the same, flow with the system. For want of bread and gravy, casabe and catarra will do nicely. You should try catarra. I have acquired a taste for it as I have for the Amazonas. I think of catarra as the flavour of the Amazonas—hot and unexpected."

"I know I have to adapt to survive here, but I'd rather not eat ants and cyanide, Pedro, thanks all the same." She sawed through a piece of meat. Her knife was dull and the meat stringy and lean. Pedro had no trouble with his shredded meat. Carne mechada was prepared by boiling beef and shredding it into tender strings. It was a matter of knowing how to get things done properly.

"Debra, what was it that brought you here?"

"The adventure, the chance to see native Amazonian cultures before they are destroyed."

"The adventure and culture are here, so enjoy them. We all suffer pains when we first arrive. You will find it easier as time goes by, but never expect to accomplish tasks the way you would in your own country. Learn to bend rules, find alternatives, use what's available. It's survival." He fondled the gold medallion nested in the thick hair of his chest.

"You're right, of course, but I would rather ride in the transport with Osvaldo than bribe an official."

"Debra, what is right in my culture may not seem acceptable to you, but it's our country and our way. Palanca is a way of life. If favours and bribes were abolished the country would collapse." Pedro hesitated; maybe he was opening up too much. "For example, I had some trouble obtaining an upriver permit. I made a deal with Máximo and, like mágico, the permit was granted."

"What kind of a deal?" Debra looked up at him, eyebrows raised and fork poised delicately above her plate. She smiled, catira pava, deliciosa!

"I have connections, Debra. No, the activity was not illegal. Suffice it to say I am not entirely comfortable with the arrangement."

"Well, what is it you're doing? I won't repeat it to anyone, promise."

"I too have an interest in native culture. I have a curious

collection of native artifacts. You see, most native groups burn their dead and crush the bones. The Piaroa, however, clean the skeletons of their dead and then lay them to rest in caves."

"Yes, but what does that have to do with you or Máximo?"

"Much can be discovered about ancient cultures by examining their dead. Although I am by no means an expert in forensic anthropology, I collect remains."

"Why, that must be very interesting." Debra had become quite animated. "Really, if age and cause of death could be determined for past civilizations and compared to present-day mortality patterns, much could be discovered about the health impacts of acculturation. A study like that could benefit the Piaroa, perhaps providing them with evidence they need for cultural preservation." Debra looked at him. "I still don't understand where Máximo fits in," she persisted.

"Shhh, please, Debra. I've told you all this in the strictest confidence. I have trusted you. You see, Máximo learned of my collection and he told me that he knew of others with an interest in obtaining such artifacts—forensic anthropologists, of course."

"Then why all the secrecy? Are you stealing remains?" Debra's animation was replaced by a suspicious look. "Burial sites must be sacred or protected or something."

"Debra, do stop talking so loudly. It's not as if I'm breaking the law. I have permission from Capitán Máximo. You see, he arranges for transport to the buyers and gives me a percentage of the profits."

"Profits! You're exploiting the Piaroa. How do you know the people who buy them are really forensic anthropologists? It sounds like the bones go to morbid curiosity collectors, if you ask me." Debra's eyebrows pulled together, making small furrows on her forehead.

"I didn't ask you. And what makes you a local saint? Are you not exploiting natives too?"

"I beg your pardon?"

He resented her superior attitude. She thought nothing of

coming here to serve her own interests and yet she felt fit to criticize him. He saved lives in this town; so what if he took a few bones in return? Who would miss them? "Didn't you say you wanted adventure? The natives are a tourist attraction to you."

"There is a huge difference between observing a culture and pilfering its graves."

"At least I don't experiment with human beings as if they were guinea pigs."

"I don't either, and I don't appreciate the implication."

"Then tell me, what exactly do you call the medical research done by INSA? Where does Velázquez get all his publications? He uses patients as living tissue and parasite factories to supply institutes abroad."

"We may take clinical specimens but we also provide a badly needed diagnostic service."

"Maybe so, but don't try to tell me that you obtain informed consent from your research subjects, people who are considered to be at a stone-age level of development, because I know differently."

Pedro Aguirre understood the fundamental principle of informed consent very well. Human subjects should understand the research to be conducted, their role, the foreseeable positive and negative consequences to them, alternative choices, the qualifications of the researchers, and the fact that their consent to participate could be withdrawn at any time with no adverse medical effects. Research subjects should never be manipulated or coerced by the researcher in any way, as his friend Velázquez did at his institute.

They walked back to the hospital in silence. Osvaldo, waiting in the INSA jeep for Debra, could see that something had happened. That was good. He didn't like Pedro, his arrogance and his powerful friends, and he didn't want the doctora to become part of that circle. She climbed into the seat beside him.

"You are just in time, doctora," he said. "I think we can still make it to the División de la Selva's headquarters in time for your appointment."

"I'm not in the mood to look at soldiers' crotches all afternoon."

"It will help take your mind off Doctor Aguirre."

"That man. He's so repulsive. Why didn't you warn me, Osvaldo?"

"It's not my place, doctora. He is a very influential man who could make things difficult for anyone he didn't like. I know that it is safer to be seen as weak in his eyes, as weak as coffee made with used grounds. But I can tell you that he is not popular with my native friends, and if he doesn't take care he will end in trouble."

Osvaldo felt her look at him, waiting for elaboration. He had already said too much. "The División de la Selva is full of very tough men, doctora, but they are disciplined well and will give you no problems. Most of them are reclutas from the streets of Caracas. That's a good name for them. It comes from the word for gathering cattle, and that's what they become when they are in the army—cattle."

"So that's what happens to them," the doctora said. "I was on a bus in Caracas once when a gang of military policemen with guns, riot masks and clubs stormed on and demanded identification from all the passengers. I thought I was going to be arrested and put in front of a firing squad, but they were actually very polite when they saw my passport. They did drag away a couple of teenagers and a woman told me they were reclutas."

"Yes. They must have been poor, with no exemption papers. Only the poor have no exemption from military service. The rich can buy papers or bribe someone to declare them medically unfit."

Osvaldo pulled into a gleaming white gateway on the

outskirts of town. Every fence-post and treetrunk was also painted spotlessly white. Bougainvillaea were trained along the high perimeter fence and around the barracks. A friendly guard at the gate, a guachiman with a machine-gun slung casually under one arm, directed them to the hospital wing. INSA had been contacted by the army for advice on controlling a large-scale outbreak of jock itch and athlete's foot among the conscripts. Veláquez had appointed the doctora to confirm the diagnosis by taking skin scrapings. This single outbreak would add significantly to the centre's dermatophyte collection, and could probably lead to a quick publication.

A column of fifty conscripts stood rigidly in the sunlight outside the clinic. They wore heavy camouflage cotton and sweated profusely. As Osvaldo and the doctora got out of the jeep an enormous camouflaged figure stepped from a doorway and eclipsed them with his shadow. A sparkling gold right incisor belied the camouflage. The paunch was as exaggerated as the stature. Such a barriga usually indicated an excessive liking for Polar, and the florid complexion beneath the light tan confirmed this.

"Buenas tardes. Capitán Máximo Zambrano, jefe of the División de la Selva, at your service." He extended stiff stubby fingers, one armoured with a gold nugget ring large enough to be distasteful. Osvaldo wondered at the clairvoyance of the parents who had named this man Máximo.

The doctora accepted the hand. "I'm pleased to meet you, Capitán Zambrano. Doctora Debra Baumstark and my colleague, Osvaldo."

Osvaldo shook the fat firm fingers, fat and firm as last year's ñame root. The oversized ring pressed uncomfortably against one of his joints.

A grin reflected the sun. "We have been expecting you, mamita. Come inside where you may start your work."

Osvaldo frowned as they followed Máximo. "Doctora," he whispered, "it is a great lack of respect to call a señorita 'mamita'. You must not let him say that."

"I can handle him, Osvaldo. Now be quiet and help me unpack the supplies."

The first conscript entered nervously, to be confronted by the tall, attractive catira in a white coat, an imposing figure holding a glinting stainless steel scalpel over the flame of a propane camping stove.

"Lower your pants and lift your apparatus," she said in a detached voice. Her face was emotionless, plástico profesional, and Osvaldo could feel the soldier's fear as she bent down to his groin and pushed his testicles aside with a wooden tongue depressor so that she could scrape the inside of his leg with the gleaming blade. Osvaldo felt a curious aching emptiness in his own groin as he watched the operation. One quick movement could end any thoughts the teenager had of a future family life. Osvaldo noticed that the hand holding the penis aloft was missing the top joint of the index finger. "Ha!" Máximo laughed, noticing Osvaldo's eyes focused on the truncated finger. "The boy thought he would obtain a medical discharge if he cut it off. He fooled only himself."

Things went smoothly until one soldier remained motionless at the doctora's command. "Baja el pantalón y levanta el aparato, por favor," she repeated, with the same negative result. Capitán Zambrano stepped forward and loomed behind the terrified youngster, who quickly undid his belt to reveal a full erection. Osvaldo saw Debra's straight-line lips lift faintly at the corners as she stooped to her work. The soldier trembled slightly as he stared ahead at attention, the capitán behind him. Yes, Osvaldo knew from experience, when the jaguar growls, the fatigue of the burro is instantly cured and he will do what is asked of him.

The parade of crotches and feet lasted for three hours. Osvaldo then helped Debra pack the equipment and racks of labelled test-tubes back into their boxes.

"Thank you for your most professional assistance, mamita," Máximo said as he escorted the doctora to the jeep, with a hand on her arm.

114

"Our pleasure, capitán," she answered. "It must have been especially fascinating for you. I hear you have a keen interest in medicine. Forensic anthropology, isn't it?"

Osvaldo didn't understand the meaning of her remark, but there was no mistaking the reaction it produced in Máximo. The golden smile was extinguished and the flushed complexion darkened.

"We will meet again, very soon, doctora." He bowed his head stiffly and watched them as they drove away.

The doctora was making dangerous enemies. Osvaldo knew that to anger a man like Máximo was to dance barefoot on a pile of corncobs until the feet bled—bastante doloroso.

10

At seven on Sunday morning Debra awoke to high-pitched voices resonating, "Gloria, gloria, alleloooia!" from loudspeakers. In her befuddlement she thought she must have died and gone to face a higher authority, the thought of which frightened her—her agnosticism surely condemned her to an eternity of perdition—until she remembered that hymns were sung next door at the Evangelist church every Sunday from dawn until dusk. Wasn't "The Battle Hymn of the Republic" an American Civil War song? What was the spiritual significance to Amazonian native people of maintaining the U.S.A. as a single nation?

She flung the sheet off her and went to find coffee. Yadira, already up and about in shorts and yellow plastic sandals, had launched an assault on the week's accumulated dust and waged war on the grey cement floor. Yadira used a garden hose, brought specially from Caracas, to clean the floors. She blasted the floor with a jet of water and handed Debra a broom to sweep water from the hallway out the front and back doors.

"In Puerto Pedriscal, rodents are a problem if a house is not kept absolutely spotless. I loathe rodents—my allergies, you know."

Yadira claimed her throat itched because of her allergies, and every morning she scratched it by rasping air over her tongue and on down the back of her throat, making a most revolting sound. And every morning she hacked mucus up from the terminus of her throat in a choking gargle that reverberated around the bathroom. When Debra first heard her cleaning out her tubes she thought Yadira was suffering a serious attack.

Debra intentionally neglected to mention to Yadira that

she had witnessed a mouse scuttling across the bedroom floor Saturday night while they watched TV. The mouse had reached the closet door, stood up on its hind legs and groomed its face with its diminutive hands. It was cute. She didn't think one little mouse would do any harm. Even if Yadira did manage to trap it, another one would come in and take its place. Anyway, traps were messy and cruel. The little creatures didn't die immediately. You had to take them out of the trap still alive, being careful not to be bitten, and then flush them down the toilet.

Debra changed into her bikini for the chores. She not only stayed cooler but she could quickly step into the shower to rinse the sweat off. After the floor had been cleaned to Yadira's satisfaction, Debra washed her clothing in a bucket in the scrubby back yard. A rope tied from the house to a fully grown plantain tree served as a clothesline. The scorching sun baked her bare skin, already blotched with hypersensitive welts from blackfly bites. As she pinned clothing to the rope, she glanced up, through the sweat dribbles hanging from her eyelids, at the church. Prayer boomed over a loudspeaker and she saw a round white disapproving face with glasses peering at her from a small window. She wiped the sweat away and looked again but the face was gone.

Segundo rescued Debra from the house-cleaning. The imperialista was wearing a brief traje de baño that really showed off her long pale legs. She looked intriguing, if the red welts on her skin were ignored. After a quick shower she returned in less revealing clothes. He preferred her in the bikini, but he was also relieved that she had dressed modestly, as he wanted no unnecessary attention drawn to himself while out with the imperialista. The party demanded certain standards of loyalty and it wouldn't look good if he was seen cavorting with the enemy.

He headed south out of town on the Puerto Pedriscal–Olvidado highway. The savannah had been transformed to a fresh green since the rains had come. Palms flew by the window and the sky encompassed them, dramatically embellished with darkening clouds.

"Those thatched dwellings are Guahibo. The domicile's shape is specific for each ethnic community." He indicated a collection of square thatched huts, about six in all. They stood picturesquely, pale yellow thatch sides and roofs contrasting against the looming slate-grey sky. "I'll take you there later. First I have another place to show you.

"Guahibos originally came from the Colombian savannahs," he continued. "They were hunted by settlers, like wild game, across the river. But there are dangers here as well: disease, insufficient land and dependency. There is little savannah on this side of the Orinoco, and what is left is prime grazing land taken by elite landowners from Caracas for haciendas. Hence the many Guahibo slums surrounding Puerto Pedriscal."

"And do you really think you could solve their problems through Communism?"

"Their problems are complex. I am realistic enough to know that there is no single simple answer. What you should realize is that Communism is supported here not from belief in Marxist–Leninist ideology but primarily from dissatisfaction with the political system we currently have in place.

"What we want in the Communist Party is social reform, nationalistic programs for resource utilization and agrarian reform. Did you know that when we first developed our oil industry, for every dollar we made, Ooosah made ten?"

"The new Venezuelan government claims to be nationalistic."

He laughed an austere laugh. "I will tell you a story. In a land where trees grow like monuments to the sky and torrents of rain bring forth life that is connected by interdependent links intricately tying the land, plants, animals and its people together as one living organism. The people have ancient knowledge allowing them to thrive within this fertile, sometimes hostile region of the world, the one and only world to them.

"The riches are so great that invaders come to exploit and, not understanding, they divide the whole into separate organs, fragmenting society as a raindrop does light, and an illness festers like a malignancy, thinning the very life-blood. Forces from afar mutilate the land and a way of life.

"Far away, in a city churning with the turmoil of early politics, Gómez, a cruel and ruthless dictator bolstered by imperialists, rules a country claiming ownership of that land. He is unknown to the people there yet their destiny is held in the small of his palm. He sends a governor, a man named Pulido, to oversee his rape and harvest. Greed stains Pulido's hands and he is bedazzled by new opportunity. There are great distances to be travelled, transportation is difficult and supplies are scarce. This makes a suitable climate for the introduction of taxes: a tax on housing, on food, on drink, on water, on medicine, on travel by boat and even on travel by foot.

"Unrest unfolds: a sequence of explosive events, each blast triggering another. A local planter, Tomás Funes, takes centre stage, speaking of injustice and revolt. The people listen and their frustrations grow with each spoken word, until they are swollen like the banks of the Orinoco during the rains— stimulating the people to organize, to recoil and to spring for revolution. In the end there are one hundred and thirty henchmen dead and Pulido lies inert in a pool of his own blood.

"A trial begins; Funes talks of treachery, taxes on sweat and public outrage. He is exonerated. A hero of the people, with his head tumefied beyond recognition, dilated by pride and power, he becomes the new governor of the land. He is no longer the idealistic labourer. But how can a man govern that of which he knows nothing? He cannot fit fragments back together unless he knows what the pieces originally looked like. He must lead instead by gun, for there is no other way. He is for sale to the highest bidder, and imperialists have plenty to offer. The freedom fighter becomes a dictator in that land, and rubber plantations and imperialist bribes yield him great wealth.

"Men shape the new landscape, and hostility erupts. For the price of five hundred dollars, Arévalo Cedeño smuggles himself over the border and gathers one hundred and ninety-three unarmed men, and for thirty nights they navigate the treacherous unknown waters of the Arauca, Casanare, Guaviare and Orinoco. He arrives in the village of San Fernando de Atabapo to find Funes hiding in a building to which he sets fire. He takes Funes prisoner, and his henchmen execute him by firing squad in the Plaza Bolívar. Today a modest cross marks the spot where his blood was shed.

"That, querida, has been the politics of Amazonas. The people here have always been ruled by forces indifferent to the intricacies of this land and the needs of its people.

"The Communist Party germinated from opposition to corrupt dictators such as Gómez and Pérez Jiménez, both of whom depended on support from los Estados Unidos, Ooosah. Today, more than ever, people in this country are ruled by powerful outside forces, particularly one so large it is beyond their comprehension: the superpower Ooosah, whose culture swamps all that it touches, concerned only with its own interests and the puppet government installed here. That puppet has allowed Ooosah to spread its agents throughout Amazonas, and this time the external force is so inundating that the people cannot hope to fight from within. No, mi amor, we do not befriend the big brown bear and his hammer and sickle so much because we like him, but because he is the only way we can fight against Uncle Sam. You see, only one giant can do battle with another."

"You may ultimately find the bear to be a more dangerous ally than you think."

"A few cubs may be killed along the way, but in any worthwhile venture there is associated risk."

They left the jeep and walked to a dense, seemingly

impenetrable wall of vegetation. He spread the bushes apart and a narrow trail partially engulfed by brush appeared. "Don't touch any of the branches for balance. Some plants have spines known to pierce all the way through a hand," he said confidently. The trail led steeply to a granite bluff, cool and oracular, completely hidden from the highway. Segundo walked unhesitatingly into a crack in the face of the bluff, and disappeared. He poked his head back out. "Are you coming?" he asked.

"Where are we?"

"This is a special place. Piaroa spirits live here. You can feel them, no?"

Segundo loved this place. Here he felt an inner peace, a sense of contentment he felt nowhere else. It was as though unseen beings watched over him, everything so still he could hear his heart beat. This place seeped up from the ground, another reality that belonged to the very essence of the earth. The forest was so thick that the sun never penetrated to these rocks and always it felt unnaturally cool. The crack was dark inside. Debra followed and they crept cautiously towards a sliver of light at the orifice's end. A monumental slab towered above the exit, making a cave fronted by a dense forest wall. A round slab of rock, about two feet high, as big in diameter and as flat as a large table-top, lay upon sandy ground. Bowl-shaped indentations, worn to smoothness, marked the surface of the slab.

"The Piaroa wrap the bodies of their departed inside chinchorros and leave them until the bones are free of flesh. The bones are then cleaned upon that stone, the indentations worn by the domes of skulls, and finally are taken to nearby caves to communal interment sites. Mi vida, you can feel the power of the Amazonas and her people here and you can reach the spirits. That is why I brought you here." He spoke softly to Debra, almost in a whisper. The crevice in the rock was a gateway to perpetuity.

"Where are the bones?" she asked in a normal voice,

deafening, rupturing the tranquillity. Segundo had been sensing a presence so overwhelming that his heart beat strongly enough to pulse in his temples. The feeling faded like footprints in silt washed by the flux of the Orinoco. He had felt the physically departed, accumulated here over thousands of years, within every bush, tree and pebble. Now the spirits hid. A shiver chilled his body. He rubbed his hands together to try to warm them but his fingers remained cold and clammy.

"It is beautiful here, no?"

"Yes. Are the caves near? I'd like to see them."

"Those are much too sacred to show you without permission from the elders. I wish them no disrespect, and unfortunately there has been some vandalism. Believe it or not, someone has been coming here and stealing remains. We must go now."

They plunged back into the crevice. He could see only the obscure outline of Debra's shoulders and head in front of him. He heard the sound of dripping water and bats squeaking in protest at the invasion of their home. Debra gripped his arm until she reached enough light to see the ground beneath her feet.

Flecks of sunlight filtered through the tree canopy above the trail, warmed him and alleviated the tension. Debra hurried down the trail, snapping twigs and talking loudly as she went. Within seconds, swarming bees covered her. She panicked, the worst of all possible reactions. She shrieked inhumanly and ran blindly, waved her hands, clawed at them like a maniacal beast, trying frantically to dislodge them, only to attract more. Segundo knew he had to catch her before she ran into a spiny tree and really injured herself.

"Segundo, they're killing me!" she squealed like a piglet being castrated. She thrashed helplessly, unable to run quickly. He grabbed her by the waist. She struggled to free herself, arms flying and legs kicking, sobbing.

"Stop! Calm down, they won't hurt you."

"They're killing me," she shouted as she kicked the air.

"I'm going to die." Her arms and legs seethed with yellow-brown bees.

Segundo laughed. "These are only pegones, sweat bees. Stop kicking me." He laughed so hard he choked on his words. He should have warned her not to make so much noise. "If you stay still they will leave. They swarm when they hear noise, as do killer bees, but these have no sting. You're an intruder and they want only to protect their home."

Her eyes looked electric bulging from their sockets, and her tears streaked black eyelash goo down her cheeks. She stopped moving, just collapsed on the ground, panting, an injured animal in shock. Segundo sat down beside her. One by one the sweat bees left, once the threat had passed. Segundo plucked a few off. A few remained buzzing, burrowing at her flesh, digging into her scalp. He picked them off her and out of her hair the way a monkey delouses another. She released a trembly breath.

He helped her to stand and kept his arm around her until they reached the safety of the jeep. Segundo turned his head away like a true caballero as she picked the last pegones from her underwear. She still breathed heavily. "I know who it is," she said between breaths.

"Who is what?"

"Who is stealing the remains. Doctor Pedro Aguirre, surgeon and official of the coroner's office. He sells them through Máximo to collectors."

❦

"You will find the Guahibo people to be far more hospitable than were the pegones."

Segundo turned the jeep off the main highway and onto a single-track dirt road etched in the grass. In the village, a throng of lean brown children with short straight black hair, wearing little else than dust and smiles eclipsing their faces, flocked around the jeep. They flung themselves upon Segundo like pegones and he swooped up wiggly masses of arms and legs and tossed them aside until the laughter grew into cacophony. Children made Debra very nervous.

"Corazoncita, stay with the niños, they'll teach you to use a bow and arrow. I must talk to the elders." He walked towards the thatched dwellings and left Debra at the mercy of children who spoke no English or Spanish. She watched him grow smaller as he walked away from her. He didn't look back, just popped into a hut. The more nervous Debra felt, the louder the children laughed. One naked boy, belly bulging with parasites and penis dangling like a boneless thumb, placed his fingers, chalky with dust, into her hand and pulled her over to an arsenal of bows and arrows heaped beside a thatched hut. Another boy, older and more serious, picked up a bow and arrow. He expertly drew back the string, bent the bow back into an arch, squinted at a point near the horizon and let the arrow fly. It flew straight and far. He smiled and handed the bow and arrow to Debra, and nodded encouragingly. Both the bow and arrow were enormous, taller than she. The brown naked bodies scattered behind her as she accepted the weapon. She tried to emulate the boy, drew back the bowstring and let go of the arrow, which fell two feet in front of her. An eruption of laughter came from behind her and little dusty bodies squirmed out from hiding.

Segundo emerged from a thatched dwelling along with a young woman and two men, one old and one about Debra's age. The men wore khaki pants and grimy old tee-shirts and the woman an unflattering sacklike dress sprinkled with a flower print, the cotton thin and brittle with age. They smiled shyly. The serious boy took the bow from Debra and picked up another arrow, firing it effortlessly into the heart of a banana palm at the edge of the village.

"How is your bowmanship?" asked Segundo. A tiny girl, round tummy, fringe of hair tanned with dirt, looked at her suspiciously and chewed her fingernail. The rest of the children chattered incomprehensibly and gestured her to make an ass of herself once again.

"Not too good."

The serious boy held out the bow to her and nodded. She drew the arrow and string back, pulled as hard as she could. The arrow landed back end first, eight feet in front of her.

"A great amount of skill and training is needed to master the bow and arrow. The Guahibo are known as experts. It's their weapon of choice. Young boys practise first with small bows, shooting butterflies and lizards. Children in Amazonas must learn survival skills from a very young age," explained Segundo.

The woman picked up one of the smaller girls and rested her on her hip.

"This man and woman are the parents of two of the children. The older man is his father. Grandparents have a special relationship with the children; they give them their names, and they are expected to teach them and to make them gifts." The woman smiled at Segundo and he smiled back.

"They seem to be happy people," Debra said.

"They are. Rarely are there personal altercations. The community is really an extended family, related through the women. Guahibo women command great respect in the home. If a husband were to mistreat his wife he would have retribution to fear from her family."

That these people lowered their guard, allowed her to glimpse daily routines of their world, surprised her. She had never before experienced this type of acceptance from indigenous people. They invariably hid or stared silently when they saw outsiders in or outside of their communities. Osvaldo had once told her it was because many native women had been raped by criollo settlers. Her being with Segundo, a person they knew and trusted, made an enormous difference.

The woman put down her little girl, and spoke to Segundo. He replied and they laughed. Debra stood smiling fixedly. Her awkwardness and inability to communicate frustrated her.

Segundo put his hand on Debra's shoulder. "She wants to

know if you are a criollo version of an albino. There are a few albino people in this area and she thinks you resemble them."

"I'm surprised to see they've retained so much of their culture."

"Make no mistake, once change has been made and integrated into daily life it can't be reversed. Dependency has left the Territory open for the outside to move in and dominate. In the long term, we harm these people. And we won't be leaving. The ethical question is: shouldn't the people be allowed to decide for themselves whether they will adopt our goods and technology? What right do we have to tell them they shouldn't acquire things we use ourselves?"

On the trip home Debra relaxed. The pegone attack had left her exhausted. She fell into a deep, satisfying sleep, and awoke disoriented and confused, slumped against Segundo's faded red shoulder.

She looked out the window. The jeep had stopped in front of her house. Songs in high-pitched, childlike voices (the same voices or another shift?) still resonated from the Evangelist church. A sunset softened the sky, irradiating the air with an orange glow. The steeple's sharp shadow lay across the jeep.

They got out of the jeep and stood in the vanishing sunlight. "Thank you. I enjoyed the day, even the pegones," she said, examining him in the oblique light. His skin looked bronze rather than plain brown, his eyes brighter. "Possibly we can do it again sometime."

"Si Dios quiere," he replied—if God wishes.

11

In the morning, Debra worked in Reina's lab with Soledad, looking at the conscripts' cultures, incubated one week at 25° Celsius. What interested her, she explained to Soledad, was that she suspected *Trichophyton rubrum* was only now invading Amazonas, twenty years after its spread among coastal populations. Half the reclutes had *T. rubrum* infections, recognizable from the wine-red pigment diffusing into the agar. The rest were caused by a powdery white mould, *Epidermophyton floccosum*. Her recent research showed that native Amazonians, on the other hand, only rarely became infected with *T. rubrum*; their infections were caused by a wide variety of dermatophyte species such as *E. floccosum, Microsporum gypseum* and *T. mentagrophytes*. In Amazonas, invasion and conquest by the non-native world occurred not only at the macroscopic level. Even at the microscopic level an invader in a new environment proliferated—unlike native species occupying more highly specialized niches, with limits set through checks and balances. The new arrival out-competed the less aggressive native species, and created havoc until a new equilibrium could be reached, usually to the interloper's advantage.

Soledad listened eagerly, soaking up information. She was barely nineteen, had only a high-school education, yet she had become an efficient and productive technician, probably the best técnico at INSA. She carried an aura of cheerfulness about her and worked with insatiable enthusiasm, but underneath the surface a despondency brewed. Inklings of emotional distress slipped out, subtly: a jump and quick wipe under her eyes when someone entered the lab unexpectedly, an uncharacteristic lab error. Reina said Soledad was the only member of her family to work. She supported her mother, her sister and her sister's illegitimate offspring, all of them, on her meagre técnico wage. She had Colombian citizenship, and Velázquez said that if she couldn't obtain Venezuelan documents he would be forced to fire her—"the ministry's decision, not mine, you understand."

❦

Yadira drove Debra home for lunch. Heaped up on their doorstep, a complete stalk of bananas, a rolled-up paper held by a rubber band, and an envelope blocked their entrance. "What the bloody hell is this?" Yadira asked, astounded. She picked up the envelope. "I assume you are 'camarada'." She held out the envelope, then snatched it back as Debra reached for it. "I want to read it too," Yadira insisted. "It doesn't have your name written on it."

> Amorcita, corazoncita,
> I dream of you every night and day. I dream of a place where there exists only earth, sky, water and newborn primal awareness. I offer you my dreams, do not give me materiality in return.
> Tuyito solito,

Debra peered eagerly over Yadira's shoulder. A red rooster drawn in place of a signature confirmed the author's identity. The red rooster had flown his coop, so to speak. "Hilarious. Imagine, un comunista Venezolano loco in love with a capitalista gringa, of all the crack-brained things."

"This looks like a poster," she added, unrolled it, then laughed so hard she was in danger of provoking an asthma attack. Debra chuckled nervously, pretending to be amused, but Yadira suspected she really took it quite seriously. It was a hideously ornate print of a porcelain figurine. A male figure glazed with a frilly-fronted shirt and tights tipped a three-cornered hat and offered an apple to a woman sitting on a swing hanging from a porcelain apple tree.

"Tacky," Debra said, quite convincingly. "Only the trash deserves this, and I intend to put it there." But she tried too hard to be convincing. If the poster had been given to Yadira, she would have kept it, dragged it out for a good laugh every now and again. It was too funny for the rubbish.

"You must have had an interesting time with your comrade on the weekend," said Yadira. "For a Communist, he has bourgeois taste. He's rather a handsome chap, don't you think? By Puerto Pedriscal standards, that is."

Debra glared at her, and turned a couple of shades pinker, a vivid hue that only a pale blonde could turn. "Yadira, I'm not interested in him. He's so macho. Why, the very idea is ludicrous!"

"Just as well, Debra. I know for a fact that our dear boss would hardly approve. I have heard him call the Europeans and Americans imperialists, but you will notice it is London, Heidelberg and Boston, not Havana and Moscow, that he collaborates with. He would be horrified if one of his co-ordinators actually had a fling with the head of the Communist Party. After all, we do draw our salaries from a political institution, and such a liaison might threaten his precious institute."

"Yadira, I hope you're not seriously suggesting that something happened between me and that man." Debra pushed the door open with her key, her condom keychain dangling from it. "He only takes me to see patients. I'd never consider having an affair with him." Yadira looked pointedly at the paracaídas key chain. Debra continued, "I don't see why Velázquez should involve himself in the private affairs of his staff. After all, no one criticizes him for keeping a mistress."

"His mistress is not a member of the Communist Party. You are an educated person, a foreigner and, at INSA, in a highly visible occupation. They might decide you were particularly dangerous if they thought you supported the roosters." Funny, wasn't it, how something unusual could have so much more appeal than something to be easily had? It was like the national male fascination with bleached hair. Couldn't Debra see that an INSA doctor and a Communist was a bad combination, about as compatible as boiled rice with mangoes? Amor incompatible es amor imposible, Yadira knew from personal experience. That was why she was still single at thirty-seven.

"Debra, I know it can be lonely here. Just look at the men around: Velázquez already has a mistress; Fermin—I won't say anything, it would be too cruel; Amador, great if you want to risk an STD; Jeff, of course you know all about him now, don't you; Aguirre, just great if you're into necrophiles; and then there's Osvaldo and the técnicos, all really nice chaps but not what I'd seek for intellectual rapport. Then again, why not try Professor Shuttleworth? He's a handsome chap. He'll be arriving on tomorrow's flight from Caracas. Unfortunately he's already married." They sat down at the pearly formica table. "How does a cachapa sound for lunch?" Yadira asked. "And if you need a reminder, think of Wilfred, how he paid for ill-fated love."

"A cachapa sounds delicious, and what about bananas for dessert? We have plenty."

Cachapas, fresh corn pancakes sold throughout Venezuela, were especially good in Puerto Pedriscal, where the hot sun ripened the corn sweetly. At one of the Malariología houses off Avenida 23 de Enero, a woman cooked the cachapas to perfection on a wide griddle over a smouldering wood fire. They stayed moist and chewy inside, and the corn tasted of Amazonian sunshine, rain, fresh air, earth and embers. Every few years, strikingly beautiful, four-inch grasshoppers, spotted red and green, travelled throughout the Territory and demolished the crop. What the Territory gave in the way of pleasures, it could take back equally in terms of payment.

❦

After lunch, Yadira dropped Debra at the hospital. It was a Tuesday afternoon, one of the days Debra came to see patients with Amador. He knew she wouldn't like the Yabarana admitted yesterday. Unsuspecting, she walked along the grey corridors slightly behind him.

"I have to go off on an expedition next week. Soledad can bring you agar slants and help you take cultures. Anything she can't handle will have to wait for my return," she said.

Amador sighed and put on one of his doleful, broken-down looks. When he wasn't lost within his private dream-world or joking unfeelingly about a grave case, he existed inside a bleak sphere of depression and frustration. He frowned briefly, though his eyes remained soft and tired. "It's a pity. Your work has added water to my soup, made my job easier. I have come to rely upon your assistance, chama." He knew all about INSA's expeditions. Publications and Velázquez's international reputation were at stake.

"I'm sorry, Amador. It's my job." Debra said.

"Velázquez," he muttered quietly, mostly speaking to himself. "Trader of flesh, a fish-hook in exchange for a pint of blood, a flashlight battery for a skin biopsy. Equitable? I would say not. I have yet to see any long-term benefit for the Yanomami."

"Amador, what are you mumbling about?"

"You will find out all in due time, chama."

They entered the communal treatment room. Cots lined both sides of the big room. Intravenous drips hung from supports like cobwebs from beams. He had thought that after a year he would get used to it, but he had been here five years now and entering this room of collective infirmities still depressed him. In this very room he witnessed a death almost every day. He stopped in front of a bed. A male patient lay upon the plastic-covered mattress, no sheet to cover him. He wore dirty red shorts, no shirt.

"He is a Yabarana, flown in from Carmelitas. The bojote could be any number of things, including mycetoma." Amador gestured him to pull down his shorts. The day before, when Amador had first seen the mess, he had fought an urge to vomit. Maybe it wasn't mycetoma. Mycetomas usually localized in an extremity, and were caused by the introduction of fungi and filamentous bacteria through a breach in the skin. He usually saw them on barefooted victims who had stepped on a thorn. Mycetomas could be disfiguring but none he had ever seen had been so grotesque, bad enough for him to experience this level of revulsion. In fact, this turpitude of fulminant growth was unlike anything he'd come across, even in the textbooks. A verrucose, tumorous growth, reminiscent in size and consistency of a decomposing cauliflower, smothered the anus. It smelled badly of faeces and secondary infection, as if a hospital rat had crawled up the rectum and died. Amador set his face as deadpan as he could get it, and swallowed hard. Aguirre would have to remove a lot of tissue.

Debra shut her eyes. If Amador found this particular case difficult to stomach, then it had to be doubly bad for the squeamish gringa. "It's not mycetoma," she said as she reopened her eyes. "There are no draining fistulae. I don't think it's a mycosis at all." She seemed to focus on an imaginary spot beside the lesion, not directly on it.

Amador smoothed his lab coat, maintained his professional composure. "Chama, not every mycetoma drains to the surface. I agree it's not likely, but I don't think we should dismiss the possibility." Many mycoses were granulomatous, although, given the location, this lesion could have resulted from repeated STD infections, years without treatment and years of immune response. Condylomata acuminata (anal and genital warts) and condylomata lata (lesions of secondary syphilis) were both raised and granulomatous, just like smaller versions of this thing, but he'd never known them to grow to anywhere near this size.

"Condyloma?" asked Amador.

"Most likely."

"Perhaps, but can you culture and examine some biopsy

tissue for mycosis anyway? Then I can definitively rule out the possibility."

Amador filled a syringe with a local anaesthetic. To insert the needle through the tough flesh he leaned against the syringe, and the skin yielded. "Not even a weevil could pierce this skin, chama." He waited a few moments for the local to take effect, then twisted the circular biopsy blade back and forth against the lesion until it broke the tissue. He removed a circular plug. The desgraciado looked confused and frightened, trapped in an alien world where no one could communicate with him. Amador watched as Debra managed a weak smile and held the patient's hand. That was right, she always got the pleasant tasks while he got all the dirty work. The patient returned to Debra what might have been a smile, with long, stained teeth and well-progressed periodontal disease.

Debra glanced away, towards the hallway. "What's wrong with Pedro?" she asked. "I just saw him pass by. He looked terribly angry."

"Qué bárbaro! His house was broken into last night." Amador slipped the plug of tissue into a vial with a little sterile saline. "Funny, nothing valuable went missing, no money, nada. Aparentemente, some native artifacts were taken."

"What type of artifacts?" Debra asked. She continued to look at the hall where Pedro had walked by, although he was no longer there. She accepted the vial from Amador and, without looking at it, slipped it into the pocket of her lab coat.

"He didn't specify. Probably some Guahibo pottery, the kind they make for the tourists. I recall seeing some over at his place." Why all this sudden interest in Pedro? He had heard a rumour that Debra was enrollado sexualmente with the gringo anthropologist studying Yanomami over in the Topochal area. On the other hand, not so very long ago he'd seen her off to lunch with bull-horn Aguirre. Pedro hardly seemed her type—he chased anything with labia, sinvergüenza. Although Amador shared Pedro's predilection for women, whenever he travelled in Pedro's prestigious beige Range Rover he was ashamed. Pedro

133

liked to "montar un show", spreading his feathers for the hens. He always drove slowly and leaned his head out the window to call to women taunts such as "Epa, muchacha bonita. Do you have a sister?"

"You don't suppose he had some pre-Columbian stashed away?" Debra asked. "It strikes me as odd that someone should risk being caught stealing Guahibo pottery."

"Perhaps." Amador looked at the hole left from removing the plug and covered it with antibiotic cream and a dressing. Why did he trouble himself? The thing teemed with secondary infection. What good would a dab of cream do? The adhesive tape didn't stick well to the rubber-textured skin. "He hasn't revealed many details; he's been secretive about the whole incident, won't even lodge a complaint with the police."

"I don't suppose there would be much the police could do for him anyway."

Amador motioned to the Yabarana that he could replace his shorts. "I suppose not, but he had Capitán Máximo investigate. I don't trust the police here and I trust Máximo even less. I wouldn't go anywhere with Máximo, not even if I required his presence to claim an inheritance."

"I've heard that sort of thing about Máximo before."

"You'd be wise to heed the warning. Did you know the police gave Wilfred's motorcycle to the very borracho who killed him? But I'd much rather deal with them than Máximo."

"I heard that Máximo is a CIA plant. I don't believe it for a moment."

"Quizás." Amador shrugged. "Chama, before I forget, that old brujo you and the gallo brought in, he escaped. Must have been sometime last night because he wasn't in his bed this morning. He will die if he doesn't return." The vultures were closing in. Another one, too late, afraid, believing nothing could be done. It would never end—the weak, those who were unable to adapt, would eventually be killed off.

☙

The feeling that she had swallowed rancid cachapas had not gone when Debra arrived home. Extreme disfiguration and the stench of infection took some getting used to. It was next to impossible not to let the patients sense when she was repulsed by a particularly horrendous lesion. Already frightened and humiliated by a deformity, the last thing a patient needed was for a physician to shrink away in disgust. She had never noticed Amador gagging as she had done. How did he do it? She thought of Sunday with Segundo. Amazonian life oscillated between beauties and defacement, pleasures and suffering.

She sprawled on the sticky brown vinyl, her body numb. A wet washcloth covered her forehead and eyes. She propped her feet over the arm of the sofa. "Debra, we have to grocery shop." Yadira rummaged through her purse and pulled out her car keys. The metallic clinks of the keys sounded intolerably loud to Debra.

"I had an ugly case and if I see anything to do with food I'll throw up my cachapas."

"I suppose I should be thankful that I work with mosquitoes. But a trip to town might do you good, take your mind off disease. Come on."

Yadira drove a little white Volkswagen. Brown with dust, it reminded Debra of the cockroaches that scuttled around the bathroom at night. Yadira squeezed it into a gap between two towering four-wheel-drive vehicles, a brown Toyota and a beige Range Rover whose letters had either fallen off or been stolen and replaced as "Renge Rogor". The supermercado was a short walk, just beyond the row of Lebanese merchants' shops. Yadira took off down the soap and shampoo aisle. It was Debra's turn to buy the week's supply of meat. She sniffed at the counter, where the meat had dehydrated, leaving the surface covered in dark muscle threads. It reminded her of the smell of the hospital. The butcher at the meat counter grinned and waved away the flies speckling the muscle fibres.

"Señorita?"

Yadira said that only the choicest cut, the lomito, was

edible. After all, she claimed, cattle in the Amazonas had to be tough if they were to survive. None of the meat looked appealing to Debra. "I'll have two chickens cut up into pieces, por favor."

His face splayed wide open into a tremendous smile. "For you, señorita, I will cut the pollos con gusto. I have a new saw, first of its kind in all of Puerto Pedriscal."

She watched helplessly as he sawed through the chickens at high speed in a checkerboard pattern. A jolly round man in a bloodstained apron, he puckered his mouth in a whistle inaudible beneath the saw's whine. He rotated the chicken ninety degrees and continued sawing. He handed her a clear plastic bag of peachy chicken flesh covered with bone dust and flaps of yellow fatty skin, cut into chunks approximately the size and shape of ice cubes. "Maravilloso! Algo más, señorita?" He radiated sheer joy.

"No, gracias." She looked down at her cubes. The watery pink blood had collected into a corner of the bag and had begun to dribble onto the floor.

A friendly voice startled her. "Corazoncita!" Segundo wore the inevitable faded red, short-sleeved shirt.

"The gifts were very thoughtful," she said politely.

"You liked the decoración?"

"I will remember it always," she said.

He laughed. "Yes, corazoncita. Only a lady of your high social standing, a capitalista, would appreciate something so ostentatious."

"Doctor Pantaleon tells me your friend the curandero ran away from the hospital," she said. "He will die if he doesn't take his medication."

"Dios mío!" He folded his hands in front of himself ecclesiastically. "I must try to find him."

He left the supermercado hurriedly with a carton of eggs and a litre of milk. Debra watched his back as he stepped through the doors, backlit by the outdoor brightness, his shirt appearing black, not red.

12

Professor David Shuttleworth watched two teenage boys swimming in the pool at the Gran Hotel Las Palmas. They dove, splashed and gleefully threw green algae at each other. Substituting a beach ball for algal slabs, this could have been a scene from Brighton. The dusk of the exotic setting, the palms and banana trees, the week-old sunburn and the long-legged beauty beside him reminded him that it was not. He was far away from Britain, away from the straitlaced, routine academia of Cambridge, and this was the Venezuelan Amazon.

"*Naegleria*," he said, in very clipped, posh English, with a cocky smile. "The amoebae love sludge. They can gain entrance though the nose, cross the cribriform plate and invade the olfactory lobes of the brain. Death may occur within days. Diagnosis is often made *post mortem*. A pathologist friend in Africa, where I was conducting research, told me that he once autopsied a victim. When he sawed through the skull a slushy fluid flowed out. The brain had liquefied."

"How was your dinner, David?" Debra asked.

"Interesting."

He hadn't expected to be assigned a personal interpreter like his dinner companion. He'd been doing collaborative research with Velázquez's institute for the past two years now, ever since the centre had opened. It had been really slow getting things started. Everything in Latin America was done "mañana". David had had good expectations initially. No question about it, Velázquez was well educated, and a first-rate scientist. He had good funding and had attracted much international attention with the new institute. But although he'd had a grandiose vision, his domineering personality had driven away the more experienced Venezuelan scientists, and the staff left behind was young and newly qualified. David had put a lot of effort into getting his malaria projects off the ground and, together with Velázquez, had pulled off a few publications, but he now had his doubts about the long-term viability of INSA. If worst came to worst, at least the affiliation would continue to provide him with fresh isolates and clinical materials he could use back in England. He personally had nothing to lose and everything to gain by going to Puerto Pedriscal. Most of all, he was anxious to see the stone-age native cultures. He wasn't actually needed on tomorrow's expedition but Velázquez had promised him he could go.

He had spent the past week getting ready for the expedition, in agony, enough to drive a man mad. There had been the meetings, called reuniones at INSA, rambling on for hours, never seeming to get anywhere, never really accomplishing very much, and in Spanish. Debra had translated for him inadequately. He understood about half of what he was supposed to. And there had been several agonizing hours spent with that hot little number, Marisol, peering down a microscope at infective larvae. She had left her lab coat unbuttoned, probably intentionally, and the plunging neckline of her blouse had fallen forward every time she leaned over the microscope. He had been able to inspect her breasts and large dark nipples, right down to her navel, at his leisure. It had been as much as he could do to keep his hands off her.

This afternoon he had endured the worst, a slide presentation—hours in the dark—of worms, tissue sections, filaria. While Marisol's breasts were still firmly entrenched in his memory, so to speak, in the darkness Debra translated softly in his ear, her breath tickling deliciously, pressing her breast against his arm. Although it was hardly sufficient to quench the pulsing heat inside his trousers, he had welcomed the dinnertime reprieve.

"It's getting late," Debra said. David downed his last drops of beer.

"Would you care for a nightcap in my room?" he asked. Debra was practically young enough to be his daughter, only she was not his daughter. He most certainly had not forgotten about his wife and children back at home. He had never done anything like this before. His reputation was impeccable. However, the contact with her breast could hardly have been accidental and he was certain it had been a signal. This, the Amazonas, was another place, another time—an exotic culture, a different existence from Cambridge.

"It's really very kind of you to offer, but I must be getting back home."

"Certain you won't join me for a scotch? I brought a bottle of excellent malt for special guests."

"It's getting very late and I'm afraid I might not find a taxi if I stay much longer."

"I'll help, then. It's not safe for you to be out alone."

"It's really not necessary."

"My dear, a gentleman always ensures the safe arrival of his escort to her front door. Allow me to change into more comfortable shoes."

"Suit yourself," she said.

They walked down the black and white polished checkered floor, underneath the highly arched ceiling, to David's room. He gestured her in and closed the door behind them. Immediately, he stretched his arms around her. "I've been waiting for this," he said, and kissed her, his lips hard.

She pulled away. "Oh no you don't," she said, as she pressed her index finger on his lips to close them. He had expected slightly parted lips and half-closed eyes, a soft expression. Instead she stood wide-eyed, smiling. At least she wasn't angry. "Why, professor," she said in a teasing voice, "do you treat all your female colleagues this way?"

"All week you've been whispering in my ear and leaning against me, your breast pressed against my arm."

"I have not, at least not that I noticed. I'm flattered, really. But it isn't a good idea. You have no idea just how gossip can get out of control in this town."

David felt frustrated. She had been leading him on all week and now she was rejecting him. A picture of his wife and children suddenly filled his head, flooding him with embarrassment as the hopeful hormones drained from his groin. "Right, my misunderstanding. Let me help you find that taxi."

They waited fifteen minutes—no taxis.

"Looks as if you may have to spend the night in my room after all, love."

"Wishful thinking, professor." She looked up and down Avenida Río Negro. The street was dark and empty; not a car, not a single human being, just the moon, stars and shadowy mango trees, and the only sounds were faint barks of dogs and the chirps of crickets. "I have no choice. I'll have to walk home," she said.

"Don't be ridiculous. Can't you get a room at the hotel?"

"What would Yadira say if I didn't show up at home? Everyone knows Velázquez sent me here to have dinner with you. Even if I didn't sleep with you, everyone would say I did."

"Then why don't you, love?"

"That's enough, professor!"

"I'll walk you home. Perhaps Yadira would be kind enough to give me a lift back to the hotel."

They walked for fifteen minutes. Avenida 23 de Enero stretched far ahead, in a straight line. Most of the streetlights had burned out, and the street was poorly lit by the remaining few, which cast a dull orange luminescence.

"I've never walked home from town before. I think it's quite far."

"Changing the subject, would you happen to know why I haven't been paid for the supplies I brought?"

"There's been a change of governors. INSA's administrator is a political appointment, I'm afraid, and they hauled her off to jail. We're waiting for her release or for the appointment of a new administrator. Most of INSA's financial assets are frozen

140

just now."

"If that isn't typical! I'm also disappointed in Velázquez's behaviour with me. I expected him to be more attentive. Instead he has brushed me off on you."

"I thought you enjoyed my company."

"I do, absolutely. It's just that I find it damned peculiar that a man who claims to be interested in collaborative research won't give me the time of day."

"I may be overstepping my boundaries, but I think Velázquez is becoming paranoid. I've noticed a change in him lately. He's been complaining about imperialist domination of science. Maybe he's afraid you and other foreigners will take all you can from INSA and leave his name off publications."

"I've been working with that bloody fool for two years. He approached me to collaborate. We've published together in the past. An attitude like that could endanger any future relationship."

ॐ

Máximo left Doctor Pedro Aguirre's house late. The paddy wagon, a jeep marked "Policía Militar—División de la Selva", headed south from Aguirre's house, on the outermost edge of town, towards the town centre. He saw the gringa mamita with a man, too tall and fair to be a criollo, both walking stupidly, in the middle of nowhere, under a streetlight. No one ever walked through town after dark. As a matter of fact, no one in Puerto Pedriscal, apart from the indios, walked through town in the daylight. The town's pandemonium traffic, the blistering hot asphalt and dust, the viciousness of the guard dogs, amounted to very unpleasant walking. He had the driver turn around at a sidestreet and pull up beside the gringos. She was stooped over a bare foot and looked to be examining a freshly torn blister, glistening in the yellow light. "Buenas noches," acknowledged Máximo from the passenger's side. "What are you doing out here so late at night?"

She stood up, almost comical—a lopsided figure, one leg longer than the other. "I'm trying to walk home."

He nodded, very, very slowly. Her answer didn't satisfy him. Did she really expect him to believe that she intended to walk home through the abandoned streets, past the barking dogs, alone with a mute gringo, in the dark? People in this town accused him of many things, mostly true, but stupidity was not one of them. She continued walking, with only one shoe on. The driver rolled the jeep slowly on, following the pedestrians. "You live very far away. You and the señor, both of you extranjeros, no less, should not be out here so late at night. Many people let their guard dogs loose at this hour. You're lucky to get away with sore feet. I will gladly take you both home, doctora, before you get into serious trouble." The Evangelist church was probably a half-hour walk from here, and the doctora and her compañero were far from the town centre, or anywhere else extranjeros were likely to go. It didn't make any sense that they would walk all this way. She was up to porquerías, undoubtedly hiding something.

"Thank you, capitán." She and the hombre climbed up into the back of the paddy wagon and sat on the metal benches, one on either side. A heavy steel mesh partitioned the prisoners' section from Máximo and his driver. Máximo looked back through the mesh at the two foreigners, veiling his face behind iron.

The señor must surely be the scientist from Gran Bretaña that his informant had told him about. Yes, upriver permits had been issued for an expedition party including the English and the doctora. Máximo made it his business to know everything that went on in the Territory; in fact, knowing everything that went on was his business. A lot of contraband passed through the Territory from over the river, and in the past there had been friction over just where the border lay between the neighbouring countries. He knew that at this moment Brazilian gold miners were spilling over the border to Yanomami territory. To top it all off, a Communist presence existed both inside the Territory and abroad, not that it would become a real threat, at least not while he, Capitán Máximo Zambrano, was in command. A strong military presence was necessary to protect sovereignty, political stability and mineral rights. As long as he protected the Territory in his official capacity, why should he not personally benefit from inside information? Yes, there were plenty of good reasons for keeping well informed, both professional and personal reasons.

"It's a good thing for you I happened along. I have been investigating a small matter for doctor Aguirre, a matter of witchcraft, brujería. Indios—they are no more civilized people than casabe is a loaf of French bread. You and your amigo wouldn't happen to have heard anything related to the brujería now, would you?"

"Doctor Pantaleon told me about a break-in at Doctor Aguirre's house but I hadn't heard about the witchcraft. It's a shame—poor Pedro. It couldn't have happened to a kinder man."

"I suppose riding in the back there gives you an idea of what it might be like to be a prisoner of mine, doesn't it, doctora?" Máximo laughed fully, his belly jiggling.

"Yes, truly it does. I'm very thankful for your hospitality, capitán."

So the doctora feigned ignorance of the brujería. He had expected that. She had spoiled a perfectly good business arrangement. Aguirre was useless to him now, his nerve lost. Then again, all was not lost. Perhaps the gringa could become useful to him in the future, just as Aguirre and his rich Caracas relations had been. Indeed, the familia Aguirre had paid handsomely for the guns he provided to protect their hacienda.

13

Cheo woke from a deep, Polar-drugged sleep at five-thirty a.m., with Osvaldo hammering on his bedroom window and shouting his name. Fortunately, he had had the foresight, though he didn't remember doing so, to leave his expedition clothes at the base of the bed. It was still ten minutes before he stumbled to the transport jeep in his calf-length leather boots. The rest of the party, Doctora Debra, Marisol and the inglés, looked at him blearily in the darkness, as tired as he was hung over.

Only Osvaldo, his usual effervescent self, spoke on the way to the airport. Cheo tried to focus his aching brain away from the pot-holes, the oh-so-many pot-holes, and he could tell that the silence of the extranjeros was not just from tiredness. He could feel their tension at what lay ahead of them. The only blessing was that Marisol appeared too tired to talk about her stupid blackflies. He hated them, he hated Marisol's obsession with them and he hated the only job he could find in Puerto Pedriscal—caring for blackflies as if they were babies. Although his friends were jealous that he had a job, he still had to endure a lot of jokes about nurturing pests that any sane person in Amazonas would want to see exterminated. By the time they reached the airport, the sun streaked the eastern sky pink and blue. Cheo didn't see too many sunrises, only the occasional one after an exceptionally late night with his panas, and he associated them with an unpleasant day of pain ahead.

Two of the other técnicos, Salvador and Inmaculada, were already at the airport, transferring supplies from the INSA truck into a twin-engined avioneta. Cheo's brain throbbed even more as he helped load box after box, the generator, gasoline, a big tank of liquid nitrogen and even a small refrigerator. Personal gear was crammed into the tail space of a single-engined Cessna that would carry the expedition party.

An enforced wait while Osvaldo drove back to town to look for one of the pilots gave Cheo time to dig some painkillers out of one of the medical supply boxes and down them with sweet, black coffee nectar at the cafeteria. He was not surprised at the non-arrival of Antonio. The pilot had still been going strong in the bar the night before when Cheo had finally left.

Osvaldo arrived with Antonio, dressed in the same clothes Cheo had seen him in a few hours before, just after eight. Cheo climbed into the copilot's seat beside Antonio, leaving Marisol and the two foreigners to squeeze into the three tiny seats behind.

"Hola, Cheo," the pilot said. "A pleasant evening, no? I'm glad we have the other avioneta to follow. I don't think I could find my way on my own today. By the way, does anyone have a watch?" he asked loudly. "If we lose sight of the plane going over the mountains, I'll need to know how long we've been flying if we are to find La Joya."

"You mean you don't have a watch of your own?" Doctora Debra asked.

"Claro que sí, señorita! Somewhere. But I knew one of you would be sure to have one."

Cheo looked back at the others. Marisol was lost in thought—thoughts of blackflies, no doubt. The others seemed a little more pale than normal and looked at each other nervously. He smiled. This trip could actually be entertaining.

In fifteen minutes they soared over a rugged landscape. No trace of human activity marred the forest carpet crowding the sheer black granite cliffs. Ribbons of water from the high forest poured down successive tiers of rock, revealing the enormous scale of the terrain. The post-alcoholic toxins in Cheo's head didn't stop him from performing a task that could one day save his life, perhaps today. He forced himself to study the complicated ridges and valleys below to ensure that the pilot was keeping to a constant bearing. His woolly afro extended the width of the window.

"What are you doing, Cheo?" Doctora Debra asked, leaning forward, trying to peer around his afro.

"I'm noting the location of rivers for when we crash. Following a river is the only sure way to get out of the selva alive."

Even the English, with his limited Spanish, understood something of the dangers. "But surely there is little chance of crashing."

"Al contrario, doctor," Cheo replied. "Several avionetas each year disappear in Amazonas. There are terrible storms which knock the planes out of the sky, like swatted mosquitoes, especialmente in the afternoons. That's why we leave so early. Then the pilots themselves are not always responsible," Cheo continued. The pilot chuckled. "They are young and think they are cowboys, like in the movies. To fly in such dangerous conditions is exciting to them."

The doctora looked worried. "They would send rescue teams to help us if anything happened, wouldn't they?"

"If they knew where we were, doctora," Cheo assured her. "En realidad, you must help yourself when we crash. Such a little plane disappears beneath the forest canopy. I always come prepared, with my strong boots and clothes and a little bag with some food and insect repellent. Just two years ago, an avioneta carrying rural doctors dropped in the selva close to San Carlos de Río Negro. The only survivor was a doctora, a woman much like yourself. The militares found the plane a week later and said everyone was dead. They sent some bones from the crash to her family in Caracas. Then she appeared. The Yanomami had found her eating caterpillars and spiders. She was so badly bitten by insect plaga that her whole body had swelled up like a boiled plantain. The bones the militares had found were from a big capybara which must have been killed in the crash."

The extranjeros didn't ask any more questions, but looked studiously out the windows. Marisol was still lost to the world.

The mountain barrier flattened to a smooth green carpet broken only by serpentine brown rivers slithering through the dense growth on their slow way to the Orinoco and the sea. Straight ahead, a large tepui grew on the horizon.

"La Montaña de las Serpientes," Antonio said. "It rises three thousand metres above the jungle. The natives believe that their snake spirit lives on top, although I've never seen anything from up here. La Joya is at its base, and we will stop there for a while to see el Padre Francisco."

The Orinoco appeared once more on their right and Cheo relaxed, knowing he could find his way back to the main liquid highway of the region. And there, between the towering wall of Serpiente and the bank of the river, lay a large patch of bright green velvet, the improbable savannah of La Joya.

❧

Padre Francisco stood in the shade of a lime tree and scanned the sky to the north through the mosquito netting draped around his hat. The Ministry of Health in Puerto Pedriscal had radioed that an expedition party would arrive at ten with supplies to replenish the medicatura before the children returned for classes. How empty the mission was without the children. The few summer months when they returned to their families were the only time in the year when he and the hermanas could concentrate on mission maintenance and the piles of paperwork that the church and territorial government imposed on them; but he missed the quiet Yanomami and Makiritare children, their shyness developing into confidence as they came to trust him and depend on him, and the laughter which surfaced once they adjusted to their new freedom in Mary and her blessed son.

Almost twenty years he had been here, and still he thanked God in every prayer for bringing him these children. They were so different from the cynical, streetwise muchachos he had once struggled to save from the slums of Caracas. Their innocent minds grasped His teachings so easily. Not like their parents, steeped in primitive fear of thunder spirits and wind spirits, and any matter of spirits. Yes, the future lay with the children. It was his duty to teach them the benevolence of the only God and prepare them for their inevitable assimilation into Christian society. Only through Christ could they defend themselves from the corruption, alcohol and prostitution which had taken so many of their parents.

Yet, with the return of the children so near—Eduardo was on the river at that moment, gathering the first group— Francisco felt some anxiety clouding his anticipation. How many of the children would fail to return this year? Which of the few who had shown so much promise, Samuel, Matéus, Juanito, María, would be hiding in the forest with their parents? The lure of candy and cookies was not always sufficient to persuade them to board the mission's dugouts. He could only have faith that some of His teaching stayed with those who remained in the forest, and that it would be passed on to others to bring a gradual change to Christian morals.

As the plane bumped to a halt on the grass runway, Debra examined the strange figure waiting under a small tree. He was tall and stooped, in a long, once-white cassock, his face hidden behind netting hanging from the rim of a brown plastic replica of the pith helmets worn by those intrepid Victorian explorers. Within seconds of the doors opening, she understood. A cloud of blackflies filled the cabin and attached themselves to all exposed skin. Cheo pulled a bottle of repellent from a small bag slung over his shoulder, calmly wiped some over his hands and face, and handed the bottle to Debra. The supply of repellent she had been warned to bring was somewhere in the bottom of a box on the other plane. Her opinion of Cheo as the INSA clown was undergoing a rapid revision.

The cassocked figure approached as she stepped onto the iron-hard earth. "Welcome to La Joya, the jewel of Amazonas. Marisol and Cheo I know, but you two I don't think I've met." A soft, kind voice and bony outstretched hand. Debra could now make out the spaniel eyes behind the netting. "Come, the sisters have some iced lemonade prepared in the refectory. We seldom have visitors, and I'm sure you have a few moments to get me up to date with all that's happening in the metropolis."

He led the expedition members towards the school complex. Debra noticed that the pilot stayed behind, and when she last looked back he was kneeling beside one of the wheels.

The mission buildings were solid, plastered and immaculately white. Only a small steeple was taller than a single storey. Padre Francisco showed them into a large hall with tables and benches stacked at one end and a kitchen visible through serving hatches at the other. A tray with glasses and a pitcher of lemonade sat in one hatch. There was no sign of whoever had prepared it.

"It's so bare now without the children," Padre Francisco said. "You will see a very different mission if you come back here after your expedition. The children will be arriving soon. Then our true work begins. Would you care to see more of our facility?"

Debra felt the depth of conviction in this priest's soft voice, and saw the enthusiasm that sparkled in the sad eyes when he spoke of his children. She and David followed his long strides out into a courtyard in the centre of the mission.

"This is the boys' dormitory," Francisco said. "The girls sleep in that building on the other side of the plaza, and the hermanas, of course, occupy the rooms between them. We can care for more than a hundred children at the moment, and we are seeking the means to expand."

Debra stood in the doorway of a long, hangar-like room. A

double row of posts about six feet apart was sunk into the bare, polished concrete floor along the length of the room. A large iron hook was set into the white breeze-block wall opposite each post and bunched hammocks hung from most of the hooks. The room was otherwise devoid of any furniture or decoration. For some reason, the hooks probably, the room reminded her of the slaughterhouse in Puerto Pedriscal where Velázquez had sent her to help Fermin collect parasites. The impression was reinforced when she looked into the communal washroom with its long, low trough and row of spigots. She could imagine the line of small, naked brown bodies, like newborn calves, at the trough. Veal for the church's sustenance. Padre Francisco continued to talk animatedly about the mission's plans for expansion. David smiled sympathetically, uncomprehending. Debra had seen enough.

"We really must be going, padre. Thank you for showing us the mission. It's most impressive."

"You were rather abrupt with the priest," David said as they walked back to the plane. "How could such a kind man offend you?"

"I'm sure he means well, but can't you see what he's doing? Those poor children. Taken from their homes and their parents, from their culture, and dumped in this sterile place. How can they understand? To be taught that everything they know is wrong, that their parents' beliefs are evil. Christianity in action—to save a soul you first have to destroy the flesh."

Marisol had enjoyed her visit. The blackflies in La Joya transmitted *Mansonella*, a worm almost identical to *Onchocerca*, but one that caused no obvious signs of disease. Her mind spun upon the possibilities of comparing the two diseases. Doctor Velázquez would be enthusiastic when she explained her ideas to him.

Judging from the number of blackflies, the Makiritare who

lived around the mission were sure to be heavily infected with *Mansonella*, while many of the Yanomami children brought from upriver had to have oncho. Why had nobody thought of working here before? It was a natural laboratory with superb facilities at the mission's hospital. The priest and nuns could translate and also control the subjects she chose, and make them do anything she wanted. And what a stroke of luck to find Diosgracio here, just when they had chanced to drop in. She had heard of this Yanomami child raised by the mission, who had become a nurse and moved north. He was obviously infected with oncho; she could recognize that wrinkly skin and persistent scratching anywhere. He so badly wanted to be cured before his eyesight worsened that she had only to suggest that INSA could help him to convince him to co-operate with her experimental infections of blackflies in Puerto Pedriscal. There was potential here for years of work.

❦

"Epa, Antonio!" Cheo called to the pilot, sound asleep in the shade under his plane. "Vamos! The plane with our equipment will be in Topochal already."

Antonio crawled into the sunlight, blinking, stood up and stretched. "We have a problem with one of the brakes, but we should be all right landing at Topochal."

"We should be. . . ?" Debra echoed.

"Sí. The airstrip at Topochal is long and we will probably have enough room to stop before the trees."

"Probably?"

"Not to worry, doctora," Antonio reassured her, exposing his heavily tartared teeth in a wide grin. "Now, if we were going to land somewhere like Kovåta-teri, I would suggest going back to Puerto Pedriscal. Let's go! It's getting late and clouds are appearing in the sky."

They shared boiled eggs with mayonnaise and soda crackers as the plane followed the river south. Small patches of cleared forest betrayed the occasional settlement. One larger settlement passed beneath them, laid out in orderly squares beside neat plantations and a long green airstrip. "The headquarters of the New World Mission for the Alto Orinoco," Cheo said, turning around to look at the others. "Just a little beyond it is the Río Casiquiare, which joins the Orinoco to the Amazon basin. We are now in Yanomami territory. Our boats and motoristas at Topochal will take us farther up the Orinoco, away from the influence of the missionaries. They have not yet built airstrips that far upriver."

The descent to Topochal from seven thousand feet plugged Debra's ears, and she swallowed repeatedly to equalize the pressure. The airstrip had been cut from solid forest and, although it was long, the trees whizzing by when Antonio dropped into the slot made the approach seem very fast. Then they were bumping violently across the grass with the black wall of trees in front of them. Debra closed her eyes, trying to think benevolently of gentle Padre Francisco, but opened them when she felt the plane swerve abruptly. Antonio had the plane under control just a hundred yards from the end of the grass.

"Plenty of room," he shouted above the roar of the engine as he taxied back up the airstrip towards the twin-engined plane parked beside two small buildings.

Four men came out to meet them. Debra recognized one, Victor, as the pilot of the other plane. Two of the men could have been clones: short square bodies, sandals, baggy pants and shirts faded by the sun to a nondescript colour, skin burnished and grooved like old chestnuts. One wore a battered cowboy hat and the other a baseball cap with "Lagoven" written on it. The fourth man, really only a boy, hung behind the others. He too wore baggy faded clothes, but his feet were bare and no hat covered his shaved scalp and the ring of thick, straight black hair. Debra's gaze was caught for a moment by his delicate features, the steady stare of his almond-shaped eyes and his four-inch cane ear plugs.

"Pepe and Juan, our motoristas," Cheo introduced the

cowboy and his twin, "and Angel María, our interpreter. They left Puerto Pedriscal a week ago to get here before us."

"Everything is loaded in the lanchas," Pepe said. "We should leave immediately to reach the rapids before dark. The river is still deep from the rains so we will make good speed."

"Don't forget that we must stop at shabonos on the way," Marisol said. "We must collect skin snips and blackflies wherever we can. Blood samples can wait until the end of the expedition. That way they'll be fresh when we get back to INSA."

"There's nothing for you here in Topochal," Angel María told her. "The Yanomami have deserted their shabono. Even the priest and the enfermera were gone when we arrived."

"Where is everyone?" Marisol asked.

"The Yanomami must be on *wayumi*, in the forest," Angel María said in a high, soft voice. "When there is no food they go to the forest to eat. They walk one month, or two, before they return." Debra found that she could follow Angel María's simple Spanish easily. His vocabulary and grammar seemed to be on a level with her own.

Two boats were tied up at the river. A large dugout with a thatched roof over the back half was heavily laden with mounds under tarpaulins. Several oil drums filled the middle section. The other, an aluminum speedboat with a huge motor and the Ministry of Health logo emblazoned on the sides, had room only for passengers. Pepe climbed into the speedboat and indicated that the guests of honour, Debra and Professor Shuttleworth, should join him. Angel María untied the boat, pushed it into the current and jumped in beside them. The engine started with a roar and the boat arced into midstream with a surge of power. Debra looked back to see Cheo squeezing himself into a small space between the oil drums, his shrivelled leg dangling over the gunwale of the dugout.

The refreshing wind from their speed disguised the heat of the early afternoon sun directly overhead. They were now only a few degrees above the equator, the farthest south Debra had been, almost right on the midriff bulge of the earth. She felt happy. This reminded her of fun days on the Intracoastal Waterway in Florida, only here there were no "no wake" signs, or manatees hiding just below the surface. She smiled at David. He also was enjoying himself. The wind and noise freed him from the isolation of incomprehensible language. She could imagine how frustrated he must feel.

An hour later the engine suddenly died and Pepe curved the boat into the bank alongside a fallen trunk.

"Cerrito," Angel María said. "A small shabono. Yanomami will come to meet us." They waited but no one came.

"Maybe they are on *wayumi* also. Wait. I will see." And Angel María disappeared into the undergrowth at the end of the trunk.

Thirty minutes of silence followed. No birds sang. No insects chirped. The shattering sound of the large dugout joining them was a welcome relief.

"What's happening? Why are you just sitting here?" Marisol shouted.

"We're waiting for Angel María to come back from the village," Debra answered.

"We have no time to waste like this! Come on. There's a lot to do," Marisol said, and climbed onto the bank. Debra and David followed. Cheo limped at the rear, carrying a box of equipment for taking skin snips. The trail was narrow, but clear and well travelled. Suddenly it ended at a sloping wall of dried palm leaves over a wooden frame, twenty feet high and curving away into the forest on both sides. Marisol slipped through a four-foot-high opening. Debra bent almost double to pass through the door and then stood up, squinting to adjust to the sudden light in the shabono.

The circular structure was bigger than she had expected, about fifty feet across, and it seemed deserted, just like Topochal. Then a movement to one side caught her attention. A group of faces stared from hammocks, and as she peered into the roofed shade around the perimeter she saw more faces, immobile, staring. The quiet was eerie. She saw babies cradled in mothers' arms in the hammocks, but not one cried. The scrawny dogs lying on their sides under the hammocks didn't bark or whine.

Angel María appeared out of the shade and walked across the bright plaza towards them. "There is much sickness here," he said. "Many have died already and more will not last much longer. You must help, doctora."

Debra stooped over the closest hammock. A naked woman looked back impassively, with dark oval eyes and deeply yellowed sclerae. An infant lay across her chest in a palm-fibre sling, dehydrated, with hot, dry skin. Debra palpated the woman's abdomen gently and pulled down an unresisting eyelid. Blanched mucous membranes, yellowed eyes, swollen spleen. Malaria. This woman's red blood cells were being destroyed by the parasite, her haemoglobin converted into new parasites to expand the cycle and the iron by-products rejected to yellow the tissues.

"Cheo, run to the lancha and bring the big bottle of chloroquine. David, we'll need to put the worst cases on saline drips. Could you help Cheo bring a case of bottles from the boat?" She moved quickly from hammock to hammock to gauge the scale of the epidemic.

David Shuttleworth knew the intricacies of malarial parasites as well as anyone on the planet. He had made his career studying their life cycles and biochemistry until he was acknowledged by his peers as an authority. One didn't become a full professor and head of department at Cambridge for no reason. He knew the statistics, he taught them to undergraduates: the millions of deaths annually, the lost production. But his clinical knowledge came from hospitals. He had never been caught in an epidemic, and to witness its catastrophic effects first-hand was shocking. That green doctor, who had probably never seen a case of malaria in her life before, had taken charge and left him, the expert, watching her like an idiot. The walk to the boat and back would at least give him a chance to compose himself. Twice now he had felt humiliated before her.

David heard the shouting before he got back to the shabono. He ducked inside to see Angel María pulling Marisol, her Pentax camera strung around her neck, back from two crazy-looking men advancing on her. One swung a machete in front of him and the other held an axe high above his head with both hands. The men were naked but for strings around their waists tied to their foreskins, holding their penises erect. They were both short but muscular and their faces were ferocious. They obviously meant business, although their eyes were strangely glazed and unfocused.

Debra joined him. "Let's get out of here," she said. "We can't do much while this is going on." They waited outside the shabono until Angel María dragged Marisol out through the low doorway. They backed away from the shabono and the wild men didn't follow.

"We must leave," Angel María said. "You have insulted the spirits. The shamans want revenge."

"We can't go yet," Marisol said, her eyes wide and her head tilted left in defiance. "We just started work, and I need specimens."

Angel María looked at Debra. "Doctora, do not allow her. It is dangerous. The shamans believe the sickness is caused by *Shawara* demons who eat souls and are brought by the white people. When she took photographs they thought she was capturing souls to feed the *Shawara*. They have inhaled *yopo* to ask their *Hekura* spirits for help, and the spirits tell them to kill those who bring *Shawara*."

"Did you hear that, Marisol?" Debra asked. "Is it worth getting chopped up for a few snips of skin? Let's go before we cause more trouble."

Marisol turned and walked down the trail to the boats.

They started upriver towards the next village. Debra fretted about the dying people at Cerrito. David withdrew into his thoughts. What if the epidemic was widespread? This expedition had gotten off to a great start, with them almost dying on that plane and Marisol almost getting them all killed with her insensitivity and obsession. How many lives could have been saved with Debra's chloroquine tablets and saline? He imagined the British tabloid headlines if things had turned out differently: "Distinguished Cambridge Scientist Killed Bravely Fighting Malaria Epidemic."

❦

The sun and the white noise from the outboard made Debra sleepy. A lot had happened since she had dragged herself out of bed that morning.

Her dreams were interrupted by a dull thud resounding through the boat and the motor shutting off. "Coño! Carajo!" Pepe swore vehemently. "We hit something." He tilted the outboard clear of the water and a bare spindle projected where the propeller should have been. "Qué vaina! Now we have to return to Topochal, where I can radio for a replacement. The others should be here soon and they can tow us back."

David swore quietly to himself as they drifted downstream with the current. There was nothing to do, so Debra stretched out on the seats and enjoyed the tranquillity of the river without the outboard. The forest was still and not even a breeze rustled leaves. The loudest sound was the gentle lapping of water against the aluminum hull. A pair of red, yellow and blue macaws flew overhead, their long tails trailing behind. They were always in pairs; she had heard that they mated for life. All the Amazonian natives prized their feathers for adornment. How would a survivor feel after her mate had been turned into a headdress? Lonely, devastated, the way a human would feel? How easy would it be to find another mate in this vast jungle, especially when all the other macaws were in pairs?

157

"Pity we have no paddles. We could speed our progress considerably," David said. His face, arms and legs had turned an angry red. His English skin had had no chance to toughen up before the expedition.

"You ought to put on a hat, David. You're getting carbonizadoed. I've always found that sort of language thing amusing: there's a perfectly good word for burning, 'quemar', but for people they come up with 'carbonized'. Quite appropriate when you think of it."

"Very droll," David replied, draping a shirt over his head.

As they drifted around a corner, Debra noticed two plastic juice containers floating ahead of them. Pollution, even here.

"*Shori!*" Angel María called, as a small dugout paddled by two young Yanomami men slid out from the shade at the edge of the river and pulled in beside them. Angel María conversed with them in a whining, cat's meow language, very different from his voice when speaking Spanish. Conversation stopped when one of the plastic jugs bobbed. The two youths paddled quickly to the bottle and pulled it into their dugout. A large catfish writhed at the end of a short length of fishing line. A vicious blow from a club stopped its struggle.

"They are warriors from a village up the river," Angel María said. "The sickness has not reached them."

The boat spun slowly in the current behind the Yanomami fishermen for another few hours. The sun sank over the forest. The fishermen gathered their tackle and dug into the water with large diamond-shaped blades and took off upstream, leaving the expedition party alone on the river again.

Where was the other boat? It would soon be dark and Debra wasn't so sure about being on the river at night. Pepe and Angel María didn't seem to be concerned. She was glad of their presence. They gave a sense of security to their predicament.

Twilight lasted only minutes. The sky blazed gold and the forest on each side became a solid black line. Debra thought she saw fluttering shapes against the indigo sky. Vampire bats! They had to be! A large splash beside the boat made her jump.

She moved closer to David. Anacondas could reach over the side of the boat and pull her into the black water just inches away. She got down onto the floor at David's feet. Then she heard faint whines around her ears. Mosquitoes, and they had to be anophelines; only anophelines bit at night. Some of them had to be carrying malaria so close to an epidemic. She hoped enough repellent remained on her skin, but she kept moving anyway, rubbing her hands over her head and neck to disturb any that landed.

She knew her fears were mostly irrational, but she could feel panic rising uncontrollably inside her. A typical fear response, adrenalin coursing into her system, directing blood to her brain and muscles. Pepe must have sensed her anxiety. "It's a beautiful evening, doctora. We're fortunate we are on the river and not stuck in the forest. There are all kinds of dangers there at night—tigres, poisonous snakes. The Yanomami don't leave their shabonos at night when evil roams the forest."

The sound of a motor coming towards them brought a palpable wave of relaxation through Debra's body. They were saved. A light probed the darkness and blinded her.

"Aquí, Juan!" Pepe shouted. "We have lost the propeller."

"We also had problems," Juan explained when he pulled alongside. "The gasoline is mostly water and dirt. We had to dismantle the engine to clean it."

"But it gave us a chance to collect some specimens, didn't it, Cheo," Marisol said enthusiastically.

"You mean to tell me that you went back to the shabono after what happened? Are you crazy?" Debra asked.

"Well, we didn't exactly go back," Marisol clarified. "We just waited outside the shabono for anyone who came out. Cheo took skin snips while I caught feeding blackflies. It was quite safe, really. And I think we got some people with good infections."

Debra couldn't think of anything to say. Marisol's bravery, or stupidity, astounded her. Was there nothing she wouldn't do for those damned blackflies?

Juan threw a rope to Pepe and they headed back down the river. How the motoristas could find Topochal in the dark was a mystery, but they did. Debra could just make out the path in the starlight when she climbed out of the boat. She grabbed a branch for support and seconds later a searing pain stabbed into her forearm. She clutched her arm and another burst of pain hit her.

"Something bit me!" she screamed. Juan jumped on the bank beside her and undid the cuff of her shirt. Angel María held a flashlight. Debra felt faint as the pain spread up and down her arm. She saw something fall out of her sleeve and Angel María swung the light onto a one-inch ant.

"Un veinticuatro," Juan said. "The pain from those bichos lasts for twenty-four hours. Mala suerte, doctora."

They slung their hammocks and mosquito nets in the empty medicatura. Debra lay down and tried to think of something besides the pain. Her forearm had swelled to twice its normal size, and it throbbed. Pepe and Juan cooked dinner, a disgusting blend of boiled macaroni and canned tuna, and the others set up the microscope to examine the skin snips that Cheo had collected.

"Maravilloso! Incredible! Look, professor." Debra lifted her head to see Marisol moving aside from the microscope to allow David to peer down. "I have never seen such quantities of parasites in a skin snip," Marisol chirped, almost breathless. "There are hundreds. My blackflies are sure to be infected."

"Debra, you should see this," David said. "She's right, there are hundreds. From just a snip of skin the size of a freckle. Can you imagine the parasite load this bloke must have in his whole body?"

Despite her self-pity, the excitement in the others' voices caught her interest and she swung out of her hammock and crossed the room to the microscope. It *was* incredible. At low magnification the skin's edge filled only a small part of the field. The rest of the field was alive with minuscule wriggling worms. Her theoretical knowledge had not prepared her for such a sight. No wonder these people itched.

❦

David slept poorly. Six hammocks criss-crossed in one room didn't leave much personal space. Pepe's deep, irregular snores close to his head on one side and Marisol's incessant muttering and sighing in her sleep on the other side did little to comfort his jangled nerves. His burnt face hurt and the lotion Debra had given him to soothe the inflammation stank. How the others could sleep so well in hammocks mystified him. He couldn't get comfortable. He first tried lying lengthwise, which, with the deep curve of the hammock, meant lying on his back. That soon gave him stomach cramps, and his legs tried to bend the wrong way at the knees on the uphill curve. Lying diagonally in the hammock allowed his body to straighten a bit, but there was no support for his head and his hips had to twist in a way that was bearable for only a few minutes. The short night was interminable.

At first light, just before six, Juan and Pepe woke simultaneously. David sat up stiffly and watched them prepare a quick breakfast of manioc and black coffee. He accepted Juan's offer of coffee and used the thick, sweet liquid to wash down crackers and jam. He followed the motoristas outside. Juan and Pepe unzipped their flies in front of the door and urinated onto the hard earth. David found the seclusion of bushes at the side of the building to relieve himself, wondering as he watched the stream of urine bounce off the ground whom he was shielding his activity from.

When he came back to the front of the building, Pepe and Juan were halfway down the trail to the river. He didn't follow. He felt awkward in their company, unable to understand more than a few basic words—which were meaningless when he didn't know the context. He looked across the airstrip at the lightening sky above the dark forest and felt his solitude. His friends and colleagues three, four thousand miles to the north-east would be getting ready for lunch, and would no doubt talk enviously of him. After all, very few Englishmen had the opportunity to experience such an exotic location. He had travelled widely in Africa and Asia and he was familiar with the loneliness of the traveller, but he had never felt as isolated as now. Almost no one knew precisely where he was: the few people here and a few others in Puerto Pedriscal. He was completely at their mercy. If he were to die here today—dysentery, drowning, a single machete blow—his death would cause only the slightest inconvenience. Debra had told him the story of a young German researcher killed by a truck in Puerto Pedriscal just a couple of months ago. Already the German was forgotten, his memory reduced to a few funny stories about his love affair. How easily he himself could become an anecdote—the English professor with his bungled attempt at seduction and his stupidity of not wearing a hat in the equatorial sun, "only mad dogs and Englishmen".

David crossed the airstrip to the Topochal shabono, which was just visible through the trees. It was very much like the shabono at Cerrito, only this one really was deserted. He walked around the perimeter of the plaza looking at the few hammocks still hanging beside the cold fireplaces. Had their occupants died? Surely they would need beds if they had fled. The shabono was surprisingly devoid of belongings. Only a couple of damaged baskets and indefinable bits of animals hung from the roof supports. It was as though the place had been abandoned permanently. He found the atmosphere depressing, and left the shabono on a good trail that led him to a large clearing dotted with an assortment of plantain and banana trees. One bore a large bunch of fat, deep red-brown bananas that looked ripe. He pried one off and bit into its sticky sweetness. There were pineapples, manioc, palms and lots of plants he didn't recognize. There seemed to be no shortage of food in this garden, which confirmed his suspicion of a flight from disease. He knew that many peoples who hadn't had much contact with modern civilization had no microbiological concept of disease, instead believing in evil spirits and hexes. If their shaman could not cure the sickness, it would be logical to them to escape it by fleeing the target of the witchcraft. With his scientific understanding, he theorized that an instinct to flee might also lead people away from an infected area.

He continued into the forest on another trail, one so obvious that he had no fear of becoming lost. The ease with which he walked through tropical jungle surprised him. Just a flaky layer of brown leaves covered the forest floor, and very little undergrowth grew between the buttressed treetrunks. A couple of crude shelters on the trail testified to recent occupation; the palm-leaf coverings were still green and flexible. Under the forest canopy it was darker than he had thought; to take a photograph he needed the camera lens wide open for a thirtieth of a second. After about an hour he came to another shabono, well hidden in the trees and also deserted.

He arrived back at Topochal by nine. Cheo and Marisol tended the samples from the day before and Debra lay in her hammock reading a paperback.

"There you are, David. Did you sleep well?" Debra asked. "Some good news at last. A plane will be arriving soon from Puerto Pedriscal with a new propeller, and we should be able to start upriver again before noon. Pepe and Juan separated lots of water from our gasoline so we shouldn't have any more fiascos like yesterday's."

David very much regretted hearing the "good" news. He had been hoping that the expedition would be cancelled and that he would be able to return to his wife and children in the familiar civilization of Cambridge. "Is it worthwhile going on? If all the shabonos are abandoned we won't be able to do much work."

"There may be people who need chloroquine, and the Yanomami fishermen Angel María spoke to yesterday said the malaria has not yet broken out farther upriver. We can do the oncho work up there," Debra answered. "There's really no reason to change our plans." She looked at him inquisitively over the top of her book. "I thought you needed *Plasmodium*-infected blood to take back with you. Where better to get it than in an epidemic area? We can likely get you some fresh on our way back."

He tried a smile that he hoped belied his tension, and felt his sun-dried bottom lip crack. "Ow! I'll be fine once we start some real work," he said, dabbing his lip with a finger and looking at a spot of blood on his fingertip. "I get a bit starved of English conversation sometimes, and the second-hand translations leave me feeling rather useless. I hear that we'll be staying with an American anthropologist upriver. I'm looking forward to meeting him." Debra appeared to be engrossed in her book.

༇

Uncomfortable as she was crammed between boxes in the dugout, Marisol smiled contentedly. The box at her feet contained the best samples she had ever collected, and she knew the expedition would only get better. Tomorrow, above the Paraua rapids, she would be in virgin territory: nobody had studied onchocerciasis in that area before, the blackfly vectors were unknown, and the Yanomami had no contact with missionaries so their diseases would not have been altered through indiscriminate dispensing of drugs. The results of this one expedition would put INSA on the map of international science, and herself at the centre.

She scratched one of the countless blackfly bites on her legs distractedly as the boat passed the fallen tree that marked Cerrito. The others had agreed with her that they should travel upriver as quickly as possible to stay ahead of the epidemic. If time allowed and more specimens were needed, they would stop at these villages on their return. A stickiness on her finger made her look down at a trickle of blood oozing from the bite. She would have to be more careful; open wounds could easily become infected, and she didn't want anything so trivial to jeopardize her work. She mopped up the blood with a piece of toilet paper and dabbed Tiger Balm on the itchiest lumps and scabs.

❦

Juan's eyes, in the shade of his baseball cap, danced between the insect doctora's back, as she leaned forward to rub her legs, and the river ahead. He was preoccupied. His penis troubled him more today. An uncomfortable itch a few days ago had grown almost unbearable, and when he urinated it hurt like peeing sand. That was what came of being separated from his wife in San Carlos for so long. A man had to get relief somewhere, and that Indian girl in Puerto Pedriscal was so pretty, and cheap. The young Yanomami girls he met upriver from La Joya had been even prettier. He would ask the americana for drugs when he could get her alone.

The level of the river was dropping. More beaches appeared each day. He had been through the rapids twice before, but never in a lancha this big. Low water could be difficult. He spun his head to a shrill whistle from the bank and saw a two-metre brown body slip into the river. His rifle lay out of reach in front of the insect doctora. A pity. A giant otter skin would have doubled his pay from this job, fed his children for a month. They were getting harder to find, and every year the price of a good skin went up. It would be worthwhile coming back here during the next rains. The tributaries this far upriver were probably full of otters. He could bring some of his friends with him. The indios around here were still wild, but they didn't have guns, so a few well-armed men could deal with them.

❦

The party reached the foot of the rapids with just enough daylight to set up camp on a small, sandy island in the middle of the river. Debra had watched the river narrow during the afternoon and here it was only a few hundred yards across. The Paraua rapids stretched the river's width, and the steady roar of turbulent water made her consultation with Juan private. She took him into her small tent and examined an inflamed and discharging urethra by flashlight. Juan laughed when she told him penicilina would clear the infection quickly—"What a joke, pene-cilina for my pene, eh, doctora? Perfect name for the drug."

Debra woke the next morning at five, chilled, and spent the next hour before dawn in a tight ball with her inadequate blanket over her head. Never before had she felt such cold, penetrating to her marrow. She shivered, wrapped in her blanket, huddled over her first coffee. Marisol's maximum-minimum thermometer sat at its night-time low of 22° Celsius, a pleasant tee-shirt and shorts temperature. If David and Marisol hadn't shivered beside her, she would have been convinced she had malaria.

"I wish I'd brought a big woolly jumper," David said. "I never thought it would be so cold in the jungle."

"I think I'll skip my bath this morning. The humidity from the river must be sucking out all our body heat," Debra said. "Where's that sun?"

Within an hour they were splashing the cool river water over their sweating heads. Pepe and Juan had organized the team to portage all the delicate and perishable supplies past the rapids. They each carried six heavy loads along the narrow path hacked out of the thick undergrowth beside the river, and then helped the men tow the boats through the quieter water at the edge of the rapids. The light aluminum boat was easy to pull, but the large dugout, even with Juan at the motor, took all their combined strength to fight the river's pull.

14

Tekiyë held back while the other Yanomami of his shabono surrounded the strangers excitedly. He had predicted long ago that Jeffyë's arrival among his people would bring outsiders to Iyëira-teri, and now this group of *nabë* was among them. He knew of the *nabë* from stories passed from shabono to shabono, of their cannibalism, of their gifts. Two of these *nabë* were as he expected, brown skin, darker than his people's and wrinkled like palm fruit, and taller than the tallest warrior. One *nabë* woman had hair dark like his people, but skin lighter. But the others. . . . One was black like charred wood, with hair thick as the tail of the *wixa* monkey. One was big and hairy like Jeffyë, but with skin redder than fresh onoto paint. Another, with breasts like a woman, was as tall as the longest arrow, with hair and skin as white as plantain caterpillars, and eyes that reflected the blue of the sky. It also surprised Tekiyë that a Yanomami from farther downstream than he had ever journeyed, from well beyond the birthplace of the Stream of the Urinating Jaguar, travelled with these *nabë*.

Jeffyë talked with the caterpillar woman and the others in a strange language, and more quickly than Tekiyë had ever heard him speak. When Jeffyë had first come to them he could not speak. The children had taught him simple words and even now, after the passing of many palm harvests, he spoke no better than the smallest child. Tekiyë alone had opposed the presence of Jeffyë in Iyëira-teri. The others had encouraged Jeffyë to stay, eager for his gifts, the fish-hooks, light-sticks, metal pots, machetes, showing him how to eat and sharing their harvests and game with him when they saw he was too clumsy and stupid to feed himself. He even allowed people to call him by name. He had no familial relationship for others to refer to him by, but he should have known how bad it was to be called out loud by name. Jeffyë was big, ugly and strange. He did not tie up his penis—he had no foreskin to tie it up with—and he had hairs on his arms, legs, chest and groin.

Jeffyë had given some men machetes in exchange for building a structure where he slept alone, as closed and dark as the isolation hut for girls when they became women. Later he moved his hammock into the shabono, but he would still shut himself in his dark hut for long periods. No Yanomami had seen inside, and Jeffyë would become very angry if anyone tried to look through the door.

Jeffyë always carried his fire club at his side when he walked among the Yanomami. It made a noise more terrible than any thunder from the celestial disk, and the club could drop a monkey from the trees beyond the reach of the best archer. The monkey would fall instantly, a hole that bled open in its side. Jeffyë said he would do the same to any warrior who challenged him. If a warrior raised a machete or pointed an arrow in Jeffyë's direction, Jeffyë would make thunder with his great club and walk slowly to his hammock. He would recline, the back of his head resting in his hands, glaring with his ugly face at anyone who dared look his way.

When Jeffyë moved his hammock into the shabono, he began to behave even more strangely. He would take food from hunters and from women returning from the garden, hang it on a strange metal basket tool and make marks on thin white leaves stuck together. Then he began to hang the children from the basket tool as if they too were food. That was when some of the other men and shamans came to Tekiyë's side. This activity was surely a ritual of *nabë* cannibalism. Now other *nabë* had joined him, perhaps invited for a feast.

Some of Jeffyë's friends slept in their big canoe, which they tied up on the far side of the river when it became dark. The others closed themselves in Jeffyë's hut beside the shabono.

During the night, Jeffyë talked from his hammock. He said

his friends had travelled from Puertopedriscal-teri, a shabono larger than Iyëira-teri and all the other Yanomami shabonos put together. They had come to trade with the Iyëira-teri and had brought many trade goods, and the Iyëira-teri should trade with them. This pleased many people, until he said they wanted to trade for blood and skin. Tekiyë protested and he heard voices of support from other hearths around the shabono. Here was proof, from Jeffyë's own mouth, that the *nabë* were cannibals. Tekiyë had warned of the dangers of allowing Jeffyë to live among them, and now Jeffyë had brought his own people to feast upon the Iyëira-teri. There was no choice but to gather all they could and leave for the forest before they were eaten.

Jeffyë's deep, powerful voice interrupted Tekiyë. He said there was no need to fear the *nabë*. They would not hurt the Yanomami. They were here to help the Iyëira-teri fight against *Shawara* that brought sickness. They wanted only small amounts of blood, less than that lost in a woman's menstruation, and small pieces of skin, smaller than the size of an ant. With the blood and skin, they could make powerful cures against *Shawara* that got into the Yanomamis' skin and made them itch, and *Shawara* that stole old people's sight. In exchange, they would give beads and machetes and metal pots. The Iyëira-teri must welcome the *nabë* and help them.

The talk lasted all night. Tekiyë couldn't fight Jeffyë's influence. The men's greed for machetes and fishing-hooks and the women's for beads pulled them to Jeffyë's side. Tekiyë's own wife, his pretty new wife that he had to guard from the other warriors, even she supported Jeffyë. Tekiyë knew she was vain and wanted more beads. She already wore more beads than any other woman in the shabono, beads received from Jeffyë. The more beads she wore, the more desirable she became and the more fiercely he had to protect her. He would raise his machete at any man who dared touch her and he would kill any man who consumed her vagina with his penis.

The *nabë* came just when the sky became light, when Tekiyë's plantain still roasted in the fire. Caterpillar woman, her red mate and Jeffyë went from hearth to hearth, looking at people's eyes and rolling people over in their hammocks to look at the skin of their backs. Children hid behind their parents and cried when Jeffyë pulled them out to be inspected. Caterpillar woman pinched everyone with a tiny knife, making the children cry even more, then painted a pattern, different each time, on each person's shoulder with a small stick, similar to painting with onoto.

The other *nabë* woman, the charred, monkey-haired man with the thin leg and the Yanomami who came with the Puertopedriscal-teri took some old people to the edge of the shabono and picked flies from their skin. The flies were trapped in short pieces of cane, clear as water.

The *nabë* frightened everyone at first, but their strange behaviour didn't harm anyone and even Tekiyë found himself becoming curious. The women didn't go to the garden to gather plantains, and the men cancelled a hunt. A crowd followed the *nabë* as they moved around the shabono, and anyone who showed fear or squealed when caterpillar woman pinched his skin was ridiculed for his cowardice by the spectators.

When the sun was high in the sky the *nabë* shared their food—fish and game from tiny metal pots—with the Iyëira-teri and were offered roasted plantain and caterpillars in return. Only the charred, monkey-haired *nabë* ate the caterpillars.

The expedition group sat cross-legged in the shade of the shabono. A small group of Yanomami squatted with them, feet flat and knees pointed upwards close to their faces, looking curiously into the open cans of tuna. A successful morning's work, Debra thought as she dug some tuna out of a can with a cracker. A Yanomami man held out a broad leaf filled with white grubs. Cheo stuck one in his mouth and actually chewed on it. Debra grimaced. The Yanomami laughed. "Tastes just like roasted peanuts, igualito, doctora," Cheo said, smacking his lips. He reached for another.

"Interesting," David said, looking at the grubs on the leaf.

"Revolting," Marisol stated emphatically.

"At this rate we shouldn't be in your hair for more than a couple of days," Debra said to Jeff, who munched on plantain.

"That'll be a relief," he replied.

"I thought we might have more resistance, but the Yanomami are really very co-operative," Debra said.

"They were terrified when you arrived," Jeff contradicted. "They thought you'd come to eat them. It took me all last night to convince them that you guys were just a bunch of wimps. They're expecting to be well paid, by the way. You don't get something for nuthin' from a Yanomami."

"Don't worry. We brought lots of gifts with us. The idea is to share them out just before we leave," Marisol reassured him. She stood up and collected empty cans, dumping them into a plastic garbage bag.

"Do you think cutting some nodules out would be a problem?" Debra asked.

"Nodules? You don't want to cut their balls off, do you?"

"Haven't you noticed the lumps that a lot of them have on their heads? Those are adult *Onchocerca* worms just below the skin. It's very easy to cut them out, and Velázquez hoped we could take some back to INSA for antigenic studies."

Jeff thought for a moment as he picked a piece of plantain out of his back teeth with a dirty fingernail. "I think you could swing that. The Yanomami hate physical deformity. Apart from scars, that is. They're really proud of those. Any child born with a deformity doesn't make it into the shabono. I should think they hate those lumps, and if you could leave nice fat scars in their place so much the better. I'll talk to one of the shamans first. If he agrees, then you'll have the rest lining up. Getting you people finished up and outa here couldn't come a moment too soon, as far as I'm concerned."

The next day was as successful as the first. By mid-afternoon Debra had hundreds of skin samples and a dozen nodules frozen safely in the liquid nitrogen tank. Despite the success, she felt unsettled, a bit guilty about bleeding and snipping the Yanomami. In the long run maybe some useful knowledge would result from these studies, but the work was of no immediate medical benefit to the Yanomami. These people were guinea pigs advancing INSA's interests rather than their own. And Jeff's attitude annoyed her. She hadn't expected him to be romantic, not with the others so close all the time, but he hardly talked to her and when he did he was gruff. He seemed much closer to David. The two of them would lie in hammocks and talk whenever they had the opportunity.

Jeff was on edge all the time. He strutted around, his rifle always in one hand, like a great white hunter. He was obviously afraid of the Yanomami—that rifle never left his side. So much for the notion that anthropologists lived as one with the people, blending into the community as impartial observers. He was a hypocrite. He criticized the missionaries for bringing accul-turation, yet he did the same. This community was full of introduced goods, his payments for services rendered through the years. She had even caught him playing a Bach Brandenburg concerto on a small cassette player to a group of women. They giggled and looked delighted. Innocent enough on the surface, but what effect did an accumulation of such intrusions have on the community?

And his scientific justification was suspect. Having seen these people for herself, always joking and cheerful, she wondered about the accuracy of the accounts of Yanomami violence. The anthropologists dwelled on rituals and described them as everyday occurrences. If what she had seen when she looked at the field notes in Jeff's hut was any indication, his anthropological studies were pseudo-scientific mumbo-jumbo. One set of notes was a collection of estimates of Yanomami cranial capacity, information that couldn't meaningfully be correlated to anything.

Debra, carrying her towel and shampoo, walked barefoot along a narrow path that led to a creek Angel María called the

Stream of the Urinating Jaguar. Mud squeezed up between her toes, cool and slippery. The sound of tumbling water filled the forest. She saw Cheo's afro bobbing up and down as he splashed in the water amid a tangle of laughing Yanomami children. So much for a private bath. Instead, she sat on her towel on the stream-side, her feet in the water, the mud on her toes dissolving in the current.

❧

Jeff lay in his hammock, hands behind his head. From the support beam above him hung tough woven baskets, painted in circles and squiggles with onoto that had turned black with age. He heard the mocking laugh of guacharaca birds deep in the forest. David Shuttleworth lay sleeping in a hammock beside him.

The expedition party had been at his shabono for two days now and already Jeff wished them gone. At first he had enjoyed the liberation of communication uninhibited by inadequate language skills. He had especially enjoyed David's stimulating academic companionship. But now he had become irritable, aware of craving his own culture but not wanting it here, not in his shabono. Outsiders just didn't belong in his private world. He had painstakingly worked his way into this shabono and had become a community member, bit by bit, learning the language and customs, gradually immersing himself in a world radically different from his own. His association with the visitors alienated him from the Yanomami community. He loved Yanomami life. He had become so entrenched in the shabono that he no longer wanted to break contact, yet he knew it was impossible to settle here permanently. He needed both worlds. He would rather have kept the two segregated, but finances didn't permit it. Jeff's grant money had dried up and Velázquez paid him well. In addition, assisting a government organization ensured renewal of upriver permits. He couldn't stay out here without money and government permits.

Jeff looked across the central plaza, into the opposite side of the shabono. Shadowy muscular figures stooped through the small door to the shabono. They had just returned from a hunt. Tekiyë came forward into the bright light of the plaza, carrying his bow and two limp curassow birds in one hand and a sling around the other arm. He glared angrily in Jeff's direction and symbolically tilted his bow. Jeff hoped Tekiyë wasn't pissed off about Debra's surgery. That would be a major setback. That man didn't particularly trust him. Jeff had watched as Debra probed around for the nodule in his right armpit, trying to grasp the lump as it slithered out of her forceps' reach. She eventually had to give up, afraid that if she left the wound open too long it would get infected. Debra had said it would hurt after the local wore off. She'd put the right arm in a sling and had had Jeff tell Tekiyë not to use it for a few days. Tekiyë had been angry, to say the least. He now held the curassows in his right hand and had his left arm in the sling. He was a tough little shit, all right.

Jeff lifted himself out of the hammock thinking a wash would refresh him, and he wandered down to the swimming hole. He saw the blonde hair and long legs stretching into the water. Shit, she had reached it first. "Unbe-fucking-lievable! You guys seem to be everywhere I want to be. What's up?" he asked, trying not to sound too angry.

Debra jumped and looked back at him. "Oh, it's you. You startled me." She half smiled, and turned back to watch Cheo and the children. Jeff sensed rather than saw her stiffen at his presence. Although he still felt some of the old stirrings—it was hard to ignore those legs and he could almost feel them wrapped around his back—he knew they were better left in another time and place, not here.

They said nothing. Jeff couldn't think of anything nice to say. He watched Cheo run and jump into the water. Cheo limped back onto the bank and gestured the children to follow him. He galloped unsteadily, one leg shrivelled, the other strong, and leapt off his normal leg, hurling himself into the water with a big splash. Water beaded and dribbled off his afro, leaving it as puffed as before. The children shrieked delightedly. "Look, his paují-bird hair doesn't get wet," one of them cried, and they ran, hobbling on imaginary crippled legs, to throw themselves into the water. Cheo had created a herd of tiny polio victims.

Debra spoke first, her voice hardened with resentment. "I don't see why you have to be such a bastard, Jeff." She didn't look at him.

His chest rose and fell with a sigh. "I suppose I should explain a few things about anthropology to clarify matters. I make observations, Debra. It's my job. And in order to make observations, I must first gain the trust of the people, establish emotional bonds and make lasting relationships. The members of this shabono confide in me and I'm allowed to see the most intimate aspects of their lives. You have no idea how fucking hard it was to achieve that level of trust. Any intimate interaction with you could screw up everything."

She turned her head around abruptly, her eyes darkened by wide-open pupils. "Bravo, nicely done. What a lot of bullshit! If you fit into this community like a hand into a glove, then why do you carry around that rifle? You're afraid of these people, aren't you?"

"And what the fuck do you know about anthropology?"

"I may not be an anthropologist, but at least I know a hell of a lot more about science than that nonsense in your field notes. Look around you, do these people look uncontacted? You're as much an intruder as the rest of us. An impartial observer? Ha, my ass you are!"

"You have no fucking business snooping in my field notes!"

"How can you study their nutritional status when you've given them all sorts of gifts in order to be accepted here? You're the one who's screwing up his own work. You're creating your own community here. It's not natural any more. Isn't it reasonable to assume that maybe, just maybe, you provoked more fighting and raids? And haven't you increased game availability with your gun, fishing nets and fish-hooks, not to mention night hunting with all the flashlights you've brought? It doesn't take a genius. . . ."

"These people are facing extinction, Debra. As an anthropologist I have a moral obligation to help them. They trust me. I'm their voice in the modern world, an intermediary between this world and ours. I've shown you people hospitality, saved your asses here, and that's the thanks I get. You looked through my private papers. You bitch!"

"Trust? You violated that trust. You record and publicly describe the most private moments of their lives. You describe them physically in intimate detail, cranial capacity, the weight of their newborn babies. Next you'll be weighing their shit. You share those details with the world without their consent."

"I try to educate people about Yanomami life so the modern world can learn to respect them and understand the need for preserving their society. You can't fucking tell me that publications of that nature constitute a violation of trust."

"To these people, the forest is the entire world. I heard you tell David they think Puerto Pedriscal is a shabono, for Christ's sake. 'To them, there are no countries, no metropolitan giants, just trees, rivers and sky,' your exact words, Jeffrey, not mine. How can they comprehend that you're sharing their lives with millions of readers, and that because you're doing so their lives will be affected? They have no concept of written language. Would they have willingly taken you in if they understood all the potential positive and negative impacts of your contact? How can they give consent to what they can't conceive? How would you like it if, without your consent, I published a description of you playing gynaecologist? Think about that, asshole!"

"I do a hell of a lot more to help them than you do, frightening them, taking their blood and skin. And you use them for your fucking publications too."

Debra suddenly calmed her voice. "You think I don't know

that? I've been thinking that maybe none of us should be out here, myself included. None of us really belongs out here, and we wouldn't be here at all if not for you paving the way. We are all intruders."

Cheo screamed, a sound that penetrated the forest. He was writhing in the stream like a speared snake, holding his good leg at the knee. "He stepped on a ray, Debra. Do something. Now!" Jeff yelled at her above the shrieks. The children stood quietly, not moving, surrounding Cheo as he screamed. Jeff ran to Cheo and knelt down. Tears streamed down Cheo's contorted face. The screaming faded into moans and whimpers. Jeff pulled the leg straight. The ray had rammed its stinger into Cheo's ankle, all the way to the bone. He turned and saw Debra running back up the trail. Stupid bitch. He just hoped she'd gone back up to look for her medical kit, and hadn't just run off crying.

The expedition party left Iyëira-teri early the next morning, and reached the Paraua rapids by mid-afternoon. Cheo sat in the shade of a tall tree shaped like an umbrella with large waxy leaves. He kept his eyes peeled for ants; he didn't want to be bitten by a veinticuatro. The others trudged by him back and forth along the narrow trail, carrying boxes past the rapids. If not for the ray sting he would have had to help, crippled leg or not. His foot throbbed. Blood oozed into the dampness of his bandage.

The last box finally sat on shore below the rapids. The water beat upon the rocks, becoming frothy, more air than liquid. The pulverized water created a mist in the air that diffracted rainbow colours. Cheo watched as Juan and Pepe secured the thatched-roof dugout with heavy sisal ropes. Pepe positioned Debra, Marisol and the English holding their ropes on the shore, and then he waded into the rushing current alongside Juan. Bit by bit the team eased the awkward boat downstream, manoeuvring it through a deeper curved channel. Juan, holding the bow upstream, scrambled on top of a rock. Then he slipped, his rope slithering out through his fingers, and his Lagoven baseball cap fell into the water and bobbed as the current carried it downstream. The others tried to brace themselves against the current, their feet planted in the sand, leaning all their weight backwards against the pull of the rope. The dugout's bow swung into the current as if in slow motion, and hit a large boulder, and the boat tilted. Cheo thought it would capsize, but the weight of the oil drums must have served as sufficient ballast, for the boat righted itself. A tank of liquid nitrogen tipped and balanced precariously on the gunwale, ready to topple over. The current grabbed the boat and without Juan's guidance it swerved towards another boulder. The tank of liquid nitrogen scraped against the rock, and Cheo watched in fascination as the styrofoam lid floated downstream. The boat tilted and the heavy tank fell into the water. Nitrogen boiled explosively as the two liquids met. For the first time since its conception, ice flowed down the silty waters of the Orinoco River.

❧

David Shuttleworth steps into a men's accessories shop, small, familiar and comforting. He is enveloped by the smells of rich leather and quality tobacco. Back from the jungle, back in Cambridge, safe at last. A tall man strolls in, with a long stride, swinging an umbrella nonchalantly, tapping it on the floor with each step. The man is dressed in a trench coat with the collar pulled up, and a deerstalker cap. David can't see his face. "Beg your pardon," David says, "do you happen to have the time?" The man swings around. David sees a nice English face with a waxed moustache, but the glazed eyes of a Yanomami high on *yopo*. The man raises his umbrella, the tip blood-red. The man smiles. David knows from the look in those eyes that the umbrella point will stab into his heart. . . .

David woke up with a jolt, a scream caught in his throat. He stared through mosquito netting at the grey concrete walls of the medical dispensary, back in time, in Topochal. He fell back into his hammock and closed his eyes. His shirt clung to his chest, soaking wet. He must have sweated buckets during that horrible dream. He sat up again, stretched, thrusting out his chest, and looked down. He saw a patch of red, richly pigmented red, bright in the centre, deeper at the edge. Blood, his own blood, soaked his shirt. It was not sweat: blood, his blood. This time, he screamed.

❦

Debra looked at the small nick on David's shoulder. Fascinating, incredible that such a tiny nick had bled so much. An adult bat drank only about five teaspoons of blood in a meal, not very much, really. Its saliva contained an anticoagulant, of course. With its scalpel-like incisor teeth it had cut painlessly into David's shoulder, where the blood vessels lay close to the surface of the skin, and it had lapped the running blood, the two lateral grooves in its tongue opening and closing, pumping the blood into its mouth. Debra had read about them but was surprised at how little there was to see. She cleaned off the blood with a wet rag, dabbed on antibiotic cream and covered the nick with a sterile dressing.

"Good as new, almost," she said. "Angel María tells me vampire bats bite frequently out here. Not much I can do, I'm afraid. He says it happens all the time."

"Splendid! What about rabies?" David asked.

"It's a concern, though I'm told it's actually quite rare. There are, of course, some other viruses carried, but that's all academic now, after the fact, so to speak." She shrugged. "Maybe I could get you started on the rabies series in Puerto Pedriscal, just to be on the safe side. You'll have to take the rest of the vaccine back with you. Your physician in Cambridge can finish them off. You don't have to have the shots in the peritoneum any more. You can have them in your arm—duck embryo, intramuscular."

Marisol handed David a mug of hot coffee with powdered milk clumps still floating on top. "Relax, we're leaving today. I confirmed this morning with Velázquez by radio. That is, if the weather holds."

They heard the distant buzz of an approaching motorboat.

"It's probably Padre Eduardo," Marisol said. "I saw him this morning at the mission. He said he'd be collecting schoolchildren this morning." She and Debra walked down the trail to meet the boat at the river.

Padre Eduardo, a young priest dressed in jeans, a tee-shirt and a floppy white hat, sat at the back of his aluminum boat steering the outboard motor with one hand, a Yanomami baby, about a year old, slung in palm fibre against his chest. He stroked the baby's back with his other hand. He cut the engine and Debra could hear the baby cry. Juan waded barefoot into the water and pulled the boat to shore. "Malaria, the two of them are suffering badly," Eduardo said. "The baby belongs to her." He gestured down inside the hull with a nod of his head. Two Yanomami lay between the seats: a woman and a teenage boy. They looked dead. Marisol took the crying baby. Juan and the padre carried the semiconscious Yanomami to the medicatura. They laid the boy upon the examining table, the woman in David's hammock. David stood near the wall, watching silently. The woman could barely talk; her lips were dry and wrinkled. She whispered to Padre Eduardo. Debra grabbed two glass bottles and tubing from a supply box and hooked the woman to a saline drip. The boy was so weak he couldn't speak or make a clenched fist, and Debra had difficulty puncturing his deflated veins. She abandoned the median basilic vein at his elbow, hooked up a butterfly and probed the outer veins of his hands. She taped the butterfly to his hand with adhesive tape and rummaged through her supplies, taking out the bottle of choroquine.

At the sound of the motorboat, Cheo hobbled from the radio room at the mission, down the shady path towards the medicatura. He placed more weight upon his polio-crippled leg than upon the foot crippled by the ray sting. The painkiller the doctora had given him had begun to wear off. He had just finished feeding those stupid flies and peeling the cellophane-thin wings off their shit, planting each fly with exquisite care back on her six little feet. Marisol had left them all the way up at the mission, where she said the temperature was more agreeable for them. More vainas than there were pods on a blackbean bush! Better care, more supplies and better equipment were available at INSA for those stupid flies than for people.

He entered the medicatura. He heard the baby cry, then he saw the two limp, naked bodies, one sprawled upon the examining table, one in the inglés's chinchorro. Coño, they looked half dead. Getting malaria here was inevitable. He would find out soon enough if he had managed to avoid it. If alcohol didn't destroy his liver first, then disease surely would. Alcohol was a much more enjoyable way to go. Live for today. Quizás se muere mañana. So live each moment to its fullest.

Cheo looked down at his bandage. A sticky fluid seeped through. He prayed that the plane would come today and that they wouldn't be stranded by bad weather. The padre intended to lock up the mission and leave by boat in the morning, meaning no more radio access. If the plane failed to arrive today, they would be stuck here without communication. With any luck, tomorrow he would be back in Puerto Pedriscal, where he could have a well-earned drink.

Glass shattered—the sick Yanomami boy had knocked over his drip. His blood backed up into the tubing. The doctora clamped the tubing, replaced the IV stand and attached another bottle. The baby cried louder than ever. "Could someone feed

181

that baby—please? It's dehydrated and hungry and that crying is getting on my nerves," the doctora snapped. Marisol jiggled the baby, hushing him and speaking softly. She glared at Doctora Debra.

"Cheo, haga me un favor?" Marisol asked sweetly, with a head tilt. "Fix some oatmeal and milk for the baby and help me feed him."

Cheo nodded and moved unsteadily to the supply boxes.

"This boy needs a blood transfusion and hospitalization," said Doctora Debra with concern. "We must bring the woman with us too. There will be no one here to care for her if Padre Eduardo leaves tomorrow." The doctora squatted beside the woman in the English's chinchorro. She pulled back the woman's eyelid. "Since we lost that tank of nitro, I think we can fit one more person in the supply plane, but even so one of us will have to stay behind. There's just not going to be enough room for all of us."

Cheo mixed water, powdered milk and sugar in a small bowl.

Marisol cooed to the baby and he stopped crying. "Simplemente, it cannot be me. The simuliids, I must go back to the lab to look after them," she said, authoritatively. "I can also look after the baby," she said, as if it was an afterthought. The blackflies, rather than the baby, had been Marisol's first concern, noted Cheo.

"Well, I have to accompany the patients," said Doctora Debra. She turned, her face serious, and looked Cheo directly in his eyes. "I don't like the thought of leaving Cheo here, not with that open sting."

"We can't leave a famous scientist who speaks no Spanish stranded with the motoristas out on the river. We have an obligation to look after him," Marisol said. "And David needs to start his rabies shots. If the Yanomami must travel with us to Puerto Pedriscal, then Cheo is the logical choice to leave behind. He can travel downstream by boat to La Joya with the padre and catch the mission plane from there, or he can go back by boat to Puerto Olvidado with Juan and Pepe. Leave him some antibiotics, bandages and chloroquine. He'll be all right." Cheo wanted to shrink. He stood stirring the cereal. Naturalmente, it will have to be him, they said. Why should he be the one to stay behind? Malaria, it was still running wild here. What if he became infected with a resistant strain of *falciparum*? Without Doctora Debra around he could easily die.

Marisol carried the baby over to where Cheo stood. She sat on a folding chair and held the baby while Cheo spooned milky cereal into the baby's mouth. Milk and lumps of oatmeal dribbled down his chin. The baby coughed and opened his mouth as if he was choking. Marisol squealed, jumping, almost letting the baby go. "Doctora, come quickly," Cheo said. He grabbed the baby away from the stricken-looking Marisol. "Look inside the baby's mouth." The doctora opened the baby's mouth and probed inside with a wooden tongue depressor. She teased out a slender, waxy, cream-coloured worm, about eight inches long. It fell from the depressor and wiggled on the floor like a whip. The doctora picked it up in her fingers. "*Ascaris*, must have been attracted up by the sugar," she said. Pobre nene, he was so hungry his parasites starved too.

The faint hum of a propeller at ten-thirty tortured Cheo's ears. He dragged himself outside and stood next to a pijiguao palm viciously armed with long thin spines, and looked at the white dot in the sky.

This expedition had been out a week and a half, but it felt like a month since he'd had a cold Polar and buried his face in the breasts of a woman. Qué abuso! The institute echoed with "Cheo, do this. Cheo, do that. Cheo do me a favour and hurry it up!" If *falciparum* didn't kill him, he would probably be fired one day soon, after all those memoranda. He had nothing to lose. Enough! Cheo would take no more vainas from Velázquez and his precious institute. When he returned to Puerto Pedriscal, if he ever did, he would proceed exactly as the brujo had instructed. On two clean white sheets of paper he would write the name of his abusador, el enemigo manipulador de todos los técnicos, seven times. He pictured it clearly in his mind:

Doctor Diego Velázquez
Doctor Diego Velázquez
Doctor Diego Velázquez
Doctor Diego Velázquez
Doctor Diego Velázquez
Doctor Diego Velázquez
Doctor Diego Velázquez

Fold the two papers seven times each, pierce each paper closed with seven long spines from the pijiguao palm, leave one paper seven days in a freezer (any at INSA would do) and then remove it on the seventh day, burn it without opening it and blow the ashes in the direction of the enemy. The other paper Cheo would leave inside the freezer until Velázquez started to show signs of vulnerability. This, the brujo guaranteed, would bring the enemy to his knees and make him sauvecito as melting butter. Unfortunately it wouldn't cause physical harm to the recipient, but it would at least be a start.

The brujo said that if Cheo could steal an object owned by the intended recipient and place it in a gourd, and if the brujo blew ritual tobacco smoke inside the gourd, then the recipient would fall ill. The brujo said that if he so desired, brujería could even kill. For the moment, Cheo didn't really want Velázquez to get hurt, so he wouldn't use the gourd and personal object method—yet. The doctor had one chance to respect him and all the técnicos more. It would be just like plastering astringent green mango peel to Velázquez's weaknesses. Cheo plucked fourteen of the longest spines he could find off the trunk of the pijiguao palm. He then plucked off seven more, just in case.

15

The day the expedition was due to return, Yadira spotted a small grey mouse scuttling from the kitchenette across the living room and making a final dash underneath the brown vinyl sofa. She immediately drove to town and bought two dozen mouse traps from a Lebanese merchant, and a block of imported Edam at the supermercado. She distributed the traps throughout the house, each baited with a fragrant Dutch morsel. She also doused the floors with a strong, floral-smelling, bright purple disinfectant called Lavasan.

Yadira was certain that Debra's crumbs, left behind from morning toast, were responsible for the infestation. Her chest had almost immediately developed a tight sensation, not relieved by her inhaler. She couldn't believe it. All her precautions, the extra care she took to keep the house clean, were in vain, because of a couple of moments of someone else's negligence. Yadira said nothing about the infestation on Debra's first night back from the expedition. She got Debra updated on the Brazilian soap opera and went to bed. She had been accumulating resentment all day long, yet she kept her fury to herself. She knew how tiring an expedition was and Debra looked exhausted. She wanted Debra to have one good night's rest before confronting her.

At seven-thirty in the morning they sat at the little formica table, Debra behind her strong coffee and Yadira behind her milky tea and her inhaler. Yadira had had a terrible night's sleep, terminated abruptly by a loud snap from one of the traps at five in the morning. She had been up for two hours, allowing Debra to sleep peacefully until seven. She could contain her frustration no longer.

"Debra, a serious problem developed during your absence," she began. She raised her eyebrows slightly and looked at Debra from underneath her grey wave of hair. "You have undoubtedly noticed the traps."

Debra looked vacuous in the mornings before she had consumed a full cup of coffee. She blinked a few times. "I had noticed, now that you come to mention them," she said.

"It was bloody awful! The trap snapped at five this morning and I checked it. There was—you won't believe me—a rat in the trap. Not a mouse, no, a rat, I tell you. A big bloody awful fat rat with no tail. Very fat, obviously well fed. And I'm sure you know as well as I do where that rat found so much to eat. Haven't I told you time and time again that here in Amazonas one must take extraordinary cleaning measures to prevent rat infestation?" She tried hard not to sound exasperated, but it was next to impossible.

"Wonderful to be back in Puerto Pedriscal, just wonderful," Debra said. She peeled at the pearlescent formica and a small piece broke off with a snap. Yadira jumped. "I've been sleeping slung U-shaped in a hammock for two weeks. I finally get a decent night's sleep flat on my back, only to get hit with your rodent obsession first thing in the morning."

"Oh, and that's not the best part," Yadira said, as she wheezed for a breath of air and tapped her inhaler against the formica. "That was when I looked in the bottom drawer of our cooker this morning while you were still sound asleep, snoring in bed. Seeing that I was wide awake already, I decided to make an early breakfast. I was looking for a frying pan. Instead I found a rat's nest, complete with nine pink wormy rat babies, and mummy rat flew out at me, straight for my throat. You left crumbs in the kitchen, and I have to pay for your negligence."

"Sorry, Yadira, it's really not my fault," Debra answered.

"I've got bloody asthma!" Yadira yelled. "You could at least pretend to be sympathetic." She wiped her palm on her blue-jean skirt.

As annoyed as she was at Debra, she wasn't one to behave vindictively. After a silent breakfast, she drove Debra to the hospital. She didn't understand why the gringa had to be so bloody obstinate.

❦

Debra found Amador in the communal room, amid a cluster of beds filled with inert patients attached to saline drips. He stood at the Yanomami boy's bedside, fidgeting with the drip control. "How are the Yanomami we brought in yesterday?" she asked.

"Chama, the nene is fine and the woman responded favourably to treatment," he said. "Desafortunadamente, there were complications with the boy. Negligencia, of course." The Yanomami boy lay supine, his naked brown body limp, his dark hair dull against the plastic mattress. Amador put his hands into the pockets of his lab coat. "The pasante on early morning shift allowed his drip to run dry, and I found him this morning in a coma, his life again slipping away like a piece of tripe sliding between my fingers. I reconnected him, catheterized his urethra and gave him oxygen. He will pull through this time."

"Good work, Amador. Do you think he should be checked for trophozoites?" Debra asked. "It might also be useful to know his red blood cell count and haemoglobin. I can get that done up at INSA."

"You must be cautious against over-optimism. The boy's condition remains guarded, and even though he should recover, we have not tied up the goat securely. The textbooks may disagree, but in my experience *falciparum* attacks worsen with each reinfection. Judging by the severity, this was not his first infection, and it surely would have killed him had he not been found. Epidemics in the Topochal area have been occurring with increasing frequency, partly because of the influx of outsiders who are very susceptible and who may bring

187

in new strains, and partly because of the changes in Yanomami customs that these outsiders encourage. Yanomami no longer migrate regularly in the Topochal area, and they have constructed permanent riverside settlements together with foci of infected mosquitoes. This means increased human and vector contact. The boy will be returned to Topochal and he will die from his next infection. Bringing him here only postponed his death by a few months."

Miraculously, the boy sputtered and opened his eyes. He muttered incomprehensibly.

"Chama, I'll go get Diosgracio. I saw him at the out-patient clinic." Amador left Debra alone with the boy, and returned a few minutes later with the four-foot-tall Yanomami nurse she had met at La Joya.

"*Shori*," Diosgracio said to the patient, who responded with a rapid whining chatter, his voice weak. The patient tried to sit up, but collapsed back against the plastic mattress.

Debra noticed that Diosgracio had combed his thick, spiky hair to one side and glued it in place with hair gel. She assumed he was trying to hide the tonsural patch on his head that his people traditionally shaved. Had the Catholic church in Puerto Pedriscal made him hide his Indianness, or had he done it on his own, ashamed of his heritage here in Puerto Pedriscal, where Yanomami were considered to be wild and uncivilized? With his head disguised, in his new blue tee-shirt, jeans and running shoes, no socks, he had a stiff air of formality about him. "Diosgracio, I am surprised to see you here," she said.

"I am in town for a biblical reunion and to update on hospital matters. While I am here I will also assist the biologist, Doctora Socorro, with her study of onchocerciasis," Diosgracio replied. Debra noticed the big holes in his ears, empty without his ear plugs. He hadn't managed to disguise his ears. He smiled in his quiet, serious way, his mouth barely turning up at the corners. "I am very much looking forward to participating in the onchocerciasis study. It is a terrible disease. I have suffered greatly and I look forward to benefiting from medical advancements."

The Yanomami boy said something to Diosgracio. Diosgracio answered him and turned to Amador. "He is asking for a meal of plantain and boiled alligator."

"I'm afraid there is no food like that in the hospital kitchen," Amador said.

"I am on my way to the outdoor market, and if you wish I will buy some food to his liking. My people do not like to eat food they are unaccustomed to," he said.

"That would be much appreciated, Diosgracio," Amador said. He opened his lab coat, fished his wallet from his pants pocket and handed Diosgracio a ten-bolívar note. Debra tried to imagine the poor man exposing his bare back, allowing blackflies to devour his flesh for hours, as Marisol let them drink their fill before catching them. Poor Diosgracio; he had had no idea what he was getting himself into when he had agreed to help her oncho study. If he had known, surely he would not have agreed to participate. Maybe he had been manipulated by Christian charity, participating purely out of the goodness of his heart. But Debra didn't think that possible. Nobody was that kind-hearted.

Two beds down, the tall, white-coated figure of Pedro Aguirre stooped over his post-operative hernia patient, his stethoscope slung over his shoulder, the collar of his pastel blue shirt casually outside his lab coat. He picked up the patient's wrist between his thumb and index finger as if it might contaminate him. He straightened up, the wrist gingerly held in four fingers, feeling for a pulse, his eyes focused upon his watch. He suddenly squirmed and hurriedly replaced the arm upon the bed. He scratched his upper thigh, close to his crotch, vigorously, like a dog infested with fleas. He closed his eyes and exhaled, looking relieved.

"Epa, Pedro, did you invite bichaco ants to bonche in your pants?" Amador asked, looking amused. Osvaldo had once described Amador's face as a burro's ridden by three fat men. His cheerfulness surprised Debra.

"Shut up, Amador," Pedro said. He scowled. "It's no laughing matter. It's a dermatitis de contacto."

"Hydrocortisone, chamo," Amador said. He actually roused himself out of his gloomy inner realm and laughed. "That is, if you're really sure it is contact dermatitis, and not pubic crabs like the ones I hear you passed on to your wife."

Pedro Aguirre and Diosgracio did not appear particularly amused by Amador's jocularity. "Carajo, get back to work," Pedro said. He nodded in the direction of the Yanomami boy, pointing with his lips, his thin moustache disappearing under his nose. He walked slowly and deliberately out of the room, his head carried high.

❦

David sat on board the DC-10 beside Charles McCulloch. It was a relief to be seated beside someone British. Charles was a distinguished Scotsman with a full head of steel-grey hair. He worked for the British Council in Caracas, the organization which had helped finance David's trip. Charles, and most of the other first-class passengers, David noticed, had been flown here specially for the governor's banquet to celebrate the opening of INSA's new library, funded in part by the British Council. Ambassador William Cox sat across the aisle from him.

"David, you must be tired after the ball-busting time you've had of it here," Charles said in his dilute brogue. "I heard you were nearly killed by curare-tipped arrows. The British Empire conquers once again."

"It has been a rather interesting three weeks, I must admit," David said.

He had spent his final week in Puerto Pedriscal, helping the inexperienced INSA staff process the expedition materials. There had been the establishment of *Plasmodium* cultures, and blood to separate into components. He had prepared the materials he needed for transport back to Britain. Pity about the liquid nitrogen tank. INSA did collaborative research with his good friend in Liverpool, Tom Cartwright, and Tom would be disappointed that David had been unable to bring him the *Onchocerca* nodules and skin snips.

Charles unfolded the *Sunday Times* that he'd brought with him from Caracas the day before and buried his nose in its headlines as the plane sat idly on the tarmac, leaving David with time to reflect upon the last few days of his trip. Aside from lab work, there had been diplomatic duties. David hated those. Standing politely, listening to Spanish blether. Last night at the municipal building, the territorial governor had hosted a dinner party for the dignitaries with David as the guest of honour. The cream of Venezuela's scientific community, British Council officials, World Health Organization and Pan American Health Organization representatives and Ambassador Cox himself had attended. Velázquez certainly knew how to advertise himself. During cocktails, David dutifully shook hands with all the pompous Venezuelan men—tight polyester trousers, pleated and embroidered shirtfronts open to display copious black chest-hair and gold medallions—ruining good imported scotch with ice and soda water. The tables were arranged in a U-shape and draped first with gold, then with starched white tablecloths. The head table, where David sat, had a podium with a microphone and was decorated with a banner displaying the Ministry of Health's logo, a yellow cross with SAS written inside, an example of typical Latin verbosity, in which the Ministry of Health can become the "Ministry of Sanitation and Social Assistance". David discovered only too early in the evening the purpose behind that podium. Every boring Malariología official had droned on and on once he had control of the microphone, knowing full well he had a captive audience. All of them were natural performers, not a trace of shyness or modesty, each one thinking what he had to say was of earth-shattering importance. Debra sat next to David, providing her inadequate translations less flirtatiously than before, with none of the pleasurable distraction of her breast pressing into his arm.

Charles looked up from his paper. "Honestly, David, what a mercy the power failure turned out to be. Those slides of the Malariology DDT team . . . why, I felt almost tortured. As merciful as it was, it did make a right balls-up of the dinner, didn't it?" He gave a few hearty chortles.

"I was rather amused by the plastic pith helmets, personally," David remarked. "Ideal for the tropics. But that slide show was entertaining compared to some of what I've been through. Charles, you cannot imagine how much I'm looking forward to returning home. I think I've had my fill of third-world travel."

Charles returned his attention to his paper.

That slide show had indeed been agony: the brave pioneering DDT team dousing thatched dwellings with DDT; maps of infection foci; tables of statistics. The power failure that cut the slide show short had also delayed the serving of dinner for several hours, and the tuxedo-clad Indian waiters had had to wait for lulls in the speeches as they brought out food. The hot foods cooled and the cold foods warmed to room temperature, which David estimated to be in the vicinity of 37° Celsius, human body temperature.

David wiped perspiration from his forehead and checked the round air vent in the luggage rack above him, finding it to be already fully open.

David's visit had been hailed by Velázquez in his speech as a victory for medical science in the Territory. Velázquez was positively charming at the farewell dinner, with promises of further collaboration. The administrator's timely release from jail unfroze INSA's assets and enabled Velázquez to reimburse David for the supplies he had brought from England. Even if Velázquez destroyed the collaboration now, it didn't really matter to David. He had obtained what he needed for his own research projects back in Cambridge, and had survived to tell about it. He thought about the rabies shots. This trip might be his last. It had been far more stressful than he had anticipated.

He wondered how long Velázquez would manage to keep his institute afloat. The money and international support were there, but the staff were young and inexperienced, the Latin American political arena was unstable, the area isolated and the infrastructure needed to support a scientific institute lacking. David had every intention of discussing his doubts with Tom Cartwright, and with any other collaborator of INSA's who cared to listen at the next World Health meeting in Geneva.

"Charles, is it hot in here or is it just me?"

"Perhaps the air-conditioning isn't functioning. We should be off shortly."

Charles, with his years in foreign service, was evidently better acclimatized to tropical heat. A cramp growled from deep within David's bowels.

"I do believe your stomach's trying to tell you something," Charles said.

"Rightly so, rightly so."

David unfastened his tweed jacket with the suede elbow patches. He straightened his tie, which proudly displayed his Oxford graduation colours. Just as well he was leaving today, if he was going to get sick. That is, if they ever got this old tub off the runway.

"I wonder what the hell is holding us up?" Charles asked.

David looked out the window at the tufts of dry grass on the savannah, and the bunches of distant palm trees. "Not a thing wrong with the weather," David answered. "My educated guess is that it's Latin inefficiency." It was sunny and hot, the sky practically cloudless. Heat rose off the tarmac and distorted the air. David looked at his watch. The DC-10 had been sitting uselessly for an hour. An announcement in Spanish, which he didn't understand, triggered a burst of activity within the cabin. The other passengers moaned, unbuckled their seatbelts, pulled down their carry-on boxes from the overhead racks and stampeded to the exits.

"I'm afraid they scrapped the flight," Charles said.

"Splendid!"

They waited until most of the shoving crowd had disembarked before taking their carry-on bags down from the luggage rack and walking to the exit. David was only a day away from being home. So close. Would he never return to his family?

He saw Yadira and Debra standing beside the chain-link fence. His two carry-ons slung over his shoulder, he joined the group of scientists and diplomats standing on the tarmac. Yadira and Debra walked over to meet them. Yadira smiled. "Sorry about the delay," she said.

"Delay? You mean cancellation," Charles said.

"Bloody marvellous," David said. "How the hell I will make my connection?" With horror he heard the slight slip of his neutral, correct English into his native Midlands accent. It was as if someone else had taken control of his mouth. The heat, his fatigue—he hadn't spoken in that accent since he had first attended Oxford at the age of eighteen. He hoped Charles and William hadn't noticed.

"Apparently there were problems with the hydraulics," said Debra in her nasal American parody of English. "You ought to be thankful that they discovered it before takeoff. Imagine the headlines." She laughed, Charles and William joining her jocularity.

"Yes," said Yadira. "One of the passengers saw an enormous rat run down the overhead luggage rack. The pilot figured that rats had been eating the hydraulic lines, and all commercial flights to Caracas are to be postponed until an exterminator and some good mechanics can be consulted."

"Well then. It looks as though we are going to be your guests a while longer," Ambassador Cox said.

"Don't worry," Yadira assured him. In her stiff blue-jean skirt, her trim grey hair, she looked a model of maturity and efficiency, an exception among the INSA staff. "We have the situation under control. The military has a Hercules transport going to Caracas. I made a few phone calls and I've arranged

194

for them to give you a lift. If I may have the stubs for your luggage, I'll have it transferred to the Hercules in a jiffy."

Yadira left for the terminal and Debra accompanied the British trio. The sweat beads on David's forehead coalesced, then trickled down his cheeks and nose. His armpits were wet under his tweed jacket. As they walked across the shimmering tarmac to the wide-bodied Hercules, he couldn't distinguish between the heat waves and his feeling of dizziness. Debra said goodbye to the visitors and even gave David a perfunctory kiss on the cheek.

David looked back one last time at Debra through the open tail section. Then he walked past wooden crates secured with green rope netting and on through the windowless hull to the front of the cargo bay. Green canvas seats were unfolded from the wall for the distinguished passengers, a dozen seats already occupied by the more rapid dignitaries.

David sat stiffly, strapped securely with a green webbing belt. The plane rumbled down the runway, then took off with a mind-numbing noise and vibration. The landing gear retracted with a thump. His bowels grumbled more urgently than before. Warm mayonnaise salad dressing. He had known the danger lurking in the salad, but in the formal dinner setting he couldn't refuse to eat.

"William, do you happen to know where the lavatory is?" David asked.

"I take it your stomach is giving you trouble too?" William questioned.

"David, there is no lavatory on a Hercules transport," Charles said, squirming in his seat. "We should have gone on the DC-10."

David Shuttleworth and an official from the World Health Organization hung up a bedsheet from David's luggage for privacy. Charles McCulloch had found an old bucket in the back of the plane. Ambassador Cox hid behind the curtain first. Charles queued, more than a dozen scientists and dignitaries behind him hugging their stomachs, and listened to the wet farts and bursts of liquid faeces exploding from behind the sheet. It was his turn next, and it couldn't come a moment too soon. Even with intense concentration he could feel his anal sphincter giving way to the pressure. "Hurry up, William. Please."

As his bowels churned like a ruminant's, Charles decided that the next time Velázquez asked him for money he would turn down the request, whether it be for airline tickets, scholarships or attending conferences in Britain. Velázquez would pay dearly for this humiliation.

Debra and Yadira had just returned from the airport. Debra lay in bed listening to the Sunday ritual of "Gloria, gloria, alleloooia" and thinking about the governor's party the night before. Perhaps she should have listened to Osvaldo. Maybe she shouldn't allow Máximo to call her mamita. She had cramps and felt hot and cold simultaneously. Her period was due. She pulled her sheets up around her neck.

Why had the governor invited that repugnant man? During cocktails, Máximo had followed her as she tried to avoid him, his adipose jowls trembling, sniffing her out like a bloodhound. She hadn't liked his tone of voice; it had sounded vaguely ominous. As an American citizen she could count on her embassy to defend her if she had any serious troubles with him. American citizenship had its advantages.

She dozed a few minutes and jolted upright when she heard a loud snap. She leapt out of bed and looked down the hallway. A fat rat ran past her, bouncing down the hallway, a generous portion of Edam held between its teeth.

A severe intestinal cramp hit, doubling her over in pain, and she ran to the toilet. Yadira must have gotten there first because brown fluid swirled around right to the brim. Debra ran out to the back yard and, aware of the excellent view afforded to the church, pulled her pants down and squatted behind the plantain trees.

16

Segundo stood wet and naked before the cracked mirror in his bathroom, the bleach smell of Las Llaves soap wafting up from his armpits. He briefly admired his well-defined abdominal muscles: lean, no fat anywhere. He blotted his skin partially dry with a towel. The water drops he missed evaporated rapidly from his body in the heat accumulated from the day. He spread Gillette shaving cream on his face, stretched his bottom lip tightly around his teeth and shaved off the stubbled growth on his chin, tapping the hair out of the razor on the edge of the sink. He put the razor down on the sink edge. He brushed his teeth thoroughly, pulling his lips wide open to expose his strong white teeth, inspecting his reflected image to make sure they gleamed.

Even if he found the curandero, he could never convince him to return to the Hospital de los Desaparecidos. The inescapable plight of his friend disheartened him. Medical help had come too late for the curandero, but there were many other unfortunate people who needed it. The gringa capitalista had recovered from her sickness, and his strategy could work out well for both himself and those who were ill. For those fearing the hospital, a doctora in their own homes was far less intimidating.

He changed into a freshly laundered faded red shirt and blue jeans. As for himself—maybe he read too much poetry—the benefit was of a personal nature. Thoughts of romance with the gringa doctora lapidified him, solidly tenting out his zipper. He knew of the perfect medical case to draw her attention, a skin condition, something right in her area of interest. Afterward, he would show the imperialista the

Amazonian sky at night—a guaranteed aphrodisiac. Maybe then she would allow him to run his hand through her hair, starlit liquid silver flowing through his fingertips, and one thing would lead to another. He had always heard that the gringas moved quickly in sexual matters, and that virginity at marriage was not an important issue to them.

He drove through the nearly deserted streets of Malariología houses, past the kiosk and the church. A bundle of pale blue flowers lay on the passenger's seat beside him. There were no lights on inside the church, but he parked a little way down the street, avoiding the illumination of a yellow streetlight. He looked around, checking that the street was empty, before he walked quickly up to the house, flowers in his hand.

But it was the other doctora who answered the door, the antipathetic one, who Debra had said worked with mosquitoes. She looked at him acrimoniously when she opened the door, and wilted the dainty blue jacaranda flowers with her glare. "Guarupa, for the doctora americana," he explained hastily. "It is sometimes used to cure infirmities of the skin, and I thought that, being a dermatologist, she would find it of medical interest."

"Suppose I use it to cure the swelling inside your pants," she said, flaring her nostrils ever so slightly.

"I thought I might persuade the doctora americana to see a patient who has an infirmity of the skin. I believe it's a disease caused by fungus," he said boldly.

The lucent imperialist head appeared from behind the mosquito doctor.

"What are the symptoms?" Debra asked.

"The woman in question has peeling skin and itchiness in the area covered by her pantaletas." The doctora antipática looked into his eyes, hard and knowingly, and nodded before she turned, leaving him alone with the imperialista.

"We shall see," Debra said. "Allow me to put these flowers in some water." She left the door open as she took the flowers into the kitchenette, put them in a glass of water and placed them on the white table. The doctora antipática was sitting at the table and he heard the two women talk to each other and laugh. Debra returned alone, stifling laughter, slipped on her sandals and followed him out to his jeep, facilito, easy as you please.

Segundo drove through rows of Malariología houses. "You may not want to believe it, but this infirmity is brought on by a brujería hex."

"Fungal diseases are spread by contact with spores, not by hexes. People here are very superstitious. I hadn't thought you would be." She sat slouched in the front seat, a foot resting on the dashboard. He didn't want his dashboard dirtied, but the position was quite stimulating. The dirt could be cleaned off later.

He stopped at a Malariología house in a new section of town, with not a tree or a blade of grass, just dirt illuminated ochre by the orange glow of the streetlights. "This enfermedad cannot be cured by modern medicine alone. It is a hex, and only a curandero more powerful than the brujo who originally cast it can remove it. I am told a remedy can be made with cariaquito mora'o leaves, but the curandero must be powerful enough to convince the spirits to enter the leaves. This requires much skill, and it takes many years to acquire such formidable powers."

"I will see for myself. If it's a fungal disease the woman can go to the out-patient clinic tomorrow, and one of the pasantes can prescribe a cream." She eyed him teasingly, provocatively.

The brujería victim said very little. Her children were in their chinchorros, sleeping. Segundo had known Conchita for at least ten years now. She had once been a pretty young girl, of mixed native and criollo ancestry. She had been as elegantly shaped as a violin, her skin smooth and rich as the lustrous wood of a fine Stradivarius, and every man who looked at her wanted to pizzicato on her strings. A long time ago, when she was eighteen and Segundo twenty-two, he had fallen madly in love with her and they had been intimate. Even back then he hated the idea of marriage, but he might have done it for her. Fortunately, before it came to that, she had the good sense to find another man more readily available for marriage than Segundo. She was now a middle-aged widow. What had once been a violin had widened into a violoncello and finally to a double-bass, and she had three children who ran like wild peccaries. She, alone, ran the business she and her husband had scraped together with hard work and determination. In her back yard, she sold fried fish with casabe bread and catarra sauce, Polar beer, Coca-Cola and cigarettes. Every night she had to fight off the borrachos who pinched her bottom and made lewd comments. Behind Conchita's wrinkles he could still see a glimmer of her old prettiness, in her eyes and in her smile. It was a good thing he hadn't married. A man could not be married to both a cause and a woman at the same time.

Conchita told Segundo in her broken Spanish to turn the other way. Debra conducted her examination and he squinted, just barely turning his head but not his shoulders, so that Conchita wouldn't notice. Nervously the woman lifted up her floral print dress and pulled down her yellow nylon underpants. Blisters the size of sweat beads and dried crust covered the hairless groin area like a burn, and the skin was inflamed red. "Ah," said Debra as she bent over the groin, "the condition is classic. It's caused by a cellular immune response to a foreign antigen."

Segundo, always a gentleman, turned back to face the two women only after Conchita had again covered her blistered crotch under her sacklike dress, looking like a meat-filled, doughy hallaca tied too loosely within its banana leaves. "It's a dermatitis de contacto," said Debra. "Many substances, such as chemicals found in some plant species, can elicit this type of reaction. In this patient's case, an irritant must have been present on her underpants, maybe the fabric dye or perhaps a change in laundry detergent, and she has become hypersensitized. We had a case identical to this at the hospital this week."

"You know, in a way you're right," said Segundo, impressed by her expertise. "The hex is cast when the brujo sneaks up to a clothesline and blows a powder made from groundup pica pica plant onto the victim's underwear and then whispers words to evoke natural spirits."

"So you knew the cause. A little test for me?" said Debra. "There is a scientific explanation for everything, even for brujería."

"Yes, though I also know your medicines will do little to counteract the powers behind the curandero's words," he replied.

Debra smiled and turned to Conchita. "You can go see Huevo de Pava tomorrow and he can sell you hydrocortisone cream. The ailment should clear up in about two weeks."

"Thank you, doctora, but I prefer to see my curandero tomorrow," Conchita said. "He will know what to do."

The two women, Segundo realized, were very close together in age. Maybe the doctora was even a little older. But one lived a life of poverty, tragedy, hard work and early childbirth; the other lived a pampered life of wealth and education. One woman looked twice the age of the other. Their lives were there, reflected in their faces and figures.

"Dios te bendiga, Conchita," Segundo said. He patted her shoulder and kissed her creased cheek.

"Sinvergüenza," Conchita said. She puckered her mouth up like an old man's anus and winked at Segundo. "You forget how well I know you. I can see what you're up to, perfumed and shaved like a patiquin. Your hen is waiting. Go now, go and fertilize her eggs. You can do it without any help from me."

❦

Debra wondered where Segundo was taking her. They travelled on a dirt road, through a tunnel of trees and past the city limits. She suspected, yet did nothing to stop him, that he was taking

202

her somewhere secluded so that he could make a sexual advance. She twirled her hair around her finger and looked through the front window at darkness and two spots of passing dirt and gravel illuminated by the headlights.

"Amorcita, have you ever looked at the stars in Amazonas? I am talking of the bright stars, the ones you see from outside town limits?" he asked. He didn't look at her.

"It's getting late and I must work tomorrow."

"This will only take a moment. Then I'll drive you home."

He parked on the roadside and doused the lights. He got out and stood in front of the jeep. Debra waited a few seconds before following him. She pulled herself up onto the hood beside him. He leaned against the front grille, looking relaxed and confident. The stars were brilliant in the cloudless night. Debra had never seen so many stars in the sky at once, from faceted gems to pinpricks, packed like pulverized glitter.

"If you search the sky you will see a satellite," he said.

"With the naked eye? Without a telescope? They'd be far too small."

"I will show you one." He scanned the sky for a minute. "See, I told you." He pointed. "There it is, that point of light you can see, the one moving across the sky."

She strained her eyes but saw nothing. "You're teasing me." He sat up on the hood beside her, moved his head close to hers and positioned her head to where he was looking. She first saw it in her peripheral vision, the faintest dot, but perceptibly moving, moving much faster than she thought a satellite would. Once she knew what to look for, she could see the moving point of light quite clearly in the centre of her field of vision. "I see it now," she said excitedly. "Are you sure it's a satellite?"

"I swear on my brother's grave, mi cielo, a satellite it is. In all probability it was put into orbit by your country."

A satellite, she could actually see a satellite with her bare eyes, a man-made object in space. Segundo had found one so quickly. There must be many, so many of those objects flung into the outmost reaches of the world. What was it she had heard they were planning to call the Star Wars satellites? Brilliant pebbles, was it? A pretty name for machines of destruction.

At that very moment, far beyond the Paraua rapids, Yanomami who had never even seen an outsider would be able to see it too. They too would see the moving pin-point of light, product of a technology far beyond their comprehension. How had they adapted their age-old myths to include the proliferation of moving stars? If they interpreted them as portents of doom, they were probably right. Malevolent *Shawara* spirits. A melancholy came over Debra; modern man could encroach upon every aspect of the earth, there was no area left untouched. When she had made the decision to work in Amazonas, she had thought the wilderness would swallow her whole, but there was her world above her, for everyone everywhere to see. She wished she could blink the satellite's existence away. She was like that satellite. Although earthbound, she too was a technological presence that didn't belong here.

Segundo placed his hands on her shoulders, turned her to face him, pulled her close and kissed her, a long kiss. Her melancholy and the cumulative effects from the previous courtship displays—the convoluted gesturing, the subtle physical messages—all culminated in this moment of her physiological readiness to couple. The stimuli from nerves to brain triggered a burst of chemical excitants targeted to various cellular receptors, causing a tingling sensation in her body, one in which stimulus perception differed from the actual point of origin.

Segundo fumbled with a button on her shirt. She slid her hand down to his thigh. The visions of Jeff Marshall returned and she fuzzily remembered the unprotected sex and the subsequent anxiety waiting for her period to come. She fought hormonal dictate with great difficulty, and her lips and hand froze. "Segundo," she said, her eyes fully open. "Do you have protection?"

"Protección?"

"You know, anticonceptivos?"

He moaned, drew his body up erect, as straight as a rod. "Ay, coño! No es posible! The yucca is peeled, quartered and salted. We are ready to fry, and we discover the corn oil is missing. You don't use pastillas anticonceptivas? I thought all women from Ooosah took those pills."

She pulled away, buttoned her shirt and smoothed her clothing. "No, and furthermore, I refuse to buy anything at the pharmacy. Everyone knows Huevo de Pava is a gossip. Just imagine what people would say if the one and only gringa doctora in town were to purchase contraceptives. You'll have to buy something before we meet again."

"Coño, amorcita mía, and you think it's easy for a man to buy paracaídas from Huevo de Pava?" he groaned, and looked down at his lap. "You cannot imagine the state of agony you have left me in."

17

Fermin Cabrera had noticed Debra change in the months since her arrival at INSA. He remembered the blisters from her high-heeled shoes and her squeamishness at embalming Wilfred. She had been useless at handling a crisis, though she had been quick to learn this most important skill at INSA. She had learned to manage her emotions, and now tackled the daily crises professionally. But her new-found confidence also brought an ability to annoy people in positions of authority, definitely not an asset at INSA. She did, for example, continually annoy the doctor. She said all the wrong things, and blurted out questions clearly antagonistic to Doctor Velázquez at Technical Commission meetings. Fermin knew that, even if he deliberately set out to anger him, he wouldn't be able to raise the doctor's blood pressure nearly so much. Fermin suspected that she angered him intentionally. Once he heard her call the doctor by his first name and the familiar form of "you" in the same sentence. "Diego, si tu puedes," she said. Fermin remembered the look on the doctor's face. It could have sharpened a picota stake, the kind of stake used in early colonial days to display heads severed from criminals, yet it didn't intimidate her. She continued to provoke him in her overtly innocent, disrespectful way. One day the doctor would explode, and Fermin hoped he would be there to see it—from a safe distance.

Osvaldo had deposited Fermin and Debra in front of the slaughterhouse. They passed through the gate of a fourteen-foot concrete barricade shielding the airport traffic on Avenida Orinoco from the horrors behind. A jagged ridge of broken glass topped the barricade to dissuade hungry slum dwellers from entering the matadero at night to steal meat.

A few months ago Fermin had begun a new research line that required materials from the matadero, and he had been having some difficulties getting started. He just couldn't find any worms. He didn't know where to look. "Debra is much more adept at recognizing tissue abnormalities than are you, Fermin," Velázquez had announced at one of the numerous Comisión Técnica meetings. "Her expertise will be essential at the matadero where she will assist you in the examination of bovine carcasses for *Onchocerca gutterosa* pathology. We will use the worms in our antigen study, and it is of paramount importance that we begin to look for animal reservoirs of *Onchocerca* species." Fermin and Debra had visited the matadero on several occasions now, and her assistance was not really needed any more. She had shown Fermin how to recognize the worms threaded along the huge nuchal ligaments at the back of the neck. The doctor nevertheless continued to assign her this duty, and Fermin suspected that he did it as a sadistic punishment for antagonizing him. Debra had tried repeatedly to argue with Velázquez. "I am not a veterinarian," she had stated emphatically on more than one occasion, but Velázquez had held firm. "The matter is not open for discussion, Doctora Baumstark."

"Velázquez insists that animal pathology can be very interesting," Debra said, looking distastefully at the pile of rubber boots and aprons lying on the iron-pigmented dirt. "He claims that disease is often far more progressed in livestock than in humans, because the pathology is frequently only discovered during post-mortems. I have now seen both human and animal pathology in Amazonas, and I can verify that they are equally unappealing."

Fermin pulled on his black rubber boots and slid the straps of a black rubber apron over his neck, covering his lab coat. "Debra, if you want some advice, I think it would be best if you didn't provoke the doctor at Technical Commission meetings. It is best to blindly follow his wishes and not be argumentative." Fermin paused, then added, "It also helps if you are not overly ambitious."

"I hate this job," Debra said. "I hate wearing smelly rubber boots and sloshing around in blood. At least with humans I feel I'm doing some good. It's hard to imagine I'm doing these poor cattle any good."

"Come on, Debra, let's get this over with," Fermin said. "The more work we complete in one day, the less frequently we have to come." She slid her feet into the boots and tied the apron around herself. Fermin opened a rusty latch and they walked through the door into the large concrete structure.

ॐ

The heavy smell of blood brought a metallic taste to Debra's mouth. The building echoed with the bellow of an angry steer; they were just in time to see the quick thrust of a short knife behind the head that paralysed the steer by severing the spinal cord and knocked it down onto its knees. This was followed by exsanguination: a swipe with a longer knife across the side of the neck severing the jugular and carotid vessels. There was no attempt to save the blood. It flowed out in rivulets and pooled on the grey cement floor. It was washed into gutters with a hose.

The process, though barbaric, was at least quick, relatively painless and probably not too stressful to the animals. Lives ended abruptly—the breathing and feeling creatures were transformed into skinned slabs of muscle for the dinner tables of Puerto Pedriscal's financially secure. But the next animal didn't fare so well. A zebu steer fell, only stunned by the first cut. With wild eyes rimmed by white sclera, the hump of fatty tissue on its withers wobbling, nostrils flaring in fear, he was bled and dragged across the floor to the butchering site still struggling. A beer-bellied man finally took an axe and chopped hard three times, behind the horns, terminating its distress.

Carpets of flies covered the still carcasses in seconds,

turning them black. Skinning and dismemberment followed quickly. Men, almost indistinguishable from the meat, in their bloodstained clothes and covering of flies, hoisted and dragged carcasses, dismembered parts, muscles sheathed in membranes, meagre subcutaneous fat, blood vessels as thick as fingers. They tramped through puddles of partially coagulated blood, with bare feet and rolled-up pants. Dogs sneaked in through the open passageways on both sides of the building, ears pulled back, tails tucked tightly between their legs, mangy, cringing, cowering, snatching scraps of tissue and lapping up blood.

The men rolled the severed heads and attached necks over to one side of the building, where Debra and Fermin conducted their search. They probed through the strong nuchal ligaments, pale, almost as thick as Debra's wrists—suspension cables for the cumbrous weight of bovine skulls. Debra looked for tissue abnormality, strands of semi-translucent vermicelli. They detached parasitized ligaments and slipped them into plastic freezer bags.

"Yet another treasure of the Amazonas," Debra said, smiling grimly, a clot of blood on her nose, as she gently lifted a worm with a pair of forceps and slid it into a vial.

"Keep your eyes skinned, Debra. Maybe you will discover a new species. You can call it *Onchocerca velazquezii* in honour of the doctor."

Debra laughed. "I couldn't think of a better name for a worm."

They squatted on the bloodstained concrete floor, bent over the massive bovine heads, for hours. Dark dried blood gummed Debra's hair. Clotted strands hung in her eyes. Blood smeared Fermin's glasses and stained his clothing where it was unprotected by his rubber apron. Debra lifted the sleeve of her lab coat to peek at her watch and left a sticky red thumbprint on the white fabric. Osvaldo would soon come. What a relief. Her back ached and she stood up straight to unstiffen. She glanced out the rear passageway, past the frightened eyes of the steers, to a holding pen where a group of native people sat on bare dirt and manure around an open fire topped by a huge iron cauldron. "Those people are here as usual."

"Sí, Debra. Very poor indios. Not everyone in Amazonas can buy meat at the supermercado. How they can eat that offal, the feet and other crap that no one else wants, I don't know. It's survival, I suppose."

The people hovered over the pot, one of them stirring with a big stick. One looked up, a very old man, his body weak and frail. He ducked his head down quickly, as if he saw and recognized Debra and didn't want her to see his face. She squinted, filtering out the glare of the outside sun. She was quite sure then that he was the ancient curandero, Segundo's tubercular friend, the hospital escapee. The spiritual leader of his people now scavenged for indigestible keratinized protein and viscera. And how many of those around him had he infected with his improperly treated tuberculosis? Antibiotic-resistant strains were probably incubating in him as she watched. The medical system, with its oath to help humanity, had failed miserably with him and his people.

❧

After Osvaldo had dropped the doctora and Fermin off at the matadero, he had continued down Avenida Orinoco in the direction of the airport, a great cloud of dust billowing behind him. He showed the guard at the chain-link fence a document and he was ushered through the gate onto the broiling asphalt.

He watched the DC-10 grow from a small dot on the horizon until it taxied to a stop, looming high above his head. He stood in the shade of the jet and watched the passengers disembark as usual, shoving, pushing, kissing and hugging. Amid all the turmoil, a closed crate big enough to hold a one-ton Brahman bull was forklifted down onto the asphalt. A deep, throaty growl rumbled from inside the crate, and Osvaldo wondered if the wooden spars could contain the immense animal. Velázquez's dog's name was Salvaje, and he was a raza pura called a mastiff. The beast had been shipped here from Ooosah solely to guard Velázquez's secluded house on its fundo and his expensive vehicle. Osvaldo had orders to handle the beast carefully, because the animal was very costly and even had papers documenting the mating of his ancestors. The dog could trace his bloodlines back farther than could Osvaldo. Osvaldo wondered why the doctor concerned himself so much about canine lineage. He looked between the slats at the royal dog and saw the red glow of reflective retinas through widely dilated pupils, a set of jaws the size of a caimán's covered by folds of rubbery black lips and a thick body covered in hide striped like a sun-faded tiger. But, papers or not, an armadillo couldn't grow a tortoise shell, and a dog was still a dog. He said sweetly, "Salvaje. Hola, Salvaje." The monstruo wagged his tail and panted, and Osvaldo smiled. Some guard dog. He signed the paperwork releasing the dog to him and, with the aid of the strongest four men at the airport, hoisted the cage onto the flatbed of the mosquito-sided pickup.

Osvaldo looked at the map Velázquez had drawn for him to locate his fundo. Verdaderamente, it was a mess. Down Avenida Orinoco to the Indian statue, turn onto Río Negro, first paved left turn and then the second (was it?) dirt road. Osvaldo followed the map as best he could, past identical rows of Malariología houses along the identical streets and out of town on a thin forest track where he forded a small stream. He drove half an hour, recognizing no landmarks matching those described by Velázquez. He headed back to town, having to back up for a long way on the narrow track before he could turn around. Qué rollo! The big dog howled unceasingly. Osvaldo parked on the side of a paved street in front of some Malariología houses. He took another look at the map. He had followed it correctly. The big dog continued to howl. Osvaldo got out of the truck and spoke to the dog in a soothing tone of voice, "Salvaje, tranquilo. Todo está bien. Seguro, pana, todo está bien." He stuck a finger through the bars and the dog whimpered, and licked him with his sloppy wet tongue. Idiota,

Velázquez, this big friendly monstruo was mansito, as dulce as sugar-cane. If he really wanted a dog to guard his fundo, then he would have been much better off with one of the tough Puerto Pedriscal street dogs than this blue blood prince of dogs. The dog was just another example of Velázquez living the high life, another way of showing others his importance. Funny, not a soul was to be seen out on the street, but Osvaldo thought he saw faces deep in the shade of their windows.

He had no choice but to drive back to INSA. The doctor was most displeased that his guard dog had not been delivered. He now had to drive Salvaje to his fundo himself, and the crate didn't fit through his Land Cruiser's tailgate. The dog sat placidly in the back seat of Velázquez's personal jeep, purchased with World Health Organization funds, panting, drooling and leaving snail marks on the side windows. Velázquez rolled down his window, complaining bitterly about the smell and the dog hair and drool on his upholstery. The last words Osvaldo heard Velázquez yell before he drove off were "Osvaldo, estúpido, necio, débil, imbécil!" The doctor's abuse was unwarranted. Had the doctor been born a zebu bull, he would surely urinate ten times more than any other, even if it meant drinking ten times more water, just to prove his dominance.

Osvaldo looked at his watch. It was the hour of the burro, when the sun is highest in the sky, a time when a man rightly belongs at home in his chinchorro, sleeping off the good food his wife has prepared for him and maybe even some amor afterward. Now there was no time for love, lunch or siesta. Getting lost with the royal dog had taken up all his time and he had to take the técnicos down the hill. He would have time only to grab a quick pastry and fruit shake at the Lunchería Manos de Dios, and then drive back to the matadero to pick up Debra and Fermin.

ॐ

Osvaldo drove blood-covered Fermin and Debra and their sixty-three worms up the steep INSA hill. Pandemonium had struck the institute. Hundreds of people milled about: criollos, campesinos, peasants, indigenous people, pushing, shoving, straining to barge through the laboratory doors; filling the little Plaza Bolívar and the dirt parking lot, tenfold worse than the crowds that met the daily DC-10 flight from Caracas. From the collective babble, individual shouts were discernible:

"We demand to see El Hombre Salvaje!"

"We know you captured him."

"We saw the crate. We heard him growl."

"You have hidden him. We have the evidence; the cage is still here."

"You will be cursed if you hurt him."

"Disaster will strike us all down."

"The director is so secretive, that he does not talk to his mistress during conjugal climax."

"What the hell is going on?" Debra yelled above the noise as she tried to shove her way towards her office.

"Doctora!" Osvaldo yelled, and pulled her back inside the jeep. "It's safer in here until we know what's happening. They seem to think we have El Hombre Salvaje here."

"The hombre what?"

"The Wild Man of Amazonas, doctora. A half-ape, half-man creature, taller than any known man. He comes in the dark of night. He jumps on top of jeeps passing through the selva to look for women. He steals them to become his brides and he has relaciones matrimoniales with them. Yes, it's true. His women and their children become wild too. He is the spirit of the wild, the essence of Amazonas; that which cannot and will not be tamed. No man is to gain dominion over him, for it is said that once he has been dominated, the rains will cease to fall, even the great Orinoco will dry up, and the land will crack and peel away like sun-baked clay in a dry streambed."

"Osvaldo, es pura superstición," Fermin said.

"Mentira, Fermin, I know it to be true. Doctora, I saw the Hombre Salvaje myself one night. The doctor had me drive the INSA jeep all the way to Caracas to pick up supplies. I drove at night as well as day to save time. The monstruo jumped my jeep at night before I reached Caicara de Orinoco. He left without harming me only after he discovered there was no woman with me, but he smashed the windshield of the jeep."

"Osvaldo, I know you made that story up as an excuse; you really drove to a bar in Caicara and a borracho smashed a bottle through the window," Fermin said scornfully.

"Osvaldo, I have to agree with Fermin," Debra said. "That's a lot of nonsense. Your description of this wild man fits half the macho men in Puerto Pedriscal. Why should they think we have him up here, anyway?"

"I'm not certain, doctora," Osvaldo said.

"Not even a whore's idea," Fermin added. "They said something about a crate. . . ."

Just then, the crowd flowed in a wave to the back of the complex, where the animal house was located.

"Look, I have better things to do than listen to this," Debra said, climbing out of the jeep. "I must get to my office for some case sheets. One of you two call the police, and then let's get out of here and leave it to them."

She was surprised to find Diosgracio waiting in her office. The strands of long hair that had been plastered with grease across his tonsure had been pushed aside and it was once again exposed, identifying him as Yanomami. He seemed unperturbed about the turmoil outside as he started to speak in a calm voice. But as he continued talking, his volume increased and his eyes narrowed and it became clear to Debra that he was actually very agitated. The kind and gentle convert was transformed into a Yanomami warrior. "I endured weeks of abuse exposed to the sun, barely a bite to eat, allowing blackflies to suck, to suck my blood dry, while the biologist doctora trapped them. I am educated, a nurse, yet I have been treated as an ignorante. I know that biting can aggravate the condition, increase the infective load, but Doctora Socorro assured me I would be compensated medically afterward. I

214

thought she had knowledge of a new experimental treatment. Instead she tells me that my compensation is the knowledge that I have assisted in an important study that may eventually contribute to control of the disease." He continued in a crescendo, "I demand from you, doctora, Coordinadora de Servicios Medicales, compensation in full, treatment for my ailment."

"Diosgracio, I'm sorry," she sputtered. "There is no safe treatment. I don't understand why you were given the impression there was. With the parasite load you have, any drugs would be lethal. You may eventually go blind without treatment, but that's better than dying." Marisol—the conniving, manipulative bitch. "I will speak to Doctor Velázquez," although she knew full well Velázquez would be pleased with Marisol's initiative. He had probably even sanctioned the experiment.

"If there is no treatment, then don't trouble yourself! God will be your judge." Diosgracio opened the door and left.

Debra grabbed the papers she needed and ran for the jeep, seething at Velázquez and Marisol. They deserved judgement from someone.

❦

Yadira had escaped home by the time the first of the curiosity seekers arrived at INSA. When bloodstained Debra staggered through the door, muttering something about retribution, Yadira prepared her a strong Cuba Libre and then set about convincing her that what she needed was to get out of the house. In fact, why didn't she come along to look at a house that was up for lease? Debra had another drink while she washed and changed, and she seemed much more relaxed as Yadira drove her little white car past the streets of Malariología houses to an older section of town with houses pre-dating the Malariología era.

The exterior was much prettier than their own house, with

breeze-blocks painted white, blue trim, the big waxy leaves of an almond tree shading a front porch, and a round water tank that looked like an oversized beach ball on the roof. The landlady said it had been vacant for two weeks, that she was looking for good tenants. As they climbed the few stairs to the front door, a smell wafted up to Yadira's nose, similar to the meat counter at the supermercado but stronger, stickier and more offensive. The olfactory gradient increased towards the door. The landlady unlocked the door and pushed it open. In the entranceway, the bloated corpse of a dog, four stiff legs pointing in the air, face frozen in a mortiferous grin, welcomed them. The paint around the metal door was gouged with claw marks.

Yadira aerosolized her throat with epinephrine before she was steady enough to drive home. That night the two of them sat together on Yadira's bed watching the Brazilian soap opera on TV and drinking more rum and Cokes than they should have. After her fifth, Yadira felt her head swim. Her eyes seemed to float away from where she wanted to look and then jerk back to the object she'd been trying to focus upon.

"Debra," she said laughing, "we may as well keep this house because we'll never find anything better. We can take the lease over from Velázquez. As much as I hate rodents, I can tolerate them better than dead dogs."

18

No one at INSA could accomplish much in the weeks following the Hombre Salvaje incident. Even after a week there were still enough people milling about, pushing their way into the labs, to disrupt research. Fantastic rumours buzzed around the town.

"It's government collusion with the CIA."

"The CIA bribed the scientists to capture and kill the Hombre Salvaje so that Ooosah can enter the Amazonas to steal our minerals without fear of his retribution."

"The ministry built their mosquito hospital on top of Cerro Orinoco so that they could hide a secret laboratory deep inside the mountain."

Just when only a few die-hards remained and things started to get back to normal, disruption struck again, in the form of bright spotlights, a furry microphone and a sixteen-millimetre movie camera.

Velázquez had hired Raúl to make a documentary, *INSA: A Triumph of Medical Science in the Venezuelan Amazonian Rainforest,* to promote his centre on national television. Raúl had made a few propaganda documentaries for national organizations, and making this small operation look good on film would be child's play.

The centre certainly looked impressive: the white tile work benches, smartly white-coated staff, hi-tech machinery and gleaming glassware, with the amazing backdrop of river, forest and huge skies for panning shots. Velázquez instructed the staff—even his driver, the secretaries, the librarian and the

217

maintenance man—to wear spotless white lab coats. Attractive young researchers posed behind flasks of coloured water and laboratory equipment, looking as if they were doing things of mind-boggling scientific importance. Raúl was impressed with Velázquez's eye for images to impress the viewing public.

Raúl captured some good footage in the first week: Marisol trapping blackflies feeding on her own legs, shaved smooth, of course; Blancanieves pipetting blood into small vials; Fermin prodding a slender nematode with a dissection needle, making it wiggle through saline solution, occasionally squinting up at the camera from behind his wire-rimmed glasses (the shots of him teasing apart human faeces could be dropped quietly later). Velázquez suspended Debra's clinical duties for the week and posed her (an example of international collaboration), hour after hour, performing clinical examinations on Salvador, including snipping biopsies from his back. No one escaped the camera's inspection. Yadira paraded the dreaded *Anopheles* mosquitoes, mounted on pins, and Reina collected sputum from a hacking victim. Cheo was perfect as a counterpoint to the blonde americana—even a poor, crippled black peasant could find a home in the INSA family.

Raúl cultivated his image as a cosmopolitan film director carefully, even to the sunshine-yellow bandanna around his neck and his attentive, attractive sound technician at his side. Self-exiled from Argentina, he had spent several years at the London School of Economics before moving to Berkeley, where marijuana and mushrooms had amplified his imagination and awakened his aesthetic senses, leading to a career in film-making.

Even for an accomplished filmmaker like himself, there were always unanticipated glitches to deal with on a new project. A sudden sneezing fit from Yadira had blown the wings off a mosquito he was filming in close-up. Her technician, Inmaculada, had had to take over. The change of skin colour of the hand in close-up, from tan to almost black, made for terrible continuity. It would be interesting to see how many people noticed it in the final cut. Also, he had run off several minutes of Marisol looking down the microscope before he noticed the stupendous view of her cleavage in the background. That would go into his private collection. Some of the staff didn't look like credible enough scientists, to his way of thinking. "If you removed some of your eye makeup and wore stunt glasses it would help you look more intellectual," he recommended to Marisol.

"Hire a bimbo to take my part," Marisol retorted. Throughout the filming she tilted and twitched her head to the left, and Raúl knew it would have to be edited out.

That was about the time when Raúl learned that Soledad cultured fungi, and asked her where he could get his hands on the narcotic mushrooms that he'd heard grew like weeds in Amazonas. Soledad reacted as though he were a venomous snake. The staff in general treated him like a nuisance and tended to shy away from the intruding eye of his camera. Firm direction and multiple takes were necessary to get any kind of natural action. By the week's end he knew he had angered almost all of them. He was glad when the weekend arrived. He decided to go off on his own, filming sights around town for filler material. The sound track would be added separately. Some local colour would liven up the film. The sacrifice of the staff, living in such a difficult, isolated environment, would surely arouse sympathy in the viewing public. Maybe he could catch some of the INSA staff about the town, and record their unrehearsed movements—catch them behaving in a less stilted manner.

❦

Yadira was tired that Saturday morning, after an awful night's sleep. She had jumped up screaming in the dark when something heavy landed on her chest, something about the weight of a huge rat. Only when her hand tingled as the blood flowed back to it did she realize that it had been her own numb arm flopping across her body.

She sipped her milky tea, inhaler in hand, as she watched Debra flutter to and fro from bedroom to bathroom. Debra wore a short skirt and flat sandals and had made up her face. She had even curled the ends of her hair. Yadira knew this extra effort was for Debra's special plans for the day, plans Debra had foolishly thought she'd kept secret. The last lascivious message embedded in bananas had been so obvious. Yadira had been wheezing and depending on her inhaler more and more ever since the rat infestation, and she was too indisposed to tease Debra about the fruit drops and clandestine messages. Despite the tackiness and inanity of the prose, Debra obviously enjoyed the rooster chap's attentions. In the last message Segundo had written some suggestive romantic prose requesting that his camarada go away from the antipathetic mosquito doctora's watchful eyes and meet him instead over at Tarzan's house. Yadira knew that the lightning-prone house perched high atop the granite boulder was such a conspicuous landmark that even the silly gringa would be unlikely to get lost. The monosynaptic spark inside the blonde-fringed cranium was fully occupied by reproductive cravings: no synapse was available for higher thought. Debra flirted with danger, trapping herself inside love like a flea trapped between the teeth of a comb.

"Debra, where the bloody hell are you off to without a car?" she asked, although she already knew the answer.

"Just out for a walk," Debra answered.

"Then you won't mind if I come along," Yadira said.

Debra stammered and turned pink.

"Just kidding. You are mad, Debra! Puerto Pedriscal is no place to take a walk. There are vicious receptionist dogs fronting every house. You'd better take a stick to whack them with." She stopped to spray her throat; damned rats, leaving hairs and dander all over. "You know, Debra, some of us are not so fortunate. Some of us have to work, rather than cavorting around town in the presence of dubious company. I, for one, must spend all weekend in the lab examining mosquitoes for *Plasmodium*. I couldn't get a bloody thing done all week with that druggy filmmaker and his brainless assistant snooping around."

Debra headed for the door. "Bye," she said with a cheery wave as she stepped outside.

Earlier in the week, Yadira had overheard Rosalia and Milagros comparing Doctora Debra's virtue to the purity of a burned paper, and they weren't exactly virgins themselves. Debra's affair was no secret at INSA or elsewhere in Puerto Pedriscal and the gossips eagerly awaited the next titbit. Despite Yadira's warnings, the scatter-brained woman had far exceeded the limits of good taste.

ะี

Debra walked south, in the direction of town, with determination. It was going to be a long walk, but she had set out with plenty of time to spare. She walked past the kiosk, and turned a corner into an alley that led to Avenida Orinoco. A vagrant squatted, his pants bunched at his ankles, relieving himself, and she negotiated a precarious detour around him. She walked through the dusty heat along Avenida Orinoco, turned onto Avenida 23 de Enero, shaded by the mango trees, and threaded her way carefully through town, dodging growling dogs. It was a gloriously sunny day with a bright blue, cloudless sky, scalding hot but beautiful none the less. Although she sweated profusely, there was a springiness to her step.

She was happy because she had a feeling that today would finally be the day she and Segundo went through with "it". If Segundo had bought condoms, she would consent. She hadn't been able to concentrate properly on her work for several weeks—ever since the night they had watched satellites together. She would have consented long ago, but Segundo kept putting off a trip to the pharmacy, stalling, always with some lame excuse why he hadn't yet purchased them: he'd forgotten his wallet at home, supplies had run low and Huevo de Pava had failed to restock the brands he most liked (and he had very definite likes: the Ooosah imports were far too small to fit him, he didn't trust the natural skins with the black sheep drawn on the wrapper because he said it was like sliding his penis into a sausage wrapper, he trusted only reservoir tips with plenty of room to expand, he liked only the British brand wrapped in the golden package), he was bigger than most men (had she not noticed?) and so paracaídas were uncomfortable, latex smelled like burning tires and the fumes gave him terrible headaches, he would lose sensitivity, he would lose his erection if he had to stuff his penis inside a thick rubber shield that constricted the blood flow, did mi cielo not know that Ooosah manufactured all their export condoms a whole four cubic centimetres smaller than those made for national consumption and openly publicized the fact (a CIA tactic to make other nationalities feel inferior, to subtly demonstrate international superiority and dominance), was corazoncita absolutely certain she didn't use birth control pills, did amorcita not own a diaphragm, and what about those metal and plastic uterine contraptions that all americanas wore? "Mi vida, you mustn't be embarrassed to tell if me if you already use a contraceptive method, because I won't think less of you as a woman. In fact, I greatly admire a woman with the courage and audacity to come prepared." Once, a tree had fallen over the road and he had been trapped outside town in the forest all day, unable to reach the pharmacy before it closed. Another time, the supply barge containing the condom shipment, he claimed, had been so heavily overloaded with Polar beer that it had sunk.

She could stand it no longer, so excruciating was the torture. He tempted her and then held back. Why did he resist? He sometimes trembled, he wanted it so badly—every bit as much as she did—but he rambled on and on about the rhythm method and wouldn't listen to Debra's solid medical reasoning against it. Last time, he had pleaded with her to try a contraceptive powder made from ground-up white butterfly wings—she could easily capture the butterflies by herself if she urinated on the riverside, as butterflies were attracted by the salts in urine. That was the final straw. She finally cracked down and made him promise on *The Communist Manifesto* to buy condoms in time for their next meeting, even if he had to drive for three days and three nights without sleep to Ciudad Bolívar just to find one large enough (the organ in question looked about average to her, but she would never tell him so). With luck, today would be the day.

After a half-hour, she reached the town centre with enough time to spare for a snack at the Lunchería Manos de Dios. There she could freshen up, treating herself to a fresh banana shake and some cholesterol-laden, delicious, meat-filled, deep-fried corn pastries. Cholesterol was the precursor molecule of the sex hormones, and she hoped that she'd be putting hers to good use.

ॐ

Proverbs, 11:22—*Like a gold ring in a pig's snout is a beautiful woman who shows no discretion.*

There she was, the scientist, a false teacher, seductress of the unstable—everything his own pious wife, Esther, was not—sitting alone at a table, tempting even the straw in her fruit juice to sin with the caress of her tongue. A serpent transparently veiled with blonde, angelic hair.

Ronald resented the interference of those atheists in his work. The influence of the heretic Marshall could be felt at many of the missions. How could a pagan people who hadn't seen God's guiding light distinguish between the just plans of the righteous and the deceitful advice of the wicked. The innocent could be easily tempted into sin.

Outside the safety of the church lay corruption and peril—alcohol, scientific lies and lust—exemplified by her kind. Sometimes Ronald wondered why God tolerated someone who destroyed modesty and held in contempt good old-fashioned values to wander among the weak. God have pity on America.

She looked up, met his eyes steadily. "Hello. Would you care to join me?" she asked in English.

Ronald took a seat opposite her. God had hope even for transgressors, hope that they might be reached and turned back to Him. Ronald sat stiffly, sickeningly aware of his own discomfort. He could see without a doubt that she was a conniving woman who tempted men into sin, like Bathsheba, the adulterous wife of Uriah who tempted David. He removed his glasses, cleaned them carefully with a hanky he kept in his shirt pocket. She looked less shocking, more blurry, that way. He put back his glasses, spreading the SnugFit hinges to pull them past his temples, and her clear blue eyes snapped back into focus.

"I'm Debra." She held out her hand. Ronald accepted it with the smallest amount of trepidation.

"Deborah, who foretold the deliverance of the Israelites from their oppressor."

"Excuse me?"

"Ronald Elliot," he replied sternly, false confidence in his voice.

"I've seen you many times at the airport with your mission colleagues, but we have never had the opportunity to talk. I'm curious why so many of you are in Amazonas."

"It's our duty to bring the Gospel to this land, following the example of the brave men and women of our own country—the Puritans who quieted the wild call of Massachusetts with the Lord's music, and the circuit riders who week after week on horseback forged a path to the wild west. Now we bring the refuge of His word to this last wilderness frontier."

"Sounds like a lengthy agenda. You must be planning to stay here for a very long time."

"We will stay for as long as it takes us to change them."

"Change who?"

"Only through exposure to the Gospel of Jesus Christ, and

to biblical principles, can the spiritually disillusioned be saved. Then and only then can they grow throughout their lives and achieve eternal salvation," Ronald answered calmly.

"And how exactly will you achieve this metamorphosis?"

"We teach discipline and respect. The Gospel teaches alternatives, brings people hope through God's word."

"I don't intend to be disagreeable," she said—to Ronald, her voice sounded edgy—"but despite the strong mission presence here, I have yet to see any material benefit to evangelized native communities, even in rudimentary health care. What do you have to say about that?" She shut her jaw tightly and looked at him straight on, asking for a confrontation.

"The Bible says if you seek his kingdom and his righteousness then you will receive all. He intended for true believers to prosper, to not want for anything, material or otherwise. The fish's mouth will open wide to all those who trust in Him, if they have taken a vow of faith. Jesus Christ, our Lord and Saviour, gives believers seeds to sow. He provides, and will bless those with prosperity who are truly deserving. He willingly sacrificed the bread of His own body and the wine of His own blood for our consumption. If the Indians pray hard enough, and if they truly believe, whatever benefits they so desire they shall so receive. Plight is but a deficiency in faith."

Debra looked at him, her mouth slightly open, as if she couldn't think of an intelligent response. She slowly closed her mouth, then said, "I thought you Christians were supposed to be charitable."

"I don't expect you to understand. You are not versed in His word. We are all, yourself included, solely responsible for ourselves. What the Gospel offers is the means for people to become whatever they were meant to be. The Gospel shows us a better way, it allows us to better ourselves and allows us the joy of forging a relationship with God."

"So that's why you keep them at that church all day, singing and praying nonstop, when they could better spend the time looking for food. Sounds like oppression, if you ask me, hollering at them over your loudspeaker about the fires of hell."

"They must earn salvation to achieve happiness in heaven. They don't have to accept the Gospel. We don't force them. God says we must show respect to those in authority over us. We would not represent Him if we didn't ask the Indians to demonstrate faith. How else can we determine which of them has accepted God's word?"

As Ronald left the table, feeling more composed, he added, "I pray for your salvation, but you must change your perverse ways, for depravity does not go unpunished and to oppose His rectification is sheer stupidity." She sat blinking for a few seconds, then shrugged. "I will pray for you," he repeated.

Those like her who were governed by instinct and not by His wisdom would one day be held accountable for their actions; Ronald could scarcely begin to imagine what sort of punishment would best befit her crimes.

Debra finished her shake and pastry in fuming silence. What had she thought to accomplish? What had made her think a rational conversation with that smug pig was possible? He reminded her of Segundo when he jabbered endlessly about Marxist philosophy, or Marisol and her blackflies. There is no discussion with fanatics entrenched in their own version of truth. At least she knew how to distract Segundo from his stream of thought. She left the lunchería determined not to let that narrow-minded Ronald ruin her day. Stepping out the doorway, her stride quick and angry, she bumped into Raúl, the goddamn filmmaker.

"Whoa, baby, slow down. What's the rush?" he asked, rearranging his yellow bandanna; its corners were tied into knots to make a scalp-shaped pouch, and his thick, dark curls protruded from the sides. He was without his pretty assistant, but he carried his sixteen-millimetre camera.

"Sorry, Raúl, I really can't stay to chat. I'm afraid I'm late for an appointment. Nice day, isn't it? Very good to see you." She hurried off in the direction of Avenida Río Negro.

❦

Segundo had been waiting on the shady front porch of Tarzan's house for ten minutes. Perhaps she had stood him up. She had been so upset last time they met. He didn't blame her, for he knew he had given more mixed signals than the malfunctioning traffic lights at the Indian statue. But she finally did arrive. He watched her legs with relish as she climbed the long staircase bolted to the granite.

"No wonder this place is uninhabitable," she mused, looking up at the scorch marks on the sheet-metal walls.

"Hola, amorcita!" She climbed the last of the stairs and joined him on the porch. They stood for a moment looking down at the town while she caught her breath. Then they embraced and kissed, un lenguazo salty with sweat from her top lip.

"I have news for you. I found the curandero," she said, detaching herself from him. "He was outside the matadero, begging for scraps of meat."

"Scraps are better than none at all."

"He should be in the hospital, where he can receive treatment. He's dying, you know."

"Maybe I shouldn't have forced him to the hospital against his wishes. Maybe he should be allowed to die with dignity, according to his own beliefs. He wasn't able to accept your medicine. You may find the younger people are more willing to accept change. It's too late for him. If I return him to the hospital, he will only run away again." They held hands, looking at the street fifty feet beneath them, the roofs of houses and the tops of mango trees.

"What about the tuberculosis he's spreading to his people?"

"Corazoncita, there are already so many infected that he'll make little difference."

"You don't understand, Segundo. He didn't complete his course of medication. He may spread resistant strains of the bacillus and that puts everyone at risk."

227

"He won't go back. I'll speak to him, but the only way I could get him to return would be to club him over the head and carry him in unconscious." They didn't speak for a moment. "Come on, let's get out of here," said Segundo.

He drove through town, onto the Olvidado highway. He thought it would do them both good to relax on an excursion before they became more intimate. He drove for about thirty minutes out of Puerto Pedriscal, past a hacienda, mile after mile of light green savannah fenced off with barbed wire, massive black beasts grazing placidly behind the fence. "Water buffalo–cattle crosses," he said. "They are owned by a rich Caracas family, la familia del Doctor Aguirre. The cross was introduced because buffalo are well adapted to the heat and seasonal extremes of wetness and dryness." They continued down the highway until they reached a black mountain, a monolithic dome of granite with a smaller dome to one side. "That's La Tortuga. You see it resembles a turtle, the shell and head. I guided a scientist up there once. A French Ph.D who specialized in the study of lichens and mosses. He collected one hundred and three different species of lichens; some he said were unique to Amazonas and some he thought to be unique to that mountaintop."

The ascent was up long slabs with tiny fingerholds that sometimes flaked off. Segundo stayed behind Debra to give her support when she needed it, and enjoyed the view up her short skirt. Debra had tied her blouse up under her breasts and the sweat glistened on the small of her back. Vultures circled overhead in thermals generated by the sun heating the black granite. The summit was a mixture of thickets and bare dark rock. Segundo and Debra peered into strange pockets in the rock where water had collected and tiny black-and-yellow frogs had taken up residence. To the west lay the great Orinoco River, the metallic surface reflecting blue sky. Beyond stretched the Colombian grasslands, and far in the distance to the west there lay a distant vertical escarpment with twin waterfalls, the limit of his Piaroa friends' territory.

He led her down an easier way into the forest, to a spot where a stream deepened into clear pools on gently sloping granite, water falling over rock like transparent silk. They sat together on a natural bench in one of the pools and sipped a very smooth rum, he in his bathing suit and Debra in only a bikini bottom. "This is all very pleasant, Segundo," she said, "but I think you're stalling." She wouldn't allow him any further delay, and he didn't think he could withstand the congestion in his groin any longer.

"I still haven't had time to buy the paracaídas, mi amor," he confessed.

"No more excuses. We're going to buy them right now." She climbed out of the pool and put on her clothes. "Come on. I'm not letting an erection that size go to waste." It was time for him to face the inevitable.

He drove back down to town, turned on Avenida 23 de Enero and stopped first at the outdoor mercado to buy some fish for their dinner. The stalls and aisles were busy and Segundo worried that the fish would be picked over.

"How about the caribe?" Debra asked.

"Amorcita, it's not the best-tasting fish."

"Maybe it would do you some good," she said. Segundo heard the taunting tone of her voice. "It has some very interesting qualities."

He bought her the caribe. It really wasn't his favourite fish; it had a slimy texture that repulsed him, and there was even a nice rayado catfish for sale. But he wouldn't refuse her today. The last time had been too traumatic. Her previous tolerance and humour had evaporated when he'd teased her about grinding up butterflies and she had finally broken down, her tears searing his heart spirituously as aguardiente. He had held her sobbing on his chest, smoothing her hair, trying to soothe her with whispers, but she didn't stop, leaving wet darkened patches on his red shirt. "I don't understand. If you really loved me the way you claim, then you'd go straight to the pharmacy," she cried, beating his chest with her clenched fists, and he promised he'd buy the paracaídas in time for their next meeting.

It wasn't that he didn't want to be intimate; he wanted nothing more. It shamed him to admit his cowardice, it wasn't manly, but the mere thought of going into the farmacia to buy paracaídas from Huevo de Pava made him limp with embarrassment.

He parked around the corner from the pharmacy and left Debra sitting in the jeep. He waited until the pharmacy was empty of customers and then entered. At first he looked furtively at the shampoos, soaps and toothpastes. "Buenos días, Señor Gallo," Huevo de Pava said amicably. "Can I be of service?" Naturalmente, the paracaídas were not out on display.

"I require anticonceptivos," Segundo replied, in the straightforward tone of voice that he usually reserved for giving proletarian speeches.

Huevo de Pava nodded slowly with understanding, the gaps in his teeth displayed annoyingly in a beatific grin. "Ah, amigo, and what sort of *an-ti-con-cep-ti-vos* would you like?"

"The safest, of course," Segundo said rapidly without hesitation, upon which Huevo de Pava pulled out a large selection of birth control pills. "No, no, hombre." Segundo felt his palms sweat and his chest become tight. "I need the latex type, the type for the man to use."

Several customers, women, waited behind Segundo for his transaction to finish. Huevo de Pava grinned, the freckles dotting the bridge of his nose dancing gaily. He dumped out an assortment which he arranged, ever so slowly, interminably, in a long chain the length of the glass countertop: the British Dorados, the natural skins, the gringo Ramses and Trojans, the capitalist Shelks, smooth ones, ribbed ones, those with reservoir tips, every colour of the rainbow, including cheerful yellow. "If I may make a suggestion," said Huevo de Pava. "These"—he held one up towards the heavens, in the light, for all the world to see. "These are designed specifically with the woman's pleasure in mind. They have small ridges to stimulate." The women behind Segundo snickered and Segundo felt his ears grow hot. Segundo selected the Dorados and asked for a hundred of them. "Remember," Huevo de Pava advised, slowly and clearly, "preservativos are best used before the expiration date, so you must use all of them expediently." Coño, next time Segundo travelled to Ciudad Bolívar he swore he would buy a lifetime's supply, to hell and carajo and back with the expiration date.

He handed Debra the large paper bag as he climbed into the driver's seat. "My, my," she said. "It looks like you're planning to make up for lost time." This bandit woman had stolen his heart, she held it in her bare hands and squeezed until it bled when she wanted something from him. He couldn't believe it, he had succumbed to the lure of a capitalist.

They ate the fried caribe washed down with premium rum, under the watchful eyes of Communist workers. He told her of the horrific experience at the pharmacy. Her laughter and the warmth of the rum soothed his bruised ego and they retreated to his hammock. To make love in a chinchorro required great skill. She was inexperienced, but Segundo taught her, his knees embedded in cloth, how to use the confined space, the yielding and the enveloping folds. He had heard it described as two cats trapped inside a pillow case, but with his experience he guided his amorcita to the depths of ardour. Afterward they lay together, wrapped inside his chinchorro like a bat and its young engulfed by wings.

19

A small boy sat on a vinyl examination table in the out-patients' clinic, his father nervously watching Amador examine him. Neither father nor child spoke Spanish. Flaking scabs and pustules encrusted the boy's entire face. Impetigo? Probablemente. The boy kept his head lowered. Amador tried to lift the chin, but it resisted. What should be simple cases could be so difficult. Amador's best hope of ensuring a complete course of treatment with antibiotics was to admit the boy to hospital. But then the father would believe the condition to be fatal, and they might go into hiding. Without an interpreter, Amador had no way of explaining the treatment to the father. He could only hope the father understood that they were to return daily until the condition had properly cleared up. He nodded as though he did.

Amador smiled and ruffled the boy's hair, and the boy jumped off the table and hugged him tightly. Amador allowed the boy to bury his contagious face into his lab coat, and he caressed the scabby, grimy hair at the back of the head with his bare hand. Debra pried the child from around Amador's waist and led father and son to the door.

Amador didn't like the helplessness he felt when he succumbed to sympathy. Countless silent faces, case histories, lesion after lesion—impersonality helped maintain his sanity. He tried to shut out the pain and suffering from his mind, but sometimes lost his emotional control. He couldn't always reduce people to medical specimens. The boy looked back at Amador as his father pulled him by the hand out the door. The dark eyes searching from behind the scabby mask stayed with Amador.

Debra unbuttoned her lab coat. "Amador, remember to wash your hands." She draped her coat over her arm.

"Before you leave, chama, there is another case I want to discuss with you, and I trust you'll keep it in the strictest confidence. Pedro Aguirre, the gran cacao—you remember, he had a dermatitis in the crural region?"

"How could I forget? He was scratching himself like a mangy dog." She laughed. "A classic contact dermatitis, wasn't it?"

"Clásico. De repente, a reaction to laundry detergent. But, it's the strangest thing. He has been using hydrocortisone for weeks now. Nada. The cream has been no more effective than would be toothpaste." The way Pedro carried on like a billygoat rutting for young nannies made him wonder—might not the condition be related to Pedro's insatiable sexual appetite? The lesion, however, was unlike any sexually transmitted disease known to Amador.

"Has he tried prednisone?"

"Prednisone soothed the itch initially, but now the fire in his groin is burning as badly as ever."

"I wonder," Debra said. "I saw the most peculiar case the other day. Someone showed me a typical case of contact dermatitis that he said was caused by brujería. He claimed that our medicine wouldn't cure it. What do you think of that, Amador?"

"If you believe that, then I would say you've been out in the Amazonian sun for too long."

"The superstition is based upon fact. The brujo sprinkles ground-up pica pica on underpants drying outdoors on a clothesline. If the irritant was administered on a frequent basis, I think the patient would react despite treatment."

"I'll pass that along to Aguirre." Amador picked up a large cardboard box containing plastic vials, each partially full of sputum curds, and placed it up on the examination table. "Chama, could you take this box of moco to Reina?" He rubbed his chin. "Have you been skin-tested? You know, with tuberculosis as common as it is here, you should, and you should think about getting a BCG inoculation if you're negative. You'll convert eventually; everyone does. It's better to receive the attenuated BCG strain first rather than a drug-resistant one. It may not provide complete protection, but it would at least improve your immunity."

"You're right, Amador. I'll have Reina test me right away." Debra put her lab coat inside the sputum box and carried it out the door. He heard her footsteps fade down the hallway. There had been symbolic paraphernalia left at Aguirre's doorstep suggesting brujería. Maybe there was some truth to Debra's suggestion. "There are dangers other than tuberculosis that one should worry about. Take care of yourself, chama," he said out loud to the empty room.

❦

Reina looked at the wall clock. There was just enough time before lunch for her to perform a skin test on Debra. She walked around the Plaza Bolívar to the storage room, where she rummaged through the -20° freezer and found a vial of purified protein derivative which she would use to conduct the test. It was in a wire basket near the very bottom, and while she was looking she found something else as well, something that made her skin prickle. She put the PPD in one pocket of her lab coat and the spine-pierced paper in the other.

She returned to her lab and filled a tuberculin syringe with 0.1 millilitres of diluent containing approximately five units of PPD. Debra sat on a tall stool beside the tiled lab bench. Reina rubbed Debra's skinny white forearm with an alcohol-soaked cotton ball and injected the PPD subcutaneously. "Ouch! You could have let the alcohol dry first," Debra said.

Reina dropped the spine-pierced paper into Debra's lap. "What's that?" Debra asked, staring at the paper.

"Open it. See for yourself."

Debra pulled out one spine from the folded white paper,

then another and another, seven in all. She unfolded the paper and smoothed it on the white tile. "Reina, all it has on it is 'Doctor Diego Velázquez' written seven times. What's it for?"

"I am not sure but, lamentablemente, it appears someone wishes harm to befall the doctor," said Reina.

"It is brujería," Soledad said without looking up from the laminar flow cabinet, her voice muffled behind a surgical mask. She dotted bacterial culture onto a glass slide with an inoculation loop. She flamed the tube, capped it and flamed the loop, then twisted around to face Reina and Debra, only her bright eyes showing above the green mask.

"If I discover who planted it in the freezer, I'll issue a memorandum condemning his behaviour," Reina said.

"Reina, you don't seriously believe in this brujo stuff?" Debra asked as she fingered the paper.

"No, Debra, I do not. But I am concerned that a staff member should harbour ill wishes against our director. You're an extranjero, you can't possibly understand the implications of allowing such disrespect."

Reina put her lab coat down over her chair and put on her sunglasses. She turned to look out of the louvred glass windows overlooking the Orinoco. Soledad, minus the surgical mask, stood at the sink facing the windows. The finished cultural smears were ready for staining. Reina saw Soledad wipe her eye; she had been crying again. "Soledad, aren't you going down with the transport for lunch?" she asked.

"I'm not hungry, Reina. I really would rather stay up here and stain these slides, and I also have to digest sputum samples."

Reina worried about Soledad—so many problems for a teenager to cope with. It made her own burden of troubles with Ignacio seem almost manageable. Ignacio would move to Puerto Pedriscal when he finished the ratification of his Madrid medical degree in Caracas, so that they could again live like a normal married couple. Yesterday she had telephoned him from the CANTV station. She had waited three hours for her call to connect. Alone in a dark wooden stall like a vertical coffin, facing the impersonal grey telephone, she had heard his distant voice: "I had some problems." He had failed the internal medicine exam on his first try, and now pathology. He might never ratify at this rate. She didn't want to eat alone today. Even Debra's company was better than none. "Would you like to have lunch with me at my house?" she asked.

"That would be nice. What would you like me to do with this so-called brujería?"

"Leave it on the bench for now. I want to show it to the doctor when he returns from Caracas."

❧

Soledad knew the brujería had been done by Cheo. All the técnicos knew. But she would never tell Reina. Soledad too felt resentful towards INSA and the doctor. Cheo's poison had spread throughout the centre, a bitterness like black tobacco juice. Soledad folded the paper and resealed it, sliding the seven pijiguao spines back into their original holes. The paper had a damp feel to it—freezer condensation.

If only there had been alternatives. But a week ago Velázquez had given her notice terminating her employment. The ministry would no longer allow a Colombian to work at the centre, not without a constancia indicating application had been made for Venezuelan citizenship. Even if she had the money to travel to Caracas, constancias were next to impossible to obtain without money to bribe an immigration official. She would have to complete Cheo's brujería. She put the spine-sealed paper into a Pyrex beaker.

Soledad didn't know what else she could do. She had her mother, sister and illegitimate niece to care for. How could she do it without a job? She couldn't focus on her work. She couldn't eat, sleep. She wanted to scream, to tear her hair out by the roots, to gouge herself with her fingernails, but she couldn't. At night, when sleep eluded her, she craved the fresh air of a walk. She couldn't even do that—it was too dangerous. She had hit bottom, absolute bottom, nothing could be any lower. The comfort of being held closely, feeling loved, that was what she had wanted. Instead, in seven more months she would have yet another mouth to feed, and that would be impossible without her wages. Soledad removed the bottle of absolute alcohol from the refrigerator and poured a capful into the beaker with the paper. She lit a match and dropped it onto the spiny paper. Blue flames engulfed the paper and it shrank, edges glowing red, turning brown and then black. The beaker's contents burned to completion. There was no turning back. Carbon ash, thin and light as the wind, rested at the bottom.

She walked outside into the full noon heat and shook the black ashes out on the sidewalk. Ash scattered in the rising heat. Most blew towards the central courtyard, where the weeds had grown so tall that only Simón Bolívar's metallic forehead and sculpted bronze hair protruded above them. A curl of carbonized paper hit a support beam and stuck there.

Soledad returned to the lab, ignored the slides at the sink waiting to be stained and dumped some methylene blue powder, used to stain cytoplasm, into the beaker that had once contained the brujería, the black residue still at the bottom. She poured fifty millilitres of distilled water into a graduated cylinder and added seventy percent ethanol until she had brought the total volume up to the hundred-millilitre mark. Then she poured the alcohol-water mixture into the beaker containing the dye.

❦

Debra and Reina walked from the parking lot towards the laboratories. Debra's stomach didn't feel quite right. Lunch with Reina had been a fiasco—Reina had cried for the duration because she missed her husband in Caracas and she wanted nothing more than to join him, but she couldn't afford to leave her job. Reina didn't mention the brujería, and Debra was disappointed because she wanted to know more about it. Reina made spaghetti for lunch, a poor choice in Puerto Pedriscal because it always came infested with weevils. The adult weevils weren't a problem; most of the black bodies could be shaken out before boiling and the few remaining floated to the surface of the boiling water and were easily removed. The white larvae and eggs embedded in the spaghetti strands were not so easily discernible, didn't float to the surface and were too small to be picked out with a fork. Debra had managed to eat her helping by not looking too closely at the plate.

They walked past the new library to the sidewalk around the Plaza Bolívar. Debra's white jeans brushed against a support beam outside the door to Reina's lab, and something sooty smudged her pants and white running shoes black. "Shit," she said in English as she tried to brush the marks off.

"Debra, watch your mouth with those groserías," Reina said as she opened the door to her lab. Her English was better than Debra had thought.

Soledad was at the microscope, didn't bother to look up to greet Reina or Debra.

"Soledad, methylene blue isn't used for a Ziehl–Neelsen stain. Where did it come from?" Reina demanded. She was obsessively fussy about lab cleanliness. Debra had noticed that if Reina had no lab work, she would repeatedly clean imaginary dirt from the benches to maintain the appearance of productivity in her lab.

Soledad looked up, backlit from the louvred windows. "Fermin was here. He used it and he used that beaker too."

"Typical male cochino," Reina snapped. She tossed her sunglasses onto her desk and they slid across the surface until they hit the wall.

❧

Yadira and Inmaculada left the lab early that day. They spent all night catching anopheline mosquitoes.

"Hello! Hello!" Yadira said when she arrived home at seven the next morning. No answer, how odd. Debra couldn't have gone up to INSA, the transport never came that early. She had probably taken advantage of Yadira's absence to sneak off and spend the night with the rooster chap.

Yadira dragged herself to the back of the house and collapsed into a chinchorro. Her chest constricted uncomfortably.

Catching anopheline mosquitoes was an unpleasant task. Sitting up all night inside a thatch hut, dusk till dawn, twelve consecutive hours. Biting frequency peaked twice, once shortly after darkness fell and again just before sunrise. During daylight hours, the mosquitoes disappeared, hiding in cool, moist vegetation. Catching them meant missing sleep, and that was that.

She and Inmaculada had fought off sleepiness and fatigue. They had talked, but only softly. When a mosquito pricked, they waited a few seconds for complete proboscis insertion, then turned on a torch covered with red cellophane and sucked the mosquito into a mouth-operated trap. The procedure was risky for the researcher because it required actual biting to occur. The researcher had to take antimalarial drugs prophylactically or risk malaria. Although no one else at INSA did, Yadira and Inmaculada took chloroquine because of their added risk. Yadira swore that it aggravated her allergies, but what a choice: lungs ruined by chloroquine or a liver ruined by malarial parasites.

She dozed off and woke up when her flatmate returned.

"Yadira, Soledad died this morning," Debra said, her face bleak. No warning, no preliminary comforting words—blunt.

Yadira gasped. "What? How?"

"I've been at the hospital with Amador all night. Yesterday, during lunch hour, Soledad drank a solution of methylene blue dye. Reina noticed the blue stain on her teeth and tongue and Soledad admitted what she had done. I don't think she meant to kill herself, poor girl. I think she was just pleading for help. Amador did all he could to save her. Last night, he said the only chance was to send her to Caracas. But the methylene blue seeped inside her cells so quickly that she took on a blue tinge by late evening and one by one her biological functions shut down. He couldn't stabilize her. She died at five this morning. It was so senseless."

Yadira felt as if she might choke. "Why?"

"Velázquez apparently terminated her employment. I think she was pretty desperate. But unfortunately that wasn't all. Aguirre discovered that she was about two months pregnant. He has agreed to keep quiet about it, and he wrote 'accidental poisoning' on the death certificate."

Yadira couldn't breathe. She felt herself swoon and she knew that vasodilatation had caused her blood pressure to plummet. Debra managed to help her into her little car and drove her quickly to the hospital. All Yadira could do was make squeaking noises.

❦

Debra stayed with Yadira, dozing off and on in an uncomfortable vinyl chair beside her bed. Yadira had been given epinephrine, put on a saline drip and then dosed heavily with antihistamines. She slept soundly.

Debra watched a succession of patients coming in and out of emergency. No matter what the ailment, they received a saline drip. A child with a sprained ankle was hooked up to a drip; likewise a woman who had miscarried. Often, the drip was the only treatment given. The newly graduated physicians who staffed the hospital on obligatory rural medical service were, for the most part, completely unprepared for anything serious.

A stretcher rolled in, a man strapped down, screaming and thrashing, arms and legs tied to the sides of the stretcher. He too was placed on a saline drip, while the rural pasantes fluttered around him unable to decide what to do next. He screamed and moaned nonstop for half an hour. Debra almost wished the poor man would die and be relieved of his suffering.

"What's wrong with that patient?" Debra asked one of the pasantes.

"He attempted suicide, swallowed a can of Baygon insecticide."

The moaning and groaning gradually diminished, stopping after an hour.

At noon Amador's sleepy face appeared at the door.

"Chama, we made arrangements to send Yadira back to Caracas on tomorrow's flight. Her allergies are so severe, I think it safest to remove her from the source of the antigens to which she is hypersensitive. Go home now, chama, and get some rest. There's nothing you can do here"

Debra didn't ask him how the Baygon victim was doing. She really preferred not to know.

20

Diego Velázquez looked at the signatures beside the official mosquito-logo stamp confirming the attendance of co-ordinators at the thirty-eighth meeting of the Technical Commission. All the co-ordinators, except Yadira, of course, would attend: Reina, Marisol, Fermin, Blancanieves and Debra.

The loss of Yadira and Soledad so soon after Wilfred gave Velázquez good reason to be concerned. His small centre could not sustain such staffing losses, and those people would have to be replaced as soon as possible. He also had finances to think about. Medical research was expensive, and he really needed that Tropical Disease Research grant from the World Health Organization to sustain his institute for another few years. He had just completed a very convincing proposal, an entire year's work. Before the opening of his new library, he had spoken to officials in Geneva and they had said INSA looked promising. They had all but confirmed the grant. He was ninety-nine percent confident he would get it. But first the staff. His institute would be in good shape if he found replacements before the fiscal year's end. It should be easy to find two postgraduates at either Universidad Central or, preferably, Universidad Simón Bolívar. A couple of years at INSA was a good stepping-stone for any young scientist. As for refilling the technical position, he just had to dangle a small salary at the local high school. Employment was difficult to come by here in Amazonas.

He glanced at his wristwatch—5:37. The co-ordinators would be sitting waiting for him by now, his space at the table's head respectfully empty. He stood up, newspaper in hand, turned off the air-conditioner and switched off the lights. He strode past the new library to the conference room.

The chairs to either side of his were left conspicuously empty. Velázquez took his seat and unfolded the newspaper before him. Ever since Soledad's death a month before, INSA had been as solemn as a morgue. A few days after the initial shocked silence, wailing and mourning began in earnest and institutional productivity began a slow decline. Grief, however, could be turned into an incentive for work, the useless energy expended mourning rechannelled into research. He cleared his throat softly, his hands folded on top of the newspaper.

"In the past months, each of us has suffered a great sense of personal loss and personal responsibility, myself included. This is a natural reaction to tragedy. We are isolated here and our institute is very small, so in a sense we are one close-knit family. We must, however, now help one another to continue past our personal grief and allow the healing process to begin.

"I want each and every one of you to read this newspaper article. These are difficult economic and social times for all of Venezuela. It should come as no surprise that many of our young people are troubled and confused, particularly in our rural communities, and this has prompted many to take their own lives. Suicide among young adults has reached epidemic proportions. None of us should feel in any way responsible for another's choice of action. The suicide epidemic is a social problem and this institute is in no way responsible. We must recover and continue with our personal and professional duties. At such a time of loss, hard and dedicated work is therapeutic. Our grieving for our lost comrades can be a monument to their memory, a monument of achievement. Think of the lives we can save by applying our knowledge and skills in medical science. Those lives saved can be a testament to those we have lost. Venezuela needs us, Amazonas needs us. People need this institute to eradicate the misery of tropical illness from their lives."

He remained silent for a few moments to allow for maximum impact, his head raised proudly and his eyes resting briefly, personally, on each co-ordinator, but not inviting verbal

243

response. He continued in his metered voice, "In order to accomplish immediate research goals, we will be undertaking two expeditions in the near future. The first, two weeks from this date, will be a study of an outbreak of respiratory disease—mostly tuberculosis—in a Piaroa community, to be conducted by the Coordinadora de Microbiología, Reina, and in light of our technical loss, Salvador will assist. The other expedition, after the Christmas season, will be undertaken in the Yanomami territory of Porohóa to obtain more specimens of *Plasmodium* and filariae and to conduct more experimental infections of simuliids. Marisol, Coordinadora de Biología de Vectores, will be in charge of that expedition. Cheo, as usual, will assist. Naturalmente, medical expertise is required on both occasions and attendance by the Co-ordinator of Medical Services is both requested and required. I expect everyone"—he hesitated, to emphasize his concluding remark with a sweep of his gaze around the table—"*everyone* to dedicate utmost concentration to the preparations for these expeditions."

ಃ

Debra sat cross-legged, head bent down, on the battleship-grey floor of the living room, two large beetles waddling in front of her. Tonight's meeting hadn't droned on for too long, thank goodness, and even Marisol had had little to say.

Wilfred's death had been a shock. Everyone felt guilty about disliking him, and emotional recovery had just begun when Soledad killed herself. Her death had been much more traumatic. All of the technicians had known her for years. Everyone, without exception, liked her—even Debra, who had hardly spoken to the girl. Her death was so senseless—and so ugly. She remained conscious and lucid, with her blue-stained teeth and lips, until just before she died, scared and confused. INSA echoed with questions and "if only" scenarios. Why had no one been aware of her desperation? Why did no one know about the man in her life? If only they had recognized the warning signs. If only she had confided in someone. If only they had been closer friends. If only they had spoken to the ministry on her behalf. Had she really wanted to kill herself or had she been pleading for help? All the laughter in the miserable institute had been extinguished along with Soledad. Poor Cheo was hit the hardest. He had hardly spoken a word to anyone since her death. He seemed, for some reason, to feel more than his share of responsibility.

If Soledad had been born in the U.S. she would still be alive. In Latin America she had been trapped in the grip of poverty. In the U.S. an intelligent girl like her would have had choices and opportunities. She would be attending university at this moment, probably on a scholarship. She would not be bloated, decomposing, packed six feet under parched, iron-stained earth. Huevo de Pava was at least partly to blame, because his gossip made it so shameful to buy contraception.

Velázquez, the detached son of a bitch—how Debra had grown to despise him! Yet the ceaseless mourning had been emotionally destructive, and the preparation required for an expedition would perhaps enable people to refocus their thoughts. Nevertheless, Debra had her own very personal reason for not wanting to leave Puerto Pedriscal, even for a few days. Her endorphins were flowing so copiously that a few days would seem like an eternity. She looked down the hall to the back door.

She prodded the larger beetle, about four inches long, with a twig. It grasped the twig with a powerful set of clawlike mandibles and she dragged it about a foot across the floor before it yielded. She wondered how many pounds per square inch of pressure those mandibles could exert. A grillo, that type of little cricket that liked to live indoors, chirped loudly from the corner. It had been driving her crazy for days now. The shrill noise reverberated around the otherwise silent house. Even the rats seemed to have gone—probably taken the flight to Caracas to be with Yadira. Just bugs for company now.

If only Segundo weren't so prudish. He could come to the

house freely, without fear of gossip, now that Yadira wasn't here to intimidate him. Nevertheless, he remained paranoid. What was his problem? His jeep was practically undetectable at night when he hid it behind the plantain bushes. She sometimes managed to beat his objections down (although it meant getting him to the stage where he wouldn't be able to walk anyway) and persuade him to stay all night, but he always made sure he left before sunrise, sometimes without even waking her to say goodbye.

Was this love, the way he filled her thoughts more and more? Her initial lust (still as potent, thank goodness) had deepened into a "relationship"—trust, care, friendship. How could she feel this way about a macho Communist? Maybe he came with the environment of Amazonas. Her sense of values and judgement had definitely taken a beating lately. The tropical sun seemed to foment confusion; the relentless heat coagulated grey matter like boiled eggs.

❦

Segundo killed the jeep's headlights before he reached the Evangelist church. He saw a light on in a room at the back of the church, and he didn't want to be spotted driving up the alley to the plantain bushes. Pebbles and clumps of hardened clay crunched deafeningly underneath the tires, but nobody appeared at the lit window.

He entered the house by the back door without knocking first, as he now did routinely. A knock to announce his arrival might also alert the next-door neighbours, a dangerous move. He found his capitalista on the floor playing with two enormous brown beetles. He had always thought her to be just a little strange, but ever since the poor young girl at INSA had died and the doctora antipática had taken ill her behaviour had become even stranger. Many nights he found her padlock-faced, lips clamped, too mournful to grieve. Playing with bugs—surely this time she had gone completamente loca, her mind spinning

246

fast, faster, around and around and around like a perinola top.

He bent over her shoulder to watch the two bichos. "Maybe they are a mother and her child," he said.

"The mother has nothing to do with her babies after the eggs are laid, and then they hatch into grubs. I think it highly unlikely that a female would recognize her young after it had metamorphosed from its larval stage. I thought perhaps they might be a pair, male and female, but they aren't very interested in one another. See?" She looked up at him, oddly hypnotized, then back down at the bichos. She pushed a twig into the larger beetle's mandíbulas and dragged it face to face with the smaller. The bichote let go and the two stood doing nothing. Their eyes were placed on the sides of their heads and Segundo wondered if they could even see each other head on. "Maybe they are different species, not completely related to one another. They won't even fight. Look how pretty they are," Debra said. They weren't exactly pretty. Long brown dates, antennae even longer than the bodies, and mandibles capable of removing a human finger.

"Then maybe it's not their mating season. But it's ours." Segundo pulled her up off the floor, and carried her, slung over his shoulder like a load of tubers, to the bed, the one in the big bedroom, sheets still crumpled from their night before.

They made love in the soft blue glow from the television. She was wild, insatiable. Each night she wanted more from him, and her inner heat fuelled him to plunge to greater depths. Her body, slick with sweat, shone in the dim light. The small electric fan beside the bed whirled steadily, drowning out their rhythms, inadequate to cool their passions or to dry the damp sheets and their wet bodies. Afterward Segundo, satisfied as a fat rooster, propped upright with pillows, looked down at her languid body stretched naked beside him, her navel a pozo—a clear Amazonian pool. He dreamed of shrinking and swimming in that miniature pool of their combined lust, its soft cream beaches cushioning the pains of corporeal reality.

"I have to go on two expeditions soon. I'll miss you." She

rolled over and lay on her stomach, her cheek against the pillow. The little pool drained into the bedsheets.

His eyes followed the ghostly female curves illuminated by the silent television screen, the twin dimples of shade low on her back. "Where are you going?"

"First a Piaroa community, then after the holidays to Porohóa, where the American missionaries are working." She lay with one arm curled above her head. "Marisol tells me the Porohóa area is very beautiful."

"A native activist group from Bolívar state is demanding the expulsion of all New World missionaries, and it's accusing them of fomenting ethnocide. It united with a progressive native faction here in Amazonas, and collectively they have been organizing a demonstration."

"Possibly a Communist ploy to create political unrest?" She smiled, eyes closed.

"It has nothing to do with the party. The activists are fed up with New World's intervention in their communities."

Debra sighed, nestled the side of her face deeper into her pillow. "They'd be far better off if they had never seen the likes of any of us, but do you honestly think a demonstration will do a damn bit of good?"

"Amorcita, without documentation to verify the accusation they don't stand a chance. They haven't one céntimo's worth of written evidence. The New World Mission has been brushing up to our monkey government and feeding it bananas for years now. Your Ooosah government has pressured the monkey to maintain a strong gringo presence, which they justify as necessary to combat the threat of Communism. I am certain that it's really because Ooosah wants control of Amazonian minerals. They are afraid Castro will get his hands on the uranium first if they don't safeguard it."

"Uranium? Here?"

"There are areas in the Territory where native people don't travel. To many native people these areas are forbidden, sacred and inhabited by spirits. It is said that anyone daring to trespass there will become very ill, and will lose all his hair and maybe even die. In reality the effects are caused by the radioactivity produced in very, very rich uranium deposits. Of course, everyone in the Territory knows that New World missionaries are operatives of the CIA. They are here to grab the stakes, to safeguard the uranium for Ooosah."

"Well, Segundo, if they are CIA agents, they're not very good at their jobs," Debra objected. "They waste a lot of time trying to convert people to Christianity. I've spoken to the missionaries myself. They are fanatical, but no way are they CIA operatives."

"It's their cover."

"They actually think they're helping people, saving them from an eternity of burning damnation. They have the very best of intentions. One of them even foolishly tried to convert me. You can't go around spreading unsubstantiated accusations, Segundo. That CIA rumour is absolutely ridiculous." Debra yawned and her eyes watered.

"As soon as they learned that they might be expelled, the missionaries took action to prevent it. People who demand expulsion are accused of being agitators of Marxism and threatened with incarceration. That sounds like CIA tactics to me. Mi vida, what do you know of the CIA? Do you know about the murder of Allende? Do you know about all the legally elected Latin American governments that have been ousted by the CIA? Do you know how many trees in our selva were chain-sawed using World Bank money given in the name of democracy to fight Communism?"

"All right, Segundo, you made some legitimate points, but in the missionaries' case I think you're way off base, and your accusations are nothing more than exaggerated rumours." She reached over to him and rested her hand upon his brown knee. "Relax, go wash off and we can get some sleep. We can even cuddle together if we don't get too hot."

"I will tell you a story." Segundo played with a strand of her hair as he spoke, his voice a caress. "Once upon a time—in a banana republic where millennia of volcanic eruptions and weathering of rock created fertile black volcanic soils—there lived a people defenceless as small bugs, seventy-five percent illiterate and with an average life-span of forty. The land and its people were visited by a hungry banana spider, United Fruit Company, offspring of a much larger arachnid, Imperialist Ooosah. United Fruit spun her silk fine and soft and the web grew, insidiously at first. It sparkled with pearls of morning dew and the bugs, hypnotized by its attractiveness, didn't notice the first tiny ants hanging in the silk. But Jacobo Arbenz Guzmán was idealistic and observant, and he took notice of the giant spider and realized that she consumed all the little bugs accumulating in her web, that the spider sucked the very blood from them until they were hollow shells. He knew the glittering web meant certain death for the defenceless.

"By this time the United Fruit web spanned the land. Silk clung to every resource, all the way from the sky to the finest root hairs, to every grain of rich dark soil. The web had grown so large that it no longer glittered with dew in the sunlight. It attracted dust loosened by the republic's turmoil. The web, caked in dirt, had grown to the point where it trapped all the sun's rays and soaked up light, shadowing the ground beneath it. The spider had entwined the entire economy, even the railroad, telephone and mail.

"The bugs decided that the spider had overstayed her welcome. They elected Arbenz as president of the republic, legally, by their own will, by democratic vote. Arbenz had wings and he flew around the web with agrarian reform and nationalization. Bit by bit he snipped individual silk strands. At the edges of the web, the first light filtered through the mat of silk, shining onto the soil once again. The silk looked fragile, but its tensile strength—tough, stronger even than steel—surprised Arbenz. The silk wasn't only tough but pliable, it could adjust, anticipating the movements of defenceless bugs and their winged leader. The spider bent the tempered steel will of the bugs until she broke it. As Arbenz chewed at individual silk strands with his bare teeth, United Fruit spun her web straight across the continent to the mother arachnid, Imperialist Ooosah, who classified the winged gnat as a pro-Soviet Communist. Ooosah's CIA was instructed to swat the legally elected gnat and replace him with a pro-Imperialist dung beetle, Colonel Castillo Armas.

"On a day bedazzled by sun filtering through the web, on a budget as short as a poor man's telegram, the CIA falsified a coup with a few hundred men, two American volunteer bombers, a handful of Molotov cocktails and phony radio broadcasts. Arbenz tumbled, tangled in the silk; he believed his government under siege. Castillo Armas, feeling the gnat thrashing against the sticky silk, homed in to assist in the kill.

"To maintain the illusion of democracy, there was an election, a blasphemy in the name of free choice. Ooosah ensured that their dung beetle, Castillo Armas, was the only bug to crawl in the race. He was elected, naturalmente, and he too sat entrapped by the web, on the promise that he wouldn't be consumed. With his back legs he rolled balls of dung to fertilize United Fruit's bananas. He promptly retied their severed strands of silk, all the assets that had been painstakingly cut by Arbenz's national reform. The bugs paid back in full with their blood, sweat and poverty. Their juices were once again sucked out and their desiccated skeletons adorned the web. Four thousand bichitos, most of them simple peasants, were arrested for being suspected Communists. Civil rights and the constitution evaporated. A delightful parade was given in mother arachnid's Nueva York, to honour the triumph of democracy in Latin America, the so-called democratic election of dung beetle Castillos Armas. You see, querida, what else can. . . ."

Segundo looked down at Debra deeply asleep, a smile on her face, and her eyeballs twitching beneath her eyelids as she dreamed. He shrugged. He had at least tried to educate her.

He walked to the bathroom and pulled the string, turning on the lightbulb. A cockroach, startled by the sudden

251

brightness, scuttled towards his foot, a fat egg-sack dragging from her ovipositor. Frightened by the illumination, she sought the security of darkness, the darkest thing in the white tile bathroom—Segundo's foot. Instinctively he stomped. She crunched under his bare foot, flattened, feelers and legs still moving slowly. Segundo picked her up with toilet paper and dropped her into the toilet bowl. He unrolled the paracaídas, heavy with semen, wrapped it in more paper and dropped it in the waste basket. He thought briefly of the life that might have been, trapped in impermeable latex. Over the sink, he soaped himself and rinsed with cold stabs of water from the Neblina River.

He returned to the bed and lay down on his back beside her, looking up at the ceiling. She lay on her side, her legs tucked up. Quietly, he said the padrenuestro once, ten avemarías and one gloriapatria. The relaxation from his recent release of sexual tension had evaporated. Penance, he knew, would come later. His imperialist querida had closed her eyes to all the dangers that surrounded them. In Amazonas there was no peril greater than innocence, ignorance, one and the same. He watched her ribs lift with a slow and regular rhythm. She snored very softly. She didn't believe that either, stubbornly refused to believe that she really did snore. Even if he were to tape-record her and present her with audio evidence, she would insist it was someone else. God willing, she wouldn't get herself into serious trouble. He too had become trapped inside a spider's web, the silk so luxurious that he couldn't, wouldn't try to free himself. Would that his ideological beliefs or his faith in God were stronger than the hold she had on him.

21

The Virgin Mother and Child hanging from the rearview mirror swung as the taxi came to a halt and deposited Jeff Marshall at the base of the INSA hill. The driver refused to go one inch up the steep hill, so Jeff dragged himself up the hard-packed dirt road, foot by foot. His vision blurred, his muscles cramped, his head felt as if it had been split wide open. He had a fever now. The machete wound on his left shoulder ached. He had tied some strips of cloth from his shirt around the wound to keep the flies out and to stop the bleeding. He should have cleaned the wound, but there hadn't been time. He had left everything behind at the shabono, his medical supplies, food, tape recordings, even his field notes, years of his life. At least he still had his life. There had been just enough time to reach his boat without being killed, and he had quickly outdistanced the angry Yanomami in their small dugouts.

A Malariología DDT team had been at Topochal when he arrived. They had flown him back to Puerto Pedriscal in their Cessna. Their suspicion and questions worried him. Why was he injured? How long would he be staying in Puerto Pedriscal? In which Yanomami area did he conduct his research? He estimated that he had a week at the very most to get the hell back to the U.S.A. before the Venezuelan authorities came after him.

He reached the halfway point of the hill and thought he might faint but he forced himself on, dragging one fucking leg up at a time. He didn't sweat much any more. His shirt was stiff with dry sweat. If he could just hang on, pull himself together a little while longer, then maybe he would make it out of this infernal country.

He collapsed just before the guardhouse, underneath a dead tree streaked with chalky white bird-droppings. He opened his eyes and saw two sets of inquisitive, round black eyes—glass beads—set into wrinkled, rubbery, blood-red faces fringed with black feathers. The two turkey vultures simultaneously tilted their heads from side to side as Jeff moaned. One untucked its wings, flapped them slowly and hopped nearer. Jeff wasn't yet ready to become carrion. He crawled a few feet forward.

ॐ

Osvaldo and the INSA guard dragged Jeff Marshall, slung over their shoulders, into Debra's office. His body slumped heavily to the floor. His clothes were filthy and stiff, one sleeve stained with dried blood.

Debra squatted beside him. She pinched his skin and the pucker remained for a second before slowly flattening. Jeff moaned. "He's badly dehydrated. We must rush him to the hospital," Debra said to Osvaldo.

"But doctora, he walked all the way up here looking for help. Doctor Yeff was asking for you. He looks to be in a very bad way. He may not make it to the hospital," Osvaldo said.

"But I have no authorization to treat him."

"This is emergency first aid. The guachiman and I will corroborate that. Don't worry."

She hooked Jeff to a saline drip and cleaned the deep slash in the deltoid muscle. At least Jeff had had the sense to cover it up, and it wasn't infested with maggots. He didn't move when the suture needle pierced his skin.

He had recovered sufficiently in a half-hour to grumble. "I'm not in the mood. Leave my groin alone."

"You're having muscle spasms. Pressure on your thighs and abdomen will help to relieve them," Debra said. "You should really be checked into the hospital, Jeff."

"No hospital. No way. I can't. I fucking well can't. I gotta go. Gotta go. Take me to the airport."

"But the wound, Jeff. It could get infected."

"I'll get antibiotics. They sell them over the fucking counter here."

"What happened to you?"

"It was nuthin'." The fear in his face belied his denial, his eyes wild, manic, like Inmaculada's the night she brought the news of Wilfred's death. Debra knew he suffered not only the physical trauma of a machete wound, but also a severe psychological trauma. But he wasn't prepared to discuss it with her, not under any circumstances.

"Debra, just take me to the airport, damn it!"

"Osvaldo, could you drive Jeff wherever it is he wants to go?"

"Yes, doctora, I will take Doctor Yeff," Osvaldo replied.

"And could you take him to see Huevo de Pava first?"

22

Reina clung to the wheel, stretched forward to look over the jeep's bulbous hood for the next obstacle. The track was overgrown and tree branches hemmed it in oppressively from both sides, scraping the jeep as it pressed forward. It lurched over a fallen branch and then sank into a pot-hole. Reina looked ahead, her sunglasses sitting on the tip of her slippery nose. "I think we'll make it," she said. She shifted into first gear and added some gas, and the extra power heaved the jeep out and over a rotting log. Debra grunted from the passenger's seat beside her. Salvador, in the back with all the supplies, swore as a box fell on his head.

The trees yielded to terracotta ground. A single churuata, tall as a two-storey building, with graceful curves thatched from tip to base, dominated the community. The churuata's simple symmetry was beautiful: a wide, round base tapering gradually to a pointed tip; convex and concave curves; a bisected raindrop, bottom half discarded. A few small rectangular thatch houses and one square, grey breeze-block building completed the village. The scene was peaceful, idyllic, dreamlike.

A flap of corrugated metal at the churuata's base clattered open and a small, dark man in colourful ceremonial finery stepped out. He walked up to the jeep to greet them. He looked very different from the time Reina had met him in the Puerto Pedriscal hospital, in trousers and a shirt. Today Melchior wore an orange and yellow feather diadem, orange mission-issued shorts, a blue and white stretch-terry sweatband around each wrist and innumerable strings of white glass beads from his neck to his groin. On his brown leathery face, slanted folds of skin partially hid near-black eyes.

"Doctoras, I am honoured to welcome you to our home," Melchior said. "I want my people free of this illness that makes us cough and grow weak, and kills our elders. I understand your medicine will help us." Melchior gave a wet-sounding hack from deep in his chest, and he spat out a gob of mucus the colour and consistency of caramelized flan. "Some others in the community do not believe you can help. Some do not trust outsiders."

"We are happy that we have, at least, your co-operation," Reina said, shaking his dry hand. "Salvador is also Piaroa. Perhaps he can help to reassure your people. We shouldn't be troubling you for more than a week."

Melchior smiled, his eyes disappearing into the folds of his skin. "I will show you around the community and then take you to the schoolhouse, which is yours to use." He graciously ushered them around the community, across compacted red earth, between the few mud and thatch houses. He was obviously proud of his community's achievements, especially of the breeze-block school where the Catholic sisters came to teach the children once a week.

"The priests have helped us to set up a co-operative," Melchior explained seriously. "We bought this truck and we can now bring our goods to market once a week." An ancient blue pickup truck, painted to mint condition, glinted in the noon sun.

Melchior suddenly smiled. "I am very happy today. Yesterday a child was born. Our children are our future." He walked around the curved thatch of the churuata to a square hut. "Many of us live together in the central churuata, but sometimes a family likes to be private." He called into the thatched hut and a young woman in a faded dress appeared at the door. She carried a tiny thing, a newborn with thick, inch-long, spiky black hair. Reina had an urge to brush her hand through the hair, but resisted it in deference to the mother's obvious shyness. The mother cradled the infant tightly to her breast. Reina had never seen a baby so embryonic, the arms and legs like sticks, pale yellow. The baby sucked lackadaisically. What was a normal birth-weight and appearance for a Piaroa baby? Surely not so small, so jaundiced. The mother smiled at them nervously and lowered her eyes to her child's face. The baby stopped sucking and closed its eyes, lips still curved around the nipple. Neonatal care was not available in Puerto Pedriscal, and the hospital was full of disease. The child's only chance was with the mother.

Melchior said something to the woman, who retreated to the hut. "Most are out at the conuco gathering food," he said. Reina suspected that many were also hiding from the strangers. As he led them around the churuata, she looked up at the thatch towering high above her head, curving away in a giant arc. She couldn't even see the pointed tip, so large was the structure. The door, the only opening, was about five feet high, protected by a sheet of corrugated metal. Reina ducked in first. She held her arms out stiffly in front of her as she stepped blindly into the churuata's void. The intense beam of light from the doorway intensified the surrounding darkness. The air inside was smoky, moist and warm.

"Forty-three people of our community live here. Even fifty or more can live inside," Melchior explained beside her. "A churuata protects from heat of day and cold of night. It is the most comfortable house in Amazonas." As Reina's eyes adjusted to the dim light, hammocks appeared, strung from support poles, baskets hung from the rafters, the dirt floor swept smooth around a few smouldering fires. So clean it was, nothing out of its proper place. Melchior coughed violently, the sound deadened by the rough walls. In the ensuing silence, his spit smacked the floor.

꿩

The next morning, Debra began her examinations of the people. Melchior brought them to the schoolhouse one at a time. She lifted up the two deflated, shrivelled sacks covering an old woman's rib cage. Holes beneath one breast, resembling old bullet wounds, discharged an exudate and small granules—the holes were draining fluid from the woman's chest, and the granules were colonies of the causative organism. Pulmonary actinomycosis, probably, which might respond to antibiotic therapy, but there was already a great deal of tissue damage.

Sickness permeated the tiny community. Aside from the expected pulmonary disease, social decay and debilitation hung like a pall over everyone. That baby already looked weaker. Amador was right—in Amazonas you had to treat a malignant tumour with a Band-Aid. What could be done? This was one village of hundreds, all equally devastated by contact with outsiders—by acculturation, dependency and introduced disease. Medical science could treat some of the symptoms, but the aetiology—who could change that? Anger and frustration tightened inside her.

❧

Salvador slid a box of sputum samples into the back of Reina's Toyota. He had never worked on tuberculosis before. Five days of hard work had provided samples for just the preliminary study. Reina wanted so much spit. She had even instructed him to collect some from the churuata's floor. All day, every day, he had cajoled and pleaded with people to cough their sputum into plastic vials, explaining over and over again how it would benefit them. The more he repeated it, the more hollow it sounded to him.

It was so long since he had used his own Piaroa tongue. He had been away too long. Few of his people lived outside their communities and even fewer had the opportunity to get an education. Salvador had been lucky to find his job at INSA, but the job had brought cultural isolation for him. This was his first experience as an interpreter, and he felt uncomfortable as an intermediary between his own people and INSA. His own people had treated him with so much suspicion. He had sold them out, become one of "the others".

Reina wedged the black carrying-case containing the field microscope securely behind a seat. "Is that all, Salvador?" she asked.

He rubbed his hairless brown forearms, tense from the exertion of carrying so many heavy boxes. "Yes, doctora, perhaps now we should go and say goodbye to Melchior."

Debra stumbled across the bare dirt carrying a box of medical supplies and her black medical bag. "No need, he's on his way. He wanted to know the preliminary results," she said.

Salvador watched the feather headdress pop out from the churuata door. Melchior stood up, his rows of white beads so heavy they appeared to weigh down his neck. Why did he wear ceremonial attire for outsiders? The doctoras couldn't possibly understand its significance; the effort was wasted on them.

Melchior offered his hand, the weariness of his tired eyes momentarily hidden behind wrinkled cheeks. Reina extended her fingers, white and pale as banana pulp. Melchior engulfed them in both his weathered brown hands.

"Thank you, doctora. I am anxious. How did the study go? We need medicine for our ailments."

"I estimate there is active tuberculosis in at least forty percent of the population, but I won't be sure until I finish the secondary phase, when I have results from the cultures."

"So many people sick with the coughing sickness?"

"Your people have very little immunity to tuberculosis. Also, I believe I discovered another contributing factor. Every person living in the churuata skin-tested positive to PPD, whereas some people in the separate huts tested negative."

"What does that mean?"

"It means, I suspect, that your churuata is ideally constructed for spreading disease. I had Salvador collect sputum from the inside. I found bacilli under the microscope, and I suspect I'll find viable organisms in the cultures I took from there."

Melchior looked confused, but he said nothing. He looked

out of place laden with his white beads, his feather headpiece, completely ineffectual against the official power represented by Reina's white lab coat.

"But the churuata—it's the central figure of our communities. It's our way of life," Salvador said, his voice escalating.

Reina turned to him. "Salvador, it's a giant incubator. The sterilizing effects of drying breezes and sunlight can't reach the interior. It's humid, it has a constant warm temperature and it traps pathogens in proximity to people."

"It served our people through millennia," Salvador retorted. "It was perfect for us—communal living providing safety in numbers, maintaining our society, sheltering us from heat and cold."

"It may well have accommodated pre-colonial conditions, but the churuata is not designed to cope with tuberculosis. The community would be better off knocking it down and constructing Malariología houses. It might be a cultural loss but it would help save their lives. I'll write about this in my report to the ministry."

"Reina," Debra said. "We should be concentrating on BCG vaccination of PPD negatives and treatment of active cases. They'd be better off living traditional lifestyles."

"Lamentablemente, medicine is not enough. Conditions have changed since pre-colonial times. Tuberculosis is here and it's here to stay. A churuata is no longer suited to the environment. Treatment is difficult to administer and next to impossible to monitor. If we are to save lives, we must get rid of churuatas."

Salvador looked at the two blonde heads—so out of place here—debating the fate of his people, each convinced that she knew best, neither asking, considering or respecting his people's opinions. Melchior looked helpless. Salvador knew what Melchior was attempting to accomplish—accept the good from both cultures. Instead he compromised, trapped somewhere in no man's land in those ridiculous mission shorts and sweat bands, crowned as a Piaroa leader. How many times could his people compromise? Each time they lost a bit more. They would compromise until they had nothing left. Did they have no choice? Were they never to be consulted?

Salvador could not be silent. He would not be one of the idle who placed his fate in the hands of others, even if they were good of heart and well intended. "What my people," said Salvador, waving his hand to encompass Melchior and the village, "and all native people really need, is to participate in any decisions made by others on our behalf. We are Piaroa, Guahibo, Yabarana, Makiritare, Panare, Macó, Piapoco, Puinave and Yanomami first. We are Venezuelans second. We want to preserve our cultures. Our throats are raw from trying to communicate to deaf ears, but we will never give up the struggle to be ourselves."

Salvador turned to Melchior. "If a cock's legs are overgrown with feathers," he said vehemently, "then it cannot use its spurs in combat. Melchior, my Piaroa brother, we must not stand here defenceless. We must pluck the feathers hindering our feet. We must expose our spurs, or we will perish. Let us stand up for our rights."

"What is it you think we can do?"

"We can start by uniting with our native brothers from Bolívar state against our oppressors." Salvador pulled out a folded paper from his pocket. He unfolded it and Reina leaned over him, looking at the print.

"I will not be party to subversive activities," she said. "Debra, when you are ready to leave I'll be waiting in my jeep. Melchior, thank you for your hospitality. I will keep you informed about the results of my study."

Salvador handed the paper to Melchior. "I cannot read," Melchior said.

"May I see?" Debra gently took the paper from Melchior's yielding fingers. She read out loud:

—DEMONSTRATION—
EXPEL THE NEW WORLD MISSION

Our native communities are being ripped apart by the New World Mission. Fanatics create fanaticism. Anyone not evangelized is accused of Satanism or possession by demons, thus fomenting disunity and distrust among fellow native brothers. Many coercive tools are used against us: false interpretation of the Bible, racist mission laws, medical advantage and technological superiority.

Coercion does not equal free will. Our sacred right to freedom of belief is violated. Our private thoughts are not our own. They are stolen: not by persuasion or logical debate, but by fear of mortal retribution. Blind fanaticism among our people results from the scare tactics, oppression and dominance that are used against us.

Blind fanaticism causes dependency and psychological disadvantage. It ultimately leads to the ethnocide of our people, facilitating the imperialistic colonization of our communities and of the entire Amazon Territory. This wave of religious fanaticism is ever expanding. Our government, acting on behalf of the United States of America, grants countless permits to New World missionaries for airstrip construction in even the most remote parts of our country, granted in clear violation of national laws. The Empire ruled by the United States of America is expanding to conquer our homelands for its own gain.

Salvador felt the initial sting of anger fade; pulling feathers from his feet felt good. And one outsider was willing to listen. Perhaps there were others willing to meet his people halfway.

ೞ

The last box of Piaroa sputum was safely in Reina's lab. Now Debra could go on home, wash the grime out of her hair, change her stinky clothes, shower, rest. Expeditions always left her drained.

"Salvador, before you and I go home we must first digest this sputum," Reina said. "First we must record the nature of the specimen: for example, mucoid, purulent, mucoid-purulent, serous, bloody. You get the idea? Then draw, with a sterile pipette, ten millilitres of material, selecting the most purulent, and place—"

"Reina, I'm going home now," Debra said loudly. Reina looked up and stared past Debra. Debra turned her head in the direction of Reina's stare.

A large silhouette filled the doorframe. The bulk and the outline of his military cap made him unmistakable. "Buenos días, Doctora Baumstark," he said. "I realize you have just returned from the selva, but it's urgent that I ask you a few questions."

"Please, capitán, do come and sit down," Debra said, in the most civil tone of voice she could muster. Máximo entered, the camouflage patches of green and brown now visible. Debra sat down at Reina's desk. He overflowed the lab stool, looming above her, took off his cap and laid it on the bench. Reina and Salvador stopped working and stared from behind the vials of sputum.

"I am trying to elicit information concerning the where-abouts of an American anthropologist, Doctor Yeff March-ell. I believe you are acquainted?" He swept back his thinning, sweaty hair with his slab of a hand.

Debra leaned back in the chair, stretching her legs out in front of her. "Yes, INSA has done some work with him in the past."

"I believe you saw him recently."

"I don't know where he is."

"Americanos, you are always above the law while you are guests in another's country. Doctora, I will say nothing about the medical services you rendered illegally, if you co-operate with me fully. Doctor March-ell is wanted for questioning in connection with a homicide. You would not want to be implicated in hampering an official murder investigation, now would you?"

"A homicide?"

"Competition over the favours of a Yanomami woman, the victim's wife. A Malariología DDT team said they flew Doctor March-ell to Puerto Pedriscal. At the airport, he caught a taxi. We questioned the taxi driver. He brought him to the base of this hill, in very poor condition, blood staining his shirt. An investigation team to his permitted study area was met with arrows. After it established contact, the Yanomami told our interpreter that a Yanomami man had died after being mortally wounded a week previously. They said the anthropologist and the victim's wife had sexual relations. The husband had threatened the anthropologist with a machete, as is their custom for such an offence, and he received a shotgun blast in his chest in return. Doctor March-ell fled downstream before retribution could be taken. Not only did he fail to report this incident, but we now know he fled to Caracas. We would like to be clear about your involvement with the fugitive."

23

Christmas had come and gone and Debra still hadn't managed to contact her parents in Miami. Every night she sat at the CANTV telephone centre, with its wooden cubicles lining an entire length of wall, waiting for the operator to shout, "Cubículo dos, Doctora Baumstark!" and every night was the same—expectation deteriorating to frustration fading to resignation, and then home to wait for the solace of Segundo's skulking arrival. Perhaps tonight would be the night. She looked at the passive faces opposite her, several now familiar companions in the nightly vigil.

The turkey would be sandwich scraps by now, but the rum and eggnog would still be flowing liberally. Family and friends in sweaters against the chill of full-blast air-conditioning—Christmas wouldn't be Christmas without a log fire, her mother always said—Mother wiping waterspots off her Waterford crystal before it disappeared until the Fourth of July, and Father, slurring his words ever so slightly, grumbling about liberals and declining family values.

Christmas in Venezuela was certainly different. Which was worse: the cloying, twee, "Silent Night" approach or the raucous gaita with its pounding migraine rhythm? They were equally bad. The season of legitimized hypocrisy and cultural confusion. The Lebanese merchants had hired a skinny, dark Santa Claus, his fake beard not quite concealing his own Fidel-like growth, to ride through town in a pillow-stuffed red satin suit on a pathetic parasitized burro and hand out candies. Children and parents stared silently as Saint Nick's meagre procession passed by.

It was also the season of the priests' annual talent show at the municipal building—the social event of the year, and one Yadira had told Debra she couldn't miss. How right she had been! The extravaganza raised the spirits of everyone at INSA. Velázquez, never missing an opportunity to promote himself and his organization, smiled his gracious, frozen smile at the Catholic TV channel camera as he walked slowly down the aisle, nodding this way and that, to his seat in the front row amid the other town dignitaries. INSA's research staff sat in the row behind their leader, except for Debra, who preferred the back with Osvaldo and the técnicos, where several bottles of rum passed from hand to hand.

The performers were enthusiastic, inept and hilarious—schoolgirls in semi-random formations performing traditional dance, proof that order can sometimes come from chaos; a ventriloquist whose dummy's mouth moved less than his did; a juggler's clubs bouncing into the audience—encouraged by polite applause from the front rows and rowdy cheers from the back.

Doctor Amador Pantaleon, accompanied by Inmaculada on the cuatro, sang a gaita, surprising Debra with his sensitivity and the beauty of his voice. The eruption of partisan support took him to first place in the men's solo category, only to be ousted by the final performer, the priests' secret weapon, a diminutive Piaroa boy almost invisible in front of the cardboard cutout pink curtains. The crowd hushed to catch the thin, high voice, its source, like a bird's, difficult to pinpoint. "Silent Night"—in Piaroa. Amador was the first to break the spell as the tiny voice faded, by striding onto the stage and lifting the boy above his head like a trophy, conceding his own defeat.

The celebration, minus Velázquez and his entourage, continued afterward in the bar Ayúdame a Vivir—Help Me Live. Cheo even managed to convince Debra to dance with him. She must have been drunk; she usually avoided embarrassing herself like that. Foreigners' hips just couldn't swivel enough—although the way Inmaculada's and Cheo's groins ground together in mutual masturbation was definitely interesting.

267

Cheo grabbed Debra after he finished with Inmaculada, and shuffled her around the floor, his erection bumping erratically halfway up her uncoordinated thighs.

The next day at INSA, despite some pale and suffering faces, Debra could sense a dramatic change in the técnicos. The wake had been completed and life could recommence.

"Doctora Baumstark! Cubículo uno, por favor."

ॐ

"Hola, chama! Look at this, a true beauty." Debra took the otoscope from Amador and inserted it deep into the patient's ear. Beauty of a sort—a miniature garden of puffy blooms of phialospores, ripe with brilliant green spores, planted in clumps of earwax. She removed the otoscope and smiled at the patient, a middle-aged man obviously unsure of whether or not to be proud of an ailment that gave such pleasure to the doctors. It reminded her of the confused, pretty young woman in Caracas surrounded by six physicians enthusing about her outstanding facial leprosy lesions.

"A saprophytic floral arrangement, Amador?"

"*Aspergillus*, one of the *fumigatus* group, I think. A culture would confirm it," Amador said. "That is, if you people at INSA are still doing mycology."

"We're trying to cope. Velázquez has decided to cut back on diagnostic services and to redirect most effort towards research."

"We say here that when the pivotal point of a difficult situation is reached, even a mother monkey will abandon her young. It's survival, I suppose." He bent over the ear and resumed his work, flushing out debris from the external auditory meatus. After he finished, he sat upon the examination table beside the patient, his foot crossed over his knee. He pulled out his prescription pad and a pen from the upper pocket of his lab coat, scribbled and handed a sheet to the patient. Then he slapped the fellow on his back good-naturedly and said in his sleepy voice, "Chamo, you have got to use this medicina twice daily. Don't be stingy with it, use it generously. You may not see the cheese on the toast immediately, but you'll relish the flavour later, when your itching goes away."

A nun, draped head to foot in black and white, entered the examination room next, the only flesh visible a doughy face constricted by cloth so tightly sealed that her flesh puffed, red and angry, over the edge, and oedematous fingers protruding from her sleeves.

"Buenos días, hermana," Amador said. "What seems to be the problem?"

"I have itching and redness. It pinches me. It's merciless, doctor."

"Where does this itching occur, exactamente?"

"I am so ashamed."

Amador nodded as if he understood perfectly. The nun lifted up layer after layer after layer of her habit, from the heaviest outer black, thick and stiff like canvas, to a final soft white cotton made almost translucent by perspiration. There were so many layers that Debra had to help hold them up for Amador to gain access to the inner reliquary—big white nylon briefs, elastic, bound to the flesh as tightly as surgical gloves, trapping sweat and preventing evaporative cooling. Despite her agnosticism, Debra had the sensation that a forbidden zone had been reached, that they had violated a consecrated area where only God was permitted to go. The lesions had definite, raised, actively scaling, erythematous borders. The sister had jock itch. Layer by layer the habit fell back down over the plump, sweaty flesh. Amador wrote a prescription. "Ketoconazole. Use it liberally, sister, on all the areas that itch: the armpits, under your breasts, anywhere there is redness and itching. It will take a long time, but you will be cured," he said solemnly, refraining from his usual slang.

"Thanks be to God for providing knowledge to restore health," said the nun. She smiled softly and turned to Amador. "I want to repay your kindness with some advice." She pointed to an inconspicuous tuft of hair on the back of Amador's head. "You would be wise to cut off that tail, young man, for it is the mark of the Evil One."

"But sister, with all due respect, it's just fashion," Amador answered.

"The Devil tempts us in subtle ways." She handed Amador and Debra religious pamphlets. "Dios les bendiga." The black figure waddled out of the room, cloth sweeping the ground. Debra slipped her pamphlet into the pocket of her lab coat without reading it. The cruel confinement of that habit was far more demonic than Amador's harmless tail of hair.

"I'll be on my way," Debra said, smirking. "I don't feel safe being in the same room with the Devil's tail." She unbuttoned her lab coat and hung it over her arm.

Amador winked. "Chao, pescao!"

Pedro Aguirre walked down the corridor about ten paces in front of her. She saw his arm move up and down as he scratched himself on the upper thigh. As he turned to enter the communal room, Debra caught his eye. He scowled.

Debra smiled. If Amazonian people couldn't cure tuberculosis, malaria and onchocerciasis with their natural remedies and incantations, wasn't it fitting that they could retaliate by inflicting an ailment that eluded modern medical treatment? His punishment constituted justifiable retribution. He should go and see a brujo, ask for forgiveness and beg to be cured.

❦

A scrawny man with a swollen belly sat on a stool beside the lab bench. Blancanieves sat at her desk looking at brown sludge in a small glass bottle—her leishmanin. The protocol for its preparation had been complicated. *Leishmania donovani* grew only inside host cells, so it had to be cultured in medium containing fresh rabbits' blood. A colony of rabbits was maintained at INSA for that specific purpose. Velázquez's preference for cardiopuncture to collect blood provided Blancanieves with a steady supply of dead rabbits that she sneaked to the técnicos for their families. Rabbit made a delicious sancocho, they said. Parasites from the cultural concoction then had to be lysed. A machine called a french press was recommended by the protocol. INSA had no such device, and Blancanieves was stymied until she discovered an ingenious alternative in a textbook. She put the parasites into a plastic bag, dunked them into liquid nitrogen—the nitrogen boiling violently at -196° Celsius—and then ground them, frozen to a solid more brittle and fragile than glass, in a mortar with a pestle. There were other steps in the protocol, too—centrifuging, shaking, mixing, that sort of a thing. Her innovation and perseverance had resulted in the final product in front of her. Even Doctor Velázquez was impressed. Now she was ready to test the leishmanin antigen and, according to Doctor Velázquez, that would require both positive and negative controls.

Blancanieves gently swirled the bottle to suspend any particulate matter. In the Amazonas the sandfly vector of *Leishmania donovani* was common, but leishmaniasis—thought to have been introduced to the New World by the conquistadors' dogs—was not often diagnosed. Medical experts in Amazonas had no idea how prevalent the disease was. Doctor Velázquez intended Blancanieves to unearth exposure rates so he could publish the results. The most efficient way would have been with *in vitro* ELISA assays using blood samples, but unfortunately Blancanieves hadn't managed to get the imported ELISA machine to function. It would hum and look as if it knew what it was doing, but all the figures that came out of it were nonsense. Wilfred had wasted months tinkering with it before his death, and he thought Puerto Pedriscal's electricity might be to blame. Now she had the antigen ready for the tests and she couldn't test it without the machine. At least, that was what she had thought until yesterday, when she had read in a new journal about *Leishmania* antigen used in skin tests on humans.

She peeled the paper wrapper off the one-millilitre disposable tuberculin syringe. A skin test could be used both scientifically and diagnostically, the literature said. If antigen was injected subcutaneously six weeks to one year after recovery from leishmaniasis, ninety percent of patients would react positively with a localized cellular immune reaction at the injection site—a positive control. In contrast, the skin tests were supposed to be uniformly negative in those with active visceral leishmaniasis—a negative control. It was a harmless procedure, no different from the PPD test used to identify exposure to the TB bacillus.

Blancanieves punctured the grey rubber seal of the bottle containing her antigen with the bevelled needle. This was her first big research responsibility, and she must please the doctor. Marisol said she was stupid, she knew, and had told the doctor so on many occasions. Marisol thought herself better educated just because she'd graduated from that snobby private Universidad Simón Bolívar. Now Blancanieves had the means to prove Marisol wrong. What luck it had been this morning that, just one day after reading about subdermic skin tests, she should practically stumble across this patient wandering around INSA's Plaza Bolívar asking for help. His Spanish wasn't too good, but Blancanieves understood enough to know that he had come to INSA because he was afraid to die at the hospital. His facial lesions—distinctive lumps, non-ulcerated nodules, hard and rubbery to her touch—were textbook classics, referred to as post-kala-azar dermal leishmaniasis. If Debra or Amador later confirmed her diagnosis of visceral leishmaniasis—his belly did indeed look very swollen—then this man would serve perfectly as a negative control for her leishmanin test. Furthermore, after treatment and recovery he would also serve as a positive control. She would test him once a month until he converted. It would be exciting. She might even publish this as a case study. How long would it take him to convert? Wouldn't the doctor be surprised that she had had the foresight to think of appropriate controls and publication possibilities all by herself? Marisol would eat her words. Blancanieves would ask the patient to return tomorrow so she could see if he had developed an indurated welt, twenty-four hours after the injection. She could do her own research all by herself, with no help from anyone.

The thin needle slipped below the skin of his forearm with no resistance.

❦

Osvaldo drove the jeep, bouncing over pockets in the red dirt road, through the tunnel of trees, past the feathered roosting sentinels, past the pox-faced guachiman and onto the plateau parking lot. A figure danced up and down like a vulture over its carrion underneath the geometric designs of INSA's acronym—a bottom-heavy figure, jumping, waving its arms excitedly. "What," Osvaldo asked the doctora beside him, "what in the name of El Señor is Blancanieves so excited about?"

"Is Amador at the hospital?" Blancanieves asked, before he could open the door. Osvaldo's stomach muscles tightened.

"He probably just left for his lunch," Doctora Debra answered calmly.

"Something has gone wrong," Blancanieves wailed, "something is terribly wrong. I tested a man just a few minutes ago with my leishmanin and he isn't well."

For Osvaldo, the next fifteen minutes passed in a succession of jumbled images: running to the laboratory, a Guahibo man lying on the floor; the doctora screaming about a chemical she called epinefrina as she knelt on the floor beside the Guahibo; Blancanieves crying; himself and Salvador hauling the poor man by his arms and legs, head fallen back, to the jeep; a blurred trip back to town. "Go to the pharmacy. It's closer," Doctora Debra said as they plummeted down the hill.

Osvaldo bounced the front wheel up onto the curb—there was no time to parallel park.

Huevo de Pava slid a tube of hydrocortisone cream into a small white paper bag. Pedro set twenty-three bolívars upon the glass. He had bought so many tubes that he knew the price without asking.

"Still no improvement, eh, Doctor Aguirre?" Huevo de Pava grinned and nodded knowingly. "Más nada? Preservativos? I guess not, at least not until that itching clears up, eh, doctor?"

"Button your lips or I'll suture them shut for you," Pedro responded coolly. He gingerly picked up his white paper bag by the very top, his little finger held out delicately.

A giant mosquito, body slanting downward, proboscis pointing like an arrow to the flesh, pulled into view. The yellow jeep jumped up onto the curb in front of the farmacia. The passengers tumbled out on the pavement and staggered through the pharmacy door.

"Anaphylactic shock. Hurry!" the gringa, Debra, shouted.

Huevo de Pava ran back to his storeroom and returned with a hypodermic needle, syringe and epinephrine, which he slapped on the glass countertop. Pedro grabbed the epinephrine and shoved his way through the pharmacy door, past Debra and Osvaldo, and out to the jeep. Those scientists had been playing around with their human guinea pigs again, but Pedro and Velázquez were good friends and Pedro would surely cover for him, as usual. They were just indios, but even so, eventually someone would start to ask questions. Velázquez was lucky it was Pedro here and not Amador. Amador wasn't nearly so understanding.

❦

Jeeps and trucks whizzed by, stirring up choking clouds of dust. Fortunately, the epinephrine and antihistamine administered by Aguirre took effect quickly. Though still shaky from his ordeal, Blancanieves' experiment sat up in the passenger's seat.

Pedro stood beside him, feeling his pulse, looking at his wristwatch. Pedro had handled the crisis expediently and efficiently, Debra thought. Yet, despite his professionalism, the detached manner in which he accepted this medical emergency as normality troubled Debra. He hadn't even asked how the emergency arose. The question of negligence never seemed to enter his mind. He didn't reprimand anybody for the near fatality.

"Crisis over, eh, Doctor Aguirre?" asked Huevo de Pava. He leaned casually against the doorway, weight upon his left shoulder. In his freckled hand he held a small white paper bag. "We can relax once again and get back to our ordinary affairs. Don't forget your hydrocortisone, doctor. The sooner you get better, the—"

"This patient is no longer in danger," said Aguirre, looking at Debra as he snatched his white paper bag. "Take him to emergency, he can rest there." Doctor Pedro Aguirre left abruptly, heading down Avenida Río Negro.

Huevo de Pava turned to Debra. "Doctora, did your friend the gallo find his purchases to his liking? I aim for the highest customer satisfaction, if you know what I mean."

24

Raúl sat in the front seat of the Cessna 152 single-engined aircraft beside the pilot, Antonio, and looked through the viewfinder of his camera. He was getting excellent footage. The forest stretched out in front of him, to the right of him, underneath him, and behind him. It stretched and stretched, on and on, to eternity. If he zoomed in with his telephoto he could detail the tops of individual trees, branches and trunks, and the flutter of birds. He had never expected it to be so vast. A flight over tropical rainforest was well worth the delay at the airport.

They were supposed to have taken off at eight in the morning, but they hadn't departed until ten-thirty. They had spent two hours at the airport snackbar eating meagre ham and cheese sandwiches with the crust cut off, no butter, squeezed flat by the grill, dry and thin like cardboard. The only other people at the airport were some American missionaries and a Communist wearing a red shirt handing out propaganda. The Communist looked somehow familiar, but Raúl couldn't quite place him.

Raúl panned his camera from the treetops to the Cessna's wing and into the cockpit. He paused on each of the three crammed into the rear seats. The crippled black technician sat squeezed in the middle. He had a compass and notebook and he leaned over Marisol so he could see out the small window. His afro brushed against Marisol's face; her nose crinkled and she pressed her head back into the seat cushion. Debra leaned her head against the window, her hair fallen forward. Debra! The connection! The Communist at the airport—he was the man she had been kissing on the porch of that strange house built on top of the black granite boulder. He had it on film. Raúl had thought the impromptu coverage cute, a gringa and a criollo, personal-interest stuff, the kind of footage that transformed cardboard characters into real-life believable people. Red—the red shirt—that was what had made the man so damned recognizable. Raúl stroked his greying goatee. Velázquez would soon have videotape transfers. What would he think of this new political angle?

"Cheo, get that Brillo pad you call hair out of my mouth," Marisol pouted.

"You'll thank me if we crash," Cheo said. "I'll know where the river lies."

"Relax, Cheo," Antonio said. "We flew over Kováta-teri more than ten minutes ago. We'll land at Porohóa in a few moments."

The plane dropped and Raúl's ears popped. Debra pinched her nostrils shut and opened and closed her mouth a few times.

"Raúl," Marisol said, "You'll love Porohóa. It's very beautiful. There are many blackflies and the people are heavily infected with oncho. You'll have plenty to film." She tilted her head flirtatiously. She had already given him plenty to film: he would enjoy that footage he was saving for his private collection. He pointed his camera out the window and let the film roll. The forest swept by underneath, so close now, and he felt a prickly warmth rush to his fingers and toes. Only a thin, light layer of aluminum separated him from the treetops. The tiny machine was almost in the canopy, and then suddenly the forest opened into velvet-green savannah marred by a straight, tan line surrounded by houses.

❦

The planes had landed some two hours earlier and the Ministry of Health scientists would have finished unpacking by now. Jim stepped down from his tidy little house and walked the well-worn trail through the grass towards the mission garden.

He and his wife, Peggy, had no children at the Porohóa base. Their three lovely daughters were grown up and married, living at home in Virginia, bringing beautiful grandchildren into this world. Without another American family for companionship, life was lonely out here. Jim and Peg welcomed outside company. Stanley and Beverley Elliot, over at Kovätateri base, had their ten-year-old, Bobby, and little Joanne to enrich their time. Stan's young daredevil brother, Luke, visited frequently—whenever Luke could fit in time between mission-supply flights—relieving the burden of isolation and sharing responsibility. Yes, Stan could well afford to be more choosy about company. But Stan's aloofness wasn't just because he had a family here to keep him busy. The eldest Elliot brother, Ronald, ran the mission headquarters in Puerto Pedriscal, and Stan considered himself to be a cut above missionaries outside the Elliot oligarchy.

Ronald Elliot disapproved of outside interference in the affairs of the mission, under any circumstances. He had protested vehemently against the construction of ministry medical dispensaries at Porohóa. While Ron recognized the political necessity of co-operating with the ministry, he instructed Stan and Jim to do so only minimally, extending as few hospitalities as possible. Stan took what his brother said to be the Gospel truth. According to Ron, healing should be strictly a Christian duty, a tool to convert those still trapped in darkness. Medicine was first given to mankind by God Himself in the form of miracles—breathing life into the near dead and making sicknesses and disabilities vanish as if they had never existed—miracles performed by His son Jesus Christ, winning the first converts over to His side. Christ then passed wondrous abilities to his twelve apostles. They were given restorative powers for the infirm, and God facilitated His Christian conversions by creating large-scale epidemics, physical catastrophes and mass starvation. "Christian faith," Ronald insisted vehemently, "was cast from the healing of morbid human flesh." It made sense. If God did indeed have absolute control of His creations, then it was He who created disease. But God would never permit His children to suffer needlessly, would He? Did He allow humanity to become diseased as part of His greater plan? Might not disease have been bestowed upon mankind to guide them along the path to peace and salvation through faith in Our Lord Jesus Christ? For as the Apostle said: "Whom the Lord loveth he chasteneth."

On the other hand, it could also be argued that periodic visits by the ministry's rural nurse, however irregular, made working for the Lord a lot less hazardous. Independent, secular health care had saved the lives of some of the Indians. When first contact had been made, many Yanomami had died of the common cold. They weren't used to the white man's diseases, and pioneering missionaries had to race with death to save souls. Ministry sick-nursing took away some of the urgency of soul-saving. Ronald, however, encouraged what Jim considered to be an outdated attitude. "Relinquishment of life is not in vain if His word is heard above the jungle clamour. Even one hundred Yanomami dead to save one soul is not undue sacrifice," Ronald had argued at one meeting. Yet God had permitted medical aid to come here. He hadn't struck ministry planes down from the sky. It was His will. If Stan and he were to continue saving souls, should they not fully co-operate with the ministry's health-care workers in order that His work be done? God would want them to be hospitable to the ministry staff, so that travel and construction permits were granted. He would deem it to be in His own interests.

Jim walked across the savannah to the perimeter of the mission garden and took the partially concealed trail that led to the medicatura.

Stanley and Ronald over-reacted. True, there was still the presence of darkness. There were still many Yanomami who resisted, but Evangelism was firmly entrenched throughout this community. They had made such progress. The Indians now depended on missionary contact for so much in their lives, for batteries, salt, fish-hooks, machetes. The Lord had made possible the impossible: deciphering the Yanomami language and expressing complex philosophical and theological concepts in the primitive tongue.

Forty years in Amazonas. Forty years of mission contact with the Yanomami, and Jim had been here from the beginning. Evangelization was a long and never-ending process. Years spent learning the simplest greetings from Makiritare, who had limited trade with the Yanomami. Years spent flying over shabonos broadcasting friendly messages through a loud-speaker and dropping gifts into the forest, brave Christian pilots sweeping so closely over the crowded treetops that many became martyrs in the name of Jesus Christ Our Lord. The harrowing journey through the forest of the upper Orinoco, beyond the influence of the Salesian missions, to found the first permanent presence of God among the Yanomami. The toil, sweat, bribery to elicit the help of the unconverted to clear virgin jungle for the mission's first airstrip, the first of many. It was all so long ago. Twenty years since the discovery of the natural savannah of Porohóa, an oasis of light in the dark forest. The frightened Indians had fled first contact, and gifts were left at the forest margins for many months before the savages came to trust their new neighbours. Jim and Peg had rarely left Porohóa—a sabbatical to Virginia every five years or so, the odd trip to Caracas to arrange permits and for medical and dental overhauls. His daughters had been born in the now comfortable house in Porohóa, then just a shell. Jim understood better than the new, young missionaries. Bringing the Gospel to the underprivileged Indians had been his life. God had trusted him to do this job, and he would weep for ever in Heaven if every attempt possible wasn't made to bring the Gospel to the Yanomami. If that meant moving more slowly, saving lives and therefore more souls, and even co-operating with the ministry, then so be it.

Jim had put on weight in the past few years. Peg didn't mind. She said the grandfatherly look suited him. When he complained about the passing years, Peg would hold his "gruffly bear head" between her two hands and kiss his receding hairline.

Jim's heavy feet struck solidly upon the ochre clay path. He approached the medicatura, painted white at the top and blue at the bottom, and tapped on the open blue metal door. Hearing no answer, he peered around the doorframe. Two of the scientists, Marisol and her assistant, Cheo, he knew. They were at the back, setting up a microscope. The two sitting at the nurse's desk, a hippieish-looking man with a small beard, wearing a bandanna tied over the top of his head, and a woman, blonde, hair limp from heat, obviously an American, he didn't recognize. What was an American woman, not affiliated with the mission, doing out here?

She wore a green tee-shirt dampened by sweat and clinging blue jeans. "Can I help you?" she asked.

"I, er. . . ." Jim wrung his hands behind his back. "My wife has prepared sandwiches up at the house. We wondered if you people might like to share our humble meal."

"Hola, Jim! We would love to," Marisol answered.

ॐ

Raúl was surprised at how nice Jim and Peggy were, after all the complaining he'd heard from the INSA staff about mission contact. They sat down to lunch in a U.S.-style kitchen complete with frilly lace curtains, round colonial-style table, refrigerator, deep freeze and oven. The table was set with cheerful placemats—a farm scene, a mother hen with a brood of fluffy yellow chicks in the foreground. Peggy served Spam sandwiches and freshly squeezed lemonade with real ice cubes. A generator hummed outside, running nonstop.

For dessert Peggy produced, as if by magic, juicy pieces of freshly baked apple pie right under her guests' noses.

"Apples," Debra sputtered incredulously, her eyes wide.

"I haven't had fresh apple pie since I left California," Raúl said.

"Yes, we are blessed with many comforts," Peggy replied. She wiped her hands on her flour-coated apron before sitting down again. She was a pleasantly plump woman wearing a paisley print dress, grey hair tied in a knot behind her head. "Our pilots bring us everything we need, including apples sometimes." She beamed, looking over the bottom magnifying lens of her bifocals.

"Misses Peggy, your torta is maravillosa, not of this world," Marisol chirped in Spanglish.

"Call me Peggy, won't you."

"Sorry, no ice-cream, I'm afraid," said Jim. "We make do with what the Lord provides. There's no way of getting ice-cream down here by plane. Peg would have to make it homemade, and we have too much hard work to do."

"It must be difficult sometimes to live out here, so isolated," Raúl said. "Puerto Pedriscal is bad enough, but it's nothing compared to this."

"It can be lonely at times, especially without the children." Raúl followed Jim's eyes to the collection of family photos on the wall, every person strikingly blond. "But helping others in need has its own rewards." He took a big bite of pie, smacked his lips. "Delicious, dear."

Raúl glanced past Cheo's afro, on through the hatch into the living room, filled with matching brown and gold, floral print, velour chairs and sofa, a tan shag carpet and those ridiculous knick-knacks that Americans invariably collected. He spotted more photos of wholesome-looking Americans adorning the bookshelves—lots of baby and first-grade school prints, chubby cheeks, missing front teeth, blue eyes and flaxen hair. He returned his attention to the kitchen. His eyes rested on two wooden plaques above the sink, carved with inspirational messages. One was decorated with hands held in prayer and read, "You'll be glad or maybe mad, but you'll never be bored, if you are become one with the Lord," and the other, adorned with an angel above, "If you're not committed you're just taking up space."

"You have a very nice house. I never expected to see anything so comfortably American out in the middle of nowhere," Raúl said. Marisol glared at him as if telling him to shut up.

"Christ not only sent us here to teach the Gospel," Peggy explained. She rested her arms on the tabletop, her fingers reverentially positioned in front of her empty dessert plate. "Christ sent us that we might help transform these impoverished communities. Through us the Yanomami are shown a positive example of how the Lord intends us to live. They learn to build safer houses and to escape the dangers of the jungle. Through positive example and teaching we try to save them from the delinquency of their superstitious beliefs, their use of infanticide and hallucinogenic drugs. They are entitled to better, better than a life of darkness spent wandering among vines and trees, eating insects and worms, are they not? We present an alternative way of life to these people oppressed by wilderness. There is a better way, and we help them aspire to more in order that they may learn to help themselves."

❦

A wet vibration of gas escaping from a tight aperture resonated in the air. Debra breathed shallowly, but the noxious fumes still reached her scent receptors. The Yanomami man lay placidly face down underneath her hands on the examining table, gunning hot gas into her face, as she snipped away tiny pieces of his skin. His companions, watching every move, smiled as a unit, displaying the black tobacco wads in their lower lips.

Cheo looked up at the sound. He sat at the nurse's desk in front of the microscope, where he mounted skin snips on microtitre plates and counted the number of emerging parasites. "Doctora, you need to wear a mask. February is the season when the Yanomami eat pijiguao fruits and little else. With such an abundance of food, it's an important time for

283

celebration. The women make a weak alcohol drink from chewed up plantain and saliva, although it's hardly what I'd call a tanganazo, not like alcohol absoluto. They bonche all the time with the other shabonos in the area. Unfortunately, so many festivities, well, they bring a lot of smelly peos."

Debra gestured to the man to get up, to let him know she was finished. He sat up and held out his hand. Cheo dropped a hypodermic needle into it and the man slipped the needle, in its plastic sheath, into the hole in his earlobe. He grinned like a child on Christmas morning. No fish-hooks, no twine, no machetes, no beads, no batteries were traded here, just hypodermic needles. At first, Debra had been mystified. Then Cheo had explained that the hypos were used by the Yanomami to dig out niguas from the soles of their feet and under their toenails. They would consent to almost any medical procedure to procure the needles. Niguas, chiggers, *Tunga penetrans*, were a painful scourge from the soil of the shabonos. The tiny fleas burrowed into the skin, and gravid females could grow as large as a pea. Debra could see the crusty black sores on almost every pair of feet that crossed her table. The flea's ovipositor protruded through the skin, making a black dot in the centre of each capsule where she both discharged ova and respired. Debra saw very few complete sets of toenails.

"Cheo, we should stop now and get started with the cryopreservation. I'm sure Raúl is sick to death of filming Marisol's blackflies. We can rescue him and think about what we might like to have for dinner."

"We usually eat macaroni with tuna, doctora."

"I was afraid you'd say that, Cheo," sighed Debra.

❦

Cheo ate his last bite of macaroni, sitting in the medicatura on the cement floor beside Debra, and sipped a clumpy mixture of powdered milk and water. Too bad the gringo missionaries hadn't invited them up to their house for dinner. He would have liked more of that postre Señora Peggi called apple pie. Cheo had never tasted an apple before. The fruit grew nowhere in Venezuela, as far as he knew.

Marisol and Raúl sat in the folding chairs, using the nurse's grey metal desk as a table. They had been talking so much that they had barely touched their macaroni. Cheo listened to Marisol's animated chatter. Could it be that she had captured a new admirer? "Yes, I did for a while have a boyfriend in Caracas. We broke up. Maybe it was all for the best. I never could travel to visit him very often, and the visits interrupted my research. I have much more time for research this way, and marriage would have interfered with my postgraduate studies. You see, I have applied for a scholarship from the British Council, and I hope I'll be studying in London next year. I must make personal sacrifices. It's much better this way, realmente it is." Marisol tilted her head charmingly at Raúl. He rubbed his tidy little goat's beard.

"I pity your boyfriend," Raúl said. "To lose one both pretty and intelligent." He leaned closer to her.

Marisol pushed a piece of macaroni around her plate with her fork and looked down at the insipid pasta-tuna mixture. "It happened many years ago," she replied softly.

Cheo could hear the pain break through her lies. He remembered a very different story. Marisol had been so wrapped up in her blackflies that she had only made time to see her boyfriend, Hector, twice in a year. Hector had actually been seeing another girl for the whole year before his "sudden" wedding. Marisol was devastated. The agony of rejection threw her deeper into her blackflies and farther away from reality. The stupid girl never did understand what had happened to her relationship.

"I saw the damnedest thing," Raúl said. Even a bat flying at noon could see that he was tactfully changing the topic. "Jim, surrounded by a group of Yanomami. He had his back to me and he didn't see me. He was pointing to this poster nailed to a tree. The Yanomami were all riled up over the thing, whining and yelping away in that strange language of theirs. I walked up closer to film it and I saw it was a coloured drawing of naked Yanomami with bows and arrows, screaming and burning in a fire. I couldn't believe those people were so panicked over a drawing."

"Raúl," Marisol said, "don't you know these people have no tradition of drawing? They can't tell the difference between a photograph and a drawing. Don't you see? They believed it. Drawings of our philosophy and concepts are accepted as truth by the Yanomami. They'll believe anything represented to them visually like that."

Marisol turned around and her bright brown eyes met Cheo's. She blinked twice in succession and tilted her head slightly to the left. "Cheo, you're finished eating. Good! You feed the blackflies. They're hungry and I'm not yet finished."

Doctora Debra smiled at him and winked. "I'll take your plate, Cheo," she said.

Cheo stood up, handed his plate to her. He walked over to the large blue plastic crates and pulled out the first vial. A blackfly, gummed by her wings to bloody shit, helplessly waved her six hairline legs at him. Cheo picked up microforceps and began to delicately peel her cellophane wings away from her shit. The wing ripped off. Coño! He felt a rabiotada rise from his stomach to his throat, like the poison water squeezed from sour manioc. He impaled the fly with the needle-sharp end of his forceps. Stupid flies, they made people itch and go blind. Good for nothing! Kill them before they kill us! He breathed deeply and closed his eyes to suppress his rage, and picked up the next vial. He had better not kill any more or Marisol would surely notice.

ૐ

Raúl hadn't slept well the first night in the medicatura. Antonio's teeth squeaked as he ground them in his sleep (a sign of parasitosis, Marisol offered by way of explanation) and mosquitoes droned incessantly outside his net. Raúl had stuffed wads of saliva-wetted toilet paper in his ears at midnight in an unsuccessful attempt to mute the sounds. He spooned his breakfast, an unappetizing mixture of raw oatmeal, sugar, powdered milk and water, into his mouth. He wasn't hungry.

Debra sat on the ground in the shade cast by the medicatura, some supply bags beside her. She wore her hair twisted and pinned up off her neck and she was absorbed in a paperback book rested upon her bent knees. Debra, it seemed, was not very communicative in the mornings. They were alone and they had been waiting for an hour and ten minutes. Marisol had used the delay to wash at the river. She hadn't wanted company.

They were supposedly flying to Kováta-teri mission. The plane was to have taken off—he looked at his watch again—an hour and twelve minutes ago, but a bolt had come loose on one of the Cessna's ailerons. Antonio, of the musical teeth and no brain, carried no tools with him, not even a flathead screwdriver. Cheo, some twenty minutes ago, had finally come up with the bright idea of going to the mission to borrow tools. No wonder these bush pilots so frequently crashed. A fifteen-minute flight delayed over an hour for want of a stupid wrench. And the light was perfect for filming now, right now. By the time they arrived at Kováta-teri the sun would be too high. He spooned more oatmeal into his mouth. It tasted like cardboard. He looked at the sky, already blue, the sun rising higher above the horizon.

The provocative figure of Marisol in tight blue jeans appeared around the bend in the trail. She was eating her pants, as a friend in California had once called it, as she walked towards him, the inviting swelling of labia on each side of the crotch seam pulsating with every step. That seam must be. . . . "OK, we can go now," Marisol's voice interrupted his reverie.

Raúl slung a bag with photography equipment over his shoulder, grabbed Debra's supply bags in one hand and his camera in the other and headed down the path to the airstrip.

Kovätä-teri mission and the doughnut-shaped shabono filled his viewfinder as the plane circled for the sixth time. "That's enough, Raúl," Debra shouted. "I'm feeling sick from this spinning." When the plane bumped to a stop at the end of the airstrip, Raúl saw a manicured scene from the suburban U.S.A. surrealistically implanted into lush tropical vegetation: a foreground of two fenced yards, two neat white houses with shady porches, a hand-operated water pump and flowerbeds, contrasted against a background of buttressed trees spreading like umbrellas, draped in lianas.

Two American men in tee-shirts and blue jeans waited in front of the houses: the younger nicely built with sandy blond hair, "My Boss Is a Jewish Carpenter" written across his chest; the other balding, barrel-chested. Two spanking-new Yamaha motorcycles gleamed in the sun beside them.

"Raúl, Debra, Stan and Luke," Marisol offered, pointing out faces to go along with the names. Luke, the young blond, smiled briefly. Stan seemed tense.

"We need you to take us to the shabono and translate to the Yanomami about what we'll be doing," Debra said.

"We have only a short time before lunch to introduce you around the shabono," Stan said abruptly, no niceties. "We'll meet you there. Walk down the airstrip 'bout a hundred yards. The trail to the left leads up to the shabono. Can't miss it." The two missionaries jumped on the motorcycles, rifles strung across their backs. They ripped the still air and silenced the birdcalls as they roared off, leaving a thread of dust behind them.

Raúl, Debra, Marisol and Cheo followed on foot. The path off the airstrip was as wide as a single-lane road. They passed a dirt clearing with a small medical dispensary, the ministry's yellow cross painted on the bare cement.

The two motorcycles were already parked in front of the circular shabono, the riders nowhere in sight, by the time the scientific party arrived. Marisol ducked into the low opening first. Raúl followed her, his viewfinder pressed to his eye, Marisol's tight behind momentarily filling the frame. The shabono contrasted with the orderly mission. Raúl filmed nonstop as he walked around in the shade of the thatched lean-to. The sun beating down upon the central plaza, bleaching the dirt almost white, sent the light meter off the scale if he swung the camera out of the shade. Chinchorros, really just strands of palm twine fastened at both ends, were strung around fireplaces. The Yanomami all had bowl-shaped haircuts and some had a shaved patch at the back of the scalp. An old man lay diagonally in his hammock wearing only a string, face brown and wrinkled, a wad of tobacco bulging his bottom lip, eyes closed, chest striped with protruding ribs. A woman squatted, feet close together, soles flat upon the dirt, skirt pulled above her knees, knees bent up almost beside her ears. She roasted a few plantains in the embers of a fire. A naked brown child limped across the central plaza and hid behind a group of hammocks. Half-dead, skeletal dogs lay in the shade panting, eyes closed.

Debra, a stethoscope hanging around her neck, separated from the group with Stan to take care of health disorders. Luke stayed with Marisol and Cheo. Raúl was pleased; this general footage of activities around the shabono would provide the documentary with excellent snippets of the Yanomami lifestyle and living conditions. Afterward, he might film Debra at work with her medical duties, the philanthropic activities of the research institute. The people were absolutely filthy. Raúl could barely discern the colour of their few rags of clothing under the dirt. He fixed his lens upon a Yanomami woman sitting on the bare dirt. The shaved patch on her head had grown out to about an inch in length and the stubble stood straight up. The rest of her black hair fell straight around the overgrown patch in a fringe. Her dingy dress was unbuttoned and lowered over her shoulders, exposing her breasts. A fat baby suckled at one nipple and a spotted fluffy ocelot kitten suckled at the other. Raúl zoomed in closer to the woman, saw her eyes almost closed, her expression serene. The kitten knew not to bite, its tongue curled around the nipple. A plethora of good footage here!

Just when he was ready to move on to something else, a group of Yanomami men burst into the shabono yelling and waving their bows and arrows victoriously above their heads. Luke evidently understood whatever it was that had been said, and so, it appeared, did every other man in the community. A flood of brown barefoot men, and two fully clothed Americans complete with running shoes and rifles, competed to exit the small opening. "Yeeeooowww! Roast pig tonight, way ta go!" screamed Luke. Raúl followed his journalistic instincts and ran with the mass, camera glued to his eye, film rolling.

Raúl stood, sun beating down upon him, in the middle of the wide dirt path, left in the machine-gun wake of the two motorcycles. The forest dampened their mufflerless bellow. The Yanomami men ran, hot in pursuit. The speed of the bare feet pounding the beaten soil impressed Raúl but, even so, the Yanomami were left far behind in the dust of the motorized Americans.

The forest echoed with the explosive cracks of rifles and then all became still. Suddenly a wild pig with bristly grey hair and small curved tusks appeared from the forest. The pig trotted quite calmly straight towards Raúl and his camera, grunting softly. A Yanomami appeared at the forest edge. He drew his arrow back smoothly, without hesitation. The arrow hit the peccary's side. The animal responded with an angry squeal, but another six-foot shaft already flew towards it. This one thudded into the pig's neck. Arrows dragging from its neck and side, the pig slowed its trot to a walk and then fell, wheezing loudly, a yard from Raúl's feet.

The motorcycles returned, the two Americans heavily laden with bristle-covered carcasses strung together by cords wrapped around small cloven hoofs. Luke dropped three carcasses onto the trail between the motorcycles. Stan dumped two more on top of the heap. Yanomami men appeared from the bushes carrying only their weapons—fifteen fully armed hunters had killed only the single peccary lying inert at Raúl's feet.

Stan spoke to the Yanomami men in their tongue. It sounded rapid and fluent to Raúl. The bare-chested Yanomami men spoke among themselves in their nasal whine. One of the men, the one who had struck down the peccary, nodded to Stan. Stan took from his pocket a plastic bag containing a small handful of a white crystalline substance. The hunter accepted the bag and dragged his peccary over to the pile of carcasses caught by Stan and Luke.

"Can we examine the cadavers for parasites while you take off the skin?" Marisol asked in heavily accented English.

"I don't know," Stan said. He turned to Luke. "What do you think?"

"Can't see what harm it would do," Luke said. "Don't want my niece and nephew eating worms and getting sick. Maybe a good thing to let them check it out." He looked at the dead pigs and scratched his blond head. "Say, we got us enough meat to last more than a coupla months, Stan. What ya say we give the Yanos a head or two?"

For the next three days the expedition party worked at Porohóa, where people were more heavily infected with oncho parasites, which Marisol said ensured better infection rates for her blackflies. Debra spent her time snipping skin, removing nodules and conducting eye examinations. If she looked through the cornea and anterior chamber into the large ocular cavity, she could see microfilariae floating in the vitreous humour. Marisol had her examine eyeballs from the dead pigs and save those infected with microfilariae in a specimen jar.

The final morning of the expedition, Jim asked Debra to see a sick child. They walked past the mission garden, its patch of avocado trees laden with ripe green teardrops. They turned onto a wide path and walked up a slight incline to dense forest and the outer wall of the shabono.

The Porohóa and Koväta-teri shabonos were dirtier than those in the Topochal area. Mission aeroplanes brought load after load of supplies in, but never took garbage back out. Contact meant frequent flights, trading and accumulation of garbage. Plastic bottles, rags, spent flashlight batteries, cans and pieces of corrugated metal littered the shabono. This junk would never degrade, at least not in her lifetime.

They crossed the central plaza and approached a family grouping of hammocks around a hearth of five logs, the centre charred black. "This girl is very special to Peg and me. Her grandfather was the first Yanomami here to be baptized. If you could help her, I'd be very grateful." Debra could see the smooth tan flanks and buttocks of a teenage girl through the twisted moriche strands of the hammock. Jim leaned over the hammock and spoke quietly. The patient sat up and looked around at Debra. She was thin, the bowl-shaped black hair complementing her dark almond eyes. A crusty malignant melanoma on her right cheek marred an otherwise beautiful face. A secondary lesion opened from the cervical node. "It's malignant, Jim," Debra said, "and it's metastasized to her lymphatics. I can't do anything for her."

"Nothing?"

"She could be flown to Puerto Pedriscal. Even so, there's no oncologist there on staff, and I doubt any treatment would be effective at this stage. No one there speaks her language and she'd be all alone. She will die soon. She'd be better off spending her last days here with her own people in familiar surroundings. About all I can do is give you something from the dispensary to ease any discomfort."

"I'll discuss it with her father," Jim said.

Two dirty little girls, hair caked stiff with oily dust, appeared from nowhere. One had lost all her toenails to niguas; the other, most of them. The girls smiled and laughed. "They are her sisters," Jim said, smiling down at them.

A woman in a loosely fitted dress spoke to Jim. "There are

two sick babies over here," Jim translated. The first baby, about a year to eighteen months, Debra estimated, had fallen into a fire, and his abdomen was burned over a large area. Debra cleaned the wound, did what she could with her limited supplies. The other baby had a nasty-looking wound on her scalp. Jim held her as she cried loudly, and waved the flies off it. "His mother says it's a machete wound," he explained. Debra cleaned it, picked out maggots, while Jim held the baby still. She wailed in Jim's arms. Interesting the way Yanomami babies hardly ever cried. Their mothers kept them tight to their bodies at almost all times. Rarely were they separated. At the slightest whimper, a breast was offered, the cries were silenced. Jim handed the baby back. The mother, lying in her hammock, cradled the baby against her chest.

"You know, Jim, what the real problem is here? Contact. Contact with you, with us."

"I did not give that child cancer, or drop the baby in the fire. We're on the same side. I want good health. I want the same things for these people that you do. I too try to save them from disease. And we have also brought them from spiritual darkness and fear to see God's light."

"By showing them pictures of hell? You don't need to threaten them with hell—you created it—right here! Look at the filth."

"But they don't understand cleanliness. We teach them hygiene."

"They wouldn't need hygiene lessons if you left them alone. You teach them to be ashamed of their bodies. You make them wear clothes. Of course, you don't supply them with enough clothing to change—that's why they're infested with lice."

"They have lived like this for thousands of years. It's a long path out of darkness. We must work one step at a time. You can't expect us to make significant change overnight."

"You do make significant change! That much you *have* managed. They lived here very well for thousands of years, until you came along and mucked up their society and created dependence. While you created your stable Christian base, you catalysed change, and every change you make threatens the social institutions that allow their survival. You stopped the *wayumi* migrations so you could have your flock around you all the time. Now the parasites accumulate in the soil and water, disease-transmitting vectors are rampant, and let's not forget about soil and game depletion. Just look at the kids, for Christ's sake—some of them can't even walk, they're infested with so many chiggers."

Debra panted, her chest tight with emotion. Jim blinked at her. He showed no sign of anger, only blissful Christian devotion—sympathetic eyes, brainwashed smile, devoid of real human emotion—the missionaries all had that same look. Never outwardly angry or sad, always such perfect control, as cloned as Malariología houses. "I'm a doctor, Jim," she said, concentrating consciously on her breathing. "I can see things that you can't. I can see the malnutrition—oedematous hands and feet, wasted muscles and subcutaneous fat, chronic diarrhoea and anaemia. Caterpillars and spiders may look awful to you, but they're a hell of a lot more nutritious than the rice and salt you provide."

"We are preparing them for the arrival of civilization. Don't you think it's better they learn good ways from people who love them than learn prostitution, alcoholism and violence? Shouldn't they learn how to defend themselves? We teach them how to live, how to trade and how to survive in the modern world. We are teaching them before others come to destroy them."

"By making them work slave labour in the mission? I saw your 'bank'—jam jars each labelled with a name. I saw them pay inflated prices for salt, batteries, machetes and twine. Stan called it a good Christian work ethic. I call it exploitation!" Debra choked on her last words. "You're softening them for the blow, making them vulnerable, making them dependent. Look at what you're doing. Open your eyes, you fool, or are you too drunk with the Spirit of the Lord to see?"

"People, Debra," Jim replied kindly, "people have spiritual as well as physical needs. What good is it to feed the body if the soul is starved?"

"You simply have no idea of the harm you cause. Or do you? The body just a cup containing the soul for God's consumption—Porohóa an internment camp, a camp where people wait for death. You're no different from Nazis—justifying systematic ethnocide through your unrestrained zeal."

"Come, Debra. I'll walk you to your plane. Remember, I've sacrificed my life to help these people. We're on the same side, really we are."

The aetiology of social decay and disease walked in front of her, a grandfatherly man with receding grey hair and a fixed smile. He might as well have been a six-foot, antibiotic-resistant bacillus secreting deadly exotoxins. He and the others were surely as lethal. It didn't matter what she said. She couldn't reach him, and he was the most approachable one she'd met. She could offer the Yanomami no therapy for this ailment. Nothing was strong enough to counteract this infection. There was no vaccine to prime their defence mechanisms. A radical mission-ectomy was needed. After all, a disease gone rampant required drastic treatment.

❦

The plane to carry the equipment back to Puerto Pedriscal arrived just before midday. They had expected Victor's twin-engined Mooney. Instead, another Cessna taxied up the airstrip. Antonio greeted the pilot as he climbed out of the cockpit: "Hola, Roberto. Congratulations on finding us. You have never flown to Porohóa before, no? Where's Victor?"

"He had a bit of an accident," Roberto replied. "You know how that old Mooney of his was always losing an engine? Said it was his way of saving fuel. It happened again when he was bringing a load of meat from San Fernando de Apure. He thought he could land with the one engine, but wouldn't you know it, the other died too, just as he was crossing the river. Smack, straight into the rocks. Quite a bonus for the caribes."

"Is he all right?" Marisol asked, wide-eyed.

"Are you joking? They couldn't tell him from the cargo. His wife won't know if she's burying Victor or a tenderloin."

Antonio lowered and raised the wing flaps as the aeroplane stood on the packed earth at one end of the airstrip. Raúl sat in the seat beside him, his camera ready in his lap. He turned around to face Marisol, her shoulders squeezed between Debra and Cheo. She frowned as she shoved against Cheo, gaining an extra inch or two of space. "What were those little bags of white stuff?" Raúl asked. "Those ones they traded with and sold at their 'store'. Was it some kind of drug?"

"Those," Marisol said, "those were bags of salt. Sodium chloride, plain and simple. The Yanomami have never had salt in their diets. Once they acquire a taste for it, they'll do practically anything to get hold of it."

"They're addicted to salt?" Raúl asked.

"Of course they are," Debra interjected in a flat voice. "And nobody ever stops to ask what it might be doing to them."

Antonio turned the key and the propeller chugged, turned slowly and died. He tried again. The propeller chugged, then the engine roared to life. "Maybe water in the fuel," he said. The plane bumped across the nubs of grass. It picked up speed, the bumps became vibrations, the trees whizzed past and they had a floating feeling as the plane left the ground. "I hope there isn't too much water," Antonio mused. "That gas has been sitting around an awful long time."

"Maybe Raúl would like to hear the story about the rural doctor and the capybara remains," Cheo said. He opened the canvas bag at his feet and pulled out his compass, a pencil and his notebook.

"Shut up, Cheo!" Marisol hissed.

"We are only immortal until we die, doctora," Cheo laughed.

296

25

Debra lay in her bed, alone, her thumbs pressed hard into her temples. Three acetaminophens, each laced with eight milligrams of codeine, hadn't shifted the headache. Early morning sun crept into the room, making the dingy bareness stand out. The poor, simple man had slept for two nights in the room next to hers, on Wilfred's bed—the death bed, as she had come to think of it. During the night, through the concrete wall, she had sensed an invisible force seeping up through the mattress and infiltrating Elio's body. Debra sometimes used the bed as an ironing board, and she felt the iron's heat draw something from the mattress, scorching it into her clothing. It was silly, utterly superstitious and totally irrational. Scientifically she knew better, yet she continued to be plagued by the ridiculous feelings. She got up, threw on some clothes that were lying on the floor.

Urine pooled on the bathroom floor again. Debra crinkled her nose. How had Marisol managed to manipulate her into taking on this unwelcome house guest? "Please, Debra, just a few days. Blancanieves and I have no room in our house and the institute can't afford to put him up at the hotel. Don't be selfish. You have three bedrooms. Don't worry, you won't have to cook for him. He will be my responsibility." So far it had been damned inconvenient. While Elio stayed in the house Segundo wouldn't spend the night with her, and tomorrow she was expected to go on another expedition to Porohóa. No sooner had she returned from the last, it seemed, than Velázquez had ordered her back. And all because Velázquez and Marisol had somehow managed to convince an unsuspecting onchocerciasis patient to come here and "volunteer" for Marisol's cross-infection studies.

Elio was illiterate, a simple man with eleven children, from a small coastal fishing village. One look at him and Debra knew the research volunteer had absolutely no idea what he'd gotten himself into. For three days now he had smiled submissively when spoken to, and when he did speak it was only to answer, "Sí doctora, sí doctora," no matter what the question was.

Obviously he had never used a toilet before. When and if he managed to hit the bowl instead of the floor, he didn't flush. He didn't seem to know about electric light either; no light appeared underneath the bathroom door when he went in at night.

Debra soaked the urine up with a sponge. The bathroom was beginning to stink. Marisol would be scrubbing it from top to bottom with disinfectant when Señor Elio left, whether she liked it or not. He was supposed to be her responsibility, after all. Debra washed the urine from her hands, soaping thoroughly.

Señor Elio sat in the kitchenette, at the pearlescent formica table, wearing a khaki shirt and brown polyester pants, his straight black hair parted on the side and slicked back with water. He just stared through the kitchen window at the church, looking very confused, as if he didn't quite know what to do with himself. Marisol had told Debra not to cook for the man. The day he arrived Marisol had asked him what he liked to eat for breakfast and he'd answered, "Bread, doctora, but only if it's not too much bother." Marisol had brought him one loaf of bread, two days ago.

"Café?" Debra asked.

"Sí, doctora," answered Elio. He grinned, no incisor teeth in his upper jaw. Probably none in the lower jaw either. Marisol said he was thirty-four. Debra would have guessed his age at closer to fifty. At what age had he started reproducing to have spawned so many children? Eleven, imagine that! She shook her head.

She poured the coffee sludge through a cloth filter—the

Venezuelan sock method, she called it—and handed Elio a mug of black coffee. "Leche?"

"Sí, doctora." Elio nodded, his lips pulled tightly back in a nervous grin.

"Señor Elio, better drink quickly because Doctora Socorro will be here soon."

"Sí, sí, claro, doctora."

That was another thing that irritated Debra. She had to be close at hand—as a medical witness—because a human research subject was involved. The dull ache pulsated from her temples through to the back of her skull. Maybe she could sit nearby, under a shady tree, and read her book.

Marisol heard the engine of her jeep protest with a horrible racket. "I forgot the clutch again. Never drove standard before I came to work here," she said cheerfully. She could hardly wait to see the results from the experimental infections on Señor Elio and compare them to those from that Yanomami nurse, Diosgracio. It would mean a few long, uncomfortable days collecting blackflies from Señor Elio's back, but it would be well worth the effort. "We'll set up at Velázquez's fundo," she said. "It's near the Carinagua River, where we'll have privacy, and lots of blackflies."

Debra got out to open the gate to the fundo. Velázquez's big brindle dog, brain no larger than an iguana's egg, lumbered up the road, tail wagging and saliva stalactites dangling. Debra stooped to pet him and Marisol drove on through the gate.

She set the equipment out beside the stream, under the stingy shade of three palms. Proximity to water meant there would be plenty of blackflies. She positioned Elio on a stool, stripped from the waist up and slumped forward. Debra and the big stupid dog arrived. If that dog was given the slightest encouragement, Marisol knew, he stuck to a person like an ectoparasite. He had better not get in the way drooling all over

299

her equipment and sticking his big drippy nose into her box of blackfly vials, or he'd be sorry.

Debra sat down, leaned against a treetrunk and opened a book. The dog lay down beside her. "What do you think you're doing, Debra? We're here to work." Marisol sat on one of the two stools at Elio's back. She held the mouth of a glass vial over a little fly and brought it down carefully. The fly flew to the back of the vial and she snapped a plastic cap over the entrance. A minute blood blister surrounded by a raised welt was left on Elio's skin where the fly had sucked. "The blackflies must have their fill. Wait until their abdomens are fat and red, but trap them before they withdraw their proboscises. If you help, we'll catch twice as many flies. It will save me time and then we can all finish earlier."

"If you needed help, why didn't you bring Cheo?"

"Cheo has to prepare things for tomorrow's expedition."

Already, five flies sucked at Elio's back, at various stages of blood fill. "Come on, Debra. I really do need your help." Debra threw down her book, sat down on a stool beside her, picked up a vial and positioned it over a fly with a bright red bead for an abdomen.

"The one I have in my vial is *Simulium sanchezi* and the one you just trapped is *Simulium exiguum*," Marisol said animatedly. She knew them all so well, there were so many colour variations and so many slight differences in behaviour. Fascinating creatures. She would really miss her field work if she went off to Britain for her graduate studies. It would be a good move career-wise, but such a waste of valuable time. Why, she knew more about simuliids in this area than any academic authority. It was irritating that she had to obtain those official letters to get the full scientific respect she deserved. If she did get the British Council scholarship, it mightn't be too bad. With any luck, she should be able to do the field-work part of her Ph.D research here while maintaining her position at INSA. At least the British didn't have the obsession with courses that the Americans had, so she wouldn't have to spend very much time in London—a few months, a year at most. She slid another vial over a fly, capped it and put it in the plastic box. And Raúl would be waiting for her in Caracas while she did her Ph.D. He was so different from Hector. After she defended her thesis, maybe she could look for a job in Caracas, where she would be closer to him. There was no reason a woman couldn't achieve both marriage and a successful career. The future looked all right.

"Elio, you should be proud. You are making a huge contribution to medical science," Marisol said. "Through this work, you are helping to combat disease. You will help maybe thousands of people. You have no idea how invaluable your contribution to humanity is." The reflection of the palm trees danced on the rippled stream. A gentle breezed cooled her as the blackflies sucked Elio's blood and with it, she hoped, many microfilariae. There were lots of flies today. It was a great day. It would be a great year.

"Why does Elio have to go to Porohóa?" asked Debra, as she placed a vial in the box. "Why can't you do the experimental infections here?"

"I thought you knew. On the coast there's *Simulium metallicum*, in Topochal *amazonicum*, in Porohóa *pintoi* and *incrustatum* and in Río Negro *cuasisanguineum*. I need to discover if Elio's strain of oncho is equally infectious for different species of *Simulium*. I want to see if the infectivity of an oncho strain differs according to its area of geographic origin. I already have half the information from Diosgracio. This is going to make a great publication."

❦

They finally stopped for lunch. Elio's stomach grumbled. The doctoras hadn't fed him anything for breakfast, only one cup of coffee. He stuffed bread and cheese into his mouth. He shouldn't have come. The fly doctora smiled at him—she was pretty but dangerous, like a heron waiting for a fish to come her way. What could she want with all these flies that made his back itch so badly?

Years ago, Elio's skin had started to itch and wrinkle. He'd started having trouble seeing close up to repair his nets, and each year he could see less. Then, just two weeks ago, he'd gone to the big University Hospital in the capital. It took almost all the money he had saved for his family. An important doctor visited him in the hospital and said he could help him fight the itching disease that was making him go blind—if Elio would help the doctor for a few weeks with an experiment. Elio agreed because of the money offered. He couldn't say no. He hadn't believed his ears when the doctor had told him how much, more money all at once than he earned in a year from selling his fish.

Now they made him sit for hours allowing flies to bite him, and they wouldn't let him move or swat. When they first let flies bite him he wanted to protest, but he didn't know how. He was afraid of these big important people from the government. They had brought him so far from home in a big plane. He couldn't get back to his family without their help. If they took him away to this Porohóa place, matters could only get worse. Even if he was afraid of them, he must do something to stop this, and he must do it now. Tomorrow would be too late. But it took all his courage to speak. "Doctora, I think maybe my children need me at home."

"Elio, your children are fine. We gave a large sum of money to your family," the fly doctora said.

"I think maybe I should go home, not go to this Porohóa place."

"You are a little nervous, and that's understandable, Elio," the fly doctora said. "Porohóa is very pretty. He'll like it, don't you think?" She turned to face the foreign doctora, who was eating a piece of bread. The fly doctora turned back to him, smiled and twisted her head. She broke a little piece of bread off and played with it in her fingers. "Elio, you will like it. Honestly you will. I wouldn't lie to you."

"I think I would like home better."

"Elio, the more you co-operate, the sooner we can return you to your family."

"Don't worry, Elio. We will take good care of you, promise," the white doctora said. He had never seen a real gringa before. He had only heard about them, that they sometimes worked as spies. He didn't trust her. He didn't trust any of the doctors, especially that big doctor, the one called Velázquez, who had come to talk to him while he was at the hospital. He had said they'd take him where many indios were sick with the same disease he had, in that Porohóa place—friendly indios—that they wouldn't hurt him. And he had said the work they did would stop many people from itching and going blind. These científicos claimed they didn't lie, but they had lied already. They said they fought the itching sickness but they had done nothing. They had said they wouldn't take him far and they had sent him, on the big plane, farther than he'd imagined existed. The houses looked so small, then disappeared as he flew up above the clouds. Now he was in a place where the indios didn't even speak Spanish. Elio had never been so frightened in his entire life, not even the time his fishing boat overturned in a storm and he almost drowned. Where was this Porohóa place? Farther away, so far away no one except these doctors had even heard of it.

How did fly bites on his back keep the skin on other people from itching? Or help their eyesight? All morning the flies bit him and now his skin itched more than ever. Maybe they thought, if the flies bit him and were full, they wouldn't bite the other people. It was their own skin they wanted to save. He wished he had never taken all that money. It would feed his family for many months, but why would someone pay a man so much money to sit while flies bit him? They didn't fight sickness. They made sickness. He would return the money so he could go home—except that his wife had used half of it to buy a television. They were now the only family in his village with a television. But what good was the television if he was here where he couldn't watch it? Maybe the doctores had tricked him. Maybe they'd never intended to return him to his family. If he didn't obey them, they might get really angry and do something worse. They might keep him prisoner for ever, and torture him. Yet he had no idea how to get back to his village. If he wanted to see his family again, maybe he had better pretend to do as they said. He could escape later, when they weren't watching him. Elio stopped chewing, no longer hungry.

"Can I have a cigarette?" he asked quietly.

"The smoke will repel the flies, Elio," the fly doctora answered. "Wait until later, then we'll be finished faster."

❦

The shower felt especially cold after the horribly long day in the heat. Debra wrapped herself in a towel. She shivered and clamped her jaw shut to prevent her teeth from chattering. It was time for dinner, but she had no appetite. Shit—a knock at the door! Never a moment's peace. She dripped, wearing only her towel, to the door. Marisol. As if she hadn't seen enough of her for one day. "I came to take Elio for dinner," Marisol said.

"Well, you're a little late. He walked over to the kiosk for a beer five minutes ago." She rubbed her arms to warm them.

Marisol frowned, hands on her hips. "How could you let him, Debra? How could you be so irresponsible?" A ligament jumped out on the right side of her neck as her head jerked left.

"He's a grown man and he can have a beer if he damn well pleases. I'm not a baby sitter. Now if you'll excuse me. . . ."

"You know he's probably an alcoholic. He'll get drunk, then be hung over and useless in Porohóa tomorrow. Have you any idea how hard it was to convince him to go with us? I had to take him up to Doctor Velázquez's office. We both spoke to him for over an hour. Debra, if you have jeopardized my research I'll . . . I'll. . . ." Marisol clenched her fists so tightly that her knuckles were white. "Where did he get money to buy beer?"

"I gave him fifteen bolívars. For the past three days you practically bled the poor man dry, and you expect *me* to tell him he can't go and have a beer down the street. He's a volunteer, not a prisoner. He begged me."

"Fifteen bolívars is a lot of beer."

"You know, Marisol, I couldn't care less. Helping you torture that man all day and cleaning up his urine every morning has made me sick. Just get lost and let me rest."

"That's right, think about yourself." Marisol spun around on one heel, her fists still clenched. From the doorway, Debra watched her storm through the weeds to her jeep, heard the gears grind as the jeep lurched forward. It stopped abruptly just down the street at the kiosk, under the sign of a frosty Polar bottle. Marisol strutted right into the centre of the men grouped around the counter, pushing and shoving.

That woman was out of her mind, in another plane of existence. Debra reached up and touched her forehead, hot and wet. The symptoms had begun when Elio first came: malaise, headache, muscle aches, lack of appetite. Working in the heat of the day, trapping blackflies—it was understandable. She dragged herself to the bathroom and looked in the mirror. Her skin was dry around the mouth, her face pale and sort of doughy, yet her flesh seemed to be flaming. She pulled her bottom eyelid down. Was it her imagination or was it exceptionally pale? The ammonia scent of Elio's urine wafted up to her nostrils. Her stomach churned. She dropped onto her knees in front of the toilet and vomited.

༃

"Feeling better now?" asked Reina. She sat at her desk covered with paperwork. She had to fill out this stack of bureaucratic ministry nonsense. Company, anybody's, relieved the monotony.

305

"Thank you, much better now the chloroquine has taken effect and I've slept for two days," Debra answered. She placed a box of sputum vials down on the tile lab bench. "Maybe I picked it up on the last expedition."

"Have some coffee." Reina nodded in the direction of the thermos at the sink. "There's a cup on my chemical shelf. What a pity you couldn't go on the expedition to Porohóa. Really, a doctor should accompany an expedition party."

"To tell you the truth, I'm awfully glad not to go. Marisol will manage fine without me."

Reina saw Doctor Velázquez walk past the louvred windows. He opened the door.

"Buenos días, doctor." Reina glanced up from her papers for a second, then looked back down, resuming her writing. What could he want? He never stopped in her lab for casual visits. He only came when he wanted something.

"As usual, we have a crisis on our hands." Reina heard the tremble in his voice, almost imperceptible. He spoke slowly and succinctly, as if to steady it. "I've been talking on the radio to Marisol. Señor Elio is missing." Velázquez picked up a test-tube from a rack, looking vacantly at its contents.

"Missing? How long? When did this happen?" asked Reina, her pen frozen to the paper.

"Since yesterday. Marisol said he became very unbalanced while on board the Cessna. He kept saying he was no longer in Venezuela; he was convinced he'd been abducted to another planet. Marisol and Cheo did succeed in calming him down, and on the first day the experimental infections were conducted smoothly, as planned. Marisol also conducted experimental infections the next morning. At lunch-time, Cheo sharpened an axe and chopped firewood. Marisol said Elio looked oddly at the axe, then calmly stated that he needed to relieve himself. He walked into the forest and hasn't returned since. The situation is complicated by the fact that the Yanomami at Porohóa are at war with the Yanomami at Kovära-teri. For the moment they are unwilling to track him. Cheo and Marisol

306

would become lost themselves if they tried to find him without a guide. I had no recourse but to report the disappearance to the División de la Selva. Capitán Zambrano was extremely co-operative, and he's launching a rescue party first thing tomorrow morning. This crisis could have serious political repercussions for our institute. I will, of course, keep you abreast of developments." He turned around, his head carried straight, and with the vestiges of his dignity proceeded out the door.

"My God," Reina said. She felt sick to her stomach. "He must have gotten lost in the forest. It's so very easy. You step into the forest a little way—when you try to retrace your steps, if you miss your tracks by a little you will pass the village without knowing."

"Maybe he's hiding. He didn't exactly enjoy being bitten all the time."

"Poor Elio. If they don't find him soon, he will die. What can a fisherman know of survival in the forest?"

"I think maybe we all share responsibility in this."

"None of us could have predicted that this would happen."

"I never stopped to think how an uneducated man would react to being surrounded by half-naked people with arrows and curare-tipped darts. I should have. Even for me—and I'd been intellectually prepared for the experience—it was overwhelming."

"He must be frightened. It's cold in the forest at night, and he's all alone." Reina put her pen down and stared at the wall in front of her.

❦

Diego Velázquez drove north on Avenida Orinoco. The sun sank in the sky like a stone thrown into the river. Orange streetlights flickered on. The day was only a pink smudge on the horizon. Another night approaching, and still no trace of Elio. Each night that passed narrowed the possibility of his survival. Even the military search party hadn't been able to find him.

Nothing had been going well for Velázquez. Last week he'd discovered that he had been turned down for the WHO grant. He would appeal. Surely there had been a terrible mistake. He had been practically promised that money, so necessary for the long-term development of his institute. And now a research volunteer had disappeared. If any grant-giving institution heard of this fiasco, he'd be ruined.

All was not lost. Marisol had returned safely from Porohóa, naturally badly shaken by the ordeal, but she had collected sufficient blackflies from Elio to continue with her research. Furthermore, Velázquez had managed to keep the crisis under control, at least for the time being. He mustn't allow any leak to the press. Unfortunately, the ministry's ham radio had broken down while he was speaking to Cheo and he had had no choice but to ask the New World Mission for use of their radio. The fewer people who knew the sordid details surrounding this scandal, the better—and now he had no alternative but to let the missionaries in on his secret.

On impulse, he turned his shiny black Land Cruiser around, drove past the kiosk and parked beside the Evangelist church. She was American. Perhaps she could visit with the missionaries, distracting them while he spoke on the radio. He walked up the steps to her house and knocked. She answered the door dressed only in a bikini, a Polar in her hand.

"Debra, I require your immediate assistance. You must accompany me to the mission headquarters. Please dress appropriately and brush your teeth." He waited for her on the doorstep. Her personal behaviour didn't please him—the video proofs were shockingly indiscreet. But he'd deal with that matter after he had eliminated the crisis at hand. He would confront Debra at a more suitable time, perhaps at a Technical Commission meeting. He didn't like to pry into the personal lives of his staff, but now INSA was jeopardized.

She reappeared, wearing blue jeans and a shocking pink, loose-fitting shirt that hid her figure. For once she had done as he asked.

The mission headquarters were four blocks away. Ronald Elliot wasn't friendly, even to his compatriot. His eyes magnified behind the thick lenses glared suspiciously. He didn't speak English with Debra as Doctor Velázquez had anticipated; instead, each appeared to be antagonized by the sight of the other. "We have prayed for the lost man," Ronald said in Spanish. That imperialist missionary shit knew too much. Of course, he spoke regularly with the missionaries in Porohóa, but why hadn't Marisol and Cheo covered up the situation better? Elio might still return on his own.

Ronald led them down a hall; past a comfortable, conservative, American-style living room; past an office; and past a bathroom. Velázquez glanced at the fluffy green bath mat, matching toilet-seat cover and a box of Kleenex sitting on the ceramic tank lid. He entered a room at the end of the hall, about the size of a walk-in closet, brightly lit by an overhead fluorescent light, with a ham radio set covering a large folding table.

Ronald sat down and picked up the mouthpiece. "Yankee Victor—One, Bravo, Oscar, Tango," he rattled off. He spoke in English with another missionary at the Porohóa base and a few moments later Cheo's voice, distorted by short-wave radio squeals, crackled into the room. Ronald stood up and allowed Velázquez to sit. The snoopy missionary stood right beside him, where he could overhear everything. He knew far too much already and he wanted to know more.

"Cheo, can you briefly update me on the situation? Over," said Velázquez.

"Doctor, the Yanomami stopped fighting today and tracked him, no problem. They could plainly see every footprint. Incredible, doctor, incredible. They explained to us everywhere he had been and everything he had done: the hombre stopped to rest and he knelt, his three fingers touching the ground here, his weight only upon his toes there; he stopped to drink and these marks were made by water as it dribbled through his fingers; he sat on a banana leaf, see the depression made by his buttocks; he slid on a patch of mud and grabbed this thorny branch, see the blood drops underneath it; he took a pee, there are a few butterflies left. Qué vaina! Once they started tracking, it took them less than half an hour to find him. Over."

"Then the crisis is over? I'll send the pilot to pick you both up tomorrow morning. Over," said Velázquez.

"Thank the Lord," Ronald said.

"Doctor, there is one complication"—crackle, squeal—"over."

"Cheo! Tell me. Tell me now! Over!"

"Señor Elio is dead. Aparentemente, se suicidió. He ripped his shirt into strips and knotted them together. He tied a noose to a branch on a young tree, a tree with low branches that grew in a small clearing where there was light. His knees were touching the ground. He knelt down to do it. Coño, he could have stopped it at any time, if only he'd stood up. It takes a lot of balls to die like that, doctor, you know what I mean, when you could stop it any time. Poor hombre, you got to admire his courage. Must have thought we were going to feed him to the Yanomami when he saw me sharpen that machete. Must have decided then that it was better to do himself in. Over."

"Cheo, that is sufficient. Give me the details tomorrow. I'll send a plane for you. I'm certain the military will take control of the situation. Over and out."

"The militares are trying to send the body back to you. It is badly decomposed. They say he died shortly after he disappeared, days ago now. The official cause of death being suicide eliminates the need for further investigation and clears INSA of any responsibility. Clear-cut, no vainas, it was his choice, they say. They want Aguirre to confirm. That is, if they can fly the body out. That's all. See you tomorrow, doctor. Over and out."

How fortunate that the military hadn't implicated INSA in any way. In return for a bottle of imported scotch, Máximo could be counted on. Suicide. Velázquez had never considered that possibility. The missionaries weren't likely to cause problems now that INSA had been absolved of responsibility, now that the situation was in the military's hands. The missionaries would never respond in a manner antagonistic to the military. They co-operated with the military so they could obtain upriver and construction permits. Diego felt confident that he could trust them to keep quiet about the situation.

"Thank you, Ronald, for the use of your radio," said Velázquez.

The missionary's lips formed a straight, flat line. "No problem," he answered.

Velázquez looked around the room and found himself uncomfortably alone with Ronald. "Where is Doctora Baumstark?"

"She asked to use the bathroom. She should be back soon." The two men locked stares, neither willing to concede to the other. Ronald broke the uncomfortable contact to switch off the radio. A minute slowly ticked by, second by second, then Debra walked in. She smiled at them both demurely, blushing to match her pink shirt. His luck, Velázquez reflected, had run out the day he hired her. Everything had gone beautifully until she arrived. Never an asset, always a liability. He should start looking for another medical doctor when he returned to Caracas.

ॐ

Velázquez watched Antonio stagger out of the Cessna onto the tarmac and vomit, heaving until he could compose himself. "It wasn't worth the double wage," Antonio gasped. "The military poured lime on top of it and sealed it in plastic bags. But even so, I made a forced emergency landing in La Joya. I threw up on the airstrip there too, until nothing came out. I had to take half an hour's fresh air before I could fly again. I didn't think I would make it."

Pedro Aguirre walked up to the plane, took one whiff. He retreated, pulled out the certificate, signed it on the spot, no questions asked, with not so much as a glance at the cadaver. "Cause of death—self-inflicted strangulation," he said. "I trust the military investigators. I don't need to see it to confirm."

"Considering the gravity of the situation, I don't think it would be wise to fly it all the way to the coast, as requested by the widow," said Velázquez.

"Suicide for the pilot," Antonio said.

"We will bury it without further delay, in unconsecrated ground, at the back edge of Puerto Pedriscal's cemetery," said Velázquez. "It will draw the least attention there."

❦

Señor Elio was gone. Marisol didn't trust Cheo with the blackflies; she suspected him of killing some of his previous charges. They were irreplaceable, and she cared for them herself. With exquisite care, with the needle-sharp ends of her microforceps, she peeled the fly's wings off her bloody faeces and planted her back upon her shaky legs. She was a pretty little thing. Marisol held a magnifying glass a few inches from the vial to marvel at the complicated details of the fly's anatomy—she was olive-green, her minuscule thorax had three segments, her two pairs of wings were iridescent and all eleven segments of her tiny abdomen were visible now that she had concentrated her blood meal. The filter paper was dotted with bloody faeces—excess water and digested by-products. It was kind of eerie to see little dots of Señor Elio left behind, when the man himself was dead. The dots were Elio's legacy—his life had not been in vain. He had made an everlasting contribution to science. Thank goodness she had collected enough flies to complete her research before he had killed himself.

❦

That evening, Velázquez took expert control of the situation at the fortieth Technical Commission meeting. He sat at the conference table, his hands folded in front of him. "The research subject, Señor Elio Pérez, had a drinking problem. Alcohol abuse caused his delusional state of mind and hence his suicide. In fact, I am told that at any time he could have prevented his death merely by standing up. Furthermore, I am informed that such a death would be prolonged. This proves that the decision to die was Elio's and his alone. INSA, although it is in no way responsible, will do its part to help his wife and eleven children. I will offer two of his children technical positions here at the institute. In the long run, the family will be much better off without him. He couldn't hold a steady job because of his disabilities, and therefore he did not adequately provide for his family's needs. With two técnico wages, the family will be more than adequately compensated.

"On a more serious note, this institute has found itself to be in a very grave situation. The WHO grant will not be awarded to INSA, contrary to expectations. At this very moment I am directing all efforts towards an appeal and alternative funding, although I suspect imperialistic manoeuvring against me. There is no need for panic yet. We must make some essential cutbacks, however, at least until I can get finances back under control. We will not have funds to provide continued antibiotic therapy to the Piaroa study village. We must focus upon international collaborative projects that bring us independent money. This may sound harsh, but I assure you we will be able to serve the Amazonian people better by thinking of the long-term viability of the institute."

❧

Euphoria—the high of adrenalin and endorphins, chemical messengers triggered by completion of a task involving risk. Debra sat upon her bed, papers scattered everywhere. She squinted to read them in the inadequate light. The papers contained abundant information: biblical translations, international communications, drawings of Yanomami, shipping documents, journals, expansion plans and bank statements; a plethora of evidence supporting the Indians' accusation.

How easy it had been to slip into Ronald's office. Velázquez and Ronald hadn't suspected a thing. Salvador would surely find this information interesting.

INSA, clearly, was falling apart, and wasn't much of a threat. No need to sabotage it; it was shooting itself in the foot. Jeff Marshall was gone, a threat that had eliminated itself. Aguirre—his itching crotch would keep him occupied for a long time to come—would no longer desecrate graves, and the dead could rest in peace. That left the missionaries. The New World—the greatest threat lay there. Something had to be done immediately, something to stop the destruction. Irreparable harm had already been done, but it was not too late for those who were still inaccessible. Padre Francisco's intrusion could be dealt with at a later date.

She eagerly read a quote from a version of the Bible intended for translation into Yanomami:

> The Yanomami lived in a bad way. Jesü wanted to show them the good way to live. He wanted to make them happy. When they died, Jesü wanted them to live in a pretty shabono in the sky, in a forest where there were no *Shawara* demons, only sweet fruit, fat vegetables and plentiful game. This Jesü wanted because he loved them. The Yanomami did not understand. They did not believe Jesü. They did not love Jesü the way he loved them. They accused Jesü of bringing *Shawara* demons and they nailed him to a big tree with no food or water. They shot at him with their arrows, and he died in this way.
>
> God is angry. He seeks revenge. His wrath burns like fire. The Yanomami killed His only son. God has

the power to send them to a land where the Yanomami will perish for ever in flames like the funereal pyres in their shabono plazas. In this place the Yanomami will live inside those flames for eternity. The Yanomami should be punished for what they did to Jesü. God is more powerful than all the *Hekura* spirits dwelling inside shamans.

But God is not bad. He does not want to hurl them into the flames. If the Yanomami repay God, He will not seek revenge. They must only believe that God exists and they must say they love His son Jesü. That is what they must do to repay Him. They must live the good way God wants them to live. That life will make the Yanomami laugh and be happy. God loves the Yanomami.

ॐ

Segundo waited inside his jeep. A full moon lit the sky. A light shone inside the church. He waited, partially hidden by the shadows of the plantains, for half an hour, glancing at his watch every few minutes. The light finally went out. The American missionary with the wide chest and glasses came out the front door with Capitán Zambrano. What could those two be doing together? They descended the steps to the sidewalk and walked around to the other side of the church, where the streetlight had burned out, to the dark outline of a jeep that Segundo hadn't noticed. The jeep made a U-turn and when it passed under the streetlight he saw "Policía Militar" emblazoned on its side. Segundo watched the red tail-lights shrink down the street. It was safe now.

He entered through the back of her house, through the metal door that she left open for him. He found her, lunatic, sitting on her bed, rummaging through papers in semi-darkness, laughing gleefully to herself. The room was illuminated only by a lightbulb in the hallway. Four empty

315

Polar bottles sat on the bedside table.

He stood in the bedroom doorway, leaning against one arm, blocking the hall light.

She looked up from the papers. "I have evidence, papers documenting New World Mission activities. What do you think?"

"I think that whatever you do, you should do it without me. The authorities would just love to associate this with the party—a clandestine Communist ploy to create political instability, they would say."

She picked up a half-empty bottle, took a swig and put it back down upon the floor. "Never mind. I intend to give them to Salvador. Beer?"

"Where did you get them?"

"It was easy, I took them straight out of the mission's own headquarters."

"Sangre de Jesús! You don't understand what you've done. Do you think the missionaries and government are playing games? Politics is not a bolas criollas match!"

"Nobody saw me. I walked straight into an office and slid them inside my shirt."

"Clandestine activities can backfire if they aren't carefully formulated."

"You'd know all about that now, wouldn't you?"

"I'm serious. After the overthrow of the Pérez Jiménez dictatorship, the Communist Party enjoyed popularity as never before. During that time the party split, between conservative-leftists and extremists. The extremists were young, politically inexperienced, mostly university students, and under urging from Cuba they instigated clandestine activities designed to overthrow the ineffective, moderate government of Betancourt. Much blood was shed: rural uprisings, a campaign of terror throughout the city, Molotov cocktail parties, burning vehicles, street riots. Students fired arms from the Central University campus. Civilians, police and students alike were killed. The riots were silenced by tear-gas and gunfire. In the end, the violence was no worse than an ant bite to Betancourt. But the party was officially outlawed, and many students, party senators and deputies were arrested. All the public support gained during Pérez Jiménez's overthrow was lost. We moved away from terrorism, denounced our clandestine activities and regained our status as a legal party, but we never regained public respect. The bloodshed and violence were useless."

"I do not see the relevance to this situation."

"Maybe I'm so averse because of my personal loss. I was a child at the time of the Communist uprising. My older brother was studying law at the university. The police gunned him down. I beg you not to take this any further."

"I love you, Segundo, but sometimes I think you are nothing but pure proletarian talk."

"A rooster's tail brushes the ground when he walks. He leaves a trail that he can't rub out. A fox can sniff out the trail no matter how discreet the rooster has been. You surely left a rooster's trail behind you, and there are dangers that you continually refuse to see. I just saw Zambrano and Señor Elliot leave the church together in a military jeep. Do you think they were having a church social, at this hour? And by the way, I know that the captain is a practising Catholic."

"Oh no, not more CIA nonsense, please."

"Do you want more proof? I'll give it to you. The military was in an uproar last month because Venezuelan military clothing was discovered among New World Mission supplies, in barrels marked 'combustibles'. What do missionaries want with our military clothing, I ask you? To wear it? Or did they purchase the supplies for another purpose? Do they have a secret agenda?"

She laughed so hard she snorted. "Segundo, Americans love camouflage and military gear. Myself, I can't fathom why. I suppose it's just fashion—maybe patriotism. In my country, they actually sell the stuff to the public in huge surplus stores. The missionaries were probably silly enough to think tough clothing would be ideal for the jungle environment. I'll bet they were surprised when they put it on and roasted to death. Hell on earth." She giggled and took another gulp of Polar.

"Mi vida, you do not understand. It is against our federal law for civilians to wear military clothing. The missionaries didn't purchase the supplies legally, for they couldn't have. They needed an inside contact. They put themselves at considerable risk, and why do that for fashion? Some high-ranking militares took serious offence. Initially there was talk of arrests, but then all charges were mysteriously dropped. Some say the CIA and the Ooosah embassy negotiated secretly with Venezuelan government officials on the CIA payroll. I tell you, it's too dangerous to go after the missionaries."

"But these papers are needed if the New World Mission is to be expelled."

"Can't you see? No complaints against the missionaries will be taken seriously. The government will never throw them out if they can blame the demonstration on leftist militant activity."

Segundo sat down on the bed beside her. She kissed his cheek. He felt like a bow stretched too far—ready to snap. He had no erection that night. He lay against the pillows, held her tightly in his arms, her blonde head against his red shirt. They fell asleep fully clothed.

Debra needed groceries, and Osvaldo drove her down to town during the lunch break.

"I can go no farther, doctora," he said. "The demonstrators are blocking the street."

"This will do fine, Osvaldo. Can you meet me back here in, say . . ."—she looked at her watch—"twenty-five minutes?" She walked down pitted Avenida Río Negro, with the crowd, to the main plaza. The sun baked hot and white, directly overhead, reflecting blindingly off the two-storied white buildings of the administrative centre. The Plaza Bolívar was packed with people chanting and jeering, spilling around the municipal council, the Ministry of Justice and the Judicial Police station. She reached the deep shade of the mature mango trees in the main plaza. Beside the omnipresent effigy of Simón Bolívar, banners waved—"Fuera Misión Nuevo Mundo", "Goodbye CIA", "Viva la Libertad", "Yankee go home". Debra watched for a few minutes. She smiled, satisfied, then turned and dodged between demonstrators to the opposite end of the plaza. She reached the end of the shade, stepped out again into the bright sun and headed for the supermercado.

She chose some Cheez Whiz, rice, withered vegetables and eggs. She picked up a bagged loaf of bread emblazoned "Holsum, Always Fresh!" and peered carefully through the writing. The loaf was sooty grey with *Rhizopus*, the same fungus the comatose diabetic had had—the one with rhinocerebral zygomycosis, one of the first patients she'd seen here, as a matter of fact. "I took those papers for you," she said to the loaf, and returned it to the shelf.

Velázquez entered. His Technical Commission—what remained of it—sat on either side of the conference table. A VCR and television occupied one end of the table. He took his seat at the other. So many responsibilities. People depended on him for their monthly paycheques. He made life-and-death decisions. Research, applied correctly, could save the lives of so many. All of it, all he had striven for, could be ruined by one careless person, by one indiscretion. It wasn't easy. Never before had he been obliged to take disciplinary action against one of the Technical Commission—many times with the técnicos, of course, but never with a co-ordinator. He placed a videotape in front of him, and made eye contact with each co-ordinator in turn. All lowered their gaze submissively. Except Debra, who stared back even after his gaze had passed on. Had she any idea? In light of all the serious financial and staffing problems faced by his institute, further scandal would not be tolerated. This was her last chance. If, after this meeting, she did not modify her behaviour drastically, it would be the beginning of the end for Doctora Baumstark.

He cleared his throat discreetly. "As you know, I do not pry into the personal lives of my staff," he began slowly. A tapping at the door interrupted his flow.

Rosalia, in her high-heeled shoes, ruffled blouse and skin-tight short skirt stretched tightly over her padded thighs, blinked behind her glasses. "Doctor, I hate to interrupt, but Capitán Máximo is here to see you and the Co-ordinator of Medical Services. He says it concerns a matter muy urgente."

"Debra," he said. She stood up. He guided her, his hand on the small of her back—dry now, unlike her first day at the institute—around the corner to his office. Máximo obscured the office door, running his hand down a length of chain hanging from the roof. He smiled, his gold tooth lustrous. "Buenas tardes, doctores." He bent stiffly over his stomach bulge to pick up his tasteless black and white cowhide briefcase.

Velázquez stood aside to allow Máximo and Debra to enter the office ahead of him. His office was dark, the outside light blocked with aluminum foil. He switched on the fluorescent overhead lights and the air-conditioner, took his seat behind the expanse of his desk and arranged himself, his temples pulsing. What was this all about, and how much imported scotch would it cost him? What sort of scandal had Debra gotten herself into now? He folded his fingers together, his hands resting on the desktop. Máximo squeezed into a chair, his barriga distended over his belt and onto his lap, and put his cowboy briefcase on the floor at his feet. Debra moved her chair a few extra inches away from Máximo, her eyes open wider than usual, before she sat down.

"Doctor," Máximo said, "as you know, I have been investigating an uprising. I inadvertently uncovered a triangular link between the demonstrators, the Communist Party and, quite unexpectedly, a staff member of your institute. . . ."

"Please continue, capitán. Let me assure you, I and my institute will co-operate in any way."

"The New World Mission has always claimed that the periodic demonstrations held against them were really part of a larger Communist conspiracy intended to destabilize legitimate government in the Territory. Naturalmente, at first I did not pay heed to this claim. Ridiculous, I said." Máximo picked up the black and white case and placed it across his lap.

"Please, capitán, continue."

Máximo opened his briefcase and rummaged through it. "Fortunately, the missionaries had the foresight to photograph the demonstrators. They were hoping that we could identify persons of known affiliation to extreme leftist militant groups."

He slapped an eight-by-ten glossy black and white

photograph on the desk. It was upside down to Velázquez, but even so it clearly showed Doctora Baumstark in the Plaza Bolívar, standing beside a banner that read, "Fuera Misión Nuevo Mundo". She was smiling, clearly participating in the demonstration. "I am shocked, capitán," Velázquez said.

Debra laughed nervously. "I was buying groceries, I was on my way to the supermercado. In any case, I'm not a member of any leftist organization," she stammered.

"Nevertheless," Máximo said, turning to her, "for quite some time now we have been aware of your close ties to a prominent member of the Communist Party. The affiliation was first brought to my attention by an esteemed member of our community, an educated man who is a most reliable source, Oscár Candido Bobadillo, none other than our pharmacist. And the connection was substantiated further by another citizen who, from the Evangelist church, spotted the Communist's jeep hidden behind the bushes at the back of your house on numerous occasions. I checked out the latter tip for myself."

"I'm an American citizen. This is outrageous. I have no political ties in this country."

"I have a videotape of Doctora Baumstark in intimate circumstances with this man," volunteered Velázquez hurriedly, "confirming the connection between them. I will gladly hand it over to you, if you will be so kind as not to implicate my institute. INSA was not associated in any way. If the doctora was somehow involved, then you have my personal assurance that she acted alone."

"I went to the grocery store. I'm romantically involved with a man who is a member of a legal political party. So what?" Debra said, her voice stronger. "You have no proof I did anything wrong."

"Is that so?" Máximo smiled. "I am informed that important documents have been stolen from the New World Mission's headquarters. They were missed, doctora, directly after you and Doctor Velázquez used the mission radio.

Aparentemente, you were the only person to leave the radio room unaccompanied. I really don't understand how you thought you could get away with it." He wet his smiling lips with his thick tongue, and Velázquez estimated that this incident of Debra's would cost him at least a case of scotch and, worse, perhaps, a social occasion with the repugnant man. "Do you think we Latin Americans are so stupid, doctora?" asked Máximo.

Debra sat with her mouth open slightly. "No, no, of course not. But this is all circumstantial. You have no proof of any involvement at all."

Velázquez leaned forward in his chair. "I assure you, I had no prior knowledge of Doctora Baumstark's militant activities. I do not condone such activities, nor will I harbour militant extremists in my institute. You cannot imagine my shock."

"Just as well, doctor. Doctora, we don't need proof. You will be leaving with me."

"I'm an American citizen," Debra repeated. "And I demand to contact my embassy."

"Don't worry, we contacted your embassy for you, and we are taking your citizenship into consideration. We are being lenient with you. No official charges will be brought against you if you co-operate. You will be put under house arrest—no secret visitors, you understand—but only until we can safely escort you out of the country. The passport you left at Extranjería for the nationalization process will be returned to you at the international airport. You are fortunate the application for Venezuelan citizenship hadn't yet been processed. We are much tougher on our own." Máximo tilted his cap at Velázquez. "Doctor. I knew I could rely upon your co-operation. I'm sorry to tell you at this time, but you will be short yet another technician. That Piaroa boy, Salvador Uribe, he is no longer in the Territory. He was a trouble-maker. But not to worry—I have a nephew who is interested in science. He would make an excellent addition to your staff. We must get together socially, discuss his appointment over a drink.

323

Soon, I hope."

"Salvador! What did you do to him?"

"Doctora, the matter is no longer of any concern to you."

❦

Debra thought a sip of rum would calm her nerves. She sat at the formica table, alone with a glass and the bottle. It had been humiliating, utterly humiliating. She took a sip of warm liquid gold and saw the room swim through her tears. She mustn't cry. A little more rum should do it. How would she contact Segundo from the U.S? Would she ever see him again? Probably not—he'd never be given a visa for the U.S., and her name was on the *persona non grata* list here. Maybe in a neutral country, maybe if she changed her name. She gulped more rum, her throat burning, the heat running down her oeso-phagus and spreading through her chest. And what had they done to Salvador? Zambrano was capable of anything. Her eyes would be swollen tomorrow if she cried. Her lips were numb. No phone here. She couldn't contact anyone.

❦

Ronald Elliot lifted a box of canned goods and dried apples into the twin-engined aircraft with "Wings of God" written on its side. Luke Elliot, sandy blond hair shining, sauntered out of the terminal, his flight plan in one hand, a grilled cheese sandwich in the other.

The DC-10 to Caracas stood nearby on the tarmac. Ronald watched a military jeep pull up to its side. Captain Zambrano rolled out and lumbered around to the passenger's side of the jeep and opened the door, and she stepped out. She wore sunglasses. Zambrano handed her something that looked like a newspaper, and they shook hands. She walked up the stairs, paused at the top and looked around. Ronald felt her stare from behind her sunglasses. She shook her head slightly and stepped through the door.

"Lady doctor's not bad-lookin'," Luke said. "Too bad she has to leave."

Ronald glared at his young brother. "She had an unsettling effect, particularly on unmarried men in your age group," Ronald said. A drop of sweat hit the right lens of his glasses and blurred his vision. "It is written in the Bible, Luke, the prophecy of Deborah. You see, don't you, how it has once again been fulfilled? The hand of God is risen. History is repeated." Ronald breathed easily, the weight lifted from his shoulders. The enemy had been delivered. He took another deep, relaxed breath. Darkness had been banished and judgement given. Wake up, Deborah, wake up, hear the righteous sing your song—thanks to you, the enemy has fallen dead, his head is crushed and his brow is pierced.

Debra looked out the window at the blue sky and fluffy white clouds. The sky looked darker blue through her smoky lenses, the clouds more dramatic. The polarization made every contour visible. Passengers walked across the tarmac, carrying bags and cardboard boxes. They shoved and pushed their way on board, squeezing boxes and bags into the overhead luggage racks.

Debra's eyes hurt; they had almost swollen shut, and her head throbbed. Nothing was more sickening than a bad hangover. She had hoped to see him passing out his pamphlets, one last glimpse, even if Máximo wouldn't let her say goodbye. But he wasn't here today. She looked into the pouch ahead of her and felt comforted by the sight of the moisture-proof vomit bag. The DC-10 taxied to the runway and the passengers crossed themselves. She would find a way to get in touch, a letter addressed to one of the técnicos, who would surely deliver it to him for her.

She looked across the savannah. The plane began to roll along the runway, picking up speed. The land swept away beneath her. The great Orinoco, its reflected blueness and white rapids, filled the window. The landing gear retracted with a dull thud.

The stewardesses would be bringing Coke soon. Maybe it would help her stomach. Painkillers with codeine—two, with Coca-Cola—should make her feel better. The newspaper Máximo had given her lay folded in her lap. "A little something for your reading pleasure, doctora," he had said. Peculiar thing for him to do. She opened it. Some kind of local publication— she hadn't known one existed. Her Spanish had improved so much that she didn't need her pocket dictionary at all. The bolívar had plummeted to fifty-three to the dollar and was predicted to stabilize at sixty. She flipped the page and the word "carbonizado" caught her eye. Such a descriptive word for a burned body. As usual, there was the grisly photo: the blackened hull of a jeep. The mental image flashed back: charred skull, eyeless sockets, clumps of charcoal-like residue. Her eyes continued down the column: "The Territory is unfortunate to lose one of our most distinguished citizens in a tragic accident. His colourful red shirt will no longer greet those arriving at the airport. . . ."

Epilogue

Concepts without observations are empty;
observations without concepts are blind.
Immanuel Kant

Tekiyë's wife stirred her dead husband's ashes into the plantain soup. The Pijiguao harvest had come and gone and now it was time for the great warrior to become part of the Iyëira-teri. His soul had risen long ago to the celestial disk, along with the smoke from his funeral pyre, the day after his death—the day the Puertopedriscal-teri had interrupted the ceremony.

That day the warriors had shot arrows tipped with *mamokrima* at the *nabë* and they had fled, but they had returned soon after with a Yanomami from Puertopedriscal-teri. He said that they wouldn't harm the Iyëira-teri, that they wanted only to learn about the bad things Jeffyë had done and then they would leave the Iyëira-teri alone. There was no alternative but to speak with them. The warrior's soul couldn't be released while the *nabë* watched. After much talk, the *nabë* left and the soul rose at last. His bones were ground to a powder and she had saved it for this day.

There had been a big discussion the night of the funeral. Many warriors didn't believe the *nabë* when they said they would return. The *nabë* had lied before and they would lie again. Her late husband had tried to warn them. They had cared for the *nabë* Jeffyë when he had come to them too stupid to care for himself. In return for their hospitality Jeffyë had consumed her vagina with his penis and made a hole through her husband with his thunder stick, leaving her unprotected from beating and rape. There were no alternatives for the Iyëira-teri. The *nabë* would return. More of them would come. They should never have allowed big, ugly, stupid Jeffyë to live with them.

The morning after Tekiyë's soul had been liberated, the Iyëira-teri gathered all their belongings. Fire was set upon Jeffyë's isolation hut. The wind caught the fire and spread it to the shabono. The shabono burned to the ground.

Hunting dogs in the lead, the Iyëira-teri started through the forest as the smoke from their village died. They travelled many days upstream, constructing palm-leaf shelters as they went. They travelled far from the mouth of the Stream of the Urinating Jaguar, and chose a site for another shabono in an area so remote that they felt confident the *nabë* would be unable to find it.

ꙮ

Close to the Stream of the Urinating Jaguar, a square patch remained in the ochre dirt, once the foundation for a small hut. Part of a mud wall remained standing, and some blackened papers stuck out between partially burned support poles.

Between forty and twenty thousand years ago, ancestors of the Amazonian people crossed the Bering Strait and populated the Americas, spreading into the southern rainforests. Isolated communities evolved as distinct ethnic groups, each with a unique language and culture. Survival in the rich rainforest environment required special knowledge and skills but diet was great in diversity. Cultivation of select crops augmented the uncertain harvest of wild fruits, game, fish, insects, insect larvae and spiders. Through the millennia the selection of favoured plants in successive small plots changed the balance of the natural forest, until the Amazon jungle became a garden. A trench cut in the soil of the most remote and wild forest will usually reveal a layer of carbon below the surface— the remains of cutting and burning for the preparation of plots. The notion of untouched, virgin rainforest is a fallacy; this is the ricebowl

*of the Yanomami, and the breadbasket of the Panare. The entire
rainforest is necessary for their survival. Any fragmentation or
resource exploitation undermines their agriculture. Sustainable
development becomes an oxymoron.*

*Amazonian ethnic groups developed together in a complex social
and economic web. Most, like the Panare, the Yabarana and the
Yanomami, were hunter-gatherers and small-scale cultivators. The
Panare were primarily horticulturists. Crops were grown in conucos,
small slash-and-burn clearings maintained for a few years and then
left for the forest to reclaim. The Piaroa, whose land and culture
were usurped by the growth of Puerto Pedriscal, specialized in native
commerce. They learned other native languages and their trade
became essential to many groups. The Panare, for example, traded
their agricultural produce, baskets and cloth with the Piaroa for
curare and the hollow canes used for blowpipes.*

*The connections broke down when outsiders arrived. The Piaroa,
accessible and accustomed to trade, were seduced by metal pots and
pans, flashlights, fish-hooks, nets and guns, and the traditional
trade alliances decayed. Dependence on the new primary trading
partner and its supplies spread rapidly, bringing irreparable change.
As dependency grew, specialized skills and knowledge were forgotten
and territorial boundaries and forest expeditions deteriorated. The
entire economic base, social life, family structure, environment,
nutrition and health of communities altered irreversibly. The Panare
learned to raise cattle. The Piaroa were taught agriculture. Metal
was introduced and people abandoned the making of functional
pottery. Groups like the Guahibo, persecuted on the Colombian
savannah, moved across the great Orinoco River where it was safer
and set up makeshift communities.*

*Some groups readily accepted change. Some accepted only the
outside influence they wanted. Some imports could not be resisted:
alcohol, prostitution and new diseases to which they had little
resistance. Great epidemics of colds, influenza, chickenpox, scarlet
fever, whooping cough, viral and bacterial meningitis, tuberculosis
and malaria swept throughout the Orinoco-Ventuari region,
devastating and sometimes wiping out entire communities,*

sometimes even entire ethnic groups, such as the extinct Atures society.

When Columbus first crossed the Atlantic, six to twelve million people lived in the Amazon basin. Now only a few hundred thousand native Amazonians remain.*

*Marshall, J. 1984. "Ethnocide in the Orinoco-Ventuari Region." *La Etnología Amazonica: Actas del Seminario patronizado por el Centro de Investigación Cultural Amazonico*, Publ. Cien. no. 312, pp. 22-29.